THE TROVE OF THE PASSION ROOM

MARCIA LYNN McCLURE

Published by Distractions Ink
P.O. Box 15971
Rio Rancho, NM 87174

Published by Distractions Ink
©Copyright 2011 by M. Meyers
A.K.A. Marcia Lynn McClure
Cover Photography by
©Olga Demchishina and ©Akiyoko74 | Dreamstime.com
Cover Design by
Sheri L. Brady | MightyPhoenixDesignStudio.com

First Printed Edition: February 2011

McClure, Marcia Lynn, 1965—
The Trove of the Passion Room: a novel/by Marcia Lynn McClure.

ISBN: 978-0-9835250-4-2

Library of Congress Control Number: 2011928541

Printed in the United States of America

To Sandy Ann and Mallory,
For kindred spirits…so rare and hard to find.
For loving the past like me…
and everything old and precious…
like photographs, aged books,
truly good music, and heroic World War II veterans.
This one is for you two…
An escape to a dream—with a whole lot of truth mixed in!

PART ONE

CHAPTER ONE

"And don't let that first edition *Uncle Remus* go for any less than five hundred, girls," Louisa Dickens reminded her daughters in a whisper. She shook her head, sighed, and smiled. "Your father is famished. I don't know why he didn't have breakfast, but he needs to eat, so I'll be back as soon as I can."

"He was probably too nervous about the show today," Gwen suggested.

Louisa nodded, still amused by her husband's predictability. "I'm sure he was. He always is." Reaching behind the old walnut secretary standing in the corner, she collected her purse and made ready to leave. "Do you girls want anything?" she asked, looking to her daughters.

"Just a chocolate shake for me, Mom," Sharla answered.

"Me too," Gwen added.

Louisa nodded. "Okay. And don't worry. I'll hurry."

"Take your time, Mom," Sharla said. She watched her rather eccentric mother hurry out of the exhibiting space in a wave of graceful purple and red scarves streaming out behind her.

"I swear, she is *so* funny," Sharla giggled.

"I know," Gwen agreed, also smiling. "There she goes…flitting down the aisle. Look how everyone is watching her."

Sharla nodded. "She's hard to miss in all that red and purple."

"*Crimson* and *plum*," Gwen said, dramatically placing a hand to her chest. "She corrected me this morning. She's not wearing red and purple, Shar. She's wearing *crimson* and *plum*."

1

"Oh! Well, excuse me," Sharla laughed. "Then Mom's hard to miss in all that crimson and plum."

Gwen and Sharla enjoyed a good giggle at their beloved mother's expense for a moment. Louisa Dickens was nothing if not entertaining. Her love of history and literature was evident in everything she did—even in the names she'd chosen for her children. Sharla's sister, Gwen, was actually named Guinevere after the ill-fated queen in the tales of Camelot. Sharla's older brother Cratch's full name was Cratchit—in tribute to the beloved character from Charles Dickens's famous work. Her younger brother, Cris, was in truth christened Cristo after Dumas's legendary count. Even Sharla herself owned a version of history in her own name—Sharlamagne. Though she was rarely addressed by her full name, just as her siblings were rarely addressed by theirs (for in truth, few people outside of the family were even aware of the Dickens children's names in their entireties), she secretly liked her name. It was unusual, and she thought it was pretty. To Sharla, her name sounded rather melodic and eccentric—like her mother's very nature.

As a small child, Sharlamagne had spent hours and hours each summer's day, playing outside beneath the old lilac bushes at the back of the family's house, pretending she was not a human girl but a fairy. Her sister, Gwen, would often join her, imagining that she was, in truth, the child-princess Guinevere—destined one day to be King Arthur's bride.

As Sharla and Gwen grew, however, they began to settle into the reality of the world—just as all children sadly do. This was particularly true when their father was tragically killed in a car accident. Sharla had been only five when her father had died. Cratch had been six, Gwen four, and Cris just a baby. The family was devastated at the loss of Gregory Grinkov—cherished husband and loving father. Sharla could still remember how the smile had vanished from her mother's face that day—her sincere smile anyway. Though she'd only been five when her father had been killed, Sharla knew the pain and gaping hole branded into her heart by the loss of her father would never truly be healed.

In truth, it had taken Sharla several years to accept her stepfather, Van-Dyke Dickens—to even call him "father." Louisa Grinkov had married Van-Dyke Dickens three short years after the loss of her first husband. Sharla had been eight, and still desperately loyal to her biological father's memory. In fact, all the Grinkov children had been somewhat resentful when their mother had remarried. However, Van-Dyke was patient and very loving—though careful not to press the children—and after several years (which Sharla later realized must have been far more difficult for Van-Dyke than she ever understood at the time), the Grinkov children had fallen well in love with their new father and agreed to allow him to legally adopt them. Thus, the surname of Dickens was lawfully bestowed upon Cratchit, Sharlamagne, Guinevere, and Cristo.

Sharla still missed her father, Gregory; sometimes she even missed being Sharlamagne Grinkov instead of Sharlamagne Dickens. Yet Van-Dyke was a wonderful parent! She could not have asked for a more kind and patient man to have stepped into her father's shoes. Van-Dyke had become a true father to her, and she loved him quite as deeply as she had Gregory Grinkov.

"What're you smiling about now?" Gwen asked, pulling Sharla's thoughts back to the present.

Sharla shrugged. "Just how funny Daddy is," she answered half-truthfully. "Every time we do an antique exhibition or show, he doesn't eat breakfast, and Mom has to run out and grab him something." She paused, smiling with the amusement of her parents' predictability. "You'd think Mom would wise up after all this time and brown-bag him a snack."

Gwen smiled. "Or you'd think we would."

Sharla gasped dramatically—widened her eyes as if a sudden awareness had only just washed over her. "Are you saying we're like Mom? Will we be whirling around in waves of crimson and plum in our middle-aged years?"

Gwen laughed. "Oh, I'm certain of it!"

"Excuse me," a woman's voice interrupted from behind them.

Sharla and Gwen both turned to look at the customer who had entered the booth while they had been talking.

"How much is this carnival glass bowl?" the woman asked.

"Oh, forgive me, ma'am. I thought I tagged that one this morning," Gwen said, going to where the woman stood at the carnival glass display. Sharla watched as Gwen took the bowl and turned it over. "There," she said. "Ninety-eight dollars."

"Would you take seventy?" the woman asked.

Gwen frowned and wrinkled her nose thoughtfully—but Sharla knew Gwen wouldn't barter too much. Sharla and Gwen both struggled with standing firm on the prices of their parents' antiques.

"I'll take eighty," Gwen rather timidly counteroffered.

"Eighty will be fine," the woman said, smiling. "Will you keep it at the desk for me while I browse your booth some more?"

"Of course," Gwen cheerily assured the customer. "Take your time."

"Thank you," the woman mumbled. She turned and began to peruse the bookshelves well stocked with antique books looming at the back of the Dickens Antiques sales space.

"I'm proud of you!" Sharla whispered as Gwen sighed and began to wrap the delicate bowl in protective paper. "I don't know if I could've said eighty—maybe seventy-five, but not eighty."

"Daddy says that the stuff in the store is usually worth more than the price he sets...so I'm trying to be a better antique dealer and not such a softy," Gwen whispered in return.

"I'm working on it too," Sharla sighed. She shook her head. "But I don't know—I just can't seem to be tough about it. It seems mean to me."

Gwen nodded in agreement. "You and I need more customers like Mrs. Tanner. She never barters...just pays whatever is on the sticker."

"I know," Sharla said, her smile broadening as she thought of the dear old lady who frequented Dickens Antiques. "I adore Mrs. Tanner!" Sharla breathed a giggle. "And I think she and Mom would have been the best of friends if they'd been the same age and known each other before."

"Oh, totally!" Gwen confirmed. "Mrs. Tanner wears as much red and purple as Mom does."

"Crimson and plum," Sharla playfully corrected he sister.

"Ah, yes! Crimson and plum."

"She's supposed to drop by the show today," Sharla said.

"Mrs. Tanner?"

"Yeah. I think she thinks we have a secret room at the store where we hide stuff and save it for these antique shows," she conspiratorially whispered.

"She's so funny!" Gwen laughed. "And so rich!"

"I know. I guess being a poet is something you used to be able to make money at, right?" Sharla asked.

"*Used to* being the operative phrase," Gwen suggested.

"Exactly," Sharla confirmed. "You know…every time I go on eBay to try and get one of Mrs. Tanner's collected works, I nearly pass out. One went for seven hundred dollars just the other day."

"Dang! You'll never get one," Gwen said, frowning.

"Probably not…but I'll keep trying."

"How much are you asking for this copy of *Nights with Uncle Remus?*" the woman who had bartered down the carnival glass bowl called.

Gwen leaned toward Sharla as she pretended to get something out from under the register desk. "She's definitely one of *those*," she whispered.

"Yep," Sharla whispered in return. "She's going to barter us down on everything she wants. Start her out at eight hundred for the book… then she'll think five hundred is a steal."

"First edition of *Nights with Uncle Remus?* That would be a steal!" Gwen teasingly glared at Sharla. "Okay. I'll deal with it. But the next customer is yours, Sharlamagne."

"Agreed." Sharla smiled with amusement as she watched her sister stride across the exhibition space to the customer looking at the *Uncle Remus* book. She knew the price was lightly penciled in on the first page. It was obvious the woman just liked bartering.

Sharla sighed and returned to polishing the silver letter opener she'd begun to polish before the customer had arrived. She smiled as she glanced up to see Gwen bartering with the woman over the *Uncle Remus* book. Sharla could tell the woman had no intention of actually purchasing the book. There were so many customers just like her—

customers who enjoyed making a salesperson uncomfortable more than they enjoyed the treasure-hunt feel of antique shopping.

Sharla set the letter opener down, reached back, and tightened her long brown ponytail. People were starting to pour into the convention center, and she smiled, hoping it would be a good sales day for her parents.

Being part of a family that owned an antique store was often difficult for Sharlamagne Dickens—because even though she wished her parents success in business—knew that it was the family income—it was not easy for Sharla to watch treasure leave in the hands of someone else. And to Sharla, antiques were exactly that—treasure.

Every old thing that found its way into the Dickens Antiques shop or warehouse was priceless to her—a piece of history—a thing that had once been used, loved, or cherished by someone in the past. To Sharla, every item had a story—a tale cached deep in its core. Thus, it was always disappointing when an item was sold—especially if it went on its way with someone who only wanted it for its monetary value.

Still, there were regular customers Sharla didn't mind selling things to—customers who appreciated a thing for the same reason she did—because it had seen the past and endured to remind those in the present what had once been.

"Sharlamagne, darling!"

Suddenly rattled from her thoughts by the familiar endearment and greeting, Sharla smiled as she turned. Yet as she saw that Mrs. Elisaveta Tanner was not standing behind her but rather seated in a wheelchair, her smile faded. A man, his hands on the handles of the wheelchair, was looking back over his shoulder at something. But Sharla was too unsettled by the sight of her cherished friend in a wheelchair to pay much attention to who was pushing it.

"Mrs. Tanner!" she exclaimed, dropping to one knee before the lovely elderly woman. "What's happened? Are you all right?" Anxiety was fast overtaking her. Sharla loved Elisaveta Tanner—loved her as if she were her own grandmother! She was anxious at seeing her in the wheelchair—afraid something serious and perhaps life-threatening had overcome her.

Quickly, Sharla studied Mrs. Tanner's countenance and person. Her cheeks were rosy, her bright blue eyes as sparkling as mountain lakes. Her snow-white hair was as perfectly coifed as it ever was. There didn't seem to be any obvious illness or damage.

"Did you fall or something? Are you okay?" she asked, awash with concern.

"I'm fine, darling," Mrs. Tanner assured Sharla, offering a comforting smile. In the next moment, Elisaveta Tanner's expression suddenly brightened into that of mischief. Leaning forward, she whispered, "My grandson thought it might be fun to tool me around in this thing awhile. I'm certainly capable of walking, but Maxim worries about me so…the dear boy."

"Maxim?" Sharla asked in a whisper.

"Maxim, darling," Elisaveta said, turning and tugging at the sleeve of the young man wielding the wheelchair. "This is Sharlamagne, Maxim…the girl I told you about. We're kindred spirits, she and I." Returning her attention to Sharla, Elisaveta's smile broadened. "This is Maxim, darling…my grandson."

Rising to her feet, Sharla tried to keep her mouth from gaping open as Elisaveta Tanner's devilishly handsome grandson smiled a stunning smile and greeted, "Hi."

"Hello," she managed, accepting his hand as he offered it to her. His grip was firm and confident—warm as well.

Midnight black hair, eyes as blue as cobalt, perfectly defined cheekbones, straight nose, a chin so flawlessly squared it didn't seem real—and his lips! There was something about Elisaveta's grandson's lips that was fabulous! She couldn't quite figure it out—not in the brief moment she had to take in his astonishing good looks—but his lips were perfectly shaped, his lower lip being full but not too full and his upper lip owning that perfect outline every human being admires in another human being's lips. Sharla suddenly felt quite dowdy with her plain brown hair and rather common hazel eyes. She also wished she'd worn something besides old jeans and a brown blouse—and that she were twenty-two instead of eighteen.

"I've heard a lot about you," the young man said, still smiling at her.

"Oh, great," Sharla mumbled, feeling a blush rise to her cheeks.

The young man chuckled. "Oh, don't worry…it was all good. Grandma thinks you're awesome."

Forcing a smile, Sharla returned her attention to Elisaveta and said, "Well, I think she's awesome too."

Elisaveta reached out, taking Sharla's hands just as she always did when they met. "I dragged poor Maxim and his hoity-toity girlfriend out here today."

"Grandma," Maxim scolded, glancing behind him.

"Well, she is hoity-toity, Maxim…not at all the girl for you," Elisaveta mumbled. "Anyway, darling," she began again, returning her attention to Sharla, "there are so many exhibitors here today! It will take me a month of Sundays to see them all."

"Well then, why don't you just start right here?" Sharla asked, smiling at her cherished friend. "Maybe *we* have something to tempt you today."

"It doesn't take much," Maxim chuckled.

"Oh, hush, Max!" Elisaveta lovingly scolded. "Don't listen to him, darling. He doesn't quite understand my passion for things of the past."

"I understand it," Maxim said, as he helped his grandmother rise from the wheelchair. "I just don't know where you're going to put anything else, that's all."

Elisaveta smiled a mischievous smile, winked at Sharla, and said, "Why at your house, darling boy. Where else? You've got plenty of room."

Maxim chuckled, shaking his handsome head with amusement. "Yeah, Grandma, that's exactly what a bachelor pad needs…old lacy stuff and crystal bowls piled everywhere," he teased.

"Now run along, darling," Elisaveta said, waving to Maxim in a playfully dismissive manner as she stepped into the exhibition space. "Go dig up that painted lady of yours and meet me back here in half an hour."

Leaning toward Sharla, Maxim lowered his already low voice and said, "Maybe I should go trade in this wheelchair for a forklift. How much stuff do you think she'll buy today?"

Sharla giggled. "A lot," she answered with honesty.

Maxim breathed a quite laugh. "Fabulous," he sighed.

"Now run along, Max, darling," Elisaveta called as she picked up a small silver butter dish. "Find whatever-her-name-is before she becomes vexed with you."

"Her name is Sophia, Grandma," Maxim said, shaking his head with further amusement.

"Of course it is, darling," Elisaveta mumbled as she continued to study the butter dish.

"I'll be back in a minute," Maxim said to Sharla. "Good luck."

"Thanks," Sharla said, smiling at him. She watched him walk away—noted his uber-cool swagger and the way his jeans fit the lower half of his surreal physique just perfectly.

"Mrs. Tanner!" Sharla heard Gwen exclaim. She turned to see Gwen place an arm around Elisaveta's shoulders. Sharla giggled as Gwen continued, "Have you gone and got yourself a boy-toy? I thought you only dated older men."

"Don't be ridiculous, Guinevere," Elisaveta said, smiling. "That's my grandson, Maxim. He took pity on me today and accompanied me here, you silly goose."

"Boy-toy, grandson, or stranger…I'd be glad to take him off your hands for you, Mrs. Tanner," Gwen teased.

"He is dreamy, isn't he?" Elisaveta whispered, grinning. "Utterly leaves the women swooning in his wake."

"No doubt," Sharla mumbled as she stepped nearer to Elisaveta. She looked to Gwen. "Did that lady take the *Uncle Remus* book?"

"Nope," Gwen answered in a whisper. "She wanted me to give it to her for three hundred. Can you believe that?"

"*Uncle Remus* book?" Elisaveta exclaimed. "Where? You girls know I love *Uncle Remus*!"

"Yes. And you already have a ton of them, if I remember correctly," Sharla giggled.

"Yes, but this one might be a better copy than any of mine. Take me to it at once, ladies. How much is your daddy asking for it?"

"Too much, Mrs. Tanner," Gwen said. "We cannot let you spend so much on one book."

"I'll be the judge of where I spend my money, girls," Elisaveta reminded them. "Now, take me to Joel Chandler Harris. I grew up with *Uncle Remus* stories…I adore them! They're profoundly historical, absolute time in bottle—or rather, a book."

"All right then. If you insist, Mrs. Tanner. It's right over here," Gwen said, heading toward the bookcase.

Sharla followed her sister and Mrs. Tanner. She watched as Elisaveta's blue eyes lit up as Gwen took the book from its place in the bookcase and handed it her.

"There are times, my darlings," Elisaveta breathed, carefully accepting the book, "when I feel as if the very preservation of history itself rests entirely upon my weakening shoulders." She smiled— lovingly smiled with awed admiration—as she gazed at the weathered copy of *Nights with Uncle Remus* she held in her hands. "Hm. The binding is tight, and I don't have a blue-covered copy. The gilt on the front and spine are perfect!" she mumbled to herself. "Any missing or torn pages?"

"Nope. It's a great copy. No foxing at all, and the boards are still strong."

Elisaveta smiled—lovingly caressed the old book with dainty, aged fingers. "Joel Chandler Harris," she began, "endeavored to preserve these stories…rare mementoes of a time that historians will gravely misrepresent in the future…have already misrepresented. Generally forbidden to learn to read and write—especially in the Old South before the Civil War—African-Americans of the time owned a beautiful oral storytelling tradition. Harris did his best to preserve their stories that often included life lessons the like of Aesop's fables. Therefore, imperfect or not, these tales of Uncle Remus's are treasure. Pure historical treasure! And how can I have too many pieces of treasure?"

Sharla smiled—commanded the tears welling in her eyes to stay in her eyes and not leap to trickling over her cheeks. It was one reason so adored Elisaveta Tanner so—her rare and wonderful sensitivity to things gone by, her deep love, appreciation, and reverence for the past and the people who lived it. The same spark of understanding that glistened in Elisaveta's eyes warmed Sharla's heart as well. She secretly hoped Mrs. Tanner would buy the book, for she knew it would be cared for, preserved by, and loved by the elderly guardian angel.

"Elisaveta Tanner!" Van-Dyke Dickens cheerily greeted as he stepped into the Dickens's exhibit area. "Don't tell me you've found our *Uncle Remus*," he laughed. "I should have had the girls hide it from you."

Sharla giggled as her father kissed her cheek. "Good morning, Sharlamagne," he said, smiling at her. She thought how very much he looked like a middle-aged Sean Connery—deep-set eyes, salt-and-peppered hair, and handsome as a king. Being the rare Gene Tierney look-alike she was, her mother's good looks only complemented Van-Dyke's. They made quite a handsome couple.

"Van-Dyke, darling!" Elisaveta exclaimed as Van-Dyke next kissed her cheek as well. "Why didn't you call me when this came in? You know I'm a collector."

"You collect everything, Elisaveta," Van-Dyke chuckled, placing a firm kiss on Guinevere's forehead.

"Oh, I do not, you silly man," Elisaveta laughed. "Now, how much is the book, Van-Dyke?"

Sharla smiled and looked to Gwen. Both girls adored watching their father wriggle under Elisaveta Tanner's gaze. Van-Dyke Dickens might have been a hard bargainer when it came to other customers, but when it came to Elisaveta, his strong business sense seemed to turn to jelly.

"Now, you know I can't barter with you," Van-Dyke began. Sharla giggled as her father blushed with discomfort.

Elisaveta opened the book and peered at the lightly penciled price on the inside cover page. "It says here eight hundred dollars…I'll give you that, Van-Dyke, and not a penny more!" she announced. Ceremoniously, she handed the book to Sharla, adjusted the brilliant purple scarf at her neck, and turned back to the bookshelf. "Wrap that up for me, darling, will you? Oh, I hope I haven't already found my treasure for the day. I've only just begun to search!"

Sharla laughed as he father said, "Elisaveta, you do realize that the idea is to talk me *down* in price, don't you?"

"Oh, fiddle-faddle, Van-Dyke. You know that book is worth twice as much as I'm paying for it," Elisaveta sighed. "Run along now, while I peruse," she said, waving the same signal of dismissal as she had to her grandson. "I don't like when you hover and try to talk me out of things."

Van-Dyke laughed. "Very well. I know better than to stand toe to toe with you."

Elisaveta nodded, smiled, and linked her arm through Sharla's. "Now, Sharlamagne, darling…you know what I like. Show me what your father has been hiding in that secret room of his back at the shop. I'm simple riddled with goose bumps in anticipating finding treasure!"

Sharla giggled, cupped her hand to Mrs. Tanner's ear, and whispered, "We have a gold mourning hair brooch nearby…complete with an inscription and mother-of-pearl embellishments."

Elisaveta gasped—the pink of sheer delight rising to her weathered, yet lovely, cheeks. "Lead on, my love, lead on! And do tell more."

Sharla's smile widened. Elisaveta shared her own gentle feelings for mourning hair jewelry. Some people thought mourning hair pieces were morbid, but Sharla understood them—as did the kindred spirit at her side.

"Well, the hair-work is very delicate," Sharla began in a whisper. "Large hair feathers and rolled edges, embellished with the tiniest seed pearls you've ever seen!"

"How divine," Elisaveta sighed.

"The pin and clasp are sturdy, and there's an engraving on the back with a date of 1861."

"I must have it!"

Sharla laughed, "You haven't even seen it yet, Mrs. Tanner."

"I don't care. You know how I am about mourning hair jewelry. Someone cherished a loved one who had passed to heaven…cherished them by clinging to just one or two locks of hair, along with their memories," she explained. "I cannot possibly let such a thing fall into hands that would not continue to cherish it for those who have gone."

"You're worse than I am," Sharla said, carefully opening the small door to the glass jewelry case.

"And you'll be just as bad when you're eighty-two, darling," Mrs. Tanner assured her.

"I have no doubt of that," Sharla mumbled. "I would've bought this one from Daddy myself...but I couldn't afford it. Sometimes I think that's why he sets the price on something the moment it enters the store the way he does...so that Gwen and I will manage to save some of our salary toward college."

Sharla handed the pretty brooch to Mrs. Tanner—watched as the old woman's eyes misted with the blue fire of excitement and sentimentality.

"Oh, it's a beautiful piece, Sharlamagne! Just beautiful!" she exclaimed. "I'll take it. Have Gwen wrap it up with my book, will you?"

"Yes, ma'am," Sharla said. She glanced up to her father, who stood smiling and shaking his head with amusement.

"Any marbles, darling?" Elisaveta asked then. "I promised Maxim I'd find some treasure for him today as well."

Sharla frowned. "Maxim?" she breathed. "Do you mean the guy you brought with you today? *He's* the grandson who collects marbles? You're kidding."

Elisaveta laughed. "Not at all, darling. I only have one grandson... one grandchild, actually."

She couldn't believe it. Nearly every time Elisaveta Tanner entered Dickens Antiques, she walked out with a small marble hoard, and Sharla couldn't imagine the "grandson" for whom Elisaveta had been buying marbles since literally the first day Sharla had started working at the antique store three years before was the handsome young man accompanying her—the hottie with the nice-fitting jeans who had been wheeling the wheelchair.

"But he's...he's, like, an adult," Sharla spluttered.

Again Elisaveta laughed. "Well, I suppose that he is. But to me, he'll always be my little Maxim...and I'll always buy marbles for him.

He absolutely loves them! Especially the very rare ones. Of course, he prefers cat's eyes…multicolored cat's eyes…even if they aren't very valuable." Elisaveta paused a moment to look at a bronze cherub standing on a marble base, holding a crystal compote over its head. The compote was embellished with glistening teardrop prisms. "How much is this, darling?" She turned the compote over, squinting at the small price sticker on the bottom. "Only ninety dollars? Oh, surely your father has mislabeled this. Ask him what he wants for it, and add it to my things, please." Instead of handing the pretty compote to Sharla, however, Elisaveta simply clutched it to her bosom and continued to look around.

"What were we talking about?" she asked. "Oh, yes! Marbles…for Maxim. Do you have any here today?"

"Uh…um…yeah, a few," Sharla stammered.

"Oh, lovely! Let me see them," Elisaveta exclaimed with renewed excitement.

Sharla led her friend to a nearby table and picked up the old wooden cigar box in which she had displayed the prettiest or rarest marbles. "I like these," she began, picking out five marbles made of swirled red and yellow glass. "They're called 'blended ketchup and mustards.'" Elisaveta held out her hand, and Sharla carefully transferred the marbles to her.

"Delicious! What else is in there?" the older woman inquired. Sharla couldn't help but giggle. Elisaveta's expression was that of a toddler who had just stepped into Disneyland.

"Well, there are seven or eight caramel swirls, a few purple and green apple limited, and—oh! I can't believe I almost forgot this!" Setting the old cigar box down on the table, Sharla reached beneath the tablecloth and retrieved something she'd set aside just in case Mrs. Tanner did come to the exhibition.

"I spirited these away for you too," Sharla explained as she pulled the lid off the old candy tin to show Mrs. Tanner what was inside. "There are two hundred of them. Cat's eye peewees…and there are so many different tricolors I didn't even have the time to separate and count them. But I thought you might like them, so I stuck them under the table in case you came in today."

Elisaveta Tanner smiled. The warmth swelling in her heart spread a comforting joy throughout her already tired body. Sharlamagne Dickens was a darling, a rare jewel, an angel on earth. There were so very few young people that even noticed the elderly—especially noticed them enough to think of them often or to remember the things they liked or said. Yet Sharlamagne was different. Not only did the girl share Elisaveta's adoration and deep love for history and the people and things of the past—the girl truly loved Elisaveta. Not because she was such a good customer for Dickens Antiques but rather because she had taken notice of her, gotten to know her, liked her for who Elisaveta was—a friend and kindred spirit. It didn't matter to Sharlamagne that Elisaveta had once been one of the most renowned poets of her time or that she had money in pure abundance. Sharlamagne adored Elisaveta simply because she liked her.

For a brief moment, Elisaveta thought about altering her will—about leaving a large amount of money to her sweet friend Sharlamagne. Still, she shook her head—for she was determined not to ruin the girl's life by burdening her with the trial of wealth. There were other things she could leave to Sharlamagne—things that would mean more to her young friend than money.

Elisaveta tried to tuck the thought away in the back of her mind. She was going to see her attorney the following day to change a few things, but she would change nothing about it where Sharlamagne Dickens was concerned.

Sighing with sheer adoration for the young woman standing before her offering an old tin full of marbles to her, Elisaveta giggled, "Darling! You always know just what I want, don't you?"

Sharlamagne smiled, delighted that Mrs. Tanner seemed to like the peewee cat's eyes. "Well, I can't see a marble anywhere in the world without thinking of you, Mrs. Tanner," she said. She giggled to herself then, adding, "Though I somehow imagined your grandson to be a boy…not so grown up. To have less…less…?"

"Less sex appeal?" Elisaveta offered.

Instantly, Sharla gasped—felt her face blush deep red. "Mrs.

Tanner!" she scolded in a whisper. "Don't say the 's' word out loud like that!" Sharla glanced about—concerned that someone might be eavesdropping and end up as startled as she was.

But Elisaveta only laughed. "What? Sex appeal?"

"Shhh!" Sharla scolded again.

Still, Elisaveta continued to chortle her amusement. "Darling, I swear you're more entertaining than anything in the world. It's not a bad word. You do know that, don't you? And anyway, I may be his grandmother, but I'm not too old or too naive to know that sex appeal is exactly what Maxim has. It emanates from him like radiation off an A-bomb. But, darling, you don't need to be so uncomfortable with the phrase. It is what it is, after all, and I believe in referencing things by proper terms—calling them exactly what they are."

Sharla nodded. "Well, yes. But couldn't you have just said something like 'attraction' instead of…instead of…?"

"It's sex appeal, Sharlamagne, darling," Elisaveta interrupted. "It is what it is." She smiled, lovingly patting Sharla's cheek. "Now, I'm off to see what else your father has been hiding from me." She handed Sharla the compote she'd been holding and said, "I want all the marbles, of course. And the cigar box too. Maxim has already got too many jars sitting around."

Sharla sighed as she watched Mrs. Tanner searching through the bookshelves and cabinets, over the table tops, and in baskets for her next nest of "treasure."

"Why do you always get the easy customers, Shar?" Gwen teased as she stepped up beside Sharla to join her in watching Elisaveta Tanner's search.

"I don't," Sharla argued. "Mrs. Tanner is the only easy customer I ever get, and you know it."

"And why are you blushing?" Gwen asked.

"Mrs. Tanner said the 's' word," Sharla whispered.

"She cussed?" Gwen asked.

"Shhh!" Sharla scolded. "Not that word…the other 's' word."

Gwen rolled her eyes. "You and your taboo words, Shar," she

16

sighed. "I swear, nobody can ever tell what word is going to freak you out next. What 's' word?"

"The other 's' word," Sharla grumbled. When Gwen's perplexed frown only deepened, Sharla sighed. "Never mind. Will you just help me wrap up the rest of her things, please?"

As Sharla handed Gwen the compote and picked up the cigar box full of marbles, Gwen said, "I can't believe how many marbles she buys."

"And here's the kicker," Sharla whispered, smiling. "She buys them for her grandson. The grandson that's here with her today."

"What?" Gwen gasped. "The sexiness who wheeled her in here before?"

Sharla frowned. "Shhh!" she scolded, blushing.

"What?" Gwen asked, entirely confused.

"Just help me wrap everything, will you?" Sharla whined.

"Okay, but, sheesh! What did I say? I haven't seen you act like this since you had to read *Don Juan* last semester."

"Let's just get these things wrapped up for her, okay?"

But Gwen giggled. "Will you look at that."

"What?" Sharla asked, allowing her attention to follow Gwen's gaze.

Mrs. Tanner was rummaging around under a table, Van-Dyke Dickens chuckling as he watched.

"She's already wanting the cherub compote with the teardrop prisms...and I told Daddy she'd find that Victorian standing ashtray under there," Gwen whispered. "I swear, if they're anywhere near... that woman can smell prisms!"

Sharla couldn't help but giggle as she watched the elderly woman rummaging around under one of the display tables. In a moment, Mrs. Tanner had freed the standing brass and crystal ashtray from its hiding place beneath the table, studied the twenty U-drop crystal prisms adorning, and sighed.

"Sharlamagne? Darling?" she called. "Would you wrap up this lovely ashtray as well?"

Sharla giggled as she nodded. Gwen was right. It really did seem as if Elisaveta could literally smell prisms—and Sharla loved her all the more for it.

CHAPTER TWO

"Ew! It smells like a barn in here."

At the sound of an obviously discontented woman, Sharla and Gwen simultaneously turned to see Mrs. Tanner's grandson had returned—and with his hoity-toity girlfriend, Sophia, in tow. It was apparent by the young woman's wrinkled nose (emphasizing her expression of disgust), platform high heels, and expensive white summer dress that the drop-dead-gorgeous brunette was not accustomed to antique shows. She was hardly wearing the appropriate attire for the amount of walking required or contact with dusty or recently restored antiques.

"Should I drive the forklift in now?" Maxim asked, approaching Sharla and Gwen. He smiled, but the woman accompanying him rolled her eyes with obvious impatience.

"She's not finished yet," Sharla answered.

"But she is showing real self-restraint so far. Only one book, one piece of jewelry, one compote, one standing ashtray, and a box of marbles," Gwen offered.

Maxim nodded. "That *is* self-restraint for Grandma."

"Max," Sophia whined. "Let's go back to that jewelry booth. If I have to look at antiques, I prefer jewelry to dirty old books and trunks." Glaring at Sharla and Gwen with blatant condemnation as she quickly studied their casual manner of dress, Sophia sighed with annoyance. "I'll wait for you over across the aisle. That booth has some interesting crystal at least."

Sharla couldn't help but sneer as she watched Sophia's hips swaying provocatively as she crossed the aisle to the opposing booth.

"I'll give her this," Sharla whispered to her sister. "She can walk well in heels. That's almost a lost art these days."

"Art is right," Gwen whispered in return. "Look at that. If anything ever inspired the phrase 'shake your groove thing,' it was her."

"Jewelry, is it?" Mrs. Tanner asked, striding to where Sharla and Gwen stood. Maxim seemed momentarily distracted by a set of old carpentry tools nearby. Elisaveta glared across the aisle at Maxim's girlfriend. "Well, if she's looking to coax Maxim into buying her a ring, she ought to stop by that old porcelain toilet booth."

"What?" Sharla asked, puzzled.

"An engagement ring is what she's after, darling," Elisaveta whispered. "But I can promise her this: The only kind of ring she's ever going to get from my Maxim is the one that comes in an antique toilet."

"Grandma," Maxim scolded, having overheard what she said. Yet Sharla did not miss the amusement in his eyes.

"She's a gold digger, darling," Elisaveta said to Maxim. "And you know it."

"It's no excuse to be rude, Grandma. Or so you always told me," Maxim countered in a lowered voice, even though Sharla was certain Sophia was too far away to hear.

"You have a point, darling," Elisaveta mumbled. Inhaling a deep breath, she forced a smile, looked across the way to Sophia, and called, "Why don't you browse around with us, dear? There are some lovely carnival glass pieces over here."

"No, thank you, Mrs. Tanner," Sophia called in return, wrinkling her nose in disgust once more as she picked up a crystal bowl from a table in the other booth. "I'll wait here."

"Very well, dear," Elisaveta said. Then lowering her voice once more, she said, "Maxim, I really do not know why you brought her."

"I didn't bring her, Grandma. She knew I was coming with you today and just sort of showed up," Maxim explained. "But this is my day with you," he said, smiling and taking his grandmother's face in his hands. "So, let me talk to her and see if she'd rather go home. I mean, we will be looking at old toilets and stinky old furniture all day, right?"

"Yes. All day," Elisaveta answered.

Sharla smiled as she watched the to-die-for hunk of gorgeousness kiss his grandmother on the forehead with comfortable affection. She could tell, just by watching, that Maxim really did adore his grandmother.

"I'll take care of it, Grandma," Maxim told Elisaveta then. He sighed. "I was as surprised as you were when she crashed our party."

Elisaveta smiled lovingly at her grandson. "I know, darling. I'm sorry for being an old sour onion."

Maxim winked. "You just stay here with your little friends a minute, and I'll take care of it," he said, glancing to Sharla and Gwen.

"Of course, darling," Elisaveta agreed.

Sharla watched as Maxim winked at his grandmother—as he turned and strode to the opposite booth to speak with Sophia. He put one well-sculpted arm around the curvaceous woman's shoulders and led her away, talking quietly to her as they went. Sharla shook her head, still astounded that he was the grandson for whom Elisaveta always purchased marbles.

She sighed and quietly said to Gwen, "Why is it that guys like him are always only ever with girls like her?"

She was surprised when Elisaveta was the one who answered. "Because girls like her are the only ones with enough self-confidence and flat-out vanity to have the courage to approach and pursue men like my Maxim."

"That's exactly it," Gwen agreed. "You're always so wise, Mrs. Tanner."

"Only because I've paid attention during a long life," Elisaveta said, "though I'm sure my special abilities help me in that regard as well."

"Special abilities?" Gwen asked.

"Mrs. Tanner is a bit of a sensitive, Gwen," Sharla explained. "She feels things…senses moods…things in the past…or even the future."

Gwen's eyes widened. "You're a psychic, Mrs. Tanner?" she gasped with evident excitement.

"I would never claim such a thing, darling," Elisaveta answered.

"Though I will—on rare occasion and to only truly intimate friends—admit to having sensitivities to feelings and moods…things that have been, as well as things that will be."

"How awesome!" Gwen breathed.

"Yes. Still, we best not discuss it any further just now," Elisaveta said. Lowering her voice as a smile of pure, triumphant mischief curled her lips, she whispered, "For your mother is about to return with the food she has procured for your father."

Sharla grinned with the delighted mischief sparked in her by Elisaveta's premonitory remark. She watched with amusement as Gwen's gaze turned toward the front of the exhibition building. Not ten second later, the exhibition hall entrance doors opened to reveal Louisa Dickens floating into the hall in a whirl of crimson and plum scarves.

Sharla's smile broadened as Gwen's mouth dropped open in astonishment. "Marvelous!" Gwen breathed.

"Now, Sharlamagne, darling," Elisaveta began, linking her arm with Sharla's once more, "has your father been hiding anything along the lines of silver trinket boxes?"

Sharla giggled. "He has some over here, but he hasn't been hiding them from you."

"I'm looking for something very special," the older woman mumbled. "Something to protect a very important treasure I own."

"Well, let's see what we've got, okay?"

"Yes, darling…let's."

Sharla sighed with gleeful anticipation as she escorted the sweet old woman to the table where her father had set a display of small silver, red-velvet-lined trinket boxes. She so dearly loved Elisaveta Tanner and laughed when the woman gasped with enchantment at the sight of the collection of ornate silver trinket and jewelry boxes gathered there. Maxim was lucky to have such a wonderful grandmother. Sharla was relieved and pleased the man had decided to find a way to spend the day alone with her as they had originally planned.

Sharla frowned a moment, however—suddenly puzzled by something Elisaveta had said to her grandson. She'd called Maxim's girlfriend a gold digger. Was Maxim as wealthy as his grandmother was? Or perhaps wealthy by mere association? Maybe he wasn't wealthy at all, she mused. Maybe people simply assumed he was because of who his grandmother happened to be. Sharla secretly hoped that Maxim wasn't rich—that some snotty gold digger wouldn't trap him.

She rolled her eyes—exasperated with herself for even thinking about things that didn't concern her in the least. After all, Mrs. Tanner was right—the only girls with the self-confidence and courage to attempt to attract the attention of a man like Maxim were gorgeous, movie starlet types—and she certainly wasn't that.

"Oh, there are so many!" Mrs. Tanner exclaimed, pulling Sharla's attention back to the table slathered in silver boxes. "I'll never be able to choose just one!"

"I'll help you, Mrs. Tanner," Sharla said. "After all, we don't want you spending all your mad money here and having nothing else to spend in the other booths, now do we?"

"I want something romantic," Elisaveta said.

"We'll find just the one," Sharla said. "I promise."

"Oh, I hope so. It's such a daunting task, isn't it?"

Sharla giggled, charmed by Mrs. Tanners dramatics. She was a jewel—a rare treasure of far more worth than the historic trinkets she so loved to collect.

"There!" Elisaveta contentedly sighed as she studied the pile of carefully wrapped antique treasures Van-Dyke Dickens was loading into a large box half an hour later. "I found some real lovelies here today, Van-Dyke," she said. Reaching up to pinch Van-Dyke's cheek as if he were no more than a toddler, Elisaveta giggled. "What would I do without you, my darling? You always have just what I'm looking for, don't you?"

Van-Dyke chuckled. "I think you mean, what would *I* do without *you*, Mrs. Tanner. I'd probably be out of business."

"Oh fiddlesticks," Elisaveta said. "Now do you want me to have Maxim haul this out to his truck now, or can you keep it here for a while?"

Again Van-Dyke smiled. "Why don't you just leave it here? And then when you're finished treasure hunting for the day, your boy can back his truck up to the loading dock out back, and we'll find some muscle to load it for you."

Elisaveta playfully slapped Van-Dyke on the arm. "Oh, you quit! I don't ever find that many things to buy."

But Sharla and Gwen giggled when their mother said, "I don't know, Elisaveta. I seem to remember last year at this same event, you went home with quite a trove of lovely treasures. Didn't you fill up a small trailer?"

Elisaveta tossed a carefree wave in the air. "That was different, Louisa, dear. I purchased a few pieces of furniture last year. Don't you remember? Large pieces, in fact. I'm only after trinkets this year."

"Trinkets?" Sharla exclaimed, studying the large box her father had just packed. "Mrs. Tanner…you haven't even been to any other booths yet, and you've already got a box as big as you are!"

"Oh, that's nothing," Maxim Tanner said, stepping up behind his grandmother. "I'm sure Grandma will find ten times this much before the day is over. Right, Grandma?"

"Of course, darling," Elisaveta said. She turned and gazed up into her grandson's handsome face. Reaching up to straighten his shirt collar, she asked, "Did you see that Sophia on her way, dear?"

Maxim chuckled, slightly shaking his head with amused disapproval. "I saw her to her car, Grandma, yes. I'm all yours for the rest of the day."

"Wonderful!" Elisaveta exclaimed, linking her arm through his. "Now, are you truly going to make me ride around in that ridiculous wheelchair all day, Maxim? I'll feel positively silly."

Maxim sighed as his amused smile broadened. "No, Grandma. We'll just fold it up and park it here until you need it."

"*If* I need it," Elisaveta corrected.

"All right, *if* you need it," he confirmed with a chuckle.

Elisaveta leaned over, kissing first Sharlamagne's cheek and then Gwen's. "Well, I'm off, lovies," she said.

"Have fun, Elisaveta," Louisa said, kissing their friend on the cheek.

"And don't buy something you're not certain is legitimate, Mrs. Tanner," Van-Dyke caringly warned. "If you need a second opinion, come and get me, and I'll look at whatever you need me to. All right?"

Elisaveta reached up, once again pinching Van-Dyke's cheek as if he were a toddler. "Of course, darling. Of course."

"It was nice to finally meet all of you," Maxim said, smiling and offering a hand to Van-Dyke. "The famous Dickens family. It's good to have faces to put with names."

"Infamous more likely," Van-Dyke laughed.

"Now you girls let me know if your daddy tries to hide any good treasure from me," Elisaveta called as she urged Maxim toward the booth across the way.

"Yes, ma'am," Sharla and Gwen chimed.

"Does Mrs. Tanner's grandson look kind of familiar to you, Gwen?" Sharla asked in a whisper as she watched them go.

Gwen frowned as she studied him for a moment. "No…not really. Does he to you?"

"Yeah…kind of," Sharla admitted. She smiled then, nodded with assurance, and said, "Oh, wait a minute. I know where I've seen him before."

Gwen giggled. "In your dreams?"

"Exactly!" Sharla said, giving her sister a high five as Gwen raised her hand.

"All right, girls," Louisa Dickens said. "Enough ogling Mrs. Tanner's grandson. Back to work."

"Yes, ma'am," Sharla giggled.

With a heavy sigh, Sharla gathered up a cloth and headed over to the old secretary she'd been polishing before Mrs. Tanner had arrived. She couldn't help taking one last glimpse over her shoulder at Mrs. Tanner's grandson.

"Maxim Tanner," she mumbled to herself. "Nice name."

"Nice everything," Gwen added in a whisper.

The girls giggled together as they worked. As a rush of customers entered the booth, Sharla wondered what other treasures Mrs. Tanner would find. She smiled, thinking that her father had not been exaggerating about having Maxim Tanner back his truck up to the loading dock. No doubt she'd uncover enough treasure to fill up a room that day. She frowned a moment, wondering where in the world Elisaveta Tanner managed to put all the antiques she collected.

"Excuse me," a woman said, and Sharla turned to face her.

"May I help you with something?" Sharla asked.

"Yes," the woman assured her. "There's a ring in the jewelry case I'd like to see."

"Of course," Sharla said. "Let me get the key for us."

As Sharla hurried to where her father was working the register, she glanced across the aisle to the other booth. She laughed when Mrs. Tanner caught her eye and held up a lovely iridescent carnival glass bowl. Sharla nodded and watched as Mrs. Tanner handed the bowl to her grandson and shooed him toward the woman working the booth. Smiling, Maxim shook his head with amusement, and Sharla giggled again. Elisaveta Tanner was without a shred of self-control that day.

❦

Although sales in the Dickens Antiques booth were profitable throughout the remainder of the morning and although Sharla kept busy, not one other customer proved to be as entertaining or as interesting as Mrs. Tanner had been. Of course, Sharla was convinced that no other customer in the world ever would be as fun to deal with as Elisaveta Tanner. Still, the fact that Mrs. Tanner had stopped by so early in the day left Sharla feeling as if there really were not one thing to look forward to for the rest of it.

As the noon hour rolled around, Sharla's mother was off once more, this time in search of lunch for her husband. Sharla and Gwen always packed their own, and Sharla felt guilty for not having thought of her father and prepared a sack lunch for him as well. The customer influx had all but died as potential buyers refreshed themselves as the various food stands on the outer perimeter of the conventions center. Thus, Sharla and Gwen took the opportunity to play a few hands of Old Maid—or Ugly Old Witch as they liked to call it, being that they always used a deck of princess cards that Sharla had received on her tenth birthday. The deck was made of pink-backed cards featuring romantic images of princes and princesses and one card (the Old Maid) featuring the portrait of an ugly, old, wart-nosed witch. Sharla and

Gwen often played Ugly Old Witch during lulls when helping their parents at sales events. The cards were beginning to show their wear too, even though Sharla had always taken good care of them.

As Gwen laid down a pair of cards featuring a prince and princess kissing under a cherry tree, Sharla grimaced. "Dang! You're going to beat me in pairs alone, Gwen."

"Maybe…but I've still got the witch in my hand," Gwen said. Fanning out her remaining cards, she held them up, peered over the tops of them, and said, "Your turn to pick." Sharla smiled as her sister began to whisper, "Please pick the witch…please pick the witch," over and over again.

Holding her breath—for Gwen only had four cards remaining in her hand—Sharla chose the card to the far right. "Whew!" she breathed as she saw the card was not the ugly old witch but a prince and a princess standing in waltz position.

"Twerp!" Gwen teased as she watched Sharla lay down a matching pair.

"Um…excuse me."

Sharla and Gwen looked up to see Mrs. Tanner's grandson standing nearby. He was retrieving the wheelchair his grandmother had insisted he leave at the booth.

"Is something wrong?" Sharla asked, suddenly unsettled at seeing him intent on taking the wheelchair.

"No," he assured her with a movie-star smile. "Her feet are just starting to ache a bit."

"Oh," Sharla breathed with relief.

"She did want me to ask you—you're Sharlamagne, right?" he began, nodding toward Sharla.

"Yeah," she answered.

"She wanted me to ask you if you'd mind coming to look at something for her," he continued. "She got all wound up when she saw it and nearly bought it on the spot. But then she settled down enough to tell me she better have you look at it first."

"Sure," Sharla said, laying her cards facedown on the little TV tray she and Gwen used to play cards on. "What is it she'd found?"

Maxim Tanner shrugged broad shoulders. "Some stuff…like some old perfume bottle in a box. All I know is everything she's looking at has a silver plate on it that says Baby Doe…and Grandma got all excited when she saw—"

"Baby Doe Tabor?" Sharla exclaimed as Gwen leapt to her feet as well.

Again Maxim shrugged, though his smile broadened with amusement at the girls' reactions. "I guess there's something I don't know here then, huh?"

Sharla glanced to Gwen, and Gwen's understanding was immediate. "Go, Shar…hurry! Before someone else buys it!"

Sharla nodded to her sister. "Okay," she said, looking back to Maxim. "Where is she?"

As Maxim began to roll the wheelchair away, he answered, "Over at a little booth in the far corner. It's just one little old guy, and he's only got those few items to sell. It's kind of weird."

Sharla's heart was pounding so hard with anticipation that the rhythm was ringing in her ears. Surely Mrs. Tanner hadn't come upon items from Baby Doe Tabor's estate! Surely she hadn't. Then again, Elisaveta Tanner had an uncanny knack for finding all things rare and historically valuable.

She was nearly trembling with excitement when she and Maxim finally reached their destination—a tiny booth nearly hidden in one corner of the convention center room. An elderly, white-haired man sat in a fold-up chair at a card table. Elisaveta Tanner was chattering away.

"Here she is, Grandma," Maxim said as they approached.

Instantly, Elisaveta gasped and hurried to Sharla. "Sharlamagne Dickens! You will not believe what this gentleman has had hidden away in his attic all these long years!"

"What?" Sharla asked. "Do they really say—"

"Baby Doe!" Elisaveta whispered almost reverently. "Naturally, I wanted to purchase all the items the moment I saw them! But, my good sense, and my wise grandson here," she said, nodding to Maxim, "suggested I have you inspect them first…to make certain they are authentic."

"Let me see," Sharla said, hurrying toward the card table where the elderly man waited.

"Sit down a minute, Grandma," she heard Maxim say behind her. "You'll wear yourself out too soon, and we'll have to leave early."

"Yes, yes…I suppose I should. But wheel me over there, darling. Quickly!" she heard Elisaveta demand.

"Hello," Sharla greeted, taking the elderly man's hand and as he stood and offered it to her.

"Hello there," he said.

Though she thought it impossible for her heart to pound more fiercely, it did! As Sharla glanced down to the items haphazardly displayed on the table, her gut told her they had indeed belonged to Baby Doe Tabor.

There were only three items on the table: a perfume casket, a letter box, and a letter portfolio. All three items were covered in worn burgundy velvet, and all three items bore a silver plate engraved with the name Baby Doe.

"Would you mind telling me a little about your things here?" Sharla asked the man.

"Sure thing," the old man said. He picked up the perfume casket, carefully removed the lid, and offered the items to Sharla. "This here is a perfume casket. You'll notice there's only one bottle…though there are places for two. The story always went that these were some of the first things Horace Tabor gave to Baby Doe and that she was buried with one of the bottles. Of course, we all know that is highly unlikely, considering her circumstances at the time of her death."

Sharla smiled. The man seemed to know his history. Furthermore, he seemed smart enough to know that anyone interested in the items would know theirs as well. The perfume casket was beautiful! Lined with once-white silk, one perfume bottle was nestled in one side of it while the other side was empty.

Sharla handed the perfume casket back to him and watched as he carefully returned it to its place on the table. Next he lifted the letter portfolio.

Nodding to toward the silver plate on the front he said, "See there?

It's inscribed to Baby Doe from Horace. See that?"

Sharla carefully accepted the portfolio. Her smile broadened, her hands trembling a little as she read the inscription. It was indeed inscribed to Baby Doe from Horace.

"And last but not least," the elderly man began, offering the letter box to Sharla, "is this letter box. These things were obviously a set... probably for Baby Doe's vanity table."

Tenderly handing the letter portfolio back to the man, Sharla accepted the letter box. As she studied it carefully and inspected the silver plate on the front, she was further convinced the items were authentic.

"How did you come to own such wonderful pieces?" she asked. "And why in the world would you want to part with them?"

She glanced over to where Elisaveta sat in the wheelchair. The woman's eyes were fairly flaming with excitement.

"Well?" she mouthed to Sharla.

"Just a minute," Sharla mouthed back. She glanced up a moment to see Maxim starring at her, a delicious grin of amusement curving the lips of his alluring mouth.

"My grandmother worked for the Tabors," the man began, "for Horace and Baby Doe. It was quite a scandal, all that mess with Augusta and Horace and such. And Horace and Baby Doe sometimes had trouble hiring on help...even when they were rolling in silver and riches."

"Mmm hmm," Sharla mumbled, encouraging him to continue.

"Well, my grandmother stayed with the Tabors through thick and thin. She even stayed on with Baby Doe for a while after Horace died—until one day Baby Doe couldn't pay my grandmother her wages and offered to give her some of her personal things as compensation. My grandmother accepted some items from her and then explained to Baby Doe that she needed real wages and would have to leave her service. My grandmother sold a few things to get by—a silver, engraved letter opener that went with the letter box and portfolio, a few other perfume bottles, and some silver spoons Baby Doe had given her. But these she kept. I don't know if it was because she thought they'd be valuable one day or if she just wanted proof she'd worked for Baby Doe. Either way, before my mother passed, she gave them to me…being that I was her only child."

"But don't you want to give them to one of your children?" Sharla asked. "They're such a treasure. Both historical and monetary. Surely you'd rather…"

Sharla paused, however. She was being rude—too inquisitive. Perhaps the man needed the money the items would bring. She knew it was bad antique dealing to pry into the reasons why someone was willing to part with things.

"I don't have any children of my own," the man answered, however. "My wife and I weren't fortunate in that regard. But we did have a good life. My wife passed two years back."

"Oh, I'm so sorry," Sharla offered.

The man smiled at her. He was kind—she could see it in his eyes.

"Thank you," he said.

"So, you're just wanting to find these things a good home. Is that it?" Sharla ventured.

"Yep. I won't sell them to anybody unless I feel the person will truly care for Baby Doe's things the way my grandmother did. The way my mother and I did. I've had several people by today, but it wasn't until I met Mrs. Tanner here that I was willing to discuss selling."

Sharla glanced to Mrs. Tanner. "Yes. If anyone understands the true value of a piece of history, it's Elisaveta Tanner."

"I've got a letter here too. I showed it to Mrs. Tanner," the man said, reaching under the table and producing a worn and yellowed envelope. "It was written by my grandmother…a little story of how she came to own things that had once belonged to Baby Doe Tabor."

He handed Sharla the envelope, and she carefully removed the letter and quickly scanned it before tenderly returning it to its place and handing it back to the man. Oh, how she wished she had the money to purchase the treasures! Sharla had never wanted to buy anything more in her life. But she knew the items were worth far more than she could spend—far more than she even had in her bank account.

"Mr. Harvey has agreed to sell these treasures to me, Sharla," Mrs.

Tanner interjected. "But Maxim wanted me to have someone else look at them first."

"Daddy really should be the one to look at them for you, Mrs. Tanner," Sharla said. "I'm not really qualified to—"

"Yes, you are, darling! When it comes to Baby Doe Tabor relics, your word is as good as your father's...even with all his experience," Elisaveta assured her.

"Grandma says you're an expert on this Baby Doe...whoever she is," Maxim added.

"Whoever she is?" Sharla, the man at the card table, and Elisaveta exclaimed in unison. They all stared at him with mouths agape.

"Oh, come on now," Maxim chuckled. "You know marbles are my bag, Grandma...not perfume bottles and stuff."

Sharla giggled, bit her lip for a moment, but couldn't help mumbling, "I get it—marbles are your bag. Marbles? Bag?"

Maxim grinned and shook his head, but Elisaveta laughed. "Well played, Sharlamagne! A pun! How clever of you!"

Mr. Harvey chuckled as well, and Sharla could not keep the blush from rising to her cheeks.

"Well, what do you think, darling?" Mrs. Tanner asked her. "Are these things, in your opinion, authentic? Do you believe they did, indeed, belong to Baby Doe Tabor?"

"Oh, Mrs. Tanner...I really wish you'd let Dad make that call," Sharla pleaded. Sharla did have a lot of experience with Baby Doe Tabor items. She'd seen many fakes and many authentic pieces since working in the store with her parents. Still, she was afraid to make the call on her own.

But Elisaveta Tanner shook her head, her expression that of pure trust and determination. "No, darling. It's your opinion I'm after."

Sharla looked to Maxim, hoping he might decide to side with her in defense of his grandmother's money somehow. But he only grinned at her and nodded, reassuring her that his grandmother's decision on who should estimate the authenticity and worth of the items was final.

Sharla swallowed the lump of nerves in her throat. In her opinion, the pieces were genuine, and she would love nothing more than to see such treasures as the rare Baby Doe items settle into the loving care of Mrs. Tanner. Well, she'd love nothing more other than being able to purchase them herself. However, she also knew that if the items were authentic (and she was ninety-nine percent certain they were), then they were worth at least twelve hundred dollars.

"Sharlamagne," Mrs. Tanner urged. "Name the price of their worth, darling. Maxim's feet are getting tired, and we need to move on."

Sharla glanced at Maxim, who shook his head, obviously amused that his grandmother should blame him for her own impatience.

"I'd pay…I'd pay at least twelve hundred for them, Mrs. Tanner," Sharla managed to state. She looked to Mr. Harvey. "You should accept no less than twelve hundred dollars for all three items, Mr. Harvey. They're worth at least that."

Sharla jumped, startled when Mrs. Tanner clapped her hands together and giggled, "Marvelous!"

"But I've agreed to sell them to her already, miss," Mr. Harvey began, "for eight hundred dollars."

"I shall pay twelve, Mr. Harvey. If Sharlamagne says they are worth twelve hundred as a lot, then I know they are most likely worth even more, and I am glad to pay the twelve," Elisaveta stated.

"Oh, but…but…" Sharla stammered. She'd really done it now! Mrs. Tanner had already bartered to buy the Baby Doe pieces at four hundred dollars less than Sharla's appraisal.

"I won't hear another word about it," Elisaveta said, rising from the wheelchair and digging into her purse.

"I'm sorry," Sharla whispered as Maxim came to stand next to her and they both watched Elisaveta dole out twelve one-hundred dollar bills to Mr. Harvey. "She should've told me they'd already bartered."

But Maxim only smiled at her. "Oh, you know Grandma," he began. "When it comes to her antiques and treasures, her motto has always been, 'Why pay less?' Right? She's a penny-pincher everywhere else, but with her treasures…"

Sharla giggled, feeling somewhat comforted. "Right," she admitted.

"Now, Mr. Harvey," Elisaveta began, drawing Sharla's attention back to the transaction at hand, "if you'll just box those items up, I'll have my Maxim take them over to Mr. Dickens's booth and leave them with my other things. Is that all right with you, Maxim?"

"Of course," Maxim said.

"I could take them back, Mrs. Tanner," Sharla offered.

"Not on your life, darling!" Mrs. Tanner differed, however. "You and I are going to find a little table and have some lunch." She turned to Maxim then and said, "Seek us out when you've finished, darling… and I'll have Sharlamagne tell you the sordid story of Baby Doe Tabor. We can't have you lingering in ignorance any longer, my love."

"I guess not," Maxim said, grinning. "I don't want to be lingering in ignorance over something sordid, now do I?"

"No, you don't, darling. So hurry along and then find us," Elisaveta said. "And let Van-Dyke know I'll have Sharlamagne back to him promptly, all right?"

"Of course, Grandma. Anything you say, Grandma," Maxim teased.

"Shh! Maxim! Sharlamagne will think you're not a gentleman with all that sarcasm dripping from your lips," Elisaveta playfully scolded.

"Yes, ma'am," Maxim said, obviously amused yet again by his grandmother's antics.

"Come along, Sharlamagne, darling," Elisaveta said as she settled herself into the wheelchair once more. "Roll me somewhere quiet and isolated so we can educate Maxim on the subject of mad silver queens. All right?"

"Yes, ma'am," Sharla giggled.

CHAPTER THREE

"You see, as he lay dying, the very last thing Horace Tabor told Baby Doe was to hold on to the Matchless Mine...to never sell it or let it go," Sharla explained to Maxim Tanner. "Horace was certain the Matchless Mine would produce again...that there were still millions of dollars' worth of silver in it somewhere." Sharla paused and took a bite of the hoagie sandwich Mrs. Tanner had purchased for her at one of the concessions stands.

"And did it? Was there more silver in it?" Maxim asked, munching on a sour cream and onion potato chip.

Sharla smiled, delighted with herself for having managed to capture and keep the attention of Mrs. Tanner's gorgeous grandson with her tale-telling concerning Baby Doe Tabor. "Sadly...no. The Matchless Mine never did produce again. And in 1927 it was sold to pay a debt. Though the new owners allowed Baby Doe to stay in the nearby ramshackle cabin she'd been living in for years and years. She spent the last thirty-five years of her life impoverished and scribbling in journals about her plans and schemes to raise funds to work the Matchless Mine once more."

"She never married again? If she was so beautiful and all that, why didn't she?" Maxim asked. His eyebrows puckered into an inquisitive frown.

Sharla shrugged and shook her head. "Nope. She never did. She chose to 'hold to the Matchless,' as she put. I guess the lure of amassing great wealth again was more overpowering than the need for love...

even from her daughters. In the end, both of her daughters were entirely estranged from her."

"So she died alone and a pauper," Maxim mumbled. "After all that scandal and mess and money."

"Yep," Sharla confirmed. "In March of 1935, after a really, really cold spell. Some neighbors noticed there wasn't any smoke coming out of Baby Doe's cabin chimney one morning. They found her on the cabin floor. Her arms were crossed over her chest, and she was dead. She'd run out of wood for her stove and had frozen to death."

"Wow," Maxim breathed. "That's a rather depressing story."

Sharla smiled and nodded. "Yeah. It is, huh."

"And it's a story of the bad end that often comes of immorality, greed, and excess," Mrs. Tanner added. Sharla watched as Mrs. Tanner reached out, patting Maxim on the arm. She winked at him playfully and added, "A story of the ultimate gold digger, darling…and of what became of her."

Maxim chuckled. "So I guess old Horace Tabor—being that he was, what, 24 years older than Baby Doe—was the first sugar daddy, is that it?"

Mrs. Tanner laughed. "Well, certainly not the first, darling…but he was undoubtedly a well-documented and public example of one."

Sharla smiled, and her heart began to hammer with excitement as Maxim leaned toward her, nodded to his grandmother, and whispered, "This is why she gives me marbles instead of money…so that I won't end up like old Horace."

But Mrs. Tanner didn't miss a beat and simply said, "Exactly, darling."

Maxim laughed, took his grandmother's hand, and kissed the back of it. "You really are the best grandma a man could ever hope for."

"Only because I have the best grandson," Elisaveta cooed as she stroked his cheek.

All at once, Sharla felt as if she were intruding. And she had no wish to impose any longer.

"Thank you for lunch, Mrs. Tanner," she said, scooting her chair back from the table and quickly gathering the remains of her lunch.

"You're always too good to us…especially me."

"Are you leaving already, lovie?" Elisaveta asked. Sharla was touched by the sincere disappointment she saw in the woman's expression.

"Yes. I'm sure Daddy needs me back at the booth," she answered. "And Gwen will need a break by now."

Sharla smiled when Maxim stood from his chair and offered a hand to her. She accepted it, and his warm, firm grip sent a pleasurable quiver racing down her spine.

"Thanks for the story," he said, "and for authenticating Grandma's purchase. It was a pleasure to meet you."

"You too," Sharla managed—even though his lingering handshake caused her stomach to feel as if a motorized tire pump were pumping air into it.

Maxim released her hand then, and Sharla leaned down to hug Mrs. Tanner. "You really did find a treasure today, didn't you, Mrs. Tanner?" she asked as the woman returned her embrace.

"Oh, but, darling," Mrs. Tanner began, "I found you years ago!"

Sharla giggled and released her friend. She felt awkward, for the both Mrs. Tanner and Maxim were smiling at her as if she amused them somehow.

"Well," she said at last, "you kids have fun now."

Maxim's smile broadened, and Mrs. Tanner chuckled.

"We will, lovie," Mrs. Tanner called as Sharla turned to leave.

Sharla couldn't wait to tell Gwen about it all—about the Baby Doe pieces, about Mrs. Tanner's purchasing them. But mostly she couldn't wait to tell her that she'd had lunch with Maxim—actually touched him—held his hand for a moment. She couldn't wait until the convention center closed for the day so she and Gwen could go to the mall and talk without any parental ears lurking about. Yep! Maxim Tanner had stepped right off the "I Was Made for Loving You" boat and right onto Sharla's hickey menu!

"You and your life lessons, Grandma," Maxim chuckled as he took hold of the wheelchair handles and began to push his grandmother in the direction of a booth they hadn't looked in yet.

"Why, whatever do you mean, darling?" Elisaveta asked, feigning innocence.

"Oh, don't play naive with me, lady," Maxim teasingly scolded. "You had the girl tell me that pitiful story about that gold digger Baby Doe Tabor and her sugar daddy old man just to make a point about Sophia."

"It was silver Baby Doe was digging for, dear," Elisaveta corrected.

"You know what I mean, Grandma."

"Yes, I do, Maxim. And I know what Sophia means too. At least, I know what she means to do...and she's not for you, darling."

"How can you be so sure?" Maxim asked.

Elisaveta knew her grandson agreed with her. She knew he did. She just couldn't figure out why he kept company with girls like that Sophia.

"Because she's got nothing between the ears or in the bosom," she answered. "She's beautiful, long-legged, and buxom...but beyond that, she has no passion and no mind to do anything but shop."

"You're always so hard on the women I date," Maxim mumbled. Elisaveta knew it was a sensitive subject. Yet she worried so for her beloved grandson. She was so afraid he would end up with a woman the very image of his mother—a heartless, money-hungry, self-absorbed snob.

"Well, they're all the same, Maxim," she began to explain. "Why don't you date some nice girls for a change? Someone down to earth? Someone with intelligence, a sense of humor, and more concern for your welfare than for whether or not her skimpy dress has a designer label?"

"Oh, you mean someone like your little Baby Doe friend there. Is that it?"

Elisaveta felt the hair on the back of her neck prickle with delight. "Well, yes. Sharlamagne is a treasure. You'd be a fortunate young man if you managed to turn her head."

"She's a kid, Grandma," Maxim reminded her.

"She's eighteen years old," Elisaveta argued. "Mind you, I was only seventeen when I married your grandfather."

"Oh, sheesh! We're talking marriage now, Gran?" Maxim sighed. "Look…I'm not even thinking that way where Sophia is concerned, Grandma. I'm just having fun. I'm only twenty-three. I've got years and years before I'm even going to think about *maybe* settling down. And even then it's only a maybe. I'm not sure marriage is in my nature. You know that."

"I know that it will be in your nature one day…when the right girl finds you," Elisaveta said. "And Sophia is not the right girl."

"You see? We agree on something. Sophia is certainly not the right girl," Maxim mumbled. "But neither is some cute little pony-tailed, jail-bait, high school girl who has a knack for spending your money for you."

Elisaveta knew his temper was provoked, and she was glad. It was about time the boy allowed some emotion to surface. Still, she wouldn't press him further. He'd given her the information she'd wanted—that he wasn't thinking of marrying that nose-in-the-air, high-heeled narcissist Sophia.

"All right, darling…all right," she soothed. "I didn't mean to upset you."

"I know, Grandma," he mumbled. "Sorry for snapping at you. Really. I'm sorry. I know you're just looking out for me…that you worry. I'm sorry."

Elisaveta reached back and patted Maxim's hand where it held a wheelchair handle. "I know I should bite my tongue more often, Maxim. It's just so hard. I know you're a man now and that I need to trust that I've raised you correctly and that you'll make wise decisions… especially where women on are concerned."

"Well, I haven't always done that now, have I?" Maxim admitted.

"Let's not talk about that. Let me just say one final thing concerning the matter."

"You mean one final thing *this* time?" Maxim said. Elisaveta could hear the smile on his face.

"Yes," she laughed. "One final thing *this* time."

"And what is this one final thing?"

Elisaveta paused a moment, gathering her thoughts. At last she

39

answered, "Your babe pool is polluted by your family dynamic, darling."

Maxim laughed. "Babe pool? Grandma! Where did you come up with that?"

"Television, dear. Now listen…your parents' lifestyle and warped priorities have left you a victim…as well you know already. But what you may not realize is that it has also determined the type of women you are exposed to—the type of women placed before you to socialize with. Expand your horizons, darling. You must search outside that damnable comfort zone you find yourself in."

"And how would you propose I do that?" he playfully bantered.

"Well, look for young women with real bosoms for one thing."

"What?" Maxim exclaimed in an astonished whisper. "Grandma… are you telling me to check out a woman's—"

"Bosoms, darling," she finished for him. "And yes…but not in the carnal way you may be accustomed to."

"Sheesh! Come on, Grandma," he whined, though she could hear the embarrassment in his voice.

"You're the type of man who needs a woman who has real bosoms… the ones she was born with."

Elisaveta sighed when she felt the wheelchair stop. She felt Maxim hunker down at her side and looked over to see him intently staring at her, any amusement having entirely vanished from his face.

"You've had a *thing*, haven't you?" he asked, his voice serious and rather nervous sounding. "You've had one of your vision things…and now you think the woman who will finally rein me is a woman who has real boo—"

"Bosoms," she interrupted.

Maxim rolled his eyes. "Okay then, she has real *bosoms*…though no one ever uses that word anymore. But you've had one of your things, haven't you? One your vision things."

"Not exactly," Elisaveta admitted, rearranging her purse on her lap. "I just know you…and I know the woman you need has real bosoms." She lowered her voice then and whispered, "And your friend Sophia does not."

Maxim's eyes narrowed. "And your little antique friend does. Is that it?"

Elisaveta grinned. "So you noticed that, did you?"

"I'm a guy, Grandma. Of course I noticed." Elisaveta arched one amused eyebrow as Maxim began to back paddle. "I mean…I wasn't staring or anything. I wasn't being *carnal*, as you put it." He grimaced with irritation, stood once more, and began pushing the wheelchair again. "This is an asinine conversation. I have no plans to get seriously involved with Sophia, Grandma. Nor do I have plans to get seriously involved with anyone…whether she's had breast augmentation or not. So don't worry. Settle down, and let's go antique shopping or treasure hunting or whatever you call it, okay?"

"Very well. Whatever you say, darling," Elisaveta said.

Elisaveta Tanner felt smug—very proud of herself. She'd planted a thought in Maxim's mind, and whether it really had to do with a woman's bosoms or not, she knew how Maxim mulled things over. He'd spend the entire evening rolling the conversation around in his mind, wondering why on earth it mattered whether the women he chose to associate with had real bosoms or surgically enhanced ones. But in the end—though it may take months, maybe even years—Elisaveta knew her Maxim would figure it out. It really had nothing whatsoever to do with bosoms. It had to do with making him think—making him think about what he really needed, what he really wanted in life.

Oh yes! He'd be thinking, pondering, philosophizing for hours— and Elisaveta was glad. That was exactly what he needed to do.

"Oh, darling, look!" she exclaimed all at once. "An entire shelf of silver trinket boxes! In there, Maxim," she begged, pointing to a nearby booth.

"So Mrs. Tanner's grandson made it onto your hickey menu, huh?" Gwen asked as she swirled her purple straw around in her slushy, green beverage. "He made mine too."

"What do you mean, he made yours too?" Sharla asked. "You can't have him on your hickey menu if he's already on mine."

"Of course I can," Gwen argued. "You put Hugh Jackman on your hickey menu *after* he was already on mine. So why can't I have Mrs. Tanner's grandson on mine after you put him on yours?"

"Because he's a *real* man! You know…he's a real person," Sharla answered.

Gwen laughed. "And Hugh Jackman isn't?"

Sharla smiled. "Not really…because you have Hugh Jackman in *Australia* on your hickey menu. So it's not really Hugh Jackman—it's the fictional character he plays in the movie you like. But Maxim Tanner is real…flesh and blood," she lovingly bantered.

"That's true," Gwen agreed.

"And his flesh fits together so well!" Sharla giggled as she bit the curl off the top of her soft ice cream cone.

Gwen laughed too. "I'll second that! And that's exactly why he's on my hickey menu."

Sharla laughed, remembering the night months before, during one of their old black-and-white movie marathons, when she and Gwen had come up with something scandalous—something they'd called their hickey menu ever since. It wasn't a tangible list, nothing that was actually written down anywhere. After all, they may have been goofy enough to come up with the idea of a hickey menu, but they weren't stupid enough to have a hard copy lying around that might end up incriminating them somehow. It was just a little verbal game they liked to play in secret—just between the two of them. The hickey menu had begun as an inventory of movie stars that Sharla or Gwen playfully declared were handsome and alluring enough, romantic and heroic enough, to kiss. It had all started very benignly.

As they sat watching an old movie starring '50s hunk John Gavin (for Sharla and Gwen were both suckers for old movies, classic-looking tall-dark-and-handsome actors, and basically anything else romantic), Gwen had randomly asked, "Would you let John Gavin kiss you if he wanted to?"

"You mean, like, 1957 John Gavin?" Sharla inquired in return.

"Yeah," Gwen affirmed. "Like…say he stepped out of the movie right now and into this room and said, 'Sharlamagne Dickens, I want to kiss you.' Would you let him?"

"Heck yeah!" Sharlamagne exclaimed. "No question about that at all. How about you?"

"Oh totally! I'd totally let him kiss me," Gwen said.

Before they knew it, the girls were swapping movie stars' names back and forth—sorting the likes of Cary Grant, Howard Keel, Ricardo Montalbán, and Elvis Presley into "would you let him kiss you" categories. There were three categories: the "No question! Of course! Yes!" category, the "Maybe if he paid me a million bucks" category, and the "Not if he were the last man on earth" category. Eventually, having exhausted the list of vintage movie stars they liked, they moved on to more current movie stars. It was during that transition—from stars of the 1940s and '50s to contemporary stars—that Sharla and Gwen thought it would be quite entertaining (not to mention secretly scandalous) if another category were added to their game. Thus, the secret "hickey menu" was born.

The hickey menu consisted of handsome actors that Sharla or Gwen dared to confess (but only to one another) that they might consider receiving a hickey from. Oh, they both well knew that hickeys were considered nasty, trashy things—usually associated with somewhat skanky girls at school. Still, Sharla and Gwen had both been curious about hickeys for years—ever since their older, rather "outgoing" (as Louisa Dickens described her) cousin Vicki had secretly told them her boyfriend had given her a hickey and that it was "awesome!"

True to form, Vicki had gone into great detail over just how she received the little purple mark on her neck, explaining that she'd been "making out" with her boyfriend and he'd suddenly started kissing her neck. Before she knew it, she felt him suck on her flesh a little ("just like a vampire might before biting you," she described), and *voilà*, the result was obvious. Vicki had gone on and on about how wonderful it was—kissing her boyfriend and all. She seemed kind of proud of the bruise on her neck too, as if it were some kind of proof to the world that her boyfriend really was her boyfriend.

Well, naturally, Sharla and Gwen were disgusted. After all, Vicki was a lot more "outgoing" than was proper or than either Gwen or Sharla ever wanted to be. Still, the entire incident was something they'd discussed at length. And after having discussed it at length, they each confessed and confided (as all close sisters do) that it was a rather intriguing idea. Oh, they could never admit it to anyone else—not anyone! But they'd confessed it to each other. Therefore, as they sat discussing which actors would be allowed to kiss them, they somehow transitioned to the hickey menu.

So far, Gwen had four guys on her hickey menu. All four were actors, two of whom were the characters played by an actor instead of the actual actor. Sharla had only two—one actor, one character played by an actor. It was a silly, adolescent pastime they'd kept going for months—but only in secret. Heaven forbid their mother should get wind of such a game! Sharla and Gwen could just imagine the lecture awaiting them if she ever did. And this made the hickey menu all the more enticing and entertaining.

"Mmm mmm *mmm*!" Gwen breathed, obviously still thinking of Maxim Tanner. "If you had to bump somebody of your hickey menu to let Mrs. Tanner's grandson on…who would you bump, Shar?"

Sharla shook her head, giggled again, and answered, "Anybody."

Gwen nodded, "I'm with you." She stirred the sloppy drink in her cup. "I wonder who he looks like. I mean, Mrs. Tanner is very pretty… but I don't really see her in him."

"Except for the eyes maybe," Sharla suggested. "I think he has her eyes."

Gwen giggled. "Well, no matter what the genetics were that put him together so well, I'd let him…you know…I'd let him do a little suction action on my neck any day of the week."

"Don't say that word!" Sharla scolded, frowning.

But Gwen laughed. "I said suction because I knew you'd freak if I said suck!"

Sharla growled and gritted her teeth. "We do not say those 's' words, Guinevere Dickens."

"What is it with you and 's' words anyway, Shar?" Gwen asked. "I mean, your name is an 's' word, isn't it?"

"Oh, don't worry about it. Let just focus on that lovely 'm' word that entered our lives today," Sharla suggested.

"Money?" Gwen asked, perplexed.

"Maxim, you doof!" Sharla teased.

"Mmm, yeah! Maxim! It sort of just blends your lips together… kind of like a kiss or something."

Sharla smiled. "Yeah, it does. It's a yummy, yummy name for a yummy, yummy man."

The girls giggled for a few moments as they meandered through the mall. Neither sister owned any real interest in shopping. It was just nice to be somewhere with new things to look at—just nice to stroll along and relax after a long day at the convention center.

"My feet kind of hurt," Gwen said at last. "I think I'll wear different shoes tomorrow."

Sharla looked down to her sister's feet. Gwen was wearing a new pair of running shoes.

"Yeah, maybe it's because they're so new," she said. "You should break them in better before you wear them to something where you're on your feet so much. Wear some old ones tomorrow instead, and see if that helps. Maybe you just need to—"

"Holy cow! Look out! The 'I Was Made for Loving You' boat just docked, big time!" Gwen interrupted.

"What?" Sharla asked. Her attention left Gwen's shoes, and she looked up to see her sister standing mouth agape and staring upward. "Gwen? What is it?" she asked, looking up to the large sunroofed ceiling of the mall above them. She didn't see anything at first, but when Gwen pointed, directing her attention to a giant poster advertising the local clothing company Jeans Innovations, Sharla's mouth dropped open as well.

"Wow! What a scrumptious piece of beefcake," Sharla said as she gazed up at the poster. The poster was enormous—she guessed it was about twenty feet high and ten feet wide. The picture on it was of a tall, dark-haired guy, wearing nothing but a pair of jeans. The jeans fit low enough on his hips that the top part of the white elastic of his boxer-briefs showed just above the jeans waistband. He stood shirtless, with one hand tucked behind his head and the other casually shoved in one front pocket. His hair was wet and hanging limp over his forehead and sides of his face. The torso and arms of the jeans model were bronzed and nothing less than masterfully sculpted, with a defined musculature that would've given the Norse god Thor some serious competition.

Gwen looked at Sharla, her mouth still gaping open. "Are you kidding me?" she asked. "What? Are you blind, Shar?"

Sharla frowned, looked to her sister, and licked her ice cream cone twice before looking back to the brawny, bronzed, brunette jeans model on the poster. "What do you mean?" she asked.

Gwen shook her head in disgust. "Exactly what are you looking at?"

Sharla pointed her ice cream cone at the poster. "The captain of the 'I Was Made for Loving You' boat there. What are *you* looking at?"

"Wow!" Gwen breathed, shaking her head again. Smiling, she said, "Remind me never to hire you if I'm ever in charge of missing persons."

"Why?" Sharla asked, again licking her cone.

"Sharlamagne Dickens! Quit looking at his chest and look at his face! Seriously! Are you gonna tell me you've never seen this guy before?"

"Of course not," Sharla answered with disgust. "They put up the new posters of this guy in Jeans Innovations last month. Remember? Everyone was asking if they could buy a copy when we were in there and…" She couldn't speak then and felt her grip tighten so hard around her ice cream cone that one side of it cracked.

Gwen giggled, "Yep…yep…it's coming to her now. Slowly, but it is coming to her."

"No freaking way!" Sharla breathed as she stared into the face of Mrs. Tanner's grandson.

"You asked me if he looked familiar today, remember?" Gwen asked. Sharla nodded. "Well, I guess he should've. And I guess you must've recognized him…subconsciously at least."

"Maxim Tanner is the Jeans Innovations model everyone has been freaking out about?" Sharla breathed in an awed whisper.

"It would appear that way," Gwen said. Taking Sharla's hand, she began to lead her toward the entrance to Jeans Innovations. "Come on, Shar. I want to see those other posters again now that we know who he is."

"No food or drink allowed," Sharla read as they approached the store.

The sisters exchanged smiles. Sharla tossed her ice cream cone into the nearby trash receptacle and watched as Gwen's green slushy drink followed.

As the girls stepped into Jeans Innovations to see the walls and ceilings fairly plastered with posters of Maxim Tanner in various ultra-cool posses, Gwen asked Sharla, "So exactly where does Mr. Sexy Jeans rank on your hickey list?"

"Number one, sista! Number one. And don't use the 's' word," came Sharla's breathless-with-awe answer.

Fifteen minutes late, Sharla and Gwen leaned forward over the register counter, listening with rapt attention as the clerk told them the story of the new Jeans Innovations model guy.

"So anyway, one day, the daughter of the guy who owns this place," the perky redhead was saying, "just walks in with this new guy she's dating, right? I mean, this chick's dad owns Jeans Innovations! All of them! The ones in the malls, the ones at the factory outlets…all of them. Anyway, the owner's daughter—her name is Sophia—walks in with this guy, right? And all of us girls who work here, I mean, we were panting! The guy is so hot! You can't even imagine!" The chatty clerk lowered her voice and added, "Some of the guys who work here were even panting."

"Really?" Sharla asked.

"Oh, totally! This guy was hot! I mean, seriously…the posters don't do him justice."

"Really?" Gwen asked.

"Not at all," the clerk said, shaking her head. "So anyway," she continued, "apparently, Sophia went home and told her rich daddy about everyone's reaction when this guy walked into the store. So the owner calls up his advertising team and tells them to get a hold of the guy and get him involved in an ad campaign for Jeans Innovations, right?"

"Right?" Sharla prompted.

"Well, the way I hear it, the guy didn't want to do it at first. But then Sophia talked him into it somehow. My guess is she whined him into it. That's how she rolls…whining and batting her eyelashes and swinging her little round booty around."

Gwen and Sharla exchanged understanding glances. If the Sophia whose father owned Jeans Innovations was the same Sophia that had showed up at the antique show earlier that day—well, they could just imagine how she'd talked Maxim Tanner into modeling for her father's business.

"So? Does he come in here a lot?" Gwen asked.

The chatty clerk shook her head. "Nope. Haven't seen him since." She glanced over at a poster of Maxim Tanner modeling nothing put a pair of Jeans Innovations jeans, however, and smiled. "At least, not in person. We get to look at his picture all day though."

"Wow! That's crazy," Sharla said.

"I know, right?" the clerk agreed. "But I'll say this—sales are through the roof! I've made so much commission this month I can almost pay off my car!"

Gwen smiled at the clerk and nodded. "Cool! That's awesome! So I guess the ad campaign with sexy Romeo there has paid off."

"Big time!" the clerk confirmed.

Sharla frowned at Gwen a moment, silently scolding her for using the 's' word again.

"Are you guys in for anything particular today?" the clerk asked.

"Not really," Gwen answered. "We were just looking around and saw the posters and were wondering who the guy was."

"Well, I don't know his name…but I know every line of every muscle he's got showing!"

Sharla forced a courtesy giggle and smile. "I bet you do. You're lucky."

The clerk nodded, agreeing that she certainly was.

"Well, have a good day," Gwen said as she turned to leave the store.

"And congratulations on paying off your car!" Sharla added over her shoulder as they left.

"Thanks!" the perky redhead called after them.

"And now you know exactly why Mrs. Tanner's grandson looked familiar to you today," Gwen offered as they stepped into the mall.

"I guess so," Sharla admitted. She looked up to see several girls standing below the big mall-sized poster of Maxim Tanner, taking photos with their cell phones. "And I'm getting me some of that action." Reaching into her pocket, she retrieved her cell and pressed the camera button.

"Me too!" Gwen laughed.

As the girls stood with the others, taking photos of the giant poster of Maxim Tanner, Sharla giggled. "That sneaky little Mrs. Tanner has been holding out on us all these years."

"Yeah," Gwen agreed. "And all this time I thought those marbles she buys were for some little boy."

"Oh, it's all relative, Gwen," Sharla said. "After all, you know what they say…"

Gwen smiled and chimed in with Sharla as she quoted, "The only difference between men and boys…is the price of their toys."

"And I'm sure Mrs. Tanner has dropped quite a price on marbles over the years," Gwen added.

"Oh, definitely!" Sharla agreed, snapping one more photo of the poster. "There!" she said as she scrolled through the photos of the poster of Maxim Tanner now saved to her phone. "And I'll never look at marbles the same way for the rest of my life."

"I have the sudden, insatiable urge to purchase a pair of Jeans Innovations brand jeans," Gwen said.

"Me too!" Sharla giggled. "I did notice they're having some sales in there."

"Then let's go," Gwen said, tugging at Sharla's arm. "And every time we wear them, we can think of Maxim Tanner."

"Yeah," Sharla agreed, still smiling. "But I still had him on my hickey menu first."

"Did not," Gwen teasingly argued.

"Did so," Sharla countered.

Back and forth they bantered, as the returned to Jeans Innovations to browse, about who had put Mrs. Tanner's on their hickey menu first.

They only stopped because they saw a security guard chasing a girl as she dashed out of Jeans Innovations—a stolen poster of Maxim Tanner clutched in her hands.

Elisaveta awoke gasping for breath. The dream had been so intense—so specific! It was a common enough thing for Elisaveta, experiencing epiphany through her revelatory dreams. Yet this dream—this dream was more than just a feeling. This dream was a vision of what was to come. She had not one shred of doubt in her soul that all she had seen would be. And so she quickly flipped on the little lamp she kept on her night table, snatching up the dream journal and pen she kept next to it.

While still in the full bloom of youth, Elisaveta Tanner had learned to keep a notebook and pen at her bedside. Dreams were fleeting, especially epiphanic dreams that revealed the future to Elisaveta. Experience had taught her to write down such dreams the moment she awoke from them, else the particulars of the dream be lost to consciousness. Therefore, she quickly scribbled the details of the dream—of the revelation of future events.

She smiled, even breathed a little giggle, as she realized how entirely undisturbed she was at now knowing exactly when she would die. She surmised that most people would find such information frightening, depressing—might live the remainder of their lives in despair and anxiety. But not Elisaveta Tanner. She was eighty-two, after all. It was a good and ripe age. Besides, she had four more years to prepare, to get everything else she'd seen in order. Furthermore, Elisaveta Tanner did not fear death and dying—especially if it came peacefully as she now knew hers would. And she so longed to see Alek again! Oh, how she'd missed her beloved Alek—her lover and husband of over fifty years. He'd been gone so very, very long from her—nearly a decade—and missing him was excruciating. Elisaveta knew Alek would be waiting for her when she passed from this life to the next, for he'd told her as much in the dream she'd only just awakened from.

Hence, as she sat in her bed, smiling as she scribbled down the elements of her dream, Elisaveta Tanner sighed with pure, unadulterated joy. All would be well—she knew it assuredly now. It was true there was much to do—indeed there was. She wondered for a moment how she would ever manage to knit together all the things she needed to before her moment of passing arrived. Yet she was grateful for the heads-up given her. Now she could plan efficiently so that every little thing would be in order when the time came.

She reached to her night table again, pressing a button on the new-fangled music device Maxim had set up for her. It would take her hours to write down everything about the dream, and she had always preferred to write with music as her companion—whether it was a letter, her poetry, or the details of a dream that had been given to her. She smiled as Helen Forrest's lovely voice began to sing "I Remember You." Try as it might, no popular music of any era owned the quality of sentiment and beauty as did the songs Elisaveta cherished of the 1940s—the songs of those golden years where men were patriotic and women beautiful. Those were the years of Alek and Elisaveta—of their meeting and romance—of the bloom of their powerful, passionate, and everlasting love.

Thus, Elisaveta's happiness grew greater as she wrote in her dream journal and listened to Helen Forrest's voice floating softly through the night air—for she had been given more than just the time and circumstances of her own passing in the dream. Yes, she had been given far, far more information and affirmation than that. In this dream, Elisaveta had been given the greatest assurance she could ever have wished for—confirmation that all would be well with the one person she loved and cared for more than anything else in all the living world.

PART TWO

CHAPTER ONE

"You knew, didn't you?" Maxim asked. "You knew that you were going to…that your time was getting close, didn't you?"

"Darling, I'm eighty-six years old. Of course I knew it was coming. You didn't think I'd live this life forever, did you?"

Maxim forced a feeble grin as renewed moisture filled his blue eyes—beautiful blue eyes that Elisaveta knew so well. Eyes as blue as the heavens—just as Alek's had been.

"No," Maxim admitted. "But I hoped you would."

Elisaveta smiled and patted the back of her grandson's hand, somewhat desperately clutching her own. Maxim was so very handsome—and in so much pain in anticipating her passing. Elisaveta wanted nothing more in that moment than to comfort him. Yet she well knew the agony of loss and knew that nothing would ease his mind much.

As her grandson let his head fall forward onto the hospice bed a moment in an effort to rein in his emotions, Elisaveta placed a weak hand on his head, lovingly stroking his soft black hair. She committed her soul to remembering the feel of Maxim's hair between her fingers. It felt so much different than it had when he'd been a little boy, but the gesture still gave them both comfort—just as it had since the day he was born.

"Shh, darling," Elisaveta whispered. "Shh…all will be well. I promise."

Maxim raised his head and looked at her once more. She saw the aching weighing heavily in his countenance, coupled with fear.

"How can you promise me that?" he asked. "What will I do now? You're the only one who really knows and understands me...the only person who loves me for who I am." He shook his head. "Sorry. I sound like a whiny, selfish little kid."

Elisaveta smiled. "Not at all, darling. Not at all. And I do understand you...and I do know you better than anyone, I suppose. And as far as loving you...oh yes! I do so love you, my precious baby boy." She took his chin in one hand, forcing him to make eye contact with her. "And yet, I make the promise to you that everything will be all right and that you will be happy again. I promise you that, lovie...and has your grandma ever broken a promise?"

He grinned a little. "No. But how do you know? Have you seen it? Did you see this?" He paused a moment, studying her face. "You did, didn't you? You knew this was coming. I know you did. I can see it in your eyes. You've never been able to hide things from me."

Elisaveta smiled. It was true. Maxim could read her like a book.

"Yes...I saw this," she admitted.

"When?" he asked. "Recently?"

"Four years ago," she answered, releasing his chin—for her arm felt weak and tired.

"Four years?" he exclaimed. She could see his temper was tweaked— yet she knew his anxiety would keep it in check. "That long? Why didn't you say something? Why didn't you tell *me*, at least?"

Elisaveta rolled her eyes and breathed an amused laugh. "Oh, Maxim! You've got to be kidding! Why on earth would I have told you that I knew when my passing would happen? What good would that have done?"

"I could've better prepared myself," he growled, frowning at her.

Again she patted the back of his hand. "Darling, no one—no matter how much notice they have—can be prepared for that kind of loss. It would have done nothing but worry and depress you. You said it yourself...I know and understand you better than anyone. So it is well I know that telling you would have only done you harm. I'm the one dying. I'm the one who was grateful to have had the time to get my affairs in order. Which reminds me…"

But Maxim began to shake his head. "I don't want to talk about that now," he grumbled.

"Too bad. You need to know what's coming," she told him. "There may not have been the need for you to know when I would leave you, but you do need to be prepared for what will happen once I'm gone."

As Maxim raised an arm, brushing his face on his shirt sleeve, Elisaveta drew a tissue from the box of tissues on her nightstand. "Here, darling, use a tissue."

Maxim took the tissue, wadded it up, and wiped at his nose. "I don't want our last moments together to be about all that, Grandma," he said.

"They won't, darling. But you need to know what I've done." Elisaveta paused, inhaling a deep breath of courage. "I've left all my money to your parents, Maxim. I've left no money to you…not a penny. No cash anyway."

Maxim frowned and shook his head. "I don't care about your money, Grandma. You know that. And I don't want to talk about this now."

"Maxim," she began in her sternest scolding voice, "you must know everything. You have to be prepared for the storm."

He frowned. "What storm? You've left Dad and Mom everything, and that's what they always wanted. I'll be free at last, as the saying goes. I won't have an inheritance, and so they'll leave me alone. What storm could there be?"

"I've left them the money, most of my properties, Maxim. But you know how they are, darling," Elisaveta said. "They'll want it all. Ninety-nine percent of my wealth won't be enough."

Maxim's frown deepened. "What else is there? That's all they care about, Grandma. You'll finally make Dad the happiest man in the world…at least the way he sees it."

"There are properties and other small items I have not left to them," Elisaveta explained. "But they'll want everything, darling. That's how they are. Their greed for wealth and material substance is insatiable."

She paused, thoughtful. "Though you're right...*you* will be free of them. But you're not the only person in my will who will be gifted things, darling. And though I know *you* can well stand up to your parents, others may not have your experience and strength in that regard. So I'm asking you to champion me and my wishes in my absence. I want you to defend others to whom I have willed things from the wrath and ugliness of your parents' hate and greed...from their arrogance, self-importance, and feelings of entitlement. Will you do this for me, darling? Please, Maxim?"

Maxim's strong brow still furrowed with a frown. "Of course, Grandma. But you didn't need to ask me. You know I will."

Elisaveta smiled and patted Maxim's hand once more. "I do know it, darling. I do." Pointing to the chest of drawers nearby, she said, "There's a box...there...in the bottom drawer. Run get it, please."

"Yes, ma'am," Maxim said as he stood and strode across the room to the chest of drawers.

Elisaveta watched as Maxim retrieved the large wooden box from the drawer and brought it to her. "Set it on the bed, darling...and then get the small silver key from the key ring in my pocketbook."

As always, Maxim did as his grandmother requested.

"Do you want me to unlock the little padlock on it?" he asked as he removed the small silver key from Elisaveta's key ring.

"No, darling," she answered. "I want you to put it on your key ring, and then, when I'm gone and before my services, I want you to take this box and deliver it to my friend Sharlamagne Dickens."

Maxim frowned once more. "The little antique girl?" he asked.

Elisaveta smiled. "Yes, darling. I want you to take it to her and hand it to her personally." She wagged a warning index finger at her grandson. "And do not unlock it first. That way, if your parents question you about what I willed to whom, or about what I gave away before my passing, you can truthfully tell them you don't know."

"Well, where does she live?" Maxim asked. "Do you have an address or something for me?"

Elisaveta shook her head. "No. Just take it to Dickens Antiques between nine and five Tuesday through Saturday, and she'll be there.

She works there full-time now that's she finished with college."

Maxim nodded. "Okay. I'll do it." He set the box down on the foot of the bed, slipped the silver key onto his own key ring, and then dropped the wad of keys into his front pocket.

"Really? No questions from he who always questions?" Elisaveta teased.

But Maxim shook his head. "Nope. If you mean to pull a fast one on Dad and Mom, I'm totally down with it. In fact, I'll take pleasure in it."

Elisaveta sighed. "Don't resent them so, darling," she counseled. "They *are* your parents. They're idiots, yes…but they brought you into this world, and I wouldn't have had you without them. We wouldn't have had each other."

Sitting in the chair beside his grandmother's bed once more, he took her hand again. "You're right," he said, forcing a grin. "Now, is there anything else you want me to secretly deliver?"

"Just this," she said, taking hold of the large gold locket that hung from the chain around her neck. "I want Sharlamagne to have this as well. Help me remove it, will you?"

"Your locket?" Maxim asked, taking the locket from her and holding it in his hand as he studied it. "This is the one Grandpa gave you, isn't it?"

"Yes," she answered.

"But I thought you'd want to take it with you."

Elisaveta laughed. "You mean you thought I'd be buried with it?"

"Yeah," Maxim admitted as he helped her remove the chain from around her neck.

"Why? I'll have Alek with me from the moment I pass away," she explained. "Your grandpa is waiting for me, you know, Maxim. He's been waiting a long time. I won't need the locket anymore because I'll have him." She smiled and laughed a little. "And besides, you know the old saying—you can't take it with you. Well, that's true enough, I suspect. Why leave it buried in the ground when I know how much Sharlamagne would treasure and care for it? And besides…your father won't even miss it…*and* it is listed in my will as going to Sharlamagne, so there can be no argument if he ever does remember it at some point."

Maxim nodded. "All right then," he said, gathering the chain and locket into his palm and dropping it into the opposite pocket from which he'd dropped keys. "What else?"

Elisaveta could sense it then—sense that her time was near—that her time with her beloved Maxim was short. It was the first time since dreaming of her death four years before that she had known true and sad regret. It would be so long before she saw him again. Suddenly, Elisaveta wasn't so certain she wanted to leave him. Yet she called to mind the other aspects of that same dream—and was comforted.

She cupped Maxim's whiskery cheeks in her hands, drew his face to hers, and placed one last kiss to his lips. "I love you, my darling. And would you allow me a few moments of final nagging?"

"I love you too, Grandma," Maxim mumbled as moisture rose to his eyes again. He felt it too—she knew he did. Maxim knew she was approaching her final moments of mortality. "And of course you can nag me...for as long as you want."

Elisaveta drew a deep breath. She knew she had very little time in which to reiterate so many important things. "Wealth, Maxim...it is very rarely a good thing. Very few people can endure the trial of wealth and keep hold of their integrity, perspective, and priorities. You've seen it firsthand, I'm afraid. And though there are those of wealth who remain humble, balanced, and caring of others—my son and his wife, your father and mother—are not they. Avoid it, my darling. There is nothing wrong with ambition, enough money to live comfortably and well. But do not fall into the trap of seeking after incredible wealth and material things. It breeds unhappiness and shallow relationships."

"I know, Grandma," Maxim mumbled.

"And now I would speak what's in my heart to tell you, Maxim," Elisaveta whispered. She inhaled deeply and fancied the action was more labored than it was a moment before. "You have a passion locked deep within you—a passion only a handful of people in all the world possess and that even fewer understand. The same passion that allows you to love me so completely will also to make you the best and strongest man any person will ever encounter in all their lives.

You have the capability to love more deeply, more thoroughly, and more passionately than most, Maxim. And you need a woman to share that with you…to take that upon herself and cherish it. Furthermore, you need a woman with full as much passion in her heart, body, and soul as you have. No other woman will ever satisfy you emotionally or physically…or in any other regard there may be in life. She needs to have a kindred passion for life, for love…and for you. You, in fact, will unlock her passion for living and loving, as she will unlock yours. So find her, my darling…or allow her find you. Either way, when you do discover her, take her in your arms and make love to her every moment you are together of every day of this life! Kiss her at breakfast, smile at her always, let her know with every touch, every glance…with every breath you draw, express your love for her. Do this and she will belong to you as you never imagined a woman could belong to you. Do all this for her, Maxim…for she will love you with full as much passion and purpose as you love her."

Maxim brushed the tears from his cheeks. She was leaving him! He could feel it as surely as he felt any physical pain ever inflicted on him. He smiled a little, however, thinking that it made sense that Elisaveta Tanner's last words would be about passion and love.

"I'm not just telling you what I think you need to hear, darling," his grandmother whispered. He studied her and could see the color visibly draining from her face.

"I know, Grandma," he whispered, clutching her hand in a desperate attempt to hold onto her. "But don't leave me here all alone, Grandma. I'm not ready."

Elisaveta smiled the smile Maxim Tanner had loved for as long as he could remember. In fact, it was his very first memory—looking up as he lay in his grandmother's arms, looking up into her smiling, loving face as she cradled him and gently rocked him as she hummed.

"I'm not leaving you alone, darling," she whispered. "At least, not for long."

"I love you, Grandma," Maxim breathed.

She raised a hand to his cheek, just as she'd done some many times.

Yet her touch did not feel quite as warm as it had a moment before.

"And I love you, darling. You, Maxim…you are my happiness," she whispered.

Maxim brushed another tear from his eye, leaned over, and kissed his sweet, beloved grandmother on one soft, wrinkled cheek. He noticed that her eyes widened, seeming to sparkle with renewed vigor once more, and hope leapt in his chest for a moment. Yet it did not take but an instant for him to realize that she was looking not at him but beyond him.

"Oh, there you are, darling!" she said as tears filled her eyes. "I've been waiting so long!"

Maxim glanced over his shoulder to see nothing—nothing but the breeze lift the curtains at the open window for a moment.

"Do you see him, Maxim?" Elisaveta whispered. "Just there at the window." She smiled and raised one hand toward the window, her other still clasping Maxim's. "Oh, Alek! How I've missed you so!"

Her eyes closed then—her breath stilled.

"Grandma?" he whispered, though he knew she was gone. "Please don't leave. I…"

His own breath caught in his throat—for he felt a gentle, almost indiscernible caress travel over his check and sensed her fingers comb through his hair. And then—then he knew she truly had gone. Maxim Tanner knew then that he was, for the first time, all alone in the world.

For the first twenty-four hours following his grandmother's death, Maxim Tanner thought he might actually follow her on her journey to what lies beyond. He'd never known such thoroughgoing heartache—never imagined that losing someone he loved could knock him flat on his back as it had. The pain and agony Maxim experienced at the death of Elisaveta Tanner was almost debilitating. Yet, somewhere in the black depths of his desolation, he remembered the light she had gifted the world—the light she had gifted him—and he chose to follow the light of living as opposed to the darkness of despairing.

His grandmother had been everything to him—mother, teacher, friend, and mentor. And though his pain didn't really lessen, his clear thinking and strength had returned. Every hero in every story lost their mentor at one point. Whether it was a parent, friend, or grandmother, it seemed every hero in every book, movie, or ballad eventually experienced that same loss.

Therefore, Elisaveta's repeated philosophy to Maxim of "the hero's journey" began to pound through Maxim's anguished mind and soul, until at last, two days before her services were to be held, he woke up with a determination to live the life she'd taught him to live—to be the man she'd always wanted him to be.

Maxim's grandmother had prepared very efficiently for her death. When he'd visited the funeral home only hours after her passing, he'd been astonished to find that everything was already arranged. Elisaveta Tanner had wanted the most uncomplicated exit from the mortal world possible—a small viewing at the funeral home and then a simple graveside service. In his heart, Maxim knew her choice to forego a lavish funeral service was more for his sake than anyone else's. He knew she didn't want him lingering in his misery, and he was thankful to her for yet another gift to him.

With everything for his grandmother's funeral already in order, Maxim then looked to granting her last request of him. Thus, he stood before the doors of Dickens Antiques, holding under one arm the wooden box his grandmother had kept in her chest of drawers, the gold locket she'd had him take from her nesting in one front pocket of his jeans.

He studied the antique shop for a moment—noted how inviting it was. He wondered how much cash the owner had had to dole out in order to have the face of the building look as if it had suddenly appeared right out of Victorian London, somehow. The front of the building was nothing but windows lined with perfectly displayed antiques. He imagined that if the Old Curiosity Shop had been lettered on the building between the two windows on the second story instead of Dickens Antiques, the building couldn't have looked more authentic. For the first time in two days, he felt the corners of his mouth slightly curve upward—he almost smiled.

But then he remembered the reason for his visit—to inform his grandmother's little friend of her death. That fact sent any resemblance of momentary gladness drowning in reality.

Inhaling a deep breath, Maxim crossed the street, opened the door to Dickens Antiques, and stepped inside. He was astonished to find that the shop didn't smell like dust, must, or furniture polish the way he'd expected it to. Rather, the comforting scent of mulling spice met his nostrils, instantly soothing him and causing his thoughts to linger for a moment on Christmas Eves past somehow.

"Good morning!" a pretty middle-aged woman, dressed in a red-and-purple scarf-like dress and accessories, greeted him. "May I help you find something? Or are you just browsing today?"

Maxim forced a friendly smile. "Actually, I'm looking for Sharlamagne Dickens. I was told she'd be working today."

The pretty woman smiled. "She is indeed working today. She's just putting some books on a shelf in one of the back rooms. Just go through here," she explained, gesturing toward a hallway to the right, "and you'll run right into her."

"Thank you, ma'am," Maxim said with a nod.

"Of course," the woman giggled with a wink.

Maxim felt sick to his stomach. No doubt the woman thought he was a friend of Sharlamagne Dickens's come to pay a social call. She wouldn't be smiling at him after she knew the news he'd come to deliver, that was for certain.

As Maxim meandered toward the back room the woman had indicated, he noticed how perfectly arranged everything in the store was. Instead of looking like a hodgepodge of used junk the way some stores he'd seen in his life, this store had class. Often there were chairs and a table set up in arrangements, giving him the feeling of just having walked back in time. Various shelves displayed books and glassware, but always with an air of order. No wonder his grandmother had favored Dickens Antiques. It was an inviting, soothing, unusually serene environment.

As he entered the room at the back, he saw Sharlamagne standing on a chair, arranging books on an upper shelf of a large bookcase. Maxim paused for a moment, wishing he didn't have to be the bearer of such sad news. His grandmother had talked a lot about Sharlamagne Dickens—harbored a special adoration for her. Furthermore, he was certain the girl adored his grandmother just as much, and he didn't want to cause her the kind of pain he himself was enduring at her loss.

He remembered the antique show four years before when he'd first met his grandmother's little friend. She'd been so cute and entertaining, spinning tales of gold diggers and sugar daddies. He wondered if she still held the same intrigue with old things as she had then. Remembering the box under his arm, he suspected she did—and he suspected what his grandmother had put in the box for the girl.

"Excuse me," he said at last. Bad news was bad news, and there was nothing he could do to avoid delivering it, so he might as well get on with the task.

Sharlamagne Dickens quickly glanced back over her shoulder when she heard a man's voice. "I'll be right with you, sir," she said. "Just finishing up stocking some new books we received yesterday."

Hopping down off the chair she'd been standing on to reach the higher shelves, she dusted her hands together and smiled as she looked up. A quiet gasp left her breathless as she immediately recognized the man standing before her—Maxim Tanner. Holy cow! He was even better looking than he'd been years before when she'd met him at an antique show his grandma dragged him to. Even for the photo she still had on her cell phone of the poster in the mall, she had forgotten what a presence he was—a sheer, magnificent, masculine, alluring presence!

"Do you remember me?" he asked when Sharla only stood staring at him with her mouth agape.

"Of…of course!" she answered, nodding like a joggled bobblehead doll. "You're Mrs. Tanner's grandson. The marble boy."

He grinned, but she thought it was not a happy grin. There was something about his eyes—they lacked the blue sparkle she so well remembered.

"Yeah," he confirmed. "I…um…I have something for you," he said.

"For me?" Sharla asked, puzzled.

"Yeah. Grandma asked me to bring it over to you," he answered. She watched as he took the wooden box out from under his arm, offering it to her.

"Does she want us to sell it for her?" Sharla asked. She giggled a moment. "Though I can't imagine Mrs. Tanner parting with anything."

"No. It's not something to sell," Maxim said, handing the box to her. "It's something she wanted you to have. Oh, and I have the key for the lock here."

Sharla held her breath as a sickening sense of dread began to wash over her. She couldn't speak. As she watched Maxim Tanner remove a small silver key from his key ring, she could only stare at him, praying that the feeling of trepidation seeping into her every pore wasn't justified—that it was only a misunderstanding of what he'd said and the lack of sparkle in his eyes.

"Here you go," he said, offering the key to her.

Sharla accepted key, setting the box down on a nearby table, her fingers trembling as she endeavored to unlock the small padlock on the box. "Wh-what is it?" she stammered as tears began to fill her eyes.

"I'm not sure," he said. "Though I think it might be the—"

"The Baby Doe Tabor pieces she bought that day at the antique show," Sharla breathed as she lifted the lid of the box to see just that— the three burgundy velvet pieces (the perfume casket and bottle, the portfolio, and letter box) she'd authenticated for Mrs. Tanner years before. There was also a book in the box. As Sharla lifted the book out of the box, tears escaped her eyes, rivuletting over her cheeks. "The Complete Poetical Works of Elisaveta Petunia Tanner," she read aloud. "I've always wanted one. Th-they're so hard to come by. I could never afford…"

Without turning to look at Maxim, Sharla hugged the book to her chest and wept. Once she felt she could speak, in a whisper, she asked, "Y-you've come to tell me something, haven't you? She didn't just send you here with a present like this on a whim, did she?"

Maxim didn't answer at first—simply moved to stand next to her, took one of her hands, and pressed something into her palm.

As Sharla looked down at the familiar locket and chain he'd place in her hand, she began to cry bitter tears of loss. She gently placed the book back into the box with the Baby Doe things and studied the locket—her hands trembling so dramatically she was afraid she'd drop it.

"It was the last thing she asked me to do," Maxim said then. "To bring these things to you. She wanted you to have them."

"Wh-when did she die?" Sharla asked, for she knew now—she knew her beloved Mrs. Tanner had passed away.

"Two days ago…peacefully," he answered.

"B-but she can't have died," Sharla wept. "I didn't have the chance to say goodbye…to tell her how much she meant to me and how much I loved her." Sharla shook her heard in a gesture of denial. "She only went into that place two weeks ago!" she cried. "I just saw her last Tuesday, and she was fine!"

Maxim was a bit unsettled at how overwrought the girl seemed. Tears were streaming down her pretty face, her shoulders trembling with sobbing. He had expected her to be sad, but not destroyed the way she appeared to be. If he hadn't known better, he would've thought her pain at the loss of his grandmother was as harsh as his own.

"Here," he said, taking her arm. "Why don't you sit down a second?" He led her to the chair she'd been standing on only a few moments before. "I'm sorry. I guess I didn't realize it would be so upsetting to you."

Sharlamagne glared at him, but it wasn't a hateful glare—more of a hurt or *How could you be so stupid as to think it wouldn't be?* glare. But then her sobbing began, and Maxim was entirely unraveled. Nothing unraveled a man's calm nature more than a woman in pain and tears.

Hunkering down before her, he said, "I'm sorry. I really am. I know she meant a lot to you. And I know she loved you more than almost anything else in the world."

Sharlamagne's demeanor changed suddenly, and Maxim was surprised when he felt her palm on his cheek. "I'm so sorry, Mr. Tanner…for you loss. You must be devastated…and here I am going on all selfish and stupid."

Maxim liked the feel of her palm to his face. It soothed him somehow, in a manner he hadn't been soothed since his grandmother's death. He felt his heart lighten just a breath and offered a comforting smile to her.

"You're not selfish and stupid," he told her. "And it *has* devastated me." He shrugged his shoulders and added, "But I'm okay. And you will be too."

Instead of comforting her the way he'd hoped his words would, what he'd said only seemed to send her into more sobbing.

"I-I don't handle loss very well," she muttered between sobbing gasps. "I'll never be the same again…never!"

Maxim watched as the girl buried her face in her hands for a moment, weeping against the gold of the locket and chain she held. He knew she was right—that after such a loss of someone so beloved, no one was ever the same. Still, he was worried about the girl. She seemed so utterly distraught, and he hadn't expected it—hadn't come prepared to be the comforter when he was still in need of comfort.

"Her services are on Saturday, if you'd like to attend," he said at last—because he didn't know what else to say. "There's a viewing at French's Mortuary at noon and then a graveside service at two. I'm sure she would love to know you were there."

The girl nodded, studying the locket in her hand as she wiped tears from her cheeks. "Yes. Yes…I want to be there." She looked up to him then, and his heart panged with the empathy for the heartache he saw in her pretty eyes. "I shouldn't keep this though," she said, offering the locket to him. "It's a family heirloom. You should…I'm sure she would want you to have it."

Shaking his head, Maxim closed her hand over the locket. "She specifically told me to give it to you. She wanted you to keep it. She knew you'd appreciate it and treasure it."

Sharlamagne nodded, sniffled, and wiped more tears from her eyes. All at once, Maxim felt the urge to gather her into his arms—to comfort her the way he wished someone had been able to comfort him. But she was nearly a complete stranger to him. What would she think if he suddenly drew her against him, kissed her forehead, and told her everything would be all right? Anyway, she had plenty of family as he recalled. The Dickens family had all known his grandmother and would no doubt mourn together and comfort one another. She didn't need some strange guy making a bad attempt at consoling her.

As Maxim Tanner stood, obviously intent on leaving, an odd sort of panic sprouted in Sharla. She didn't want him to leave! He was her last link to Mrs. Tanner—all that remained of her—and she felt desperate for him to remain with her. Yet she couldn't ask him to stay. How ridiculous would that be? After all, he no doubt had many other people to inform of Elisaveta Tanner's upcoming viewing and funeral services. She had no right or reason to keep him.

"So can I expect to see you at the viewing and services?" he asked.

Sharla nodded, wiping more tears from her cheeks. "Yes. Th-thank you for letting me know." She studied the locket in her trembling hand. "I just can't believe she's gone. I swear to you, I'll never be the same."

He nodded, and Sharla felt guilty for adding to his pain when she saw excess moisture welling in his beautiful blue and very sad eyes. "I know. I'm sorry."

"It probably sounds really dumb," she began, "but is there anything I can do to help? To help you?"

He forced a grin. "Everything's been taken care of," he answered. "Apparently she had it all in line a long time ago."

Sharla nodded. "I'm sure she did."

Maxim watched the girl wipe more tears from her cheeks. He couldn't believe how affected she was by his grandmother's death. It was strange to him—and yet comfortingly endearing at the same time.

"Well, I'll look for you on Saturday then," he said as he turned to leave.

"M-Mr. Tanner?" she asked.

He turned to see Sharlamagne Dickens weeping the bitter tears of heartache, and he winced in knowing how she felt.

"Yeah?" he asked.

"On your way out, w-would you ask my mom to come back here,

69

please?" she whispered, trying in vain to control her sobbing.

"Sure," he said. And then he left the poor girl to the harsh pain of mourning. There was no more he could do for her. After all, he hardly knew her. What could he do? Nothing.

Sharla studied the gold locket in her hand. With weak and trembling fingers, she opened the locket to reveal the photographs that had been placed inside. On the left half of the locket was a portrait of a very handsome man—a man who looked very much like Maxim Tanner. The man was young and wearing a white Navy dress uniform. Sharla knew this was Alek Tanner, Elisaveta's beloved husband. She let her fingers gently caress Alek's image before looking to the portrait secured in the right half of the locket—the portrait of a young, vibrant Elisaveta Tanner. Oh, she was as beautiful as a 1940s movie starlet, and Sharla's tears increased.

Quickly she closed the locket, afraid her tears might ruin the images inside somehow. A moment later, her mother floated into the room, already shedding tears of her own.

"Oh my, baby!" Louisa Dickens wept as she gathered her daughter into her arms. "Our dear Mrs. Tanner! I can't believe it! I just knew she would live forever! Oh, she was such a kindred spirit with me…with all of us, wasn't she?"

Sharla wept against her mother's shoulder. She couldn't speak. She could only cry—sobbing with the pain of loss. Yet even for her own pain and misery, she could not help but think how more painful the loss must be for Maxim Tanner. And at the thought of his pain, Sharlamagne cried harder.

CHAPTER TWO

Sharlamagne sat nervously picking at one of her fingernails. She didn't like the attorney's office. It was far too stiff and formal—all brown and black and dull. Furthermore, she couldn't imagine why on earth she'd been summoned to the reading of Elisaveta Tanner's will.

Two days after Mrs. Tanner's funeral, when she'd first received the phone call asking her to appear in Mrs. Tanner's attorney's office, Sharla thought maybe she was in trouble—that maybe someone had seen her slip the small braid of her own hair into Mrs. Tanner's casket at the viewing and that now she was about to face charges of tampering with funeral services or something. Yet, as Mr. Rowlands's secretary began to explain that Mrs. Tanner had requested Sharla be present at the reading of the will, she breathed a sigh of relief—at least for a moment.

But now, as she sat in the office reception area, across from a man and a woman she could only guess were Maxim's parents, she began to fidget. The man in the room resembled Maxim, only with no charming smile and with an air of arrogance that permeated the atmosphere like stinky pea soup. The woman was just as bad—tall, slender, with her nose so high in the air Sharla could nearly see up her nostrils. Only the size and number of diamonds adorning the woman's fingers, wrists, and neck kept Sharla from wondering whether she could see up her nose into her sinuses if she really tried.

Maxim Tanner was nowhere in sight, however, and Sharla thought it odd. She knew how much Mrs. Tanner loved her grandson and therefore could not imagine he would not be present at the reading of her will.

Just when Sharla thought she might scream just to break the silence, a woman appeared from around one corner and said, "Mr. Rowlands is ready to see you now."

"Well," the nose-in-the-air woman said with irritation thick in her voice, "I'm glad he could find the time to settle my mother-in-law's massive estate…which no doubt afforded him a hefty profit."

"We were told our appointment was at one p.m.," the arrogant man said as he stood from his chair and rudely brushed past Mr. Rowlands's assistant. "It is now five after that hour, and my time is more valuable than he knows."

Sharla felt her mouth drop open in astonishment at the arrogant, rude, and entitled behavior of the middle-aged man and woman.

She closed her mouth quickly, however, when the Mr. Rowlands's assistant looked at her and asked, "Are you ready as well, Miss Dickens?"

"Yes. Thank you," Sharla answered as she stood and began to follow Maxim's parents.

Maxim's mother, however, stopped cold in her tracks. "Well, who is she?" she demanded, speaking to Mr. Rowlands's assistant but staring at Sharla.

"Miss Dickens has been asked to attend as well," Mr. Rowlands's assistant answered.

"Why?" Maxim's father growled.

Mr. Rowlands's assistant simply shrugged and said, "Will you all follow me, please?"

Maxim's mother took her husband's arm, looked back over her shoulder to Sharla, and shot her the nastiest look she'd ever seen in her life. Sharla literally felt as if she'd been physically slapped. Yet when Mr. Rowlands's assistant dropped back behind the snotty couple, smiled, and winked at her with encouragement, she managed to keep going.

As they stepped into a large office with shelves lining the walls and stacked with heaps of old books and papers, a man looking to be in his mid-seventies stood from his chair behind the desk and offered a hand to Maxim's father.

Again Sharla's mouth dropped open as Maxim's father ignored the man's polite gesture and simply took a seat in one of the chairs facing the table. "Let's get to this. I've got places to be," he said.

Maxim's mother didn't accept the man's hand either but, casting another irritated look Sharla's way, asked, "Why is this girl here? Who was she to Elisaveta?"

"Wow, Mom. What, are you worried Dad fathered a love child or something and that she might get some of Grandma's money and leave you with only a measly few million?"

Sharla turned to see Maxim Tanner standing in one back corner of the room. He was leaning against a bookcase, looking not only furious but so incredibly handsome that Sharla was rendered breathless and goose-bumpy.

Maxim's mother didn't even respond to him, other than to give him a scolding look. What she did do, however, was look to his father.

"Is that true?" she asked. "Is this girl some...something you—?"

"Absolutely not!" Maxim's father nearly shouted.

"Then what's she doing here?" his mother demanded, again glaring at Sharla. All at once, she quickly turned in her chair and exclaimed. "Maxim Tanner! Do *you* have something to do with her being here?"

"Yep," Maxim answered. "You guessed it, Mom. I had a fling, and Grandma changed her will to leave everything to this girl's baby."

"What?" Maxim's parents exclaimed in horrified unison as they looked to Sharla.

Sharla could only sit shaking her head. Thus, she was very relieved when Maxim finally intervened.

"Relax, Mom," Maxim grumbled. "She's just a friend of Grandma's. And you're probably freaking her out because she comes from a nice, normal, polite family. Settle down so Mr. Rowlands can hand over Grandma's money to you and make you and Dad the happiest people in the world."

"Mrs. Tanner...Mr. Tanner," Mr. Rowlands began then. "Shall we begin?"

"Yes," Maxim's father grumbled. "I cannot abide having my time wasted." He looked at his watch. "It is now ten minutes after one p.m., Mr. Rowlands."

Maxim studied Sharlamagne Dickens for a moment. She looked like a lamb chained to a post and waiting for the wolves to devour her. Again, his promise to his grandmother—to basically stand between his parents and whoever else was involved in the division of her estate—echoed in his mind. It was what she'd been talking about—protecting her little friend from his predatory, cruel, merciless parents.

Leaving his place at the back of the room, he strode to where Sharlamagne Dickens stood. She still hadn't taken a seat in one of the chairs in front of Mr. Rowlands's desk. He knew she was probably afraid to. Therefore, as he reached the place where she stood standing looking like a rabbit ready to bolt, he pulled a chair out from in front of the desk and nodded toward it. When she'd taken her seat, Maxim planted himself in the chair between her and his parents. He heard an audible sigh of relief escape her lungs and offered her a reassuring nod.

Sharla smiled at Maxim. She hoped he understood that she was grateful he'd put himself between her and his distasteful family. She felt sorry for him, for having grown up with them. Still, she remembered how much his grandmother had talked of him and all the time she and he spent together. It was then obvious to her just who had raised and influenced Maxim Tanner and who hadn't.

"Well," Mr. Rowlands began, "I have here the last will and testament of Elisaveta Petunia Thomas Tanner." Sharla watched as Mr. Rowlands unfolded a thick bunch of legal documents and began to read. "*I, Elisaveta Petunia Thomas Tanner—*"

"You're not going to read it word for word, are you?" Maxim's mother interrupted. "It's enormous. Can't you just paraphrase it?"

Again, Sharla felt her mouth drop open in astonishment.

She closed it very quickly, however, when Maxim leaned over to her and whispered, "It's like a bad film noir movie, right?"

"Yes," Mr. Tanner said. "I don't have time to sit here and listen to all the mundane details of my mother's estate."

"Very well," Mr. Rowlands said. He picked up a document sitting on one side of his desk. "If you'll both sign these, stating that you have requested to receive only the details of the will concerning you both—"

Sharla watched as Mr. and Mrs. Tanner quickly signed the papers, handing them back to Mr. Rowlands.

"Now get on with it," Mr. Tanner demanded.

Mr. Rowlands said, "Gladly." He then opened a drawer at the front of his desk and withdrew two simple legal-sized envelopes. "Mr. Tanner, it seemed your mother often had a sixth sense about things... including the approach of her passing. Therefore, two years ago, she began to liquidate all of her assets, save one small property, on which sits the house she lived in until her death and a second house that has not been inhabited for many years."

"She liquidated everything?" Mrs. Tanner asked, obviously upset. "Her properties? Investments?"

"That is correct," Mr. Rowlands answered.

"And what did she do with all the money?" Mrs. Tanner asked, nearly screeching. "Don't tell me she's gone and left it all to Maxim! Or to some damn charity or something!"

"We'll contest the will, Rowlands," Mr. Tanner grumbled. "If that's what my idiot mother did, then we'll see you in court."

"Shut up, Dad," Maxim growled.

"Actually, Mr. Tanner," Mr. Rowlands continued, "your mother left every penny of her accumulated wealth—save the one property I mentioned—to you and your wife...jointly."

"What?" Mrs. Tanner asked, though the smile spreading across her face was resplendent.

"I have here two cashier's checks," Mr. Rowlands said. "One is in your name, Mr. Tanner," he said, handing one envelope to Maxim's father. "And one is in your name, Mrs. Tanner," he added, handing the other check to Maxim's mother. "Each check is in the amount of fifteen million, two hundred seventy-five thousand, eight-hundred and ninety-one dollars. Elisaveta Tanner died a very wealthy woman."

Sharla swallowed the lump of astonishment in her throat. She never, never—not in all her life—would have guessed Mrs. Tanner was so rich.

"This is all of it?" Maxim's mother asked.

Maxim sighed with frustration. "What, Mom? Thirty million damn dollars between you guys isn't enough?"

"Well, of course…that's not what I meant at all, Maxim," Mrs. Tanner stammered.

"Yes, it is!" Maxim growled. "Geez, Mom! Grandma liquidated everything for you guys—everything but the house she lived in! She probably only kept that because you've always hated it, and she knew you wouldn't want it." He shook his head. "I cannot believe you people."

"Except for the property on which she lived until the time of her death, those checks represent Alek Tanner's life's work and Elisaveta Tanner's legacy of managing it well," Mr. Rowlands said.

"And the old house?" Mr. Tanner asked.

Sharla bit her lip—for Mr. Rowlands's face was fiery red with indignation and fury all of a sudden. "The old house and the property it sits on she left to her Maxim."

"That's all she left him?" Mrs. Tanner asked. "I find that hard to believe."

"Well, Mom…you could read Grandma's will for yourself and see," Maxim suggested with sarcasm.

"And the other house on the property?" Mr. Tanner inquired, ignoring his son. "That went to Maxim too?"

"That house and all its contents have been willed to Miss Dickens," Mr. Rowlands answered.

"Me?" Sharla squeaked.

"All its contents?" Mrs. Tanner laughed. "It's filled with nothing but junk! Nostalgic trash. Why on earth would she—"

"The Dickens family owns an antique store that was Grandma's favorite, Mom," Maxim interjected.

"Oh," Mrs. Tanner said, pointing her nose to the ceiling and mumbling. "Well, that explains it then."

"If you have no other questions," Mr. Rowlands began, "then, Mr. Tanner…our business is concluded."

"Good. I have an appointment in an hour," Mr. Tanner said, standing.

Sharla watched as Mrs. Tanner stood as well—as they both turned and began to leave the room. At the last possible moment, however, Maxim's mother turned and asked, "Will the sale of Elisaveta's house provide enough income for you for a time, Max? We…we could loan you something if you need us to."

"Gee thanks, Mom," Maxim said, shaking his head. "You know, for managing to think of me there at the last minute. But…nope. I'm fine. You and Dad have fun spending the money it took Grandpa and Grandma over fifty years to earn."

"Very well then," Mrs. Tanner said before following her husband out of the office and closing the door behind them.

Sharla heard Mr. Rowlands sigh with relief. "I don't know how you stand them, Maxim. Really I don't."

Maxim nodded and then turned to Sharla. "They're, like, the worst people you've ever met, aren't they?"

Sharla sighed and arched her eyebrows. "Well, technically I never *officially* met them."

Maxim and Mr. Rowlands both chuckled. "She caught a break," Maxim said to the attorney.

"Indeed," Mr. Rowlands agreed.

"Do you have the paper for her to sign, Carl?" Maxim asked.

"Oh, yes," Mr. Rowlands said, picking up a paper from a stack of papers on the front of his desk. "If you'd like to opt out of hearing the will read, Miss Dickens…"

"Well…would it be too much trouble to read it to me?" Sharla asked as Mr. Rowlands offered the document to her. "I'd really rather hear it, actually."

A warm, happy sensation drizzled over her as she saw Maxim smile at her—saw his deep blue eyes light up with approval. Mr. Rowlands seemed pleased as well.

"I would be more than happy to read it to you, Miss Dickens," he said. "Oh! But first…"

It was obvious he'd only just remembered something. Sharla

watched as he opened the same drawer from which he'd removed the envelopes for Maxim's parents and retrieved a small envelope.

"I'm supposed to give this to you and have you read it before we proceed with the will and its concerns with you," he said.

"Thank you," Sharla mumbled as she accepted the small envelope. As she turned it over, intending to open it, she smiled. There, on the flap of the small envelope, was seal of crimson wax. An ornate cursive capital "E" had been pressed into the wax, and Sharla let her fingers gently caress the emblem. She didn't want to break the seal, so as tears of missing Mrs. Tanner filled her eyes, she carefully peeled it off.

Inside was a small, Victorian-style die-cut note card. Brushing a tear from her eye, Sharla opened the card and read what Elisaveta Tanner had written to her inside.

Sharlamagne Darling,

This is just one final nagging note for you, dearest…to tell you one final wish I would like for you to grant for me. My wish is this, darling. Your name is Sharlamagne—not Sharla or Shar or any shortened form. Would you grant me this one last request and allow people to call you by your given name, Sharlamagne, in its beautiful entirety…for me? And know this…I could not love you more had God given you to me instead of to your own wonderful parents. You have all my heart, darling Sharlamagne.

I love you, Elisaveta.

Sharlamagne Dickens brushed the tears from her cheeks. She was rendered painfully self-conscious when she looked up to see both Mr. Rowlands and Maxim staring at her with kind expressions of understanding.

"She has a way of getting everybody all soppy, doesn't she?" Maxim asked with a wink.

"Yeah," Sharlamagne agreed.

"Are you ready then?" Mr. Rowlands asked.

Sharlamagne nodded, relaxed where she sat at last, and thought of her beloved Mrs. Tanner as Mr. Rowlands began to read, "*I, Elisaveta Petunia Thomas Tanner…*"

Maxim sat back in his chair and exhaled a heavy sigh. He'd heard the will earlier that morning—in its entirety, the way his grandmother had specified. Now he could just let his mind wander a bit—breathe easier now that his parents had what they wanted and were gone.

He was amazed at how well his grandmother knew them all—his father, his mother...himself. Just before she'd died, when she'd told him she'd left all her money to his parents, he hadn't really thought she meant literally. Of course, he hadn't been thinking of money or material things at all when his grandmother was dying. But now—man, oh, man could he see the wisdom in what she'd done. In his mind, he thanked her again for his freedom. Neither of his parents could've given a rat's rear end about the old house on Whippoorwill Lane, but Maxim loved it. He'd grown up in it—spent all those beautiful years with his grandparents and then his grandmother in it. He'd played in the yards and climbed the trees. He knew every story associated with every picture and trinket his grandmother housed in it. It always smelled like freshly baked bread or chocolate chip cookies or apples and nutmeg. It was his home, and he had no plans of selling it. He really couldn't see himself living it in—not with his grandmother gone. Besides, he'd put so much work into restoring the old, turreted Victorian manor that it had become like a person to him. Still, he was thankful to his grandmother for leaving it to him—grateful to her and happy that he could still go there and linger where he'd known so many happy days.

Maxim looked to Sharlamagne Dickens for a moment—studied her as she dabbed at the tears on her cheeks. She truly, truly loved his grandmother; he could see it in absolutely everything about her. Furthermore, he could tell it had nothing whatsoever to do with all the cash his grandmother had laid out at Dickens Antiques over the years either.

All at once then, it made sense—his grandmother's leaving the old, smaller, and abandoned house and its contents to Sharlamagne. He grinned. Yep, his grandmother was a stinker! The old house on the back part of the property was simply stuffed to the gills with a large portion of his grandmother's antique collection—her treasures! That old house was a veritable treasure trove to anyone who loved old things and history the way his grandmother had.

It all made sense to him then—in a way it hadn't when Mr. Rowlands had first read the part of Elisaveta Tanner's will concerning the bequeathing of that old house and its contents to Sharlamagne Dickens. He should've picked up on it sooner, but hearing the will read had brought his grandmother's death racing over him anew, and he'd been somewhat distracted. Now, however, he got it—he completely got it.

He remembered the antique show years before—when he'd sat at a lunch table listening to his grandmother's little antique friend telling the story of Baby Doe Tabor. Sharlamagne's eyes had lit up like stars when she'd first seen the Baby Doe items—and only continued to glisten as she told the story. Willing the old house on the back of the property to Sharlamagne was his grandmother's way of not only keeping her treasures safe, cared for, guarded and loved but also of making sure the historic and emotional value of them would endure.

There was something else Maxim thought about as he studied the pretty brunette in the chair next to him. He'd seen her do it, of course—at his grandmother's viewing four days before. Maxim had seen Sharlamagne lean over and kiss his grandmother's cheek as her body lay in repose in the casket—and he'd seen her slip something beneath his grandmother's clasped hands. He hadn't said anything. But as soon as the place had cleared out and everyone was heading to their cars for the funeral possession to the cemetery, he'd gone over to say one last goodbye to the woman he loved more than anything in all the world. That's when he lifted her hands to see the soft, thin braid of hair Sharlamagne had tucked there. It was a beautiful little thing, actually—tied with a tiny lavender ribbon at each end and soft as velvet. Maxim had smiled, woven the little braid between his grandmother's fingers and called the funeral director over to ask a quick question. The man had looked at him oddly when Maxim asked for a small pair of scissors so he could clip a couple of snowy lengths of hair from his grandmother before closing the casket lid. He wasn't even sure why he'd felt the need to do it—he just had.

The funeral director had complied and even supplied an envelope for Maxim to put the hair into. Maxim had always known of his grandmother's passion for antique mourning hair jewelry things. And even though he never planned to have such a thing crafted, he suddenly understood that Sharlamagne Dickens had put a little piece of herself to rest with his grandmother. By the same token, he'd thought that perhaps having a length of her lovely white hair would be a part of her he could keep with him. It was a sappy, sentimental, almost strange gesture—but then again, the woman who had raised him had slathered him with sappy sentiment—and a lot of it stuck.

Maxim's thoughts had begun to wander to Sharlamagne Dickens very often after that. Once his grandmother's services were over, his mind began the process of climbing out of the darkness of pain and despair. It was then that he realized Sharlamagne Dickens had turned his head. With her refreshing middle-class manner, emotion, sentiment, and thoughtfulness, she'd given him a good case of whiplash. She was kind, sweet, witty, beautiful. *And her bosoms are real*, he thought, smiling at yet another amusing memory of his grandmother.

"So…what does that mean…exactly?" Sharlamagne asked, drawing Maxim's attention back to the reading of the will. "Am I supposed to just clean out the house and…and then do what with it? You said it's old and not really habitable. So I'm not quite sure what she wanted me to do with it."

Maxim smiled. "Oh, I think when you see what's inside that old house, it will make perfect sense," he said.

Sharlamagne smiled at him. He seemed so much happier since his parents left the room. She thought how sad the fact was—yet she could see his strength. She had no doubt Mrs. Tanner had prepared him to deal with whatever was going to happen to her estate when she'd gone.

"I'll tell you what," Maxim said, leaning forward in his chair until he was nearly nose-to-nose with her. "I've got a ton of stuff I have to finish up this week. With everything that has happened, I'm way behind at work. But why don't you come over Sunday afternoon—if you have time, of course—and I'll show you just what Grandma left to you. I think it will be quite obvious to you why she left you what she did then. Okay?"

"Okay," Sharlamagne said, smiling at him. It should be a criminal act, being so attractive! She was a little freaked out at the way her heart was hammering—the way her mouth was watering.

"Let's say Sunday afternoon at three? Sound good?" he asked.

"Yeah," she answered.

"Well then," Mr. Rowlands sighed, "I've already given Maxim the title to the house and property. And here are your documents, Miss Dickens." Sharlamagne accepted the large manila envelope he offered to her. "Now the house Elisaveta left to you sits on the same property Maxim owns. However, that can be subdivided when or if both of you agree to it. All the information is in there," he said, nodding toward the envelope. "Read over it a few times, and call me with any questions at all. My information is in there as well."

"Thank you, Mr. Rowlands," Sharlamagne said, offering a hand to him. He smiled at her and shook her hand.

"Yes. Thank you, Carl," Maxim said, standing and shaking hands with Mr. Rowlands. "Call me if you think of anything else, okay?"

"I will. Have good day, Maxim," Mr. Rowlands said. "And you too, Miss Dickens. It was a pleasure to meet you."

"Thank you. And the pleasure was all mine," Sharlamagne said.

Maxim started to walk with Sharlamagne to the office door, but he paused and turned. "Oh! Carl…I need the paperwork for the copyright transfer of Grandma's poetry." He looked to Sharlamagne and winked. "Just a tiny, little detail my parents didn't want to take the time to listen to. Grandma left the rights to her work to me as well."

Sharlamagne smiled, for she couldn't have imagined a better guardian of Elisaveta Tanner's poetical works. "Oh, I'm so glad!"

"Me too. Have a good day," Maxim said.

"Thanks. You too." And she left the office—as a beneficiary of Elisaveta Tanner's incomprehensible benevolence.

❦

Sharlamagne sighed when she entered the house. The whole will thing at Mr. Rowlands office had worn her out for some reason. Still, she could smell something sweet baking in the kitchen and was instantly enveloped in the secure comfort of home. She paused at the entryway table to go through the mail someone had left on the silver tray.

"Is that you, Shar?" Gwen called from the kitchen.

"Yeah. I just walked in."

"Awesome! I have warm cookies if you want some."

"What kind?" Sharlamagne asked as she sifted through the mail.

"Oatmeal!" Gwen called.

"Mmm! I'm almost there."

"Oh," Gwen began, "and you got something in the mail."

"Yeah. I found it."

"It's all, like, fancy. A wedding announcement or something," Gwen continued to call. "But I can't think of anybody you know who's getting married that the rest of us wouldn't know."

The envelope of white linen paper was expensive-looking. There was no return address, but a metallic gold seal on the back of it was embossed with a "T."

As Sharlamagne opened the envelope, Gwen came in, wiping her hands on her apron. "So who's getting married?" she asked.

"Nobody," Sharlamagne answered as she read the very fancy invitation inside. "It's a birthday party...for Maxim Tanner."

"No way!" Gwen squealed. "He already invited you to his birthday party? You hardly know him!"

"He didn't invite me," Sharlamagne said, offering the invitation to Gwen.

Gwen read, "Birthday party for Maxim Tanner...blah, blah, blah... seven o'clock, Saturday the blah, blah, blah."

"Read the handwritten note at the bottom," Sharlamagne said, pointing to the bottom edge of the invitation.

Tears had already filled Sharlamagne's eyes as Gwen read aloud. *"Please don't be late, Sharlamagne, darling. He may need help setting out the hors d'oeuvres. Love to you, dearest. Elisaveta."*

CHAPTER THREE

"Yeah. She must've had the invitations dropped in the mail a day or so before she died," Maxim explained as he began escorting Sharlamagne up the front walk leading to Mrs. Tanner's restored Victorian house. "I'm really not much into parties...but Grandma always insisted. I guess I'll look at it as her last request and endure it." He glanced to Sharlamagne and asked, "You're coming, right?"

"Of course!" Sharlamagne assured him—though, until that very moment, she hadn't really decided whether she had the nerve to actually show up at the birthday party for Maxim that Mrs. Tanner had prearranged.

Maxim paused for a moment, sighing with satisfaction as he gazed up to the house. "It looks pretty good, doesn't it?"

Sharlamagne could not keep from gazing in wonder at the beautiful Queen Anne Victorian home before her. It was, by far, the most beautifully restored Victorian in town. She'd driven by it before, of course—just because she'd always been so intrigued by its beauty. But she'd never guessed it belonged to Mrs. Tanner.

"Grandma calls it the Pink Peony...because of the huge peonies that were growing all around it in clumps when she and Grandpa first bought it," Maxim explained. "There are still a lot of those peonies in the back garden. Grandma transplanted them about forty years ago."

"It's beautiful!" Sharlamagne whispered. "I've always loved this house...ever since I was a little girl. I just never imagined that Mrs. Tanner lived here." She shook her head, disgusted with her lack of

85

deductive reasoning. It made perfect sense that someone who loved the past as much as Elisaveta Tanner did would live in such a home. "I'm such an idiot sometimes."

Maxim laughed. "Aren't we all…at one time or another." He stood for a moment studying the house. "Well? Do you want the historic rundown?"

"Are you kidding?" Sharlamagne giggled. "Of course I do. Tell me everything."

"Okay," he began, "but remember, you asked for it." He chuckled a moment and then continued. "The house was designed by the famous Newsom Brothers and built in 1887 as a wedding gift from Humphrey Williams to his son John. In the 1920s, the Williams family sold it, and it endured being a boarding house through the late 1930s. Then it stood empty and fell into pretty bad disrepair until Grandpa and Grandma bought it in 1948. It took them almost fifteen years to finish fixing it up…at which time Grandma begged Grandpa to let her paint it a pretty peony pink." Maxim paused, smiling. "I remember when my grandpa told me that story. 'Elisaveta wanted to paint the damn house pink,' he said. 'And the fact I let her do it…well, that right there is proof a man will do anything for the woman he loves, even live in pink house like a damn china doll.'" Maxim paused to smile and shake his head at the obviously fond memory. "But the pink house, combined with the white ornate carvings, decorative flourishes, and gables, put the house on the map. I'm not much for pink houses either…but it's striking, right?"

"It's literally the most beautiful home I've ever seen," Sharlamagne confessed with admiration.

Maxim smiled at her. "Would you like to go in?" he asked.

"In that house? Not just the one in the back?"

"Sure," he answered. "Grandma would want you to see it." She followed him up the front steps and watched as he unlocked the door. "We'll just go through the front rooms and kitchen and then out the back to the other house. I can show you the upstairs some other time."

"That would be wonderful! Thank you so much," Sharlamagne said. She sensed he wasn't ready to brave going upstairs to his grandmother's private rooms—to see her personal things. Not yet. The pain of loss was still too fresh to him, and she felt the same way.

Maxim opened the door, stepped aside, and gestured for Sharlamagne to precede him in entering the house. "Thank you," Sharlamagne said, blushing at his old-fashioned manners.

The moment she stepped into Mrs. Tanner's beautiful Victorian home, Sharlamagne gasped—was rendered astonished and silenced into awe—as the ambiance and beauty of the home washed over her like some soothing summer breeze from long ago.

"It's so beautiful!" she exclaimed in a whisper. She heard Maxim step in behind her and close the door, yet her feet seemed rooted to the floor. Sharlamagne could only stand in awe, slowing looking around the entryway, into the parlor on the right and the more formal drawing room to the left. "I cannot believe how incredible it is!" She glanced to Maxim to see him smiling at her with approval. "And do you know what else?" she asked.

"What?" he asked in return.

"It feels like a home...not a bed-and-breakfast or something. It feels like you just stepped back through time and arrived in someone's home for a friendly visit. I feel like I should have a dainty calling card to leave on..." Sharlamagne paused, glancing to the small table placed near the front door. She giggled and, pointing to the small silver dish sitting on the table top, continued, "To leave on that silver calling card tray there."

Maxim chuckled, and his smile broadened. "Well, it is a home. Grandma and Grandpa didn't restore it to be tiptoed around in," he explained. "When I was kid, I played on the rugs just like any other kid would play on the carpet or floor. Grandma baked cookies and fed them to me with glass after glass of milk while I rolled my toy cars on her table. I licked the mixing bowl when she made a cake, spent the night camped out in a tent she'd make by stringing blankets over the furniture. It's a home...a real home."

Sharlamagne smiled at him, delighted by his sentiment. She sighed, imagining how marvelous it must have been for him to escape the snooty lifestyle his parents obviously led and linger in the warmth and love of his grandparents' home.

"It was actually just out back, behind the house, that Grandpa first taught me to play marbles," he continued. "That's when I first became so interested in them…because it was something I used to do with my grandpa." He shook his head and sighed. "You probably think I'm a moron, going on and on about stuff."

"Not at all," Sharlamagne assured him. "You forget who you're talking to. When it comes to sappy, sentimental, reminiscing-type stuff, I'm the queen of the morons."

He laughed. "Oh, I doubt that."

Sharlamagne exhaled another sigh of just plain wonderment as she looked around. She wanted to wander through every room, of course—study every knickknack, let her fingers feel the upholstery of every piece of furniture. She wanted to gaze at every photograph displayed on the walls or mantels, linger in the kitchen, and drink lemonade. Yet she knew Maxim's feelings were still tender and wounded by his grandmother's death. Furthermore, she didn't want to be rude and snoop through his house. Well, actually, she did want to be rude and snoop through his house, but she wouldn't. All at once she could feel Mrs. Tanner's presence again—her joy, her teasing manner. For a moment, she could've sworn she caught a whiff of the gardenia-scented perfume she always wore. Oh, how she would miss her friend!

As her eyes began to mist with tears, she was thankful that Maxim said, "Come on. We'll go through the kitchen and out back. I'm kind of intrigued to see what's in that old house myself. I haven't been out there in probably over a year."

"Okay," Sharlamagne managed. Yet as they walked down the entryway toward the kitchen, she looked up to the large, very old, convex-glass framed photograph hanging on one wall before them and stopped cold in her tracks. "Maxim!" she breathed, staring, entirely mesmerized by the beautiful and very, very rare photograph before her. "Maxim…where in all the world did she find this? Oh, it's fantastic!" She drew in a long, awed breath. "I've never seen anything like that in all my life! Not up close anyway. I love it! I kind of can't believe I'm seeing it. It's authentic, right?" In the next moment, Sharlamagne shook her head, again humiliated by her own stupidity. "Well, of course it is. Mrs. Tanner owns it."

She looked to Maxim to see a very, very pleased smile spread across his very, very handsome face. "So you like that one, do you?"

"How couldn't I? I love it!"

"Well, I'm glad," he said, looking to the photograph, "because it's a family portrait of my great-great-great-grandparents and their family. The little girl in the photo," he said, pointing to a beautiful young woman dressed in a lovely white dress and a large hair bow common near the turn of the previous century, "is my great-great-grandmother, Grandpa's great-grandmother."

Sharlamagne shook her head, almost too awed to speak. "I truly have never seen anything like that. It's so beautiful!"

Maxim smiled again. "Well, so I'm guessing you know how rare it is then and why."

She nodded. "And I love it!" She couldn't get over the beauty of the photo. The tall, handsome man in the photograph looked strong, intimidating, and almost severe. Sharlamagne knew he would have to have been a strong man in order to have endured the challenges that would've faced him and his beautiful, dark-complected wife. Sharlamagne instantly began to wonder if the woman in the photo had been born into slavery—wondered what she had endured even before she married a strikingly handsome white man. The five children in the photograph were absolutely adorable—beautiful, with coffee-and-cream skin, light-colored eyes, and rare and stunning features.

"Yes," Maxim said, interrupting her awed contemplation.

"Yes what?" Sharlamagne asked, still staring at the photograph.

"Yes, Abigail was born a slave…in 1862. My great-great-great-grandfather Dillanger Thomas was ten years old when she was born on the plantation his father owned. After the emancipation, Dillanger and his mother moved north and took Abigail's mother, father, and family with them. Dillanger married Abigail in 1878, and his mother disinherited him for it. But he worked hard and actually became a very wealthy man in New York—wealthy enough that he and Abigail and their children lived a very comfortable, and even well-respected, life."

"Wow," Sharlamagne breathed. "Oh, I love that story! I love hearing that." She leaned in closer to the photograph. "You look like her, you know," she said, pointing to the beautiful young woman who looked to be about twelve in the photograph.

"Like my great-great-grandmother?" he asked. "Yeah, I know. Grandpa looked like her too. Her name was Tandie. We have a lot of photographs of her. I'm wondering if she was kind of vain or something."

"Oh, people have always loved photographs of other beautiful people," Sharlamagne said. "After all, look at you. I remember your Jeans Innovations posters a few years back."

"Oh, man, don't bring up that," he chuckled. "How embarrassing."

"Embarrassing?" she asked, smiling at him.

"Of course," he said. "I couldn't believe how long the guy who owns those stores ran that stupid campaign. I thought I was going to have to leave town to get away from the hard time my friends laid on me."

Sharlamagne giggled. "Well, look at it this way. You can gaze at this beautiful little girl and say, 'Physical gorgeousness and being easy to photograph—two things I inherited from my great-great-grandmother Tandie Thomas,' right? So there you go. And besides, you should've seen me and Gwen the day we figured out we'd actually met the Jeans Innovations guy in real life! We were so dorky, standing there taking photos of your posters with our cell phones and stuff. We even dropped a hundred bucks each that day on jeans we couldn't afford just because we'd met you and thought we were so cool because we did."

All at once, Sharlamagne realized she was rambling on—spitting out confessions that she thought he was a hottie—that she'd thought he was a hottie from day one. Blushing, she looked up to see him smiling at her.

"Well, I feel sort of bad now…like I should hand you a hundred spot or something to cover your losses," he chuckled.

"Don't be dumb," she giggled. Then, attempting to make the entire incident seem more trivial than it really was, she added, "I'll just get you to autograph that old pair of jeans for me or something…being that I still do have them and all. Then when I'm old and gray and need a few extra bucks, I can sell them online for some quick cash."

He laughed, and Sharlamagne was delighted at having amused him. "Let's go through the kitchen and out back," he suggested, stepping ahead of her a ways.

Rather unwilling to leave the beautiful photograph, Sharlamagne followed him, awed once more as she entered Mrs. Tanner's kitchen. It was lovely, so quaint and Victorian. Only the refrigerator, stovetop, oven, and updated plumbing gave away that the room was not actually a functioning turn-of-the-previous-century kitchen.

"Do you know what else I like about this house?" Sharlamagne asked out loud, more to herself than to Maxim.

"What?" he answered.

"It's not overdone," she explained. "You know, it's not an antique hoard or anything like that. There are just enough furnishings and embellishments to make it look authentic but not too many to make it look like it was made to look authentic. Do you know what I mean?"

He chuckled again. "Yep," he said, nodding. "The house is perfect." He smiled at her then, as if he knew something she didn't and couldn't wait to tell her. "Grandma *was* something of an antique hoarder, however…and I think you're about to find that out firsthand."

Sharlamagne followed him through the kitchen and out through the back door leading to a beautiful porch, lawn, and gardens. She couldn't keep from smiling as she walked past the lovely flower beds, through the lush grass, and toward an old, abandoned-looking house surrounded by lilac bushes that hadn't bloomed yet.

As they approached the old house, Sharlamagne's heart began to hammer madly. Mrs. Tanner had loved her—loved her and valued her friendship more than Sharlamagne had ever realized before her death. Sharlamagne had been important enough to Elisaveta Tanner that she had willed her something. And not just something—the old house that stood nestled among a near forest of lilac trees. She wondered if there would be anything inside. After all, the will had stated the house and its contents were hers, hadn't it? Her heart hammered harder, and she couldn't keep from smiling with delicious anticipation.

"It's older than the other house," Maxim explained as they neared the old brick home. "Twenty years or so older. Grandpa used it for storage and things, and then Grandma just added to it. There's no telling what's in there now." He paused as they reached the front door, looked to Sharlamagne, and winked. "It's probably full of mice and spiders and dust and cobwebs."

Sharlamagne smiled back at him. "Most interesting, old, abandoned houses are," she said.

He took his keys out of his pocket and began removing a key from his key ring. "Here," he said, handing her a shiny, new key. "I had the lock changed for Grandma at her request a couple of months ago. She had me keep two copies of the key." He smiled at her as she accepted the key, adding, "I guess now I know why."

Sharlamagne's hands were trembling! What had Mrs. Tanner left in the house for her? She couldn't imagine any greater gift than having had the privilege of knowing her. And then there were the things Maxim had brought to her the day he'd come to inform her Mrs. Tanner has passed. What better treasure could there be than those sweet, beloved items?

"Go on," he urged. "I wanna see how much crap she was able to stuff in there."

Sharlamagne couldn't stop the nervous giggle of excitement that bubbled up in her throat. Quickly, she pushed the key into the deadbolt lock on the door and twisted it. As she pushed the door in, the scent of aged wood, furniture oil, and dust hit her with powerful force. It wasn't a bad smell—nothing like most old houses that had been closed up for years. It was almost a strange perfume, a mix of lavender and furniture polish, dust and old linens.

"Oh my gosh!" Sharlamagne gasped as the sunlight pierced the darkness of the room before her. "Oh my gosh!" she breathed in astonishment. The room before her was literally packed with things—with furniture and lamps, crystal bowls and china plates. There were stereo viewers with stereo view cards, old dolls sitting on shelves with old books. There were sets of silver dinner utensils, compotes, and vintage Christmas ornaments. Old pictures and prints lined the walls and mantel, table tops, and even chairs.

"Damn!" Maxim exclaimed as he stepped into the room behind Sharlamagne and looked around. "And I thought she had a lot of stuff in the house." He smiled, shaking his head with disbelief. "It'll take you a year to go through all this stuff."

"Oh, I hope so!" Sharlamagne sighed with a smile of pure pleasure.

She wondered if she'd ever known a more exciting moment in all her life. It was as if Elisaveta Tanner had known exactly what one of Sharlamagne's most elusive dreams was—as if the eccentric poetry-writing, antique-collecting lady had actually seen into Sharlamagne's mind somehow—for ever since she could remember, Sharlamagne had experienced a reoccurring dream. It did not seem to be triggered by any one thing or event; it simply came to her two or three times a year. Every few months, Sharlamagne would dream of finding an old, abandoned house—an house empty of living people but filled with the evidences of their history, of their stories, of their having once walked the earth. More frequently than she cared to admit, she literally dreamt of finding an old house or building packed with long-forgotten mementos, furniture, and historic treasures. And now, right at her fingertips, was literally a dream come true!

Sharlamagne giggled. "It's like she's my fairy godmother or something," she mumbled as she wedged herself between two large boxes stacked in the doorway of what had once been a quaint parlor.

"This doesn't overwhelm you?" Maxim asked, following her into the parlor.

"Overwhelm me?" Sharlamagne squealed, turning to face Maxim and taking hold of his arms as she smiled up at him. "It's a dream come true! I mean, in this room alone, look at the treasure!"

Releasing him, she turned back to gaze into the ill-lit room. Everywhere she could see treasure. Certainly there were unopened boxes, some looking very old themselves—and who was to know what treasure they held? But the already visible treasure was simply astonishing.

"Look," she said, pointing to one wall of the old parlor. "If you discount the sideboard there—and I can see, even from here, that it's beautiful—look at the compotes stacked on the mantel! There must twenty of them, all with dangling prisms. Can you imagine what they'll look like cleaned up? I think I'm dreaming. I must be! Pinch me so I know I'm really awake, will you?"

Maxim smiled—chuckled to himself—for he could not keep his gaze from lingering on Sharlamagne's curvaceous little butt. She wanted him to pinch her to make sure she was awake, did she? Wildly tempted to pinch her bottom, he thought better of it and reached up, pinching the back of her arm tenderly.

"Nope," he said. "You're not dreaming. You really are going to be at this for a year. But at least it looks like you might make some sweet cash on this stuff."

He was surprised when Sharlamagne turned to look at him again, an expression of something akin to disappointment on her cute little face.

"You think I should sell things?" she asked.

Maxim shrugged, feeling like he'd just suggested she drown a puppy.

"Well, sure, if you want to. I'm sure Grandma meant for you to do that—you know, to keep what you want...and sell the rest to give yourself a nice little nest egg," he answered.

She turned and slowly looked around the room. "I suppose you're right. After all, where would I keep it all? This is a big house...and it's probably stuffed like this in every room."

"You could probably consign some of it to your dad for his store," Maxim offered. "I'm sure Grandma wasn't expecting you to keep every single thing. I mean...you can if you want, of course. But there is a lot of stuff in here. It would cost you a fortune to store it all."

"You're right," she said, sighing with renewed determination. She turned back to him again. "But...how quickly do you need for me to go through everything? How quickly do you need this old house emptied? I don't want to be a bother. I'm not sure what your plans are for it, but I do think it might take me more than a couple of days to sort through, catalog, and decide what to do with everything in here."

Maxim smiled. "That's fine," he said. And it was. It was perfectly fine with him if his grandma's little pet was around for an extended period of time. Sharlamagne Dickens made him smile for some reason—really, truly, sincerely smile—and he liked the feeling. "Take as long as you need," he said. "I'll be here every day for a while anyway. I'll even help you when I can, okay? And besides, you seem to be forgetting that it's your house, not mine. You can leave all this stuff in here forever if you want. It doesn't matter to me."

"Oh, yes. I forgot," she breathed with billowing delight. "It's mine…the house too." She smiled at him again. "Okay then…if you don't mind me coming and going for a while."

"Why would I mind?" he asked. "As long as you don't mind my being here too. I'm going to work on a few things in the house over the next couple of weeks."

She giggled, a light of pure, delighted anticipation twinkling in her rather brown-spice eyes. "Why would I mind that? It's not every girl who gets to see the Jeans Innovations guy every day."

Sharlamagne's smile broadened, for she could swear Maxim Tanner was blushing.

"You're never going to let me live that down, are you?" he asked.

"Has anyone?" she teased.

He shook his head. "Nope. I guess that's what I get for being roped into it in the first place. One more albatross around my neck won't hurt me, right?"

"It's not an albatross around your neck," she said, gazing up at him. "It's a great little tidbit to add to your résumé."

He laughed, but her own comment had caused her to start thinking about something. "What is it that you do?" she asked him. "You sure know a lot about the architecture of the big house and stuff."

"Well, I better know about it. I've been helping Grandma remodel and restore it for a few years now," he answered. "I'm a contractor slash builder slash carpenter slash anything else it takes to restore old houses."

95

"How wonderful!" Sharlamagne couldn't keep from exclaiming. "And you've been working on her house? Like…doing what?"

He shrugged. "She had me redo some bathrooms and plumbing, especially in the bedrooms. I did some wall work, painting, electrical—you know, just whatever she needed me to do. It's my business, restoring old buildings."

Could he be more dreamy? Sharlamagne decided he couldn't. A gorgeous man with personality, charm, and charisma—and he restored old houses? He was heaven-sent for certain!

"Are you kidding me?" she asked as a thread of doubt wandered through her brain a moment.

"Nope," he assured her. Then he frowned a little, smiling at the same time as he studied her. "You're looking at me like that's a good thing. Most of the people I know think it's a waste of my life."

"A waste of your life?" she squeaked. She shook her head, still awed by what he did for a living and how perfectly it fit his grandmother's reminiscent soul. "Are you kidding me? It's marvelous! Oh, I love that that's what you do! Are you kidding? Restoring old homes, remodeling, and even carpentry work? Do you know how important that is?" She shook her head and continued, "I mean, anyone can be a doctor or lawyer or make a ton of money with some dumb Internet business. But knowing how to do all that—that's worth something!"

"Okay," Maxim asked with a chuckle, "what do you want?" After all, she couldn't be serious. There wasn't one person he knew, other than his grandmother, who thought his skills and business choice were worth a dime, let alone anything else. Most of his friends thought he was an idiot to be working so hard when he could just sit around sponging off his parents. Surely this girl was just stroking his ego.

"What do you mean?" she asked.

"You must want something from me to be sucking up to me like that," he explained.

Her smiled instantly faded, however. "I'm serious," she told him. "I think it's admirable, what you do. You have to love it to do it. And it adds beauty to the world and restores the glory to old buildings that have been all but forgotten. You do see the value in that, don't you?"

He nodded. "*I* do," he agreed. "But most people don't."

"That's because most people are ignorant," she said. "But I'm not." She paused for a moment, and he watched as her pretty eyes widened with wonderment. "Do you ever find stuff? Like, when you're redoing a house, do you ever find things, like, tucked away in the attic or even inside the walls?"

Maxim grinned. He had her interest like a fish on a hook—and he liked having it.

"All the time," he answered.

"Like what?" she begged.

"Well…" he said as he thought. "Well, even in Grandma's house," he began. "When I was redoing the Passion Room for her, I found an old wooden box filled with love letters under one of the flooring planks. They were all dated 1901 and were written to one of the daughters of the guy who first owned the house."

"You're teasing me," she said. "You just know that's what I would want to hear."

But Maxim shook his head. "Nope. It's the truth."

He watched as her mind appeared to shift gears a little. She glanced up to the beautiful Victorian house behind him.

"The Passion Room?" she asked. "What's that mean?"

Maxim smiled. "Oh, it's a long story. One of Grandma's eccentricities…one of the many. I'll tell you about it sometime."

"Promise?" she asked.

"I promise," he said. "But only if you promise to come to my stupid birthday thing on Saturday."

"But I won't know anyone there," she said. He could tell she was unnerved at the thought of attending. But he wanted her there. In fact, he couldn't think of anyone else he really wanted there other than her.

"You'll know me," he offered.

Sharlamagne studied him for a moment. She could've sworn there was a sort of pleading in his expression—as if he were hoping to find an ally in her somehow. How could she refuse the handsome Jeans Innovations model anything?

"Okay," she agreed. "I'll go. But then you have to tell me about this Passion Room of your grandmother's. Deal?"

"Of course," he said. "Wanna shake on it?" he asked, offering a hand to her.

The moment she struck hands with him, goose bumps raced over Sharlamagne's arms. Yet, she thought, why not pursue a friendship of sorts with him? It would be safe enough. Guys like Maxim Tanner never went for girls like her, so what chance was there of getting hurt in any regard?

"Okay, then. I'll see you Saturday," he said. "I've got to go for now though. Will you be okay here alone?"

"I'm leaving too," she explained. "This is all too overwhelming to start thinking about on a Sunday afternoon."

"I can imagine," he said, glancing around the room once more. "Well, if you wanna lock it up, I'll walk you back to your car."

"Thanks."

Sharlamagne locked the door of the house Mrs. Tanner had bequeathed to her. She still couldn't believe it—couldn't believe Mrs. Tanner had left her such a trove of treasure, couldn't believe she was walking back to her car with the gorgeous Jeans Innovations model from four years before. She couldn't believe any of it. Surely she'd wake up any moment to find it was all a dream.

Maxim Tanner opened her car door for her, saying, "See you Saturday, if not before," before closing it. She smiled and shook her head. Mrs. Tanner had done nothing but fill her life with joy and treasure-hunting since the moment Sharlamagne had met her. It stood to reason she'd continue to do it from the great beyond. It was so very, very *her*.

CHAPTER FOUR

"So," Gwen began, "are you nervous?"

Sharlamagne rolled her eyes with exasperation. "Of course I'm nervous!" she answered. "I won't know anybody there...and every other girl who is there will probably be tall, skinny, gorgeous, and perfect. How could I not be nervous?" She exhaled a disappointed sigh as she studied herself in the bathroom mirror for a minute. "I still don't understand why Mrs. Tanner didn't send you an invitation too."

"Because I have boyfriend, you ding-dong," Gwen reminded her. "You don't invite a girl who already has a boyfriend to parties for a single guy...unless you invite her boyfriend too, I suppose."

"Yeah, yeah, yeah. But why invite me in the first place? Mrs. Tanner knows I'll feel out of place."

"I'm sure she knew you would, but I'm guessing that, from what you told me about Mr. Maxim Tanner—conductor of the 'I Was Made for Loving You' train—and his family, his grandmother probably thought he needed a little normality in his life after she was gone," Gwen offered.

Sharlamagne nodded. "I've actually thought of that too," she admitted. "But I don't know how in the world sending one lone normal person into the gauntlet of a bunch of strangers at a birthday party will help him."

Gwen shrugged. "Maybe she meant for you to be an anchor."

"An anchor?" Sharlamagne asked. "Are you saying I'm a wet blanket at a party?" she teased.

"No, dummy," Gwen giggled. "I mean, this is probably the first birthday party Mrs. Tanner won't be attending for Maxim…probably since his very first one. Maybe she just wants you there to give him an anchor to her—something that will remind him of her, make him feel supported and remember the normal world. I don't know." Gwen smiled then, and somehow Sharlamagne knew what was coming next. "Or maybe Mrs. Tanner is playing matchmaker…from the other side."

"I knew you were gonna say that," Sharlamagne said, shaking her head. "You just couldn't resist it, could you?"

"Just imagine, Shar…being Maxim Tanner's main squeeze. The Jeans Innovations guy's favorite plaything."

"Main squeeze?" Sharlamagne laughed. "I swear, you have to quit reading those old *Life* magazines from the '70s that Dad has in the store."

"But I'm serious, Shar! What if Mrs. Tanner just wanted to put you in Maxim's way—you know—to try and catch his eye?" Gwen's eyes widened with anticipation. "Can you imagine it? I bet he's as good as he looks when it comes to sss…"

"Do *not* say it, Guinevere!" Sharlamagne ordered, clamping a hand over her sister's mouth. "Don't you dare say it!"

But Gwen giggled and pushed Sharlamagne's hand away. "I was only going to say *Sunday spooning*, Sharlamagne. Sheesh! Get your mind out of the gutter."

"You were not going to say Sunday spooning," Sharlamagne scolded, wagging an index finger at her sister. "You were going to say the 's' word, just to rattle me. Spooning? What? You've gone all MGM musical now? Pick a decade and stick with it, Gwen."

"Oh, just relax, Shar," Gwen said with a sigh. "Just go to the party and don't worry about why Mrs. Tanner had an invitation sent to you. Just have fun."

"Have fun? Doing what, being all self-conscious and nervous?"

Gwen reached out, straightening the necklace Sharlamagne was wearing. "No. Have fun looking at Maxim Tanner. That guy is pure confectionary eye candy. So just enjoy looking at him if nothing else.

Mrs. Tanner wanted you there for a reason. Just keep that in mind, and try to enjoy it."

"Enjoy it? Are you kidding?" Sharlamagne asked, again studying herself in the mirror.

"Well, endure it then. Whatever. Just quit being so stupid about it, okay?"

"That's easy for you to say," Sharlamagne grumbled.

"Yes, it is," Gwen teased. She paused a moment and then said, "What underwear are you wearing?"

"Oh, don't start with the lingerie thing, Gwen," Sharlamagne whined.

"I'm serious," Gwen said, however. "You know a woman only feels as pretty as her lingerie. So what are you wearing?"

"White bra, white panties...and that's all you need to know," Sharlamagne answered.

"White? Good grief, Grandma! Wearing white underwear, to an event like this?" Gwen exclaimed. "You should at least wear lavender, if not red or black. Have I taught you nothing?"

Sharlamagne giggled when Gwen slapped her smartly on the bottom and ordered, "Now you run in and change your underwear, missy! How could you even fathom going to a party in honor of Maxim Tanner wearing white underwear? That would've been criminal! You could be locked up for something like that!"

"Gwen...you're being stupid."

"No, I'm not! You can't wear white underwear with those black leggings! And your dress, it's purple, so wear your lavender bra and panties. I promise you'll feel better...more confident." Gwen paused and arched one eyebrow as she stared daringly at her sister. "You know I'm right, don't you?"

"Yeah, yeah, yeah," Sharlamagne sighed. "But I'll still feel weird in a room full of people I don't know."

"Maybe," Gwen agreed. She smiled then and added, "But at least you'll know your underwear is pretty."

Sharlamagne laughed, shook her head, and headed back into her bedroom to change her white bra and panties for her lavender ones.

After all, Gwen was right—a woman did only feel as pretty as her lingerie.

🐛

Sharlamagne swallowed hard, smoothed the skirt of her amethyst dress, and inhaled a deep breath of courage. She hadn't been able to catch Maxim at the Mrs. Tanner's house either of the two days that week that she'd stopped by. She'd gone into the house Mrs. Tanner had left to her and taken a few things out to show her dad and mom—a couple of crystal compotes, a few books, and some pieces of china—but in truth, she'd hoped she'd run into Maxim. She decided to help her dad get things in order at the store before taking any real time off to root through Mrs. Tanner's treasure trove in the old house. Yet she had stopped by, hoping to catch a glimpse of Maxim. She'd hoped talking to him again would give her a little more courage to show up at his party. But she hadn't seen him, and now she stood on the porch of his house making ready to ring the doorbell, as nervous as a mouse.

"Well," she sighed out loud, "here I go…lavender underwear and all."

She watched her own trembling index finger press the doorbell, and when she heard the Westminster chime on the other side of the door, she nearly chickened out and ran. But she didn't. She commanded her feet to stay glued to the porch and waited.

She didn't have to wait long. Only a few moments later, the front door swung open to reveal a very, very, very delicious-looking Maxim Tanner standing before her. He wasn't dressed up too much—wearing jeans, boots, and a blue-and-red plaid, mod-western shirt with pearl snaps—but he looked so good Sharlamagne felt her eyes bug out anyway.

"Hey!" he greeted. "You made it. I was beginning to think you were gonna stand me up."

"Nope," she said, forcing a confident smile. "I just had a few things to finish up at work and stuff."

"Well, I'm glad to see you. Come on in," he said, stepping aside so she could enter.

Sharlamagne stepped into the house and was instantly met by the smell of high-end catered food and expensive perfume and cologne and the sound of music and laughter wafting in from another room. Her stomach began to twist into knots. This wasn't her kind of house—large, expensive, luxuriously furnished—and she knew Maxim's other guests wouldn't be her kind of people. No doubt his other guests would be like the girl that had been with him the day she'd first met him—confident, wildly beautiful, and slathered in expensive clothes and jewelry.

"So," he began, "did you have any trouble finding it?"

Sharlamagne shook her head. "Not at all," she answered. It was then that she glanced up and over to her right. She gasped a little when she saw it—Maxim Tanner's marble collection.

"Wow!" Sharlamagne breathed as she studied the long wall of shelves stocked with nothing but jar after jar of marbles floor to ceiling. "You really have a lot of marbles."

"Yeah," Maxim said with a shrug. "Grandma spoiled me rotten when it came to marbles. She was sort of obsessed with prisms…and I guess with me, it's marbles."

Sharlamagne was awed as she stared at the vast collection awhile longer. She hoped with all her heart that most of the marbles displayed on the shelves before her were ones she or her father had sold to Elisaveta. If they were, then she could pretty much be assured that what was inside the small gift-wrapped box in her purse would please Maxim. In truth, she was somewhat anxious—worried that perhaps Maxim Tanner had lost his love of marbles when he'd lost his grandmother. Yet she knew, from her own experience as well as from observing others, that once a person fixated on collecting something, it was pretty much a lifelong fixation.

Turning to face him again, Sharlamagne smiled, reached into her purse, and retrieved the small gift box she'd brought.

Balancing the small box on one outstretched palm, she said, "Happy birthday!"

Maxim grinned, chuckled, and lifted the box from her palm. "You didn't read the invitation very well, did you?"

"Do you mean the small print at the bottom that said, *No gifts please*?" she answered.

"Yeah…exactly," he said, still grinning.

"Oh, I never pay attention to that," she explained. "That phrase infringes on my Constitutional rights."

Maxim laughed. "Constitutional rights? How do you figure that?"

Sharlamagne tossed a dismissing wave in the air as she said, "You know, my right to freedom of gift-giving or something like that."

"Oh, I see," he chuckled, studying the small gift for a moment. He looked back to her then, placed the small package on a nearby accent table, took hold of her upper arm, and began leading her out of the marble-lined room.

"Come on in," he said as he dropped behind her, still holding her arm and gently pushing her into another room. "Everyone's in here."

Upon entering the room—a room that she interpreted as being something akin to a den—Sharlamagne immediately felt out of place. She'd felt somewhat convinced she looked nice when she'd left the house. Yet now she thought herself very underdressed in her black leggings, black flats, and little amethyst dress. Everyone other woman in the room was dripping with expensive, high-end, name-brand clothing and tons of jewelry—jewelry that sparkled too perfectly to be costume. To make matters worse, every guy she could see was staring at her like she was some new plaything.

Sharlamagne inhaled a deep breath, determined not to judge the group of Maxim's friends just by their outward appearances, and smiled as he introduced her.

"Hey, you all, this is my friend Sharlamagne," he said.

"Hello," she managed to greet the onlookers.

Everyone smiled and returned her greeting. In fact, she felt much better when three very handsome young men stood up and instantly strode over to gather around her.

"Come on in, pretty young thing," one young man said. He looked to Maxim and winked. "You've been keeping secrets, man."

"And how did Maxim score such a shawty as you, baby?" another charmer asked, taking her arm and leading her to one of the sofas in the room.

"Shawty?" Sharlamagne asked, glancing back to Maxim.

He shook his head, amused. "It means, you know, fine female... pretty girl," he answered.

"Mmm mmm! Maxim sure knows how to pick 'em," another young man said as he gestured for Sharlamagne to sit down.

"You've been holding out, Maxim. What's up with that?" the first handsome young man who had addressed her asked.

"You guys are like a bunch of gorillas," a gorgeous brunette supermodel-type woman scolded as she smiled at Sharlamagne. She walked to where Sharlamagne now sat surrounded by handsome young men and offered a graceful, soft, well-manicured hand to Sharlamagne. "I'm Liz, Sharlamagne. And that's a great name, by the way."

"Thank you," Sharlamagne said, taking the woman's offered hand.

"Max and I grew up together," Liz explained. "Our parents built homes in the same development when we were in fifth grade." Liz paused a moment, smiled, and continued. "I'm surprised we haven't met before. I've always known everyone Max has. How do you know him?"

Sharlamagne glanced up to Maxim. He was staring at her with a rather mischievous grin. Yet the expression in his mesmerizing eyes would have led her to believe he hadn't even heard what Liz had asked her but was instead thinking something else entirely.

"I...uh...our family was Mrs. Tanner's...we deal in antiques," Sharlamagne sputtered. "We met Maxim several years ago, through his grandmother." It was all she could come up with—not very informative, but what else could she say? She hardly knew Maxim Tanner! Discounting all the ogling and daydreaming she had done over his Jeans Innovations posters years before, she'd only really seen him and talked with him on four other occasions. It seemed ludicrous—even to her—that she should be at a party held in his honor where only intimate friends were in attendance.

"You wouldn't by any chance be responsible for a few million of

Maxim's marbles, would you now, baby?" the flirtatious young man sitting next to her asked.

"Probably," Sharlamagne confessed, feeling somewhat relieved.

"Sharlamagne always saved the best marbles that came through her father's store for my grandma to look through for me," Maxim interjected. "Didn't you, shawty?"

"Yes," Sharlamagne admitted. "Though for a really long time I thought you were, you know…younger."

Everyone laughed, and Liz giggled, "You mean like eight or nine, right?"

"Well, actually…yes," Sharlamagne answered. She looked to Maxim to find he was not at all bothered by her previous misconception. In fact, he winked at her and laughed along with the others.

"Oh, Max and his marbles," a beautiful blonde woman sighed from across the room. Sharlamagne watched the woman's hips swing to and fro as she walked toward Maxim. Reaching up and taking hold of his chin, she asked, "Whatever do you see in those stupid marbles anyway, Max?" she asked.

"You wouldn't understand," Maxim said, however kindly.

Sharlamagne felt her face grow warm with an unfamiliar feeling of disquiet as the beautiful blonde leaned up, kissed Maxim squarely on the mouth, and said, "Well, baby…what *I* plan to give you for your birthday, you can't find in any antique store."

"Oooo!" the others in the room exclaimed in unison.

"Maxim! Man! You draw the ladies in like bees to sugar," one young man said. The man strode to where Sharlamagne sat, offered a hand to her, and said, "Ignore that lady-bait over there, honey. I'm Ian Welch, and I'm just as sexy as Maxim here…whether or not my washboard abs have been all over the mall in the past."

Sharlamagne forced a smile and shook his hand. "It's very nice to meet you, Mr. Washboard Abs."

Ian laughed and settled himself on the sofa between Sharlamagne and the other flirtatious guy. "That's me, shawty," he said, grinning at her. "You want me to prove it?"

Sharlamagne blushed. "Oh, no…I'll believe you. I'm sure if you say it's true, then it is."

"Ian, you're such an idiot," the blonde said. "I've seen your abs. Don't even pretend you can go up against Max's."

"Oh, yeah? Shows what you know, Ashley," Ian said, rising to his feet and unexpectedly stripping off his shirt. Turning to Sharlamagne, he asked, "What do you think of these?"

Sharlamagne felt her face blaze crimson. The guy was standing before her, flexing every muscle in his torso to show off his well-sculpted body.

"That's nothing," the guy on the other side of her said. Sharlamagne watched, astounded, as this man also stood and stripped off his shirt. "Look at these abdominals, Ian, you poser. Try to rank up against these babies. You'll lose."

Several other young men in the room joined the shirt-stripping, showing-off-the-abs medley, and Sharlamagne could only sit on the sofa (trapped as she was by all the shirtless men towering over her) and watch as the women in the room giggled while the men strutted around like roosters.

"You guys are pathetic," Liz laughed at last. She stood up, smiled at Sharlamagne, and said, "Sharlamagne's going to think you're a bunch of brainless gladiators with nothing but muscle in your skulls." Sharlamagne watched as Liz went to where Maxim stood, looking mildly amused. "Besides," she continued, "there's not one of you who can beat Max when it comes to muscle definition…or anything else for that matter."

But Ian laughed. "No way, Liz! Our buddy Max has been too busy remodeling that old house lately. I bet he's gone all to squash."

"That's not true," Ashley defended. Sharlamagne watched as several other well-dressed, heavily bejeweled women gathered around Maxim. "I can feel the muscles right above his ribcage here," she said, rubbing one hand over Max's shirt below his pectoral muscle. "What are they called again, Max?"

"Come on, Ashley," Maxim grumbled, stepping away from her.

"Knock it off." He shook his head at his friends, chuckled, and said, "You guys are too much, man."

"They're called obliques, Ashley," Ian answered. "And I won't believe Max's are better than mine until I see them for myself." He turned back to Sharlamagne, raised his arms above his head, and flexed the muscles in his torso. "See that, Sharlamagne, baby?" he asked. "Look at those obliques! You can't get them like that by fixing your grandma's house, now can you?"

"Ooo! He's talking trash, Max," one of the men laughed. "Are you gonna let him get away with that?"

"Yeah, I am," Maxim said. "I don't have to strut around half-naked in front of the girls to prove anything."

"Oh, come on, Max," another woman said. "Show us you still have that hot Jeans Innovations look. Don't let these guys show you up. I still have one of your posters in my apartment, you know."

Sharlamagne studied Maxim's expression for a moment. She could see he felt trapped between a rock and a hard place. These were his friends—obviously they'd known him for a very long time. Yet she sensed that her presence was making him uncomfortable somehow, that he was pausing in just letting go. The last thing on the face of the earth she wanted was for Maxim to feel uncomfortable in his own home. So as a ridiculous, but supportive, thought flashed through her mind, she knew there was only one thing to do.

Hopping up from her seat on the sofa, Sharlamagne pulled her cell phone out of her purse. Quickly she scrolled through her photos, including the ones she'd saved from her old phone. Pulling up one of the photos of the giant Jeans Innovations poster she and Gwen had photographed in the mall four years before, she held it up—looked from the photo to Maxim and back again.

"Hmmm," she said. Liz smiled as she looked over Sharlamagne's shoulder to see the photo of the poster of Maxim. "He looks about the same to me…but they could have digitally enhanced him on those posters."

"Yes, they could have," Liz said, smiling.

"Oh no, you don't," Maxim said then. "Don't you accuse me of being digitally enhanced."

Sharlamagne giggled as Maxim then pulled at the front of his snap-front shirt, popping the snaps open and stripping the shirt off over his head.

"Digitally enhanced, my ass," he playfully grumbled as he raised his arms above his head, put his hands behind his back, and flexed the muscles in his torso.

Sharlamagne couldn't believe she had the foresight to do it, but she did—she snapped a photo of Maxim Tanner flexing his incredibly sculpted muscles on her cell phone. After all, she'd been holding it up to let everyone look at the Jeans Innovations poster photo, so she figured he'd never know if she just pushed the camera button too.

"Does that look digitally enhanced to you, Ian?" Maxim asked his friend, flexing even harder. "This is what comes from hard work...real muscle."

"Hard work in the gym maybe," another guy said.

"Hard work in the gym and hard work period, man," Maxim corrected. He changed his position, flexing his biceps and pectoral muscles this time.

"Holy boxer briefs model, Batman!" Ashley giggled. "Look out, Times Square! Here comes Maxim Tanner!"

All at once, Maxim glanced up to Sharlamagne. His triumphant smile faded a little, and he ceased his impressive flexing and snatched his shirt from the back of the chair where he'd tossed it. Quickly he put it back on and snapped up the front.

"Okay, okay, you pervs," he chuckled. "Get your clothes back on, boys. The girls are starting to blush."

"I'm not blushing," another pretty brunette said. She ran her fingers through Maxim's hair and planted a kiss on the corner of his mouth. "But I thought this was your birthday party, not mine." She winked at him, and Maxim smiled and shook his head.

"Cute, Yvette. You're a real scream," he mumbled. He looked to Sharlamagne again, and she could've sworn he was blushing. "You'll have to forgive us, Sharlamagne," he began, "but we can get sort of... sort of..."

"Childish," Liz offered. She giggled. "I can remember you and Ian doing this same thing when we were in high school." Liz looked to Sharlamagne and whispered, "Boys—they never really grow up, you know."

"I do know," Sharlamagne said. "I have two brothers, and they're exactly the same way."

"Come on, you guys," Maxim said. "Let's eat some of this food. I think Grandma thought she was ordering for an army. My kitchen is packed."

Sharlamagne's heart leapt when Maxim reached through the throng of drooling females to take hold of her arm. "Come on, Sharlamagne," he said. "The kitchen is this way."

"Okay," she managed. All at once she did feel pretty—though she wasn't quite sure whether it was because Maxim had shown her special attention in that moment or because a woman really did feel more pretty wearing lavender underwear.

CHAPTER FIVE

There was no doubting the quality of the food—it was delicious! In fact, Sharlamagne lost track of how many bacon-wrapped water chestnuts she consumed. She ate too much, probably because she was so anxious. It didn't matter how nice everyone was to her—and they were nice—she couldn't seem to shake the bad case of nervousness she had. She kept reminding herself that she was wearing a lavender bra and lavender panties, but it just didn't make her feel as perfect and pretty as all the other women at the party. For one thing, they were all very, very forward—especially toward Maxim. At one point, she heard Ashley tell him that what she planned to give him couldn't be unwrapped in front of everyone. She then added, "Well…unzipped, that is," as she turned around and pulled her long hair aside to reveal the zipper at the back of her little black dress.

Maxim's eyes widened, and he shook his head a little, grinned, and told Ashley that the invitations had said *no gifts*. Still, no matter what Maxim did to kindly brush off the advances of all the very forward women he seemed to know, Sharlamagne thought there were a few too many kisses that he willingly accepted. It seemed all his friends were excessively huggy and kissy.

Oh, Sharlamagne believed in hugging and kissing—of course she did. It just seemed to her that the way all the girls had to kiss Maxim on the lips—every time they wished him a happy birthday or thanked him for the great food—was too casual. Sure, it made her feel jealous and envious inside—wildly so. But it was more the fact that it was obvious

Liz, Ashley, Yvette, and the other young women at the party simply wanted a piece of Maxim, like he was some delicious new dessert they had to have a taste of. Of course, Sharlamagne totally understood how they felt, and she wondered for a moment if that was exactly the problem. Every girl there had managed to find a way to kiss Maxim Tanner on the lips—every girl but her.

Still, she decided that whether that was true, it was the fact that it was all too casual that really bothered her. Furthermore, she understood that all the kissing the women were doing (especially Liz) was absolutely a measure of attempted seduction. Men were very physical, and it made sense that if a woman wanted Maxim to notice her, then she needed to set a little physical lure.

The men, on the other hand, seemed oblivious most of the time—ignorantly so. Sharlamagne wondered if it was just such common practice for young woman to grope, grab, and kiss Maxim that the other guys just didn't even notice it. They didn't seem jealous at all—as if they knew they didn't stand a chance with any "shawty" when Maxim was around. So why even try?

All in all, the evening was an interesting study in human behavior, if nothing else. Yet after a few hours, Sharlamagne began to grow very weary of watching all the flirting—even of being a victim of the men flirting with her. After all, with all the other shawties busy trying to lure in Maxim, it left her as the only place for the guys to focus their attention.

As a large clock in the hallway struck eleven p.m.—as Ashley again implied that the birthday gift she wanted to give to Maxim required his bedroom to receive—Sharlamagne was suddenly very tired. Glancing around the room, she noticed that everyone was involved in conversation. She'd somehow managed to slip out of Ian's clutches for a moment and saw that her chance has arrived. No one would even notice if she snuck out. Oh sure, it was rude not to thank Maxim for his hospitality and thank him for a "wonderful evening" and all, but she figured he wouldn't think twice about it. Maybe once, but not twice.

Furthermore, other than Ashley's constant assurance that if Maxim would take her to his room, she'd let him "unzip" her gift to him, Sharlamagne could tell that everyone else had followed the instructions on the invitations and not brought a gift for Maxim. Thus, she felt ridiculous, not for having brought him a gift (for she didn't believe in the "no gift" thing) but at having brought him such a corny birthday gift. She knew if she could slip away now, she could retrieve her stupid gift from the little accent table in the entryway and he'd never be the wiser. There was no way he'd ever remember her having given it to him. And if he did—well, he'd just think he'd imagined it or misplaced it or something.

Sharlamagne did feel a bit disappointed as she quickly made her way toward the front of the house, however. She would've liked to have sat and stared at Maxim a little longer—but she couldn't take the women slobbering all over him. And anyway, she'd see him again. She was bound to run into him at Mrs. Tanner's old house sooner or later. It was going to take her forever to sort through all the stuff Mrs. Tanner had left in the old house.

Quickly snatching the small birthday gift from the accent table in the entryway and stuffing it in her purse, Sharlamagne headed for the front door—and escape.

"Trying to sneak out, huh?"

Sharlamagne grimaced when she heard Maxim's voice. She could feel him standing behind her, even though she knew he wasn't really, really close.

"Was it that boring?" he asked.

"No, no, no!" Sharlamagne rather frantically assured him, turning to face him. As she saw him leaning against the wall studying her, she could almost hear the old song "I Was Made for Loving You" echoing through her mind—could almost hear a distant train whistle signaling that the conductor of the "I Was Made for Loving You" train was standing right in front of her.

"I just...I'm just...you know...it's late...and I'm kind of tired. I worked all day and...well, you know how it is," she explained. "I had fun. Really," she further assured him, though she could see he wasn't buying it.

He sort of half-grinned with understanding and nodded. "Well," he began, "can I at least have my gift?"

"What do you mean?" Sharlamagne felt the heat rise to her cheeks. Had he actually seen her retrieve her goofy gift from the little table? She'd been so careful, so stealth—at least in her own mind.

His charming half-grin broadened to a smile, and he held out his hand. "Come on," he said with a gesture of his fingers that she should surrender the gift to him. "I saw you lift it from the table. Grandma never told me you were a thief. Was all that Constitutional rights stuff just bull or what?"

"No," Sharlamagne sighed. "It's just that…it's a really dumb gift," she admitted. "Just a little thing that made me think of you and—"

"So give it to me," he interrupted. She smiled. He looked almost impatient with excited anticipation.

"Really, Maxim," she repeated. "It's just the littlest thing…"

"Give it to me now…before I wrestle you to the ground and take it from you," he told her, striding to where she stood to tower over her.

"But it's only—" she began. Sharlamagne gasped, however—rendered astonished and breathless as one of Maxim's powerful arms encircled her waist, pulling her against him.

"Where'd you put it?" he asked as he used his free hand to fumble with one pocket of her dress.

"In my purse," she said, gently pushing herself from his grasp. She could hardly breathe, and she felt overheated and kind of weak. Reaching into her purse, she retrieved the small gift and offered it to him. "I'm warning you. It really is nothing."

"It's not nothing," he said, awkwardly tugging at the raffia ribbon tied around the small box. "This little box represents your Constitutional rights, after all." He smiled, and she thought she might melt, for it sent a warm wave of delight racing through her.

Sharlamagne had the sudden urge to turn and run—and not just because she felt ashamed about the trivial nature of her gift to him. Something about his touch—it affected her far too strongly. She'd liked the way he'd taken hold of her while trying to retrieve the gift. In truth, she'd loved it! Something in her was suddenly and profoundly uncomfortable at the depth of the attraction she felt toward him.

Still, she endeavored to appear calm and watched as he unwrapped the gift. As he opened the small box, a smile spread across his handsome, way too handsome face. He chuckled as he tipped the box upside down, spilling the five rare marbles into his other palm.

"Awesome!" he mumbled as he tossed the box onto the accent table once more and began to study the marbles in the light of the entryway.

"I-I really had no idea how many you already had," Sharlamagne stammered. She was surprised at exactly how sincere his delight seemed to be. Surely he was only acting. "I mean, I knew we'd sold your grandmother a lot of marbles over the years…but I had no idea. I walked in and saw all those jars on your shelves and…and…" Sharlamagne frowned. He was still studying the marbles—closely studying them. Maxim Tanner seemed legitimately taken with her gift.

"Have these got, like, a lavender swirl in them?" he asked, glancing up to the dim entryway light with frustration.

Sharlamagne smiled. He'd noticed! He'd noticed right away that the swirl in the clear glass marble was lavender.

"Yes," she confirmed. "They're really hard to find, you know."

"I do know," he said, smiling at her. She giggled, for he looked like a little boy who'd just found the greatest treasure of his life.

"It's hard to see them in this low light," he mumbled, holding one marble up toward one of the sconces on the porch. "If I didn't know better, I'd think these weren't just clear but…"

Sharlamagne giggled again. "Do you really think, after all those years of selling marbles to your grandmother, that I wouldn't know a vintage lavender swirl in Vaseline Glass when I saw it?"

"No way!" Maxim exclaimed, smiling and holding another marble up to the sconce.

"Yes way," Sharlamagne assured him. "My dad dates them about 1920, at the height of the popularity of Vaseline—or rather, uranium— Glass products." She giggled a moment as she watched him inspect each marble very closely.

"You've got to be kidding me," he mumbled. "Vaseline Glass *and* a lavender swirl? Do you know how hard these are to find?"

115

"Yes, actually…I do," she affirmed as she watched him. It was obvious he was literally infatuated with the marbles—and Sharlamagne could not have been happier about it. "You wouldn't happen to have a black light handy, would you?"

Maxim's smile broadened again as he continued to study the marbles in the low lighting. "Shawty…do I look like a man who would just happen to have a black light on hand?" he asked.

"Yes, actually…you do," Sharlamagne answered.

He looked at her—gazed at her a moment with obvious gratitude and approval. "Am I that transparent?"

"Not really," she said. "I just figured that a man who was into marbles the way you are…well, he wouldn't be much of a collector if he wasn't always on the hunt for vintage Vaseline Glass ones, now would he? And the best way to see if something is uranium glass…" She paused, and his smile broadened once more.

"Is to view it under UV lighting—a.k.a., plain old black light," he finished.

It seemed only moments later that Sharlamagne was standing in Maxim Tanner's garage, viewing the Vaseline Glass marbles under a little lamp sitting on a work table that was equipped with a black lightbulb.

"Awesome!" Maxim breathed as he studied the unusual marbles. "I've never seen one with a lavender swirl. I mean, I've seen them online and things, but I've never owned one…let alone five. This is awesome. Seriously."

Sharlamagne smiled and couldn't keep a quiet sigh of relief from escaping her lungs. "I'm so glad you like them. When I walked in and saw your collection, I thought for sure you probably had a million of these already."

"Are you kidding? I've only seen these at exhibitions and stuff." He paused a moment, an expression of concern wrinkling his strong brow. "Where did you get these? You didn't pay what they're worth or anything, did you?"

"On my measly salary?" she asked, shaking her head. "Nope. I handled the purchase of some stuff from a resent estate Dad was interested in. These were mixed in with a bunch of vintage marbles I found in an old cigar box in the bottom of a trunk."

"What did you do with the rest of the marbles? Did your dad purchase them? Did he sell them yet?" he asked.

"Why don't you stop in at the store and see for yourself?" she teased.

"Tell him not to sell them. I want them," Maxim said.

"Don't worry," Sharlamagne assured him. "I sent them aside…just in case you did find these interesting."

"Interesting?" he mumbled, returning his attention to the marbles glowing green under the black light. "I won't be able to sleep for a week after this."

Sharlamagne rolled her eyes. "Okay, now you're just being ridiculous. I believed you when you made out that they were a big deal before. But now…now I know you're just trying to make me feel better."

"Shawty…if I wanted to make you feel better, I wouldn't be keeping you out here in my dirty garage. I think someplace more like my bedroom—or Grandma's passion room, for that matter—would be more the type of place to take you to…" His voice trailed off as he squinted to study one marble more intently. "This one has two swirl veins. Did you notice that before?"

Sharlamagne didn't answer, however. She was too unnerved by what he'd said. Apparently all of Ashley's insinuations throughout the evening had planted themselves firmly in Maxim's mind somehow and washed over onto her, and something in her body thrilled because of it. She felt weak and knew that goose bumps were breaking out all over her arms. It was weird, the way he could have such a physical effect on her without even touching her! It made her uncomfortable—deliciously uncomfortable.

"Well…well, I'm glad you like them, Maxim," she said at last. "But I really do need to be going. I have a…a thing tomorrow morning early. And…and you still have guests and stuff. So I'll just see you later and—"

"Hold on," he said, however. She watched as he scooped up the marbles, shoved them into the front pocket of his jeans, and turned off the lamp. Placing his strong hands at her shoulders, he smiled down at her. "Thank you," he mumbled. "I'm serious. It's the best gift I've gotten in a really long time. Most of my friends just buy stuff they would like to have—clothes, electronics, stuff like that. But the Vaseline Glass marbles—"

"With lavender swirls," she nervously added, thinking of her lavender underwear.

He chuckled. "Yeah…no one gives me stuff like that. Not anymore."

"Maybe it's because they're all too smart to think one more marble can bring you any joy when you've got trillions on your shelf, right?"

"Wrong," he said. "Marbles are like snowflakes, you know."

"Snowflakes?" she asked, wrinkling her nose.

"Yeah…no two are alike. A person could own every marble in the world, and no two would be exactly alike."

Sharlamagne smiled, thinking his metaphor was too adorable.

"But you already have so many in there. Like…jars and jars full," she reminded him.

"Well, my grandma always said that there are some things you can never own too many or too much of. You can never own too much love, you can never own too much passion…and you can never own too many marbles."

"Or, in her case, prisms," Sharlamagne offered.

Maxim chuckled and agreed. "Or, in her case, prisms. That's right."

The warmth of his palms on her shoulders seemed to be scalding her flesh, even through her dress. He was *so* good looking—entirely hot! Sharlamagne was again far too discomfited by the physical effect Maxim Tanner had on her. All at once, she felt the need to escape—to truly escape.

"I really am glad you like them," she said. "And…and I hope you did have a happy birthday…continue to have one really…with all your friends inside and stuff."

"What? No birthday kiss?" he asked—and she did not miss the spark of misbehavior that leapt into the smoldering sapphire of his eyes.

She giggled nervously. "Oh, right. Like I could ever compete with those supermodels in there. I'd probably flub it up and totally miss the mark," she said. She immediately regretted her rather self-deprecating remark, for the mischief that had caused his eyes to sparkle the moment before dulled and faded almost instantly.

"Thanks for the marbles, Sharlamagne," he said. "Really. They really are something I've always wanted."

You're something I've always wanted, Sharlamagne thought. But what she said was, "You're welcome. A-and I do okay at birthday *hugs* if you're up for it."

He grinned, and a small glimmer returned to the beautiful blue of his eyes. "I suppose a whole body is a harder mark to miss," he mumbled.

"Yours is anyway." It was out of her mouth before she knew it, and she blushed, hoping he couldn't see how red her face was in the low light of the garage.

He gathered her into his arms then—into his powerful arms and against the strong, well-defined contours of his body. Sharlamagne allowed her arms to slide around his broad torso, relishing the feel of every sculpted muscle. Her cheeks blazed crimson, and the goose bumps on her arms were now joined by their counterparts racing over her legs. Dang, even her scalp had goose bumps!

Maxim Tanner felt fascinating, and he smelled wildly alluring. He smelled like a man—like *the* man—like he'd stepped off the "I Was Made for Loving You" boat as well as the train! To Sharlamagne, he smelled just the way the perfect, archetypal man should smell—like fresh mountain air, a cedar forest, a campfire, a refreshing sea breeze, and a warm summer's day all blended together. She smiled when she realized her knees were nearly gelatinous. Maxim was warm and strong, and she wanted to kiss him. She wanted to have the guts those supermodel wenches in the house did—wished she could simply reach up, take his whiskery face in her hands, and kiss him square on the mouth. Not just kiss him on the lips either—actually kiss him on the mouth, on his warm, open mouth and...

"I'm serious when I say that's the best gift I've received in long time, Sharlamagne," he said, jostling her from her far too ridiculous thoughts. "Thanks again. Really."

It was her cue to let him go. She wondered if she'd been too obvious about her sudden euphoric state of mind and body. She released him and quickly stepped back out of his arms.

"You're welcome," she managed, taking two steps back from him. "And you just let me know when you're ready for me to come over to Mrs. Tanner's house and sort through whatever, and I'll—"

"Monday," he interrupted. "I'm off work Monday. How about you?"

"Monday?" she gulped. "Well, yeah…I can get work off Monday. Are you sure that's okay? I mean, it's already Saturday. And besides, if you're not quite ready to face it, I…I…"

"I'm ready," he said. "I was ready last week…but I didn't have the time off."

"Oh, okay," Sharlamagne said. "Well, you just name the time, and I'll meet you there…if that's all right."

"Eight a.m. too early for you?" he asked. Sharlamagne took another step backward as he took a step toward her. There was a new expression in his eyes that rattled her—a smolder, an intention—an intention toward teasing and flirting maybe.

"Not at all," she said. Then turning, she tossed a wave in the air and called, "Happy birthday, Maxim. I'll see you Monday," as she hurried toward her car and much needed escape.

Sharlamagne's heart was hammering so hard she was certain she would have a heart attack! She knew her blood pressure must be through the roof, even for her young age. The intoxicating scent of Maxim Tanner still pervaded her senses, and she stumbled a little as she reached her car. He was wigging her out! She felt out of control, as if she might run back to him and throw herself at him like some tramp.

"And who uses the word *tramp* anymore anyway?" she grumbled at herself. "You idiot, Sharlamagne."

Quickly, she slid into the driver's seat of her car, jammed her key in the ignition, and started the engine. She was acting like some crazy teenager in a slasher film—acting as if she really did have some lethal thing to run from. But she was already settling down, already breathing easier and thinking with a clear head.

"I'm just glad he liked the marbles," she mumbled as she pulled out of the circular driveway.

Maxim watched Sharlamagne hurry away. He grinned, thinking the little, natural wiggle in her walk was vastly more attractive than the runway model swing in the hips of most of the girls he knew. He watched her get into her car and drive away before he turned to return to the house and the party.

Maxim shook his head and breathed a chuckle at the irony of it all. There he was, celebrating his twenty-sixth birthday with a houseful of gorgeous women—any one of which would do anything he asked (and he knew they'd do *anything* he asked)—and all he could think about was that fact that the one girl he actually wanted a birthday kiss from hadn't kissed him.

Maybe his money was all he really was. Maybe it really was exactly like he thought; maybe there wasn't anything attractive about him other than his stuff and cash. Maybe the gold diggers waiting inside to try and scheme their way into his bed and bank account were all he was worthy of. He reached into his pocket and pulled out the Vaseline Glass marbles. They were warm in his hand—warm like Sharlamagne Dickens's smile—warm like the birthday hug she'd given him. The marbles made him think of his grandmother—of all the times she'd told him vast wealth was a trial, not a gift—of all the times she'd explained that Maxim Tanner was special and that somewhere there was a special girl that heaven had marked just for him.

He was tired of it all—tired of the gold diggers, tired of the money and the crap that it heaped on him. He thought of his parents and how jacked up they were. He looked at the marbles again as he entered the house. Vintage, rare, and wondrous—that's what they were. He thought of the girl who had given them to him—his grandma's little antique-dealer friend. Moisture sprang to his eyes as he remembered the look on Sharlamagne's face when he'd told her Elisaveta Tanner had passed away. He would never forget the way the color had drained from her pretty cheeks, the incredible pain that had been evident in her.

Maxim wondered if Chad Lyons had left the party yet. Chad was a real-estate broker. Maxim would have him list his house the next day. He was sick of the place anyway. His parents had given it to him when he'd turned twenty-one. He shook his head as he entered through the front door, thinking he would've much rather had parents who cared about teaching him, nurturing him, and loving him than ones who had simply given him a house as compensation for neglect.

Still, his grandmother had taught him well, and it was time he applied her lessons better than he sometimes had before. He'd sell the house—get out of the neighborhood where all that mattered was expensive cars and money. On her deathbed, his grandmother had told him to break free and be the man she knew he was—the man he'd always wanted to be.

Maxim knew his grandmother had given him the key to unlock the prison door: she'd given his parents all her money. How truly great a gift his grandmother had given him by having left her millions to his parents. He suddenly realized that he *was* free—truly free. With no prospects of their son being the cash-cow heir to the Tanner fortune, his parents would leave him alone now, allowing him to live his life in whatever way he chose. They'd never really wanted him. He suspected the only reason they'd had him was so they'd have an heir to his grandparents' fortune. How he came by his name was evidence enough of that.

Oh, Maxim didn't wallow in self-pity. His parents were what they were. His grandmother had loved him more than her own life, and that fact had always made up for the lack of his parents' true affection. He struggled with self-worth and self-esteem maybe, but not with the lack of being loved as a child or even a young adult. His parents' attitude and priorities simply irritated him more than anything else. But he was free now—liberated! He'd only just realized how liberated and shook his gloom, disgusted with himself for not seeing the true depth of his freedom before.

Still, it was probably his grief at losing the one person he'd loved more than anything or anyone that had blinded him until that moment. But now he saw it clearly—he was done with being chained to wealth and all the crap it brought. He was free.

Yep. He'd have Chad list the house for him, take the cash he would get out of it, and buy himself a little place in some little cute suburban neighborhood where kids ran through sprinklers in their front yards in the summer, men mowed their own lawns, and women drove kids to soccer games in minivans. He'd sink whatever cash was left into his business and really make good at it at last.

Maxim smiled, realizing he would finally have the time to run his own show. He wouldn't need to worry about his parents; they had what they wanted and would be happy with it, at least in their own minds of what happiness was.

Maxim wasn't discouraged, disgusted, or disinterested anymore. It was as if he'd just opened his eyes on a fresh, new day—a fresh new life. His grandmother had freed him, and he would make sure he took advantage of every opportunity she'd laid before him.

Glancing down at the Vaseline Glass marbles in his hand, he laughed out loud. "You scheming little vixen, Grandma," he whispered. "You sent her that invitation to help me get my head out of the sand, didn't you?"

Yep, Maxim knew his grandmother must've sent Sharlamagne Dickens an invitation to his birthday bash because she knew Sharlamagne would stand out in the shallow crowd he'd been associated with for so long. His grandmother had known that five Vaseline Glass marbles and a hug were exactly what he needed to realize the freedom she'd given him.

Striding to the marble wall, Maxim took down the jar that cached his most valuable or sentimentally treasured marbles. He removed the lid and carefully placed the five Vaseline Glass with lavender swirls in the jar and put it back on the shelf.

Turning toward the den then, he called, "Hey, Chad! Wanna make a sweet commission?"

CHAPTER SIX

"It was awful, Gwen," Sharlamagne whispered. "I felt like some sleazy, wanton woman."

Gwen shrugged with indifference. "So you had a carnal moment, Shar. It happens to everybody."

Sharlamagne frowned. "Not to me!" she insisted.

"Well, now that I think about it, it is true that you can't even hear the word *sex* without getting all—"

"Shhh! Gwen! No 's' words, all right?" Sharlamagne scolded.

"All right," Gwen said. She smiled, however, adding, "You know that *shhh* is actually an 's' word, don't you?"

"So is 'shut up,'" Sharlamagne reminded her.

"Come on, Shar. Settle down. It is the way God intended, you know—for men and women to be attracted to each other, physically," Gwen offered. "How else would the human race have survived if not for that?"

"We are not talking about the human race, Gwen. We are talking about me...and the fact that I had to restrain myself from, like... from, like, groping him!" Sharlamagne squeezed toothpaste onto her toothbrush, fairly jamming it into her mouth.

"Settle down, girl," Gwen giggled. "You'll get receding gums brushing so hard. And besides, you didn't grope him. You hugged him."

"Yeah, but I wanted to grope him," Sharlamagne mumbled as she brushed.

"Well, if he's still *Into the Blue* Paul Walker buff, I understand why," Gwen giggled.

Sharlamagne rinsed. "It's worse than that," she said. "He's more like *Australia* Hugh Jackman buff now. It's visible to the naked eye, of course. But I could also feel it when I hugged him."

Gwen giggled again. "Well, no wonder you're having issues. And I never thought I'd hear you use the words *naked* and *feel* in the same sentence."

"'S' word—shut up, Gwen," Sharlamagne scolded, though she couldn't help but smile. "Why is it you have all the lack of inhibition and I'm all like...like..."

"Inhibited?" Gwen finished with a smile.

"Yeah, exactly."

Gwen shrugged again. "It's probably your safety net, being that you're so carnally minded and all."

Sharlamagne growled with frustration. "I am not talking to you about it anymore, Guinevere. You cannot be serious for one lousy moment."

"Okay, okay, I'm sorry. I shouldn't tease you about it. It's obviously a sensitive subject to you...and no wonder! *Australia* Hugh Jackman buff, you say?"

"Totally *Australia* Hugh Jackman buff," Sharlamagne confirmed.

"Then, if you want my advice...grope away, Sharlamagne. I would."

"You would not, and I said I'm done talking to you about it. You couldn't be serious to save your life." Sharlamagne vigorously rinsed her toothbrush and returned it to its place in the medicine cabinet. "Something is seriously wrong with me, Gwen. I'm not kidding."

Sharlamagne inhaled a slow, deep breath in trying to remain patient with her sister as Gwen took her hands in her own. "Look, Shar...there's nothing wrong with you," she said. "He just rang your bell, that's all. I guess you didn't really realize no one ever had before." Gwen frowned slightly, with an expression of disbelief. "Seriously. No one ever has before...have they?"

"If having your bell rung means you considered for a moment being a million times more aggressive than is in your nature and kissing a guy you hardly know—actually instigating the kiss, actually risking his rejection—then yeah…I guess he rung my bell, and I guess no one else ever has."

"Even Joey Hayes your sophomore year of college?" Gwen asked, again disbelieving.

"Not even close," Sharlamagne admitted.

"Wow!" Gwen whispered. "One hug from Mrs. Tanner's grandson did you that bad? He must be *Australia* Hugh Jackman buff!"

"See?" Sharlamagne exclaimed, pulling away from her sister and turning toward their bedroom. "I'm a floozy!"

"Because you wanted to kiss him?" Gwen laughed. "Calm down, Shar. It's human nature. It's attraction. It's *supposed* to happen! And no one uses the word *floozy* anymore. You're the one who needs to stop reading the old magazines in the store."

"It's supposed to happen with real guys, not ones that just stepped off the 'I Was Made for Loving You' train, Gwen."

"He is a real guy. If anyone knows that, it should be you."

"Don't say it, Gwen," Sharlamagne warned, though she recognized that her sister had managed to lighten her mood with her lighthearted teasing. "Don't you dare say—"

"After all, you were the one groping him. If anyone knows he's real, it's you," Gwen interjected however. Sharlamagne rolled her eyes. "Why don't you grope his butt a little today and see if that feels as real as his pecs?"

"'S' word, Gwen—shut up," Sharlamagne giggled.

Gwen smiled at her sister as she slipped on a dress. "You know I'm kidding, right?" she asked. "I would've been as wigged out as you were. No one has ever rung my bell like that either—not even Braden, who I've been dating for two months. Well, no one has rung my bell like that unless you count *Reign of Fire* Matthew McCona-hottie. But he's totally not real…and I've never groped him. I wouldn't have the nerve to if I ever had the chance anyway and—"

"Enough! 'S' word, Gwen. 'S' word!" Sharlamagne laughed.

"Shar, just let go of it, and enjoying finding out what else Mrs. Tanner left to you today. Okay?"

Sharlamagne nodded. "Okay."

"But do grope him again if you get the chance," Gwen added.

Sharlamagne laughed, picked up a discarded bra from the nearby chair in their room, and tossed it at her sister.

"Don't throw lingerie at me, Sharlamagne Dickens!" Gwen giggled, snatching a pair of lace underwear out of the basket of folded clothes at the foot of her bed and rifling it toward Sharlamagne. "Save it for Mrs. Tanner's grandson!"

Sharlamagne giggled and threw the lace panties back at her sister.

"Girls!" Louisa Dickens exclaimed as she entered Sharlamagne and Gwen's bedroom with several dresses hanging from hangers. "Quit throwing your panties! I swear, I really thought you girls would grow out of this. Why do I even bother to fold them? Why do you? I just don't see—"

Louisa gasped and was silenced as a lacy pink bra hit her in the face. She inhaled a deep breath, appearing quite irritated as she said, "Now, who threw that? Girls?"

"Sorry, Mom," Sharlamagne confessed. "We were just—"

She watched as her mother bent over and picked up the lacy pink bra that had hit her in the face only a moment ago.

"Darling," her mother began, "if you're going to fling braziers at people, then you'd better get the most out of it."

Louisa laughed, and before Sharlamagne could move out of the way, her mother had taken hold of the bra as if it were a slingshot and snapped it right back at her.

Instantly, wild giggling and laughter erupted as bras, panties, and various forms of leg lingerie began rocketing around the room like fireworks on the Fourth of July.

Sharlamagne laughed with her mother and sister. All her cares and concerns about the physical attraction toward Maxim Tanner she'd experienced were momentarily forgotten.

"What's going on in here?" Cris Dickens asked, poking his head into the girls' room. "Never mind," he grumbled as a lacy red pair of boy shorts panties hit him squarely in the face. "I hate laundry day," he mumbled as the pink brazier skimmed the top of his head.

It was eight a.m., and Sharlamagne stood on the front porch of Mrs. Tanner's restored Victorian home, wondering how in the world she'd worked up the courage to ring the doorbell. But she had. She glanced to the old military-green jeep parked in the driveway. She thought it looked like a legitimate 1940s or 1950s Army jeep but didn't know the history of jeeps the way her father did. Still, she smiled; she knew it belonged to him, because driving a vintage jeep seemed to fit Maxim Tanner perfectly somehow.

She startled as the front door swung open to reveal Maxim Tanner dressed in jeans and a worn blue shirt. "Hi," he greeted. As she heard several clocks inside the house begin to chime eight, he smiled and added, "You're prompt. I like that in a marble expert."

Sharlamagne giggled and stepped into the house as he stepped aside, gesturing for her to do so. "Well, I like to get things done, and being prompt seems to help that along a little."

"I like that too," he said, smiling. "So do you want to get started?"

"Yeah. But you don't have to take me tramping through your beautiful home every time I come to work on the house, you know," she offered.

"It's Grandma's house, and she would love to have you tramping through it. In fact, you should probably take note of a few things in here. There's a lot of stuff…and if you see anything you'd like to have, just ask me, and I'll tell you whether I'm willing to let it go." He paused, seeming pleased by the way Sharlamagne's mouth was gaping open in astonishment. "Of course, I'd only gift it to you if it were for your own collection. Grandma kept her best stuff in the house for herself, so anything I give to you, I would want you to keep."

But Sharlamagne shook her head, still astonished at what he was offering. "This is all yours," she began. "Your grandma wanted you to have the house and everything in it. I'm sure she didn't mean for you to—"

"Look over here," he interrupted, taking hold of her arm and pulling her into the parlor to the right of them. "I do want to keep the house the way she left it—at least for now—but what does this room need with ten stereoscopes? That's too many, and it makes the table look cluttered."

"But…but," Sharlamagne stammered as she stared at the beautiful collection of stereoscopes on the doily-lined tabletop. Four of them were on pedestals; the others were handheld models. An old wooden box filled with stereoview cards sat with them. "They're gorgeous!" Sharlamagne breathed at last. "Wow! And in such good condition." She looked to Maxim and asked, "May I look through the stereoview cards? I'll be careful."

Maxim chuckled. "You're an antique dealer—I'm sure you will. But I will remind you that Grandma always liked for people to touch and use her stuff. I spent half my childhood rifling through that box of view cards picking out my favorites."

Sharlamagne smiled at the memory of the way Mrs. Tanner would champion handling old things—handling them carefully, of course—but she believed people should touch and care for things that represented the past. It helped instill appreciation for the people and events of long ago. Sharlamagne's smile broadened as she remembered the time Mrs. Tanner told her that the things themselves needed to be valued—that they appreciated being appreciated.

"Here," Maxim said, picking up several of the stereoview cards. "This is one of my favorites. The 3-D effect is incredible." He picked up one of the handheld stereoscopes and placed the card in position to be viewed.

Sharlamagne watched, smiling with delighted approval as he adjusted the sliding card holder.

"There," he said. "Check it out. See if you know what I mean."

Sharlamagne took the stereoscope when he offered it, pressed it to her forehead and cheekbones, and looked through the ancient scope lenses to the card.

"*Love, Courtship, and Marriage,*" she said as she read the title of the card. She smiled as she studied the scene. The scene was a Victorian parlor, complete with tables, chairs, lamps, heavy draperies, and every other lovely room embellishment of the time. In the foreground, a boy and a girl, both in their early teens, sat in chairs across from one another sharing a sweet kiss. Yet when Sharlamagne looked past the boy and girl to the standing mirror behind them to the left, there was another couple reflected in the mirror. This couple—a man and a women of young adult age—stood before a preacher and were obviously being married. To the right in the scene, there hung a large mirror on the wall. In this reflection, an older couple sat in their bed with their cheeks lovingly pressed together.

"Oh, wow!" Sharlamagne breathed. "Wow! I've never seen one like this. It's fabulous! Wow! It's an awesome 3-D type thing."

"I know," Maxim agreed. "You should take one. She has three or four of that one in there."

"Oh, no. Really, I couldn't," Sharlamagne argued, but only out of politeness. She really would love to have the stereoview card! It was very unique and obviously very rare because she'd never seen one like it before.

"I'm not kidding," Maxim began, "so don't worry about being polite or something. Just take one. Take this one and the stereoscope… or whichever one you want." She watched as he looked at the table laden with stereoscopes. "In fact, take one of the standing ones *and* two of the handhelds. That way, it'll only be seven on the table, and I can sleep better."

"What?" Sharlamagne giggled.

"I like odd numbers," he confessed. "I don't know why. But I like one, three, five, seven—you know—better than two, four, six. It's just a thing I have. And besides—" He leaned closer to her, and Sharlamagne felt goose bumps prickling her arms as she felt his breath on her neck when he continued, "She's got one in every bedroom upstairs too…at least one."

"Really?"

"Yep," he assured her. He shrugged broad (very broad) shoulders. "If you don't take a few of them, I might just end up taking them over to your dad's place to sell."

"No, no, no," she said then. "I'll take three of them from here… and a few cards too…if that's really okay."

He smiled. "It's really okay. Otherwise, I wouldn't have offered."

He glanced around the room for a moment. "There's actually a lot of stuff in here I plan to have you look at eventually. But I figure we better get your house taken care of first. Okay?"

"More than okay," she answered.

"Then let's get to it, Sharlamagne Dickens," he kindly suggested. "I promise you, you've got a year's worth of work waiting out there for you."

"I know," Sharlamagne agreed as she remembered how much stuff—how much treasure—was in the old house. "Isn't it wonderful?"

He chuckled. "If you say so," he said. He nodded to the stereoscopes on the table. "You can just come get what you want when you're finished for today, okay?"

"Okay. And thank you, Maxim. Your grandmother meant more to me than you know. And for you to offer to share her things with me...I...I..."

"She adored you," he said, smiling a sad sort of smile. "I know. And I know that she would want you to have some of the stuff in this house...as well as all the crap out in the other one."

Sharlamagne giggled as she followed him toward the kitchen and back door. Oh, how she loved lingering in Mrs. Tanner's home! Oh, how she loved lingering in it with Mrs. Tanner's handsome grandson.

"Have you got your key?" Maxim asked as they approached the old house.

"Yep," Sharlamagne said, pulling her keys out of her pocket. She'd left her purse in the trunk of the car, not wanting to be bothered with it while going through the stuff in the old house.

Maxim stepped aside, allowing Sharlamagne to unlock the door and open it. As soon as the door swung into the old house, Sharlamagne couldn't help but smile and exhale a sigh of pure delight. She was awash with wonderful sensory overload—compotes, photos, dolls, silver, beautifully crafted furniture. It was marvelous!

"Where are you gonna start?" Maxim asked. "I'd be totally overwhelmed."

But Sharlamagne smiled at him and answered, "I'll start at the beginning." Stepping into the entryway of the old house, she looked to her right. There were three old wooden crates stacked on top of each other and filled with things wrapped in packing paper. "I'll start with these," she said, trying to lift the first crate. "Wow! It's heavy," she said, taking a deep breath and trying again. But the crate was so heavy and stacked so high she couldn't lift it down safely. Shrugging, she said, "I'll just have to unpack it first."

"Here," Maxim said, stepping up and easily lifting the crate. "Where do you want it?" he asked.

"Oh! Um…just outside will be fine. Thank you."

"No problem," he said, setting the crate down on the walkway just outside the house. "What has she got in there? It weighs a lot more than it seems like it should."

"Well, let's find out, shall we?" Sharlamagne said. Her excitement was soaring! She couldn't begin to imagine what Mrs. Tanner had in the old crate that was so heavy.

Taking out the very top item, which was carefully wrapped in packing paper and then bubble wrap, she mumbled, "Holy cow! What has she got in here?" As Sharlamagne carefully removed the remaining layer of plastic cushioning material, she gasped.

"It's a rock," Maxim stated.

Sharlamagne giggled. He was too cute!

"It's not a rock," she countered. "It's a piece of a tombstone."

"A piece of a tombstone?" Maxim chuckled. "What it the hell would a person do with a piece of a tombstone? It's a rock. It might have been a tombstone—or a piece of a tombstone at one time—but it's just a rock now. Right?"

Again Sharlamagne laughed. Oh, Elisaveta Tanner was incredible— just incredible! Sharlamagne's antiquing mind had instantly known the value of the tombstone, historically. Furthermore, she'd guessed at just what Mrs. Tanner had intended it to be used for.

"Darling! Don't be such a silly goose," she said, imitating Mrs. Tanner's voice and inflections as best she could. "Here, hold this," she added, handing the piece of the tombstone to Maxim as she began to dig through the wrapped items in the crate.

"Hmm," she heard Maxim mumbled. "September 20, 1863. It's Civil War era."

"Yep," Sharlamagne said. "Mrs. Tanner told me she'd been to Georgia years and years ago, when they were replacing some old tombstones in a cemetery. I'm pretty sure you're looking at the tombstone of a man who died in the Battle of Chickamauga. And," she added as she unwrapped another piece of tombstone, "*voilà*! Bookends!"

Smiling, she handed Maxim a second piece of tombstone.

"Bookends?" he asked as he stared at the two pieces of stone in his hand.

"Yep! I remember Mrs. Tanner telling me she had retrieved some old Civil War tombstone pieces on her trip down there…and that she planned to use them as bookends for her collection of books from that era."

"This one is engraved with C.S.A.…a Confederate," Maxim remarked. "Wow, it's kind of incredible." He smiled at Sharlamagne. "So this tombstone was carved in 1863?"

"Yep. It probably came from a cemetery that was in a really bad state of disrepair. They replace the old tombstones sometimes." As she removed the wrapping from another piece, she whispered, "I think it's sad that they just toss away the pieces of the original ones. Someone carved this almost a hundred and fifty years ago, and it marked a soldier's grave for over a hundred of those years. And then it just ended up as a rock in a pile of trash."

"Geez. Now I feel bad for calling it a rock at first," Maxim said. Sharlamagne smiled as she watched him study the pieces of stone. "Bookends, huh?" He smiled then. "Grandma sure wasn't one to miss picking up a good rock…whether or not it was a tombstone."

Sharlamagne smiled and returned her attention to the crate. "I think all of these are probably pieces of tombstone," she said. "I wonder if all three of those crates are filled with them."

"Well, let's find out," Maxim said. Stepping into the house, he lifted another crate. "This one is much, much lighter."

Once he'd set the crate down next to the first one, Sharlamagne reached into it and withdrew something wrapped as the tombstones had been. "It's light," she said. "Obviously not a rock."

"A tombstone remnant," Maxim teasingly corrected. "Have some respect, lady."

Sharlamagne laughed and continued to unwrap the item. "Ah ha!" she exclaimed with an approving smile. "A book to go with the bookends." In her hands, she held an old book, and she knew at once that it was Civil War era.

"Do you think this one is filled with books then?" Maxim asked.

"Definitely," she assured him. "Here," she began, handing him a wrapped "something" out of the crate. "It's like a treasure hunt—you'll see. Unwrap it and see what it is."

Maxim grinned as he carefully unwrapped the item she'd handed him. The book was large and green and in excellent shape. "Hmm. *The Horse and His Diseases*," Maxim read. "By Robert Jennings V.S." His grin broadened to a smile. "Awesome!" Maxim nodded as he carefully opened the book. "Copyright 1863. Cool."

Sharlamagne giggled. "See? It's totally fun!" She sighed with delight and shook her head. "This house…it's going to be a total treasure trove. I can tell just by these things."

"And as I said, it's going to take us years to go through it," Maxim said.

"Us?" Sharlamagne asked as her heart skipped a beat.

"Well, yeah," Maxim said. "You can't dangle the worm on a hook in front of me and expect me not to bite. It's hard telling what else Grandma has hidden away in there." He paused and frowned. "Do you mind if I hang around here and there while you're going through stuff? I could help—you know, lift the heavy boxes and things. I won't get in your way, I swear."

Sharlamagne smiled and felt a blush of pure elation rise to her cheeks. "I would love to have you help me!" she exclaimed—perhaps with a little too much obvious exuberance.

"Great! Then what do we do next?" he asked.

"Well," she began, glancing around, "if we're going to do it right, we need to catalog everything as we go—and at the same time decide what I'm going to keep and what I'll put on consignment at the store.

I've got some notebooks in the car. I'll run back and get them."

She watched as Maxim carefully unwrapped another book. "So you say this house is a treasure trove, right?"

"Oh, yeah! Completely," she assured him. "Why?"

"Well...nothing. Just something Grandma always used to talk about," he began. "There's a bedroom in the main house. When I was remodeling it for her, Grandma kept telling me there was a trove in it—the trove of the Passion Room, she called it."

"The trove of the Passion Room?" Sharlamagne repeated. "What does that mean? And what is a Passion Room anyway?"

Maxim chuckled. "The Passion Room is exactly what its title implies—a room of passion." He shook his head. "It's a long story. Boring too. But now you've got me curious. A trove...what is that, exactly? Like a collection of objects, isn't it? Something like that?"

"Yeah," Sharlamagne agreed. "Like an assortment of things, a mass or stockpile of stuff. What's in the room? Does it look like this house does? Is it, like, stuffed with things or something?"

Maxim shook his head. "Nope. It's just a really nice room with cool paintings on the walls." He looked at her and winked. "Romantic paintings—thus the passion part, I guess." He shrugged. "Grandma told me that there was a legend or something about that particular room...that people couldn't spend the night in there without..." He paused and looked at her. Sharlamagne's heart began to pound, for the expression in his eyes was nothing less than provocative!

"That people couldn't spent the night in there without what?" she had to ask.

"Without passion flaming between them to such a point that inevitably they ended up having s—"

"Don't say it!" Sharlamagne exclaimed, clamping her hand over his mouth. "If you're going to say the 's' word...I-I..." She realized how ridiculous and childish he must think she was.

Pushing her hand away from his mouth, he simply said, "Sex? You don't want me to say s—"

"Don't say it!" she exclaimed once more, clamping her hand over his mouth again. He began to laugh—of course he did.

"You're kidding me, right?" he asked once he'd detached her hand from his mouth a second time.

"No," she confessed, feeling like an idiot. "I don't like the word. Certain words just bother me for some reason."

"Well, how cute is that?" he chuckled. "So is it just the word you don't like? Or is the actual—you know—*thing* itself?"

"It's the word," she admitted. Though before she could stop herself, she added, "I wouldn't know about the actual *thing* itself." She felt her cheeks roasting. She knew she was as red as radish. Why had she said it? She was such an idiot!

"Well now, that's even more adorable," he said. "Not to mention pitifully rare these days."

Maxim was intrigued—even more intrigued than he had been moments before. He felt like someone had just opened a window and let some fresh air into a room filled with stifling smoke. That's exactly the sensation he had whenever he was in Sharlamagne Dickens's company. He'd had that same feeling the night she'd actually shown up at his birthday party—the day she'd walked into Carl's office to hear his grandmother's will read. And now—now she'd just revealed she wasn't into sleeping around—that she hadn't *ever* slept with anyone? He loved it!

In truth, there wasn't one young woman in his circle of friends who wasn't forever and always wanting to drag him to bed. Oh, certainly he'd never slept with any of them. His grandmother had raised him well—to keep intimate things intimate *and* monogamous. But he'd pretty much given up hope that he'd ever run into a girl who had managed to keep herself…well, virginal. Yet it seemed miracles still happened—because here was one sitting on the grass right next to him.

Yep. Maxim Tanner was all the more fascinated by Sharlamagne Dickens. She was funny, clever, kind, pretty, and apparently a very chaste young woman with real bosoms. Yes—a breath of fresh air.

He could tell she felt stupid for revealing her innocence, however, and he didn't want that—not in any respect.

"I guess my grandma was even better at finding treasure than I even knew," he said, hoping the compliment would cool the blush on her cheeks a little.

Sharlamagne smiled at him. Oh, she was still painfully embarrassed, but she was also very pleased with his gentlemanly remarks. He was kind. With everything else he was—gorgeous, smart, capable, strong—he was kind as well. It only made him more attractive, and Sharlamagne had thought that was impossible.

"I'll run and get those notebooks out of my car...if you really do have time to help me," she said.

"I've got time," he said, smiling at her. "Do you mind if I unwrap a couple more things, just to see what they are?"

"Of course not! Treasure hunts are always more fun when you have someone along," she told him.

"Awesome! Thanks."

Sharlamagne nodded and then started around the big house toward the street and her parked car. He hadn't made fun of her. She couldn't believe it! Most guys she knew made fun of her when they found out she had never had the "s" word—even guys she knew had never had the "s" word either. But Maxim Tanner—he'd complimented her on the fact. Oh, she was pretty nearly certain he'd had the "s" word—probably a lot—but she wouldn't think about it. After all, maybe he was like her; maybe he'd been raised to save the "s" word for that one special woman, the one he would eventually marry. She thought of his parents then and decided that they probably hadn't taught him any such thing. But then she remembered that it was Mrs. Tanner who had done most of the raising where Maxim was concerned—and she knew how Mrs. Tanner felt about the "s" word.

"Your husband, darlings...that's the one and only person you ever give yourself to," Mrs. Tanner had told Sharlamagne and Gwen once when they were still in middle school. "The world has quit believing in that—abandoned fidelity, chastity, and the saving of intimacy for marriage. But don't you girls let the world tell you what to do. Don't you dare ever let the world determine your actions. You be your own women...and you be strong ones."

Sharlamagne smiled as she popped the trunk of her car and pulled out a couple of notebooks and some pens. Mrs. Tanner had raised Maxim. Therefore, no matter what—no matter the supermodel types that had thrown themselves at him at his birthday party or all the other women in the world willing to do anything to capture his attention—Sharlamagne decided she would go through life thinking that Maxim was just the way she was—that the "s" word wasn't something he did casually, that he was a man among men and held to a high moral standard. Oh, she knew it was a naive notion, but Sharlamagne decided to hang onto it anyway.

As she returned to find Maxim had unwrapped several books and now had them placed between two tombstone pieces, she smiled. He was *so* dreamy. So very, very dreamy!

"They'd look good on a shelf, wouldn't they?" he asked as she approached.

"Yeah. They would," she agreed.

"Well, give me a notebook and tell me what to do, Ms. Dickens," he said, sitting down in the grass.

Sharlamagne smiled and handed him a notebook and a pen. *Thank you, Mrs. Tanner,* she thought to herself. *And not just for the house full of treasure.*

CHAPTER SEVEN

All week (literally from sunup to sundown) Sharlamagne worked on going through the things Mrs. Tanner had left for her in the old house. The further she made her way into the house, the more astounding the treasure was. Each and every day she awoke with an airy, nearly delirious feeling of excited anticipation in her chest. Every morning as she drove toward Mrs. Tanner's (now hers and Maxim's) houses, she wondered what the day would bring—wondered what she would find hidden away in the old treasure trove of a house.

Even more affecting, Sharlamagne had quickly discovered that her feelings of excitement—her near fever in anticipation—had as much to do with spending the day with Maxim Tanner as it did in finding what other treasures Mrs. Tanner had left for her. In fact, as she pulled up in front of the old restored Victorian and saw Maxim's jeep already in the driveway, she thought the joy flailing around in her stomach might cause her to throw up.

As she sat in her car a moment, watching Maxim shove his keys in his pocket and saunter toward her smiling his "I Was Made for Loving You" train conductor smile, she tried to catch her breath—tried to breathe normally. She couldn't believe he'd taken the whole week off and spent it helping her. She couldn't believe he'd made them grilled cheese sandwiches every day for lunch in Mrs. Tanner's (now his) kitchen.

She couldn't believe it when he reached out and opened the car door for her, smiling and saying, "Good morning," as she stepped out of her car.

"Good morning," she offered, smiling in return.

"Sorry I'm a little late," he said. "Had to get my Saturday morning cartoons in, you know."

Sharlamagne giggled. "Oh, really?"

"Naw," he said, still grinning. "I just overslept."

"Well, I'm glad you did. You've worked very hard helping me this week. Your charitable works quota is overflowing for this month. Right?"

"Charitable works?" he asked as they walked together toward the backyard. "Treasure hunting can't be categorized as charitable works."

Sharlamagne looked up at him, and even though she tried not to, she audibly sighed as she studied his ever-refreshing good looks.

"Dust, spiders, heavy lifting?" she began. "Packing paper, bubble wrapping, old stuff? Are you trying to tell me you've caught the antiquing fever, Mr. Tanner?"

"Oh, I've always had the antiquing fever, Miss Dickens," he chuckled. He shrugged. "Admittedly not to the extent that you and Grandma have it. Maybe it's more of a cold or a sniffle for me rather than a fever. But I have it all the same. I just always felt responsible to keep Grandma in line with her purchases where and if I could." He smiled down at her. "But now that she's left all her crap to you, I guess I'm off the hook. Right?"

"It's not crap," Sharlamagne teasingly scolded. "It's treasure."

He laughed as they reached the front door of the old house. "I know, I know. And you've pulled me into your treasure-hunting obsession somehow. I'm, like, all excited to see if those old wardrobes in the back of that one bedroom are empty or filled with more crap...I mean treasure."

"Ooo! You see?" Sharlamagne giggled as she unlocked the door. "You *do* have the fever, and not just the sniffles."

Sharlamagne bit her lip with anticipation, and she and Maxim stepped into the house. The first two rooms were completely cleaned out—thanks to Maxim, Cris, Cratch, and her father's moving truck.

She couldn't believe how much stuff she'd put on consignment with her father at the store. Even more astonishing, she couldn't believe she'd had to rent a storage unit for what she'd decided to keep. She'd have to whittle it down; she knew she would—eventually. But that could wait. She had already let go of what she easily could. The rest was too wonderful, astonishing, rare, or simply beautiful to let go.

Sharlamagne found she was most excited about the seven or eight large boxes of photos she had taken back to the house—old photos—nineteenth and early twentieth century photos. She couldn't wait until Mrs. Tanner's old house was cleaned out and she could steal an evening here and there to sort through the beautiful old cabinet and folder folio photos.

But there was still way too much left to do with the other things packed in the old house for her to think about having any downtime for the next while. It had taken her and Maxim five days to clear out the first two rooms of the house, and according to Maxim, the house had five bedrooms, a kitchen, and a study left to sift through.

"You're looking a little overwhelmed there, shawty," Maxim chuckled.

Sharlamagne shook her head and sighed. "Well…I have to work at least six hours a day at the store next week. I promised Dad I'd cover while Gwen took the week off. And I'm just wondering how I'll ever get this finished."

"There's no hurry, remember?" he reminded her. "And I can come help you in the evenings if you want."

"Really?" Sharlamagne asked, hoping the joy she felt inside wasn't too obvious on the outside.

"Yeah," he answered. "I can be here about five every evening if you want to keep working. But seriously…you don't have to kill yourself trying to get everything out of here. I mean that."

Sharlamagne shook her head, amazed at his kindness to her.

"What's the matter? Still too overwhelmed even after that assurance?" he asked.

"No. I just can't figure out why you're being so nice to me. I mean… this is a lot of work," she explained.

She heard him chuckle and looked up to see him staring at her. There was a bright glint in his gorgeous sapphire blues—something like mischief, only not quite as daring as it usually was when he was teasing her.

"Well, I like you," he said, causing Sharlamagne's breath to catch in her throat. "We're on a treasure hunt, after all. And besides, you haven't once tried to borrow money from me, tried to seduce me, or anything outrageous like that…all of which is refreshingly unfamiliar territory to me when it comes to friends. So why wouldn't I want to help you?"

She smiled. He'd called her a friend! He thought of her as a friend. She was delirious with gladness—so delirious that she'd said it almost before she'd even realized it was coming out of her mouth.

"Well, I never borrow money from friends, and I haven't tried to seduce you…*yet*," she flirted. Instantly, her hand flew to her mouth. "I'm so sorry!" she apologized, covering her mouth again as if she were afraid something else scandalous would slip out. What an idiot! Here he'd just sort of confided in her that all his friends were shallow people who always wanted something from him, and she had to go and let a secret, unfamiliarly scandalous thought slip out of her mouth. Now he'd just lump her in with all his other shallow friends for sure.

"I'm so sorry," she apologized again, placing a hand on his arm. She couldn't help but notice how rock-solid his bicep was. "I was only…"

She realized then that he was smiling at her with twinkling amusement in his eyes.

"So I'm not allowed to say the 's' word," he began, "but you can imply that one day you'll try to sedu—"

"Shhh!" she shushed him as her hand clamped over his mouth. "I was…I was only…only…"

"Flirting," he suggested as he pushed her hand away. "It's called flirting, Sharlamagne." He grimaced as if he'd said a bad word. "And…I feel obligated to inform you that flirting is an 'f' word."

He was teasing her now, and she felt better. He didn't seem at all irritated with her for flirting with him, and she sighed with relief.

Playfully slapping him on the chest, she turned toward the first bedroom of the house. "You're making fun of me…again," she said.

"I'm making fun *with* you," he corrected.

And I'd like to make more than just fun with you, Maxim thought as he followed her toward the bedroom. He frowned, surprised and momentarily disgusted with himself for having such an indecent thought toward his grandmother's little pet friend. He shook his head and chuckled a little, wondering if he was disturbed by having such a thought toward Sharlamagne because she was just his friend or if Sharlamagne was rubbing off on him and he would start flogging himself for using the "s" word next. *Is she rubbing off on me?* he wondered. *Well, I wouldn't mind her rubbing against me, that's for sure*, he thought next—again shaking his head at the absurd things banging around in it at the moment.

"These wardrobes are beautiful!" Sharlamagne exclaimed, rattling him back to his senses. "Look at the detail work."

Maxim forced himself to look away from Sharlamagne, and her pretty beaming-with-admiration face, and to the wardrobe. He nodded and let his fingers travel over the wood.

"It's incredible, actually," he admitted. "They just don't make things like this anymore. Even carpenters like me. It's so time-consuming and—"

"Oh, please do not tell me you're a carpenter too," Sharlamagne interrupted. "Is there anything you're not good at?"

He smiled at her. "Yes, I enjoy carpentry, shawty," he answered. "I do remodel vintage homes, you know. It's pretty much a necessary skill. And of course there are a million things I'm not good at."

"I don't know," she said as she pulled a box away from the front of the wardrobe. "It seems to me you're like Mr. Carpenter, Contractor, Jeans Model, etcetera, all rolled into one."

"Hey, look, I don't make fun of you for being Ms. Antique Expert, the Queen of Marble Acquisitions, and the authority on Victorian love triangles, now do I?" he teased.

She giggled, and he liked that it was because of what he'd said.

"Apples to oranges, Mr. Maxim," she said as she took hold of the handles on the doors of the wardrobe. Looking to him and smiling a smile that made his smile broaden if he wanted it to or not, she asked, "Well? What's your guess? Boxes, books? Hats and clothing?"

"I couldn't begin to guess," he lied. Yep—he'd lied. He had a pretty good idea exactly what was in the wardrobes stored in the bedrooms of the old house. After all, no one knew his grandmother the way he did—no one still living anyway. Furthermore, if his suspicions were right about what Sharlamagne was about to find when she opened the wardrobe doors, then he couldn't wait to see the look on her face. Her expression would be priceless if his guess was right.

"Well then…here goes," she said, inhaling a deep breath as if she were about to find a million dollars in cash stashed away in the old wardrobe.

Maxim watched as Sharlamagne opened the wardrobe doors— watched as astonishment washed over her face, followed by a blush of pure euphoria on her soft cheeks and moisture brimming in her pretty brown-green eyes.

"Oh my gosh!" she breathed. He was sure she was going to cry. As her hand went to her chest (no doubt to still the rapid beating of her heart), Maxim quickly glanced inside the wardrobe to find that his assumption of its contents had been spot on.

Sharlamagne gasped as she saw what was in the wardrobe—what else Mrs. Tanner had left to her. "No way!" she breathed. "I cannot believe this!"

"I recognized this stuff," Maxim offered. "Grandma has shown me these dresses a hundred times."

"They look authentic…vintage 1940s," Sharlamagne said as she reached into the wardrobe and touched one glamorous dress.

"They are. They're some of her fancy dresses from way back when she was singing with the USO and stuff." He reached in, took hold of one dress, and carefully tugged the skirt of it out of the wardrobe. "Man. They really do look brand-new. There's not even any dust on them or anything." He leaned forward and sniffed the fabric. "They don't even smell musty. It's almost like she…" He paused, and understanding swept over Sharlamagne. She watched, almost afraid to touch anything for fear it would vanish and she would wake up and find she really was only dreaming. Maxim took hold of one old hanger and carefully removed a gown from its place in the wardrobe.

"It looks like she had them all cleaned before she left," Sharlamagne whispered, her eyes glistening with dazzled excitement and sentimental moisture.

"Knowing Grandma, I'm sure she did," Maxim said, handing the dress to her. "And I'm sure she didn't mean for you to be afraid to touch them."

Suddenly, Sharlamagne squealed with delight, reached out, and clasped the beautiful coral sequined gown to her, saying, "Do you think she meant to find them here like this...to touch them and everything?"

Maxim laughed. "Of course. In fact," he began, taking another dress from the wardrobe and holding it up as he looked from Sharlamagne to the dress and back, "she probably meant for you to wear them."

"Really?" Sharlamagne exclaimed. Holding the beautiful coral sequin-bedazzled evening gown against her body, she sighed. "I think it would fit. I seriously think this would fit me! Ooo, I'd feel just like Ginger Rogers in this!"

"Grandma contrived all this, you know," Maxim chuckled. "Just like she contrived bequeathing everything else she left in this house to you." He frowned a little, and his smile faded as he studied Sharlamagne again. His grandmother *had* contrived everything she'd left to Sharlamagne—and more. He thought of what had come in the mail only a few days earlier. At first, he'd assumed it was just to be expected. After all, he'd accompanied his grandmother to the event every year since he was sixteen. But now, as he studied the dresses in the wardrobe, he wondered if there were more to the fact that Elisaveta Tanner had left her collection of 1940s movie-star-type gowns to Sharlamagne.

Yet, as he watched Sharlamagne return the coral-colored gown to the wardrobe and gently remove a lavender gown fairly dripping with sparkling stuff and some sort of netting at the shoulders, he realized there would have been no one else on the face of the whole earth who would treasure his grandmother's gowns more than this girl.

"I seriously think these will fit me," Sharlamagne giggled as she placed the lavender gown flush with her body and studied herself in an old mirror hanging on a nearby wall.

"Oh, I'm positive they will," he chuckled. He considered the upcoming event for a moment. Why shouldn't he still attend it? He'd enjoyed it every year, so why miss it this year? Then he remembered something else—something his grandma had left to him—some things upstairs in the bedroom she and his grandfather had shared. He'd used a few of them before, but not the best one. Yep—an idea was forming in his mind. Still, his distrust of mankind, coupled with the lingering pain of losing his grandma, caused him to pause. He'd have to think about it. It was kind of a big thing, and he didn't want to jump the gun and do something he wasn't ready to do.

To say Sharlamagne was overwhelmed with joy at finding the stash of 1940s evening gowns would've been the understatement of the last millennium. As she replaced the gown she'd been holding and hung it back in the safe confines of the wardrobe, she knew that they were not something she could address easily. She'd have to think out what to do with them—where to store them and how to care for them. She could smell cedar and lavender and looked in the bottom of the wardrobe to see that Mrs. Tanner had made certain there was plenty of both inside the wardrobe. At least the gowns would be safe from moths until she could think what to do about them. But for the moment, she knew that her last full day off for over a week would need to be spent elsewhere.

"I'll have to leave these here awhile," she said out loud. "They'll need planning, and today I better just spend my time going through stuff that's more easily managed."

"Does that mean I can open a box now?" Maxim asked.

Sharlamagne smiled. He was like a kid in a toy store. Any time Maxim opened a box, his excitement or disinterest in what lay within spilled over onto her. His emotions were contagious that way, and she liked it.

"Of course," she assured him. "You don't have to ask me permission to open a box. I think I've told you that about six hundred and seventy-three times by now, haven't I?" she added, smiling at him.

"Well, I'm just afraid I'll open a box and it'll end up being the jewel of the collection or something. I'm sure Grandma wanted you to see everything first," he explained.

Sharlamagne wrinkled her brow in an expression of doubt. "Are you really this thoughtful?" she asked. "Sometimes you seem too good to be true." Instantly she wondered if what she'd said was too revealing of her opinion of him. He'd think she was flirting again if she wasn't careful. In truth, her desire to flirt with him had been becoming more and more difficult to keep from acting upon.

"Sometimes *you* seem too good to be true," he countered, however, and she felt better. She also began to wonder if flirting with Maxim Tanner a little bit here and there would be such a bad thing. He didn't seem offended by it. He didn't seem adverse to it. So what was wrong with a tad of playful flirting here and there? Why shouldn't she enjoy every moment she had in Maxim's company? Why shouldn't she throw a tiny lure and hope to capture his attention? Gwen wouldn't be afraid to do it. In fact, Gwen would've begun flirting with Maxim on day one. But Sharlamagne didn't have Gwen's sometimes brazen confidence. Furthermore, she really did like Maxim—she liked him a lot—a ton— far more than she should or had the right to. So she didn't want to scare him off by letting him know just how much she liked him. Still, a little flirting was harmless enough. Wasn't it?

Sharlamagne watched as Maxim took the box cutter out of his back pocket and carefully slit the packaging tape on the top seams of a small box he'd chosen to open. She admired the way he didn't just start hacking into a box. Who knew what delicate thing might be packed just under the tape? He seemed to appreciate the concept.

"Well...more doilies," he said. Sharlamagne could see how disappointed he was, and she felt bad for him—even though she smiled. "I swear...where did she ever find time to crochet so many damn doilies?"

Sharlamagne giggled at first. She couldn't help it. In fact, the expression of mingled disappointment and irritated marvel on Maxim's face was so boyishly adorable. Combined with his grumbling statement of his grandmother's prolific crocheting—well, both were so amusing that she couldn't keep from bursting into laughter.

"What?" he asked, still irritated. "I'm serious. How many doilies can one woman make? Especially one who was always as busy as my grandma was."

But Sharlamagne was still laughing. "I-I'm sorry," she gasped. "I-I'm sorry. You're just so funny sometimes! I can't help it."

Maxim's frown softened; he even grinned. "Well, I'm glad I can amuse you." Shaking his head, he pushed the box aside with his foot. "I could've sworn there was more in there than doilies. It seems too heavy to just be that...even for a small box."

Sharlamagne sighed as her laughter finally subsided. "Lift out the doilies and see if there's something else in the box under them," she suggested. "Remember Tuesday when we found that box full of old embroidered dishtowels...but they had really been used as padding to protect that crystal vase? Maybe the doilies aren't the only things in the box."

"So you're an eternal optimist, I see?" he said as he began to lift the doilies out of the box and hand them to Sharlamagne.

Sharlamagne was enchanted by the doilies, even if Maxim wasn't. In her opinion, each one was not only a work of art but was all the more valuable for sentimental reasons—for Elisaveta had made them.

"Well, there you go again...showing you're smarter than I am," Maxim mumbled. "But what is it?"

Sharlamagne watched as he drew a small, weathered wooden box from beneath the doily cache. "It's a wooden box," she answered.

Maxim chuckled, looked at her, and shook his head with amusement. "You know, you're a real smarty pants sometimes, you know that?" He kept smiling and added, "I *meant*, what could be in it? It's kind of heavy for its size, I think."

"Well, open it and find out," she urged.

"Like I said... a real smart a...aleck," he chuckled.

Sharlamagne watched Maxim open the wooden box—watched as a

broad smile spread across his face. "Now *that's* what I'm talking about!" he exclaimed. "That's something fun to find."

"I thought the doilies were fun to find," Sharlamagne teased.

"Oh, yeah? Then what about this?"

Sharlamagne's excitement was piqued as he moved closer to her and held the box so that she could peer into it. "Wow!" she exclaimed. "Wow! How fun!"

"Very fun," Maxim said as he reached into the box and removed one of the silver dollar coins it cached. Studying the coin for a moment, he continued to smile and said, "An 1885 Morgan silver dollar. It's in great condition. You could probably get over fifty bucks for this one."

He handed the coin to Sharlamagne, and she felt her heart swell inside her chest. She didn't care what the coin was worth on the open market. She thought of it as treasure—priceless treasure.

"Are there any more?" she asked.

"Are you kidding me?" Maxim chuckled. "The box is filled with him. That's why the box it was in was so heavy."

Without another word, Sharlamagne and Maxim simultaneously sat down on the floor, and Maxim placed the old wooden box between them. Over the past five days, it had become their habit—to sit down on the floor together to better study an item when they found something excessively interesting. It wasn't until that very moment, however, that Sharlamagne was consciously aware of the habit they'd formed together. The thought of it made her heart hammer faster, for it was almost as if their minds shared an invisible connection sometimes.

"Look at this one," Maxim said, withdrawing another coin from the box. "A 1923 silver Peace one. I always thought they were so cool." Handing it to Sharlamagne, he continued to dig through the box of old coins. "There're silver Mercury dimes, quarters, Liberty half dollars, Barber dimes…but it looks like it's mostly Morgan silver dollars."

Sharlamagne studied Maxim for a moment. He was so excited over the coins. It was adorable!

"So I'm guessing that, next to marbles, coins are your thing," she offered.

"I love coins," he admitted. "But they're too pricey to collect, you know what I mean?"

"Yeah," Sharlamagne agreed. "I have a few cool ones, but not a ton. These are awesome though…because it's such a stash."

He smiled. "A total stash of silver, dumped into an old box, covered up with some doilies, and stored away. Awesome!" He frowned a moment and then closed the lid to the box and turned it upside down. "I do remember this box," he said. "I thought it looked familiar."

"You've seen it before?" Sharlamagne asked.

"Yeah. It used to sit on my grandpa's nightstand," he began to explain. "At the end of the day, he'd put the change from his pockets, his keys, wallet, and watch in it. See?" He turned the box over so Sharlamagne could see the bottom. "My grandpa had a younger brother that was killed at Normandy. His name was Holms, and he made this for my grandpa the year he was eight. See the inscription?"

Sure enough, carved into the bottom of the old wooden box was an inscription: *To Alek. Happy Birthday from your brother Holms.*

"Oh, how sweet!" Sharlamagne sighed. "But…it kind of hurts me too."

"Why?" Maxim asked. "This box was one of my grandpa's favorite things. He used to tell me about his brother…how much fun they had together as boys, how brave Holms was. It always made me feel happy that grandpa had kept the box Holms had made." He chuckled as he studied the box again. "I mean, you have to admit…it's dog-ugly."

"It's beautiful," Sharlamagne argued however. "And you should have it. I'm sure it was a complete accident that it got put in here. I know your grandmother. She would never have left something so valuable in here on purpose."

Maxim smiled. "Valuable? It's not worth a dime." He arched his brows, adding, "Well, you can't get anything for a dime anymore, but it's still not worth a dime…not without the loot inside."

"It's priceless, and I want you to take it into the house," Sharlamagne said as she began to stand.

"No," Maxim said. "Grandma meant it for you…and that's fine

with me. I've got a whole house full of this kind of stuff to go through myself."

"Maxim," Sharlamagne began, "your grandfather's precious box, filled with old silver coins—I promise you, this was meant for you. Seriously, the doilies that were on top mean as much to me as anything. But this box, it's special to you…so I'm sure she would want you to have it. I'll keep the doilies; you keep the box."

Was she kidding? Maxim frowned a moment, uncertain as to what exactly to think. There was probably two grand's worth of old silver coins in the weathered box. Was Sharlamagne serious about giving the box and its contents to him? Secretly, Maxim didn't give a rip about the coins. Coins were coins. It was cool that they were old and silver—who wouldn't be intrigued by them? But, if he were to be honest with himself, he did want the box. He remembered it much more vividly than he'd admitted to Sharlamagne. His grandpa had let him root through the box on many occasions when he'd been a boy.

When Maxim was a little kid, his Grandpa Tanner would take the box off the nightstand and whisk Maxim up into his lap, and together they'd sort through the box Holms had made. There were always such interesting things to find in the box—at least the way Maxim remembered it. There were always coins or little, interesting rocks his grandpa had picked up along the way. His grandpa would always have Maxim pick out some change to put in his own piggy bank, and while Maxim would treasure hunt in his grandpa's old box, Alek Tanner would tell his grandson about his little brother Holms, who had made the box for him—about how close they'd been, how much fun they'd had growing up, all the mischief they'd gotten into, and finally how his brother had died a hero at Normandy.

In truth, he wondered why his grandmother had left the box to Sharlamagne when she knew how much Maxim had loved it. Still, he figured there was a reason—one he didn't understand maybe—but his grandmother had a reason for everything. It was no accident the box was in Sharlamagne's house.

"I mean it," Sharlamagne said, jostling Maxim from his thoughts.

"I know your grandmother, and she certainly would have wanted you to have that box. So let me keep the doilies, and you keep the box and the coins. Okay?"

She was serious. He could see it in her eyes: her sincerest desire was that the box should stay with him. Still, another thought occurred to him as she started to stand up. Reaching out, he took hold of her wrist and forced her to sit down on the floor with him once more.

"I'll make you a deal," Maxim began. "You keep the damn doilies, I'll keep the box, and we'll split the coins. That way I won't feel so bad about taking the box."

"But I don't want the coins," she reiterated, smiling at him.

"Well then, I won't take the box."

"But you have to have it! Your grandfather would want that. To me, it's just a neat old box with a sweet story. But to you…to you it's something you will always cherish…something you can give to one of your own kids one day. I really don't want it. I just—"

"We'll do it this way," he interrupted, pretending to ignore her. "You'll pick a coin, then I'll pick a coin. We'll do that until they're all divided. Then you can trot home with your doilies, and I'll put Grandpa's box on my own nightstand and dump my change and keys and stuff into it at the end of the day. How does that sound?"

He wasn't going to budge. Sharlamagne had learned enough about Maxim Tanner to know that once he made up his mind about something, then that was the end of it. She wanted him to take his grandfather's box—she could see how much it meant to him, no matter what he was saying. Therefore, there was only one thing she could do.

"Okay," she said. "I want the 1885 Morgan dollar you pulled out first."

Maxim smiled. He reached into the box and removed the Morgan silver dollar, placing it on the floor in front of her.

"Okay then…my turn," he said. Sharlamagne watched as he dug through the coins in the box. "I'll take this 1922 Peace one."

She giggled as he placed it on the floor in front of him and handed her the box. "I'll take a silver Peace one for myself. Here. 1928."

She handed the box back to Maxim, and he smiled at her. "You know…we're not going to get anything done today if we keep this up."

Sharlamagne shrugged. "Oh well. This guy I know keeps telling me that there's no hurry…that I don't have to get all my stuff out of here by tomorrow. So let's sort the coins and not worry about anything else."

Maxim smiled, and Sharlamagne's heart leapt. She'd made him happy! She knew he wanted his grandfather's box—he wanted it much more than he'd let on. She'd made him happy by giving it to him, and to her, that knowledge was worth more than the whole house full of treasure.

Thus, as she sat across from Maxim divvying up silver coins like two kids who had just raided their parents' change jar, Sharlamagne was happy as well. She couldn't imagine a better morning. Who cared what else was waiting to be found in the old house? Sharlamagne was beginning to realize that when she was with Maxim, she didn't care about anything else—not in all the world.

CHAPTER EIGHT

"I don't want you to think I'm picky or anything," Maxim began as Sharlamagne followed him out of the old house five hours later. "But I can't do grilled cheese for lunch again."

"Oh. You do realize you don't have to feed me, Maxim," she said. "I can fend for myself, you know." She was disappointed—painfully so—for she'd relished their lunches together. Not that she particularly liked grilled cheese sandwiches, but she did like watching Maxim make them—and she loved sitting with him at his grandmother's kitchen table and talking while they ate them.

"No, I mean, I can't stomach another one," he explained. "I think I burned myself out on them. They're so easy to make, you know… and I eat them all the time. So what do you think about just going somewhere for lunch? Jilly's Deli is just a few blocks down. Do you like other kinds of sandwiches besides grilled cheese?"

He smiled at her, and Sharlamagne felt as if she couldn't catch her breath for a moment. He was suggesting they go to lunch together—*out* to lunch together?

Quickly she looked down at her dusty jeans and rather ratty pink T-shirt. Her hair was pulled back in a ponytail, but after working in the house, there were a lot of strands that had escaped and were now hanging here and there around her face.

"But I look like a hobo," she began.

Maxim laughed, however. "A hobo?" he teased. "Who uses the word *hobo* anymore? I had to stop and think about it to make sure I

157

knew what you were talking about. And besides, you don't look like a hobo, shawty. You look great."

"Hmmm," she said. "Jeans Innovations model *and* a liar. You *do* have a lot of skills."

He chuckled. "So are you up for something besides grilled cheese? They have soup and salad there too. I'll drive."

"Sure," Sharlamagne said, smiling at him. "If you don't mind being seen with a hobo."

"If you don't mind being seen with a dorky, washed-up jeans-store guy who collects marbles and bums valuable coins off unsuspecting young ladies," he countered.

"Not at all."

"Then come on, Miss Dickens," he said, taking her arm and pulling her in the direction of his jeep. "I'm starving."

❦

"Yeah, it's quite a list," Maxim said as he ate a potato chip. "You know the guy in the family photo in Grandma's house…my great-great-great-grandfather?"

"Dillanger Thomas? Yeah. He married Abigail, and their daughter Tandie was your great-great-grandmother. Got it," Sharlamagne answered.

Maxim raised his eyebrows with admiration, and Sharlamagne smiled at him.

"Wow! That's some memory you've got there," he said.

"I try," she giggled.

"So obviously Abigail was African-American, and Dillanger Thomas, his family was from Ireland," Maxim explained. "So there's Irish, African-American, and British on Grandpa's side, with some South American, Egyptian, and Irish ancestry on Grandma's side. So… you could say I'm one hundred percent American mutt."

Sharlamagne smiled and said, "I've always preferred mutts. They're more interesting."

Maxim nodded. "I agree." He paused a moment to take a bite of his BLT, chew, and swallow. "What about you? Sharlamagne Dickens. Hmmm. Any famous English authors in there perhaps?"

Sharlamagne smiled. "Well, actually...Dad is my second father. My first father died when I was little. So Daddy adopted us later. My last name used to be Grinkov."

Maxim frowned a moment. "I'm so sorry about your father," Maxim offered. "How did he die?"

"In a car accident. I was five," she answered.

"How awful. I'm so sorry."

Sharlamagne looked at Maxim. There was true, sincere sympathy in his eyes, and it warmed her toward him even further.

"Thank you," she said. "Mom married Daddy a few years later... and a few years after that we became Dickenses."

Maxim nodded. "So...Russian, eh?"

"Yep."

"Your father...was he actually from Russia?" he asked. "Born in Russia, I mean?"

"Yep."

"So let's see," Maxim began, studying Sharlamagne closely. "I figure you're about...what? Twenty-one?"

"Mm hmm," Sharlamagne concurred. She could see where his mind was going and wondered if he really would figure it out.

"So your father...he would've been born in about what...the mid-'60s?"

"Yep," she confirmed.

He smiled—frowned a little. "Well, how did that work? Did he defect or something? Russia was the Soviet Union back then."

"Yep and yep," Sharlamagne giggled.

"He did? Your dad really did defect? No way!" He was enthralled by the fact—Sharlamagne could see it in him.

"During the 1988 Olympics, actually," Sharlamagne said. "He was one of the Soviet athletes. A gymnast."

Maxim sat back in his chair, obviously astonished. "I think you might just have trumped my great-great-great-grandmother's being a slave, being emancipated, and marrying the son of her previous owner."

"Never! Nothing trumps that," Sharlamagne assured him. "Certainly not a defecting Soviet gymnast."

"You're right. I win that round," he said. "But that's amazing... really. Wow."

"I think so too," Sharlamagne said. "So I'm one half Russian, and then we get into the melting pot thing on my mother's side. Let's see... Scottish, Cherokee, and French, if you go back enough generations."

"Well then, here we are...just a couple of American mutts hanging out at the deli for lunch," he said. He smiled. "I like it."

"Me too," Sharlamagne agreed.

"Okay," he said. "What else do you want to know? Ask me anything."

"Anything, huh?" Sharlamagne teased.

"Yep. I'm not kidding. I'll answer anything you ask me," Maxim assured her.

"Okay then...let me think." She sighed, trying to think of another question to use in getting to know Maxim's brain. There was so much she'd like to ask him. How many girlfriends had he had? Did he think she was pretty? What project was he working on at his work? Still, she knew she shouldn't be too intrusive.

"Well," she began, "I already know you love BLTs."

"I do," he admitted, nodding.

"Then, what about this—what's your full given name? Do you even have a middle name?"

"I do," he said.

But when he didn't immediately elaborate, Sharlamagne prodded, "And? Your middle name is?"

"Olivier," he mumbled.

Sharlamagne smiled. "Hmmm. Maxim Olivier Tanner," Sharlamagne said. "I like it!" Then she felt her eyebrows pucker into a frown of curiosity. "Olivier?" she asked, smiling suddenly with amusement.

"And here it comes," Maxim sighed.

"Olivier? As in Sir Laurence Olivier? The actor?"

"Yeah," he admitted with another sigh. It was obvious he was somewhat uncomfortable or embarrassed about his middle name.

"Do tell," she urged.

He smiled, shook his head, and began, "Grandma saw that old Hitchcock movie *Rebecca* when she was…however old she was when she saw it. Have you seen it?"

"Of course!" Sharlamagne assured him. "Who hasn't?"

"Well, then you know Olivier's character's name was Maxim. Grandma claims she fell in love with him at first sight. I was never quite sure if she meant she fell in love with Laurence Olivier or his character. But anyway, when I was born, my parents couldn't agree on a name for their only son. So Grandma intervened and named me Maxim Olivier. I've always been suspicious that she probably bribed them to name me what she wanted me named."

Sharlamagne giggled. "Maxim Olivier. I really do like it," she said. "It's very romantic…and very Elisaveta Tanner. How sweet."

"Thanks, *Sharlamagne*," he teased. He frowned a moment and seemed pensive as he studied her. "Sharlamagne what?" he asked at last. "What's your middle name?"

Sharlamagne shook her head. "No way! You couldn't draw and quarter that out of me."

"Oh, come on. It's only fair. Maxim Olivier Tanner…and Sharlamagne what Dickens?"

Sharlamagne sighed. She really didn't want to tell him. Not that she didn't like her middle name—she did. It's just that she knew it would give him more ammunition for teasing her. However, in the next instant, she decided that since she liked him to tease her, she might as well tell him.

"Bronte," Sharlamagne mumbled.

"Bronte?" Maxim laughed. "You're kidding, right? Bronte? As in Charlotte Bronte?"

Sharlamagne shrugged. "Charlotte, Emily, or Anne. Take your pick."

"Bronte Dickens?"

"Shut up, *Sir* Olivier," she said, playfully slapping him on one strong arm.

He chuckled. "Well, there's another thing we have in common. Apparently we were both named by crazy people."

161

"Eccentric people, Sir Olivier. Not crazy, just eccentric," she playfully corrected him.

He laughed again. "I swear I'm gonna name my kids Tom, John, and Mike...or Anne, Pam, and Sue. Good old regular names."

"Not me," Sharlamagne said with a sigh. "I'm going stick with unusual names with a story behind them. Not too crazy, but unique enough that people stop to think about them...and interesting enough that my kids have a fun tale to tell."

"You mean something like Cruise Efron Pitt?" Maxim teasingly suggested.

"Har har," Sharlamagne said, rolling her eyes. "No, nothing as ridiculous as that." She paused a moment, remembering something. "I did have a friend named Sandy Beach in high school. She had two brothers, Rocky Beach and Sonny Beach. I was always jealous because they had such cool names."

"Oh, like Sharlamagne isn't a cool name?" he teased.

"I admit it, I like the Sharlamagne part," she said. "But sometimes the Bronte Dickens part seems a little overdone."

"Naw. I like it. So, we've got the names down...and the ancestry stuff," Maxim said. "What next? You still have half a sandwich to go."

"Okay," Sharlamagne began, eating one of her own potato chips. "Now tell me something shocking or scandalous about yourself."

Maxim chuckled. She couldn't be serious. And if she was—well, he didn't know where to begin. In truth, he'd never done anything truly immoral, but he'd done plenty of stupid. He wasn't at all sure he wanted her to know how adolescent and messed up he'd once been. Still, he wondered—wondered just how forgiving of mankind the girl really was.

"Okay," he ventured. "Let's see if this ruffles your panties. I was in a fight club all through college."

Sharlamagne was temporarily astonished into silence—but not by his admitting to being in a fight club—rather by his metaphor using panties to gauge whether she would be shocked. Still, she recovered quickly enough.

"You mean like…one of those things where guys just show up and beat each other bloody and senseless…just because?" she asked. Now that she was beyond the shock of his asking her if the idea ruffled her panties, she was disturbed by his confession.

Maxim nodded. "Well, bloody and senseless was one thing we beat out of each other." He grinned at her, and she smiled. He was too charming for his own good—and for hers!

"Are you serious?" she asked. "I mean…I've heard of that. Isn't it brutal? Like with bare fists and stuff?"

He nodded. "Yeah…not to mention illegal."

"Did you ever get caught?"

"Nope. Though I got messed up pretty badly a couple of times. I only lost twice though. It helped that I studied mixed martial arts when I was a teenager." He paused and took a bite of his sandwich. "I was a pretty angry kid, and my dad thought mixed martial arts would help me work out my frustrations. Instead, it just kind of gave me the skill and strength to excel in the local fight club network."

"But…but you don't do it anymore, do you?" Sharlamagne inquired. The more she imagined Maxim Tanner having the tar beat out of him, or beating the tar out of someone else, the more disturbed she became.

He shook his head. "Nope. Grandma helped me pull my head out of…she knocked some sense into me a few years ago. Helped me to learn to deal with my anger in less violent ways."

Pretty Sharlamagne Dickens exhaled a heavy sigh, as if she'd been holding her breath.

"Well, that's a relief," she said.

Maxim smiled. She was a sensitive soul. It became more and more apparent the more and more time he spent with her.

"So now that you know what a bad guy I was…is that a scandalous enough confession for you?" he asked.

He watched as she shrugged. "It kind of freaks me out…just because it must've hurt you so much all the time. How could you take it?"

Maxim mirrored her shrug. "As I said, I was angry a lot back then. Sometimes I was so mad I didn't even feel the pain. I'd just wake up all bloodied and bruised…stiff and sore…and then just go work out until I felt better."

Sharlamagne endeavored to hide the true depth of her astonishment. It hadn't been what she expected—not at all. Fight clubbing? It was so vicious! She studied his face and arms quickly, relieved when she found no visible trace of permanent physical damage. Yet to think of it—to imagine Maxim Tanner so filled with frustration and anger that he would find some warped sense of solace in fighting—it was upsetting. A deep sense of pain, sympathy, and compassion squeezed her heart, and she tried not to grimace.

She studied his eyes a moment. What an awful family life he must've had. She wondered what would have become of him if it hadn't been for his grandmother's love.

"What about you?" Maxim asked.

"Me?" she asked in return, momentarily having forgotten what had spurred his revelation.

"Yeah. I took your bait and bit. Now you have to tell me something shocking or scandalous about yourself," he reminded.

"Well, I don't know if I can even begin to hang with a big dog like you when it comes to that," she mumbled.

"Oh sure you can," he urged. "Everyone has stuff like that hidden away. Go on. Tell me something that'll shock and awe me."

Sharlamagne struggled to think of something shocking or scandalous she'd experienced in her life—struggled to think at all, actually. Yet nothing would come to her—nothing like Maxim's admission of fight clubbing.

"Well…I…um…" she stammered. "I really haven't led a very interesting life…especially compared to yours, I guess."

"Everyone has led an interesting life," he countered. "I just scattered your thoughts with my revelation that I used to be even more stupid than I am now."

"Yeah. My dad says testosterone will do that to a guy," Sharlamagne teased.

Maxim nodded and laughed. "Your dad is a smart man."

"But seriously…fight club? Really, I promise…you win. I can't think of anything," she said.

"Nothing?" he prodded. "Not even something weird? Let's say it doesn't have to be shocking or scandalous. Let's just say it has to be something…you know…something."

A thought came to her then—more of a memory in truth. When she'd been in middle school, there was a game she and all her friends used to play at slumber parties. It might work to keep the conversation going with Maxim. And, oh, how desperately she wanted to keep the conversation going with Maxim.

"You mean maybe like that party game, I Never?"

"What's that?" he asked.

"It's kind of dumb but can be pretty revealing. You tell me something you've never done," she began. "Something most people probably have done…but that you've never done."

He frowned, pensive for a moment. "You mean like the fact that I've never sat down on a public toilet seat? Do you mean like that?"

"You're kidding, right?" she asked, delighted that he'd taken the bait but astonished at what he'd revealed. "You've never sat on a public toilet seat? Not even with one of those toilet seat tissues on it?"

Maxim shook his head as he popped another potato chip into his mouth. "Nope. Never." He paused, adding, "Well, not that I can remember anyway. I might have once or twice when I was a little kid." A slight frown of pondering puckered his handsome brow a moment. "Although my mother did tell me that I wouldn't even go…you know…*number one*…in a public bathroom until I was, like, four years old. So maybe I really never have sat on a public toilet seat. Boys have it a little bit easier that way, you know. Unless…you know…*number two* causes a need…but even then I'm a squatter through and through. But to my knowledge, I've never sat on a public toilet seat…ever. Public restrooms sick me out."

Sharlamagne couldn't help giggling with disbelief. "So when you were little, you wouldn't even go *number one*, as you put it, in a public restroom? Well, what did you do when your family traveled and stuff? I mean…you have to use a public restroom sometimes. You *have* to. What did you do…just hold it in all the time?" Sharlamagne shook her head. "You're lucky you didn't get a bladder infection or something. I mean, I know men are supposed to have bigger bladders…but still."

"Oh, I went number one when I needed to when we were traveling and stuff," Maxim explained. "Just not in a public restroom."

Sharlamagne felt one brow wrinkle with curiosity. "Well…if you wouldn't go, like, at gas stations and rest areas and stuff…how did you go?"

"Dad would just pull over to the side of the road and let me out, and I'd go," he answered simply. "Nothing like a little fresh air…no matter what your task is, right?" He grinned a mischievous grin and ate another potato chip.

"What if you were in town? What if you couldn't pull over and go outside?" she asked.

"Mom always kept an empty sports drink bottle or something in the car or limo. I'd just go in that."

All at once, Sharlamagne was overcome with amusement. She couldn't believe they were sitting in a booth at a local deli discussing the fact that Maxim had never sat on a public restroom toilet seat. He was so hilarious—so amusing—so entertaining—and without even trying!

"What's so funny?" he asked, smiling. He chuckled a little as Sharlamagne gasped, slapping the tabletop three times as she tried to catch her breath.

"You!" she breathed through her laughter. "You're so funny! Never having sat on a public restroom seat in all your life? That's hysterical!"

"Why is that so funny?" he asked, laughing as he began to catch the virus of Sharlamagne's glee. "Do *you* sit on public bathroom toilet seats?"

"No. No, of course not," Sharlamagne giggled. She laughed hard again as she said, "I'm a sq-squatter too…but it's just so funny!"

Maxim was laughing with her now, his gorgeous eyes dancing with mirth as Sharlamagne slapped the tabletop three more times and gasped for breath in an effort to gain some reprieve from her wild amusement.

"It's really not that funny," Maxim offered, eating another chip.

"Y-yes! Y-yes, it is!" Sharlamagne giggled, slapping the table again and letting her forehead rest on it a minute as her laughter began to subside. "Oh! My back hurts from laughing so hard."

Maxim chuckled. "Well, I'll give you this. You sure are easily entertained."

Sitting up straight in her seat once more, Sharlamagne exhaled the long, satisfied sigh that follows a good, cleansing laugh. "You're hilarious," she breathed.

"I'm glad you think so," he said. "But it didn't seem that funny to me." He paused, smiling as one last giggle escaped Sharlamagne's throat. "And besides…isn't there something you've never done? I guess everybody has something they've never done or never experienced… never seen or heard."

"Oh, I'm sure there is," she answered, swirling a carrot stick in the little cup of ranch dressing next to her plate. "Let me think." She smiled, still amused by the entire public restroom toilet seat revelation.

Perhaps it was the lingering glee raining over her, or perhaps she just wasn't really thinking. Regardless of the reason for her not being more guarded at the moment, the thought of her and Gwen's hickey menu popped into her mind, and she said, "I've never had a hickey. That's something I've never done…or had…or whatever."

She smiled when she heard Maxim cough. It seemed he had nearly choked on a bite of BLT, and she was secretly delighted that she'd so obviously surprised him.

He grinned, laughed a low laugh, and said, "I can honestly say that *that* is the last thing I ever expected to come out of your mouth."

Sharlamagne was pleased with his reaction to her confession. "I mean…I burned my neck with my curling iron once when I was in high school, and everyone *thought* it was a hickey…but it wasn't. So yep…I've never had a hickey." She dipped another carrot stick in her ranch dressing. "What's something else you've never done?" she asked, wanting to keep the conversation going.

But Maxim simply shook his head and chuckled again. "I can't think of anything else. I'm still stuck on the hickey thing." He looked at her, an expression of amused disbelief on his face. "You've never had a hickey? *That* was the first thing that came to your mind?"

"Well, yeah," she answered with a casual shrug. Something tickled her brain then, and it wasn't a pleasant tickle for some reason. "Have *you* ever had a hickey?" she asked, somewhat anxiously hesitant to hear his answer.

"Nope. Never had a hickey," he answered however. He was obviously still as utterly amused as Sharlamagne was to hear his answer. "And I've never had a curling iron burn on my neck before either," he added.

She smiled at him then, her stomach suddenly awash with butterflies as she saw the expression in his eyes turn from that of pure amusement to something else. If blue eyes could smolder, then Maxim's were smoldering.

"But if you ever decide you want a hickey...let me know," he said in a lowered voice. "I'll volunteer to give it to you."

Sharlamagne felt the blush begin in her cheeks and rapidly spread over her whole body. She could've sworn even her toes were blushing!

She managed somehow to contain her astonishment, however— veil the thrilling delight wracking her body with goose bumps—and respond, "How chivalrous of you, Mr. Tanner."

"'Always be a gentleman, Maxim. And always champion the damsel in distress.' That's what my grandmother always told me," he said, winking at her. "I'm just trying to live by, and implement, what I've learned."

"Of course," Sharlamagne said, blushing an even deeper hue of pink. "I'll keep that in mind."

"Please do," he chuckled, scrunching up his napkin and tossing it onto his plate.

Ooo! He had her rattled now. He could tell by the blush on her cheeks. Maxim was really enjoying her company. In fact, he enjoyed her company every time they were together. He had a ton of stuff waiting to be finished at work, but he just hadn't been able to pull himself away from helping Sharlamagne clean out the old house long enough to focus on any of it. It would be a hell of a week coming up—he was so far behind. And yet, the mail kept leaping to his thoughts—the event tickets. He had no doubt Sharlamagne would be a blast at the event. He'd have a great time with her. But should he go there?

The next thing Maxim knew, however, he'd started the ball rolling by asking, "So...do you have a boyfriend?"

He was pleased when she rolled her eyes as if he'd asked the most ridiculous question in the world and in return responded, "Heck no! Do I look like I have a boyfriend to you? How many girls with boyfriends do you know that could (or would) spend twelve hours a day rooting through an old house full of stuff?"

Maxim's smile broadened. He couldn't help it. She was too adorable.

"Nope. In our family, Gwen is the boy magnet. She attracts men like bees to honey," she finished with a rather revealing sigh of disappointment.

"Well, I prefer sugar myself," Maxim said. "Sugar over honey, I mean." She smiled at him as he continued. "Honey's not as sweet or something. I can't quite explain it, but I'd rather feel the texture of some good old granulated sugar on my tongue than mess with honey."

"You're just trying to make me feel better," she said, smiling at him. Maxim could tell he had made her feel better, and it gave him some satisfaction.

"So, you don't have a boyfriend then?" he reiterated.

"Nope," she confirmed.

Maxim watched the expression in her eyes change a bit as she looked at him. He couldn't quite figure what she was thinking, but he could tell she was wondering something about him.

"What?" he asked.

"Do you have a girlfriend?" she tentatively asked. "I mean...I don't want her to be upset with you for helping me and stuff."

Sharlamagne had never considered the fact that she might be keeping Maxim away from a significant other of the female persuasion. In truth, the imp in her hoped she was—that if he did have a girlfriend, said girlfriend would become enraged with him at his neglect of her and break up with him. Still, now she was curious and felt she had to know.

She couldn't help exhale a sigh of relief, however, when he answered, "Nope. Not me. Not currently at least."

"Oh," was all she could manage as a response.

"So, no boyfriend, huh?" he asked again.

"No boyfriend," she assured him.

"Then I was wondering…there's this thing next Saturday. After my grandpa died, I used to take my grandma to it every year," he explained. "Well, being the plan-ahead freak that she was, Grandma must've ordered the tickets a long time ago because I got them in the mail the other day. It's a really cool event, and I was wondering if you were interested in going with me."

Sharlamagne half expected her head to pop off her shoulders with excitement. Was he actually asking her out? It sounded like it. Sure, it was something he'd always taken his grandmother to, but she wouldn't worry about that. A date with Maxim Tanner? He could've taken her on a tour of the city sewer, and she would've jumped at the opportunity to go with him.

"I'd love to," she managed to answer. Then, realizing how eager she'd sounded, she asked, "What is it, exactly?"

"It's really awesome," he began, and Sharlamagne smiled as his face seemed to brighten with enthusiasm. "They have it out at the old airport…in one of the old airport hangars. It's a World War II night dance thing. Everyone wears vintage attire—you know, like World War II clothes. They have a band there that plays '40s music, and there's dancing, of course. One year they had this group—I guess you would call them impersonators. They had a Bing Crosby guy, a Frank Sinatra guy, and some Andrews sisters ladies. It really is something to behold. They fly in all these old planes—a couple of B-52 bombers, a P-23, and others—to do flybys, and then you can take photos in them and stuff. They have World War II veterans there you can talk to and take photos with and people dressed up in perfect vintage clothes and uniforms you can take photos with if you want. There's food and a contest for best costume and a bunch of things. But it's mostly a dance. Oh…and they do this thing where they announce the end of the war and everyone celebrates. It's something you don't get to do every day, and tickets are limited."

Sharlamagne was stunned. She could feel her mouth gaping. Was he making it up? It sounded like a dream—and to go to something like this as his date…

"You're kidding me, right?" she asked. "You really have to be kidding me. You've just gotten to know me enough this week that you've peeked into my brain and pulled out something I could only dream up, right?"

Maxim smiled and shook his head. "Nope. It's real. They've been putting it on for, like, fifteen years or something. It's cool. I think you'll really like it." He leaned back in his chair and added, "And you've already got something to wear…obviously."

Maxim watched Sharlamagne's pretty hazel eyes widen as understanding washed over her. He chuckled when a quiet squeal of excitement escaped her lips as she whispered, "Yes! All the vintage evening gowns in the old wardrobes!"

"Yep," he confirmed. "And it looked like you had quite a selection to choose from."

"I know, right?" Sharlamagne giggled. "And what about you? Did you want to borrow one of my gowns?" she teased.

Maxim shook his head. "Naw. I'll wear one of my grandpa's old Navy uniforms. There's one or two that I haven't worn yet."

She sighed with obvious delight. Yet she paused a moment.

"What?" he asked.

"Are you sure you want to take *me* to this thing?" she asked. "I'm not all glamorous and supermodel-ish like some of your other friends, and I—"

"Shawty," he interrupted, "can you really see Liz or Ashley going to something like this? I want to have fun…and I can already tell you're fun." She smiled, and he added, "And besides, you're just as glamorous and supermodel-ish as any other woman I know." Her smile broadened, and he added, "Actually, more glamorous and supermodel-ish. I mean,

I don't know one other woman who could pull off that outfit you're wearing right now." He allowed his eyes to narrow as he studied her from head to toe and added, "Mmm. Yep. You're too hot to handle in that pink T-shirt and your worn-out jeans."

He chuckled when Sharlamagne rolled her eyes and mumbled, "Oh brother. You're laying it on a little thick, don't you think, Maxim Olivier?"

"Not at all," he answered.

He noticed the way the light in her eyes brightened and saw a little spark of mischief leap to them. "Well, I will tell you this. I may not glam up as well as your other girlfriends...but I can sure show you a better time at this 1940s event than anybody else could. That I can promise."

"Why do you think I asked you?" he said, winking at her. He liked her spirit! He'd apparently touched a sensitive little nerve, and he was glad. He wanted to see her confidence show through. He well remembered it from the day he'd first met her—when she'd related the story of Baby Doe Tabor to him. She knew her stuff, and she knew she knew her stuff. He liked that about her. She wasn't cocky at all—not stuck-up, arrogant, or vain. She was even lacking in self-confidence here and there, but when she was in her comfort zone she could hold her own.

"Ooo! I'm so excited!" she admitted. "The way you describe it... well, in truth, it sounds a little too good to be true. But if Mrs. Tanner always attended, it's gotta be awesome!"

"It is. That *I* can promise," he assured her.

Sharlamagne could hardly stay seated in her chair or concentrate on finishing her sandwich. A date with Maxim Tanner? Seriously? It was hard to believe! And yet, there he sat—right across the table from her—offering more details about what could be expected at the World War II gala.

Her mind starting thinking about all the evening gowns she'd found in the old wardrobe earlier that day. Which one should she wear? The coral? The lavender? Well, she did have a lavender bra and matching panties—maybe she should wear the lavender gown. But then she remembered the lovely cream sequin-bedazzled gown she'd seen. Maybe that one would do. Oh, how would she ever find the motivation to finish the day out sorting through stuff in the old house? How would she ever manage not to explode with excitement having to wait an entire week before she could go with Maxim to the event?

"She made me learn, you know," Maxim said, drawing Sharlamagne's attention back to what he was saying. "I'm not very good at it—a little too clunky—but I can pull off a mean foxtrot and a pretty good swing if you give me a chance. How about you?"

"M-me?" Sharlamagne stammered. He was talking about dancing—vintage dances. "I'm okay, I guess. I watched a lot of Ginger Rogers and Fred Astaire and took a ballroom dance class in college…but just for fun."

"So you're not, like, a professional or anything, right?" he asked.

"Right," she giggled. She could see he'd had a moment of anxiety.

"Well, good. It'll be just plain fun then."

"That's the way it should be," Sharlamagne assured him.

"Agreed," he concurred. "So it's a date…Saturday…for the 1940s World War II dance. I'll pick you up in my grandpa's 1943 Oldsmobile. It's parked in the garage out back, and Grandma and I haven't had it out for months."

Sharlamagne laughed. She was entirely delighted by him—by all of it.

"Are you telling me you even have a vintage car in which to convey us to the thing?" she asked.

Maxim nodded. "Yep. I helped Grandpa restore it when I was a kid. It's cherry. You'll love it."

"I'm sure I will," Sharlamagne assured him.

"We just might look snazzy enough with the Olds on our side to win the costume competition," he added. "There's a trophy and everything."

Once again, Maxim looked like a little boy—a little boy excited about a soapbox derby race or something. Sharlamagne determined then and there that, no matter what, she would make sure Maxim

Olivier Tanner had the time of his life next Saturday night.

"We can drop that stuff we put in the back of my jeep at your storage unit on the way back to the house if you want," he offered.

"Oh, that would be awesome! If you're sure you don't mind," she said.

"I don't mind," he said, smiling at her. Again she noticed the way eyes seemed to smolder, even for their cool blue hue. It caused her heart to leap in her chest, and a few goose bumps rippled over her arms.

As Maxim left the table to toss his napkin and other disposable remnants from his lunch into the garbage can, Sharlamagne looked around the room. Every set of female eyes followed Maxim as he strode toward the trash receptacle—lingered on him with obvious approval and quite a bit of desire. Oh, he was handsome! She could only imagine how he'd look all decked out in a Navy uniform.

She sighed as he sat down at the table once more. Boy, oh, boy did she have something to look forward to! She couldn't think of anything in all her life she'd looked forward to more than she was already looking forward to the World War II gala. And knowing she would get to see him every day after work the coming week only sweetened it all the more.

Sharlamagne was tired. Even for the infinite pleasure she'd known at being in Maxim's company every day as they worked to clean out the old house, she was tired. Her muscles were sore, and she thought she'd never get the smell of furniture polish and old dustrags out of her sinuses. Still, it had been the most wonderful week of her life. Being bequeathed Mrs. Tanner's old house and all its rare and fabulous contents was marvelous enough. But having Maxim Tanner's undivided attention at the same time—rapturous!

As she snuggled down in bed, tired but with a mind still too alive with the wild, excited anticipation of the World War II event, Sharlamagne picked up the book sitting on her nightstand.

"*The Complete Poetical Works of Elisaveta Petunia Tanner*," she read aloud as she gently opened the old book of poetry. Sharlamagne had been savoring one poem a night every night since Mrs. Tanner's funeral.

Elisaveta Tanner's poetry was beautiful! It was soothing, romantic, serene, and visual, and it left a mark on the human heart. Thus, Sharlamagne (determined to relish every word) had limited herself to one poem a night.

Consequently, she carefully flipped through the pages of the old book, waiting for a title to catch her eye. Unexpectedly, something slipped from the pages of the book—several folded sheets of notepaper. They were old and weathered-looking, and Sharlamagne retrieved them from her lap with a gentle hand. Sitting upright and placing the book to one side, she smiled. One of her greatest delights in life was to leaf through old antique books and find the things people had left tucked in their pages decades before—even a century before. Calling cards, old photographs, pressed flowers, handwritten notations, ancient newspaper articles—the list of things Sharlamagne had gleefully gleaned from the pages of old books was seemingly endless. And now this! Something had been tucked away in the pages of the old poetry book Mrs. Tanner had left to her.

Though she couldn't wait to see what was written on the yellowed pieces of paper—though she hoped they weren't blank and at least held the beginning of a long-ago letter or grocery list—she was careful in handling the pages. Slowly she unfolded them and read aloud what was written at the top of the first page.

"*The Trove of the Passion Room?*" she whispered aloud. "The Passion Room?" She well remembered Maxim's references on two different occasions to the Passion Room in Mrs. Tanner's main house. She especially remembered when he had told her that his grandmother had always maintained there was a legend attached to the room— that a man and woman could not spent a night in the Passion Room together without passion flaming between them to such a point that they inevitably were swept away to intimacy.

"What in the world?" Sharlamagne breathed, instantly intrigued. "*The Trove of the Passion Room*," she read aloud again—for she was pretty sure she'd imagined it before. "Nope, that's what it says."

"Are you talking to yourself again, Shar?" Gwen groaned from the other bed. "Quit narrating your thoughts, shut up, and go to sleep."

"In a minute," Sharlamagne mumbled as she began to read the writing on the old pages. "*The Trove of the Passion Room is not simply a story. Nor is it only a fable, a legend, or mere nonsensical superstition. It exists. There is a trove hidden in the Passion Room…a trove that has never before in fullness been found, for it is hidden by the spell of passion that lingers within the room itself.*"

"Shut up, Sharlamagne!" Gwen growled.

Sharlamagne gasped as a pillow hit her squarely in the face, toppling to her bed and nearly damaging the old, yellowing papers in her hands. "All right," she grumbled. "I'll read to myself."

"That's why they call it silent reading," Gwen said.

Rolling her eyes at Gwen's insensitivity, Sharlamagne began again. "*The Trove of the Passion Room is not simply a story. Nor is it only a fable, a legend, or mere nonsensical superstition. It exists. There is a trove hidden in the Passion Room…a trove that has never before in its fullness been found, for it is hidden by the spell of passion that lingers within the room itself. The passion inspired of the room cannot be denied. It cannot be controlled or resisted. And as the influence of the Passion Room cannot be evaded, neither can the trove be revealed without absolute and consummate surrender to—*"

"Sharlamagne Dickens!" Gwen exclaimed then. "Maybe you don't have to be to work until eight, but I have to be up by five in the morning, and I want to be rested! Turn out the light, shut up, and go to sleep."

But there was more written on the pages. Sharlamagne couldn't possibly stop reading now!

"Fine," she grumbled at Gwen as she got out of bed, clicked off the lamp on her nightstand, and left the bedroom for the privacy of the den.

Once settled in her father's weathered lounge chair, Sharlamagne began to read the old pages once more—afresh.

"*The Trove of the Passion Room is not simply a story. Nor is it only a fable, a legend, or mere nonsensical superstition. It exists. There is a trove hidden in the Passion Room…a trove that has never before in its fullness been found, for it is hidden by the spell of passion that lingers within the room itself. The passion inspired of the room cannot be denied. It cannot be controlled or resisted. And as the influence of the Passion Room cannot be evaded, neither can the trove be revealed without absolute and consummate surrender to—*" She paused as her eyes widened. "What?" she breathed. "No way!"

CHAPTER NINE

"Wow," Maxim said as he finished reading the old note pages Sharlamagne had found in Mrs. Tanner's poetry book the night before. "Scandalous, eh?"

"You told me your grandmother had always said there was something about the Passion Room like this, right?" Sharlamagne asked.

"Something like this," Maxim confirmed. "But it sounds way more outrageous when you see it written out." He smiled and shook his head with amusement. "I'll say this for Grandma: she had quite the imagination."

"So you don't think there's anything to it?" Sharlamagne asked, half hoping he did believe what his grandmother had written. The idea of it was wildly intriguing, and even though she knew the whole precept was not only impossible but absolutely unfounded, she secretly wished such things were sometimes true.

He chuckled. "No," he answered. "It's a room. I've been in it a million times. I remodeled it, remember? It's just a room."

"Oh," Sharlamagne mumbled, unable to entirely hide her disappointment.

"However," Maxim continued. She looked up to see him grinning at her, a look of complete monkey business in his deep blues. "Now that I think about it, I've never been up in that room with a woman… other than Grandma, of course. So if you think there's something to this *legend*, as it were…I'm more than willing to drag you up the stairs and into the Passion Room and test it out."

Sharlamagne playfully glared at him, slapped him on his solid, massive chest, and giggled. "Stop it. Don't tease me," she scolded. "There has to be a reason she wrote this down...a reason she always told you the story."

Maxim took hold of her arm and said, "Well, come on then, shawty. Let's go up there and put it to the test."

Sharlamagne shook her head. "Oh, quit making fun of me," she said, pulling her arm from his grasp. "I'm just gonna pretend it's true... no matter what you say. And besides, we're burning daylight. I really do want to get a few things out of the house tonight before it gets dark, so are you gonna help me or not?"

Maxim was still smiling. He couldn't help it. He could tell by the expression on Sharlamagne's face and the twinkle in her eyes that she wanted the story to be true. She wanted to believe that if a man and woman spent the night in the Passion Room, they would be swept away on the rapturous wings of fiery, amorous ecstasy. And who was he to ruin it for her? Furthermore, why not spur the mystery on a little?

"Yes, I'm gonna help you," he said. "And by the way, I'm sure there *is* something to Grandma's tales concerning that room. She wouldn't have written it down if there wasn't."

"You're still making fun of me," she said, snatching his grandmother's note pages from his hand.

"No, I'm serious," he assured her. "I mean, she had me put a lot of work into that one room. It was crazy. I couldn't figure out why it was so important to her at the time, so she told me the story—briefly, but nothing like she wrote here. But she wanted that room updated, preserved, and perfect. So there must be something to it, right? I've wondered if maybe she was planning to turn the house into a bed-and-breakfast and wanted that room to be, like, the honeymoon suite or something. But whatever her plans were...she was very serious about that room."

"I think you're just trying to make me feel better because you were teasing me," she accused, smiling at him.

"Well, my offer still stands," he said, staring down at her. She was a really, really, really pretty woman. "And, furthermore, it would probably be a great place for you to receive your first hickey."

"Oh!" she exclaimed, blushing pure crimson. "I knew I shouldn't have told you that! You're never going to let me hear the end of it, are you?"

Maxim felt his smile broaden. "Nope. Never."

She growled at him, trying to appear angry, but he knew she wasn't. "Just you wait, Mr. Jeans Innovations Naked Man. I'll get some dirt on you sooner or later, and then, wham! What comes around goes around." She paused, her adorable brows crinkling with curiosity. "Is it 'what comes around goes around'? Or is it 'what goes around comes around'?"

Maxim laughed. "I have no idea. But you're right. We are burning daylight here."

"Yes, we are," Sharlamagne agreed, smiling at him.

Turning to head back into the old house, she paused when Maxim asked, "Hey. Do you think you could make me a copy of those pages you found? Scan them or something? They are kind of interesting where the Passion Room is concerned. And since I do own the house now, if I ever want to turn it into a bed-and-breakfast, they might come in handy somehow."

"Of course," Sharlamagne said. "But…you really don't strike me as the bed-and-breakfast type."

Maxim smiled again, glanced over his shoulder to his grandmother's beautiful Victorian, and said, "I'm not. I'm actually more of a museum type—you know, historical society stuff…tours of vintage homes."

"Is that what you're thinking of doing?" she asked. "You're not going to just live in it?"

He shrugged. "I could still live in it even if I did something like that, I guess. But it just seems too…too rare and perfect to not display it somehow. Don't you think?"

Sharlamagne giggled a little, delighted by his insight and sentiment. Clasping one of his hands with her own, she said, "Come on. I need your muscles."

"Ooo!" Maxim breathed as the spark of monkey business leapt to his eyes again. "And we're not even in the Passion Room."

Sharlamagne rolled her eyes but couldn't keep from blushing no matter how irritated she pretended to be with his flirting. "I need your muscles to move some heavy things for me, you nitwit."

"Nitwit?" he asked. "How old are you? A hundred and seven?"

"Come on," she giggled. "Let's put those rippling abs of yours to good use."

"Ooo!" he breathed again. "And we're not even in the Passion Room."

Sharlamagne playfully slapped his arm, rolling her eyes and shaking her head. "Does your mother know what a naughty man you are?"

"Absolutely not," he chuckled as he followed her into the house. "But really...don't forget to copy those pages for me, okay?"

"I won't," Sharlamagne assured him. "I promise. I'll bring them to you tomorrow." She turned to look at him. "I mean, if you're still planning to help me tomorrow evening...if you even can."

He smiled. "I wouldn't miss the chance to go through another box of doilies for all the money in the world."

"You be nice or I might not give you the old cigar box full of marbles I found earlier," she teasingly warned.

"Ooo...playing hardball now, I see."

Sharlamagne giggled as she led Maxim toward the old trunk she needed help moving in one of the bedrooms. She liked the way his hand felt in hers—warm, callused, strong. She wished she could hold his hand forever. She wished she could hug him, kiss him—really, really kiss him! She still hadn't gotten used to the way he made her feel. Just being in a room with Maxim made her feel more alive somehow—more adventurous, happier. And she wouldn't even let her mind nest one moment on how he made her feel physically. His physical effect on her was frighteningly powerful! She'd never felt so drawn to a man before—so nearly frantic to date him—to hold him and have him hold her.

But Sharlamagne figured that most women felt that way when they were around Maxim Tanner—women that weren't dead and buried anyway. Hence, she was constantly trying to convince herself that she just needed to bury her feelings and desires where Maxim was concerned.

However, there was something else whispering in her brain—an ally, as it were, advocating courage. Something in her head was always there, whispering, *Why not go for him? He asked you out, didn't he? He wouldn't have asked you out if he wasn't interested in you too.*

Thus, she'd nearly decided several times to just "go for it." She'd nearly decided that when Saturday came and Maxim arrived to pick her up for the World War II dance, she would simply kick all her inhibitions out the back door, flirt as much as she wanted to with him, just be herself, have fun, and make the evening one Maxim would never forget. But she was still uncertain, wondering how she would handle it if the gorgeous conductor of the "I Was Made for Loving You" train really wasn't interested in her and refused her ticket.

"Another trunk?" Maxim asked as she pointed to the old oval-top trunk she need help moving.

"Yeah," she confirmed. "Will you just put it in the trunk of my car for me, please?"

He smiled at her and said, "Yes, ma'am," he said. He hefted the trunk up onto one shoulder and began muttering (supposedly to himself), "She just wants me for my body. All she wants out of me is my hard-earned muscles so I can move her crap around for her. That's it. That's the only reason she keeps me around. And what do I get out of it? Not even one little trip to the Passion Room, that's what. Nope. Nothing. She just uses me as her workhorse, and I don't even get—"

He stopped his ramblings and laughed when Sharlamagne lightly kicked him in the seat of his pants.

"Be careful there, Miss Dickens," he chuckled. "I might trip and drop this trunk and spill out all your damn doilies."

Sharlamagne giggled as she watched him saunter out of the house and toward her car. He was *so* incredibly attractive! Her heart was pounding like a hammer on an anvil, and she frowned and shook her head when she realized her mouth was actually watering.

"Oh, brother," she mumbled as she carefully tucked Mrs. Tanner's pages concerning the Passion Room into her purse hanging on a nearby hat rack. "Get a hold of yourself, stupid," she muttered. "Just wait until Saturday. Just wait and see what happens. Now calm down."

She knew she needed distraction, so she pulled up the lid on another nearby trunk. Instantly, she burst into peals of laughter when she saw that the first layer of stuff in the trunk was, indeed, a trove of handmade doilies.

❧

"What are you scanning?" Gwen asked, licking the chocolate ice cream on the cone she held.

"Something I found in the poetry book Mrs. Tanner left to me," Sharlamagne answered. "Maxim wanted a copy of it."

"Ooo! Maxim wanted a copy, did he?" Gwen giggled. "What else is Maxim wanting, Shar?"

"Nothing," Sharlamagne answered.

"Oh, I wouldn't be so sure, Sharlamagne Dickens," Gwen teased. "After taking you to a big old shindig like that World War II thing, I'm sure he'll expect at least a good-night kiss."

"Well, I'm sure he won't," Sharlamagne countered. She looked over her shoulder and smiled at her sister, adding, "But I'll be happy to oblige if he does."

Gwen laughed. "Oh, I'm sure you will be happy to oblige." She licked her ice cream a few more times and asked, "Are you gonna go for him, Shar? You totally should, you know."

"He's a little intimidating," Sharlamagne answered.

"Just because he's so gorgeous? Look…if he was Joe Homely, you wouldn't pause, right? And Maxim can't help it that he was born looking like the archetypal male. So you need to just reach out and grab him. Snatch him up. Pull him to your bosom and love the snot out of him!"

Sharlamagne wrinkled her nose. "Love the snot out of him? Oh, that sounded appetizing, Gwen."

"You know what I mean, Shar. Just go for it. No fear, no holds barred. Courage, my little Padawan! Be brave, my armored warrior!"

"You're an idiot," Sharlamagne laughed. Sharlamagne removed Mrs. Tanner's pages from the scanner.

"What is that anyway?" Gwen asked.

"It's about a room in Mrs. Tanner's house. A room that's supposed to be, like, magical or something."

Gwen smiled. "Yep. Sounds just like Mrs. Tanner to have a magic room in her house." She sighed. "I miss her. She made the world a more interesting place to live."

"I know," Sharlamagne agreed. "I miss her too. So much."

❦

Gwen still hadn't come in from spending the evening with her boyfriend. Thus Sharlamagne had the bedroom all to herself.

Serenely content with the isolation, Sharlamagne started to pick up Mrs. Tanner's poetry book, intent on reading a poem out loud without Gwen nagging her about turning off the light and going to sleep. Yet she paused, picking up the note papers about the Passion Room instead. She'd been very tired when she'd read them the night before and in a hurry when she'd read them again that morning before leaving for work. She wanted to read them slowly, while her mind was still somewhat fresh. She wanted to savor the words on the page, knowing that Elisaveta Tanner had written them—knowing they referred to the room in her restored Victorian that Maxim had spent so much time and energy remodeling.

"*The Trove of the Passion Room is not simply a story. Nor is it only a fable, a legend, or mere nonsensical superstition.*" Sharlamagne read the now-familiar words aloud. (She found that certain things were more dramatic read aloud than in silence.)

"*It exists,*" she continued. "*There is a trove hidden in the Passion Room…a trove that has never before in its fullness been found, for it is hidden by the spell of passion that lingers within the room itself. The passion inspired of the room cannot be denied. It cannot be controlled or resisted. And as the influence of the Passion Room cannot be evaded, neither can the trove be revealed without absolute and consummate surrender to intimate passion itself—to pure, fiery, impetuous, and unbridled passion. Not intimate passion as the world now defines it, but intimate passion on a far deeper level—a level that is not felt by the physical senses of the body only but is instead recognized purely by the very soul.*

"It is not mere lust that will reveal the trove of the Passion Room—though lust will always be ignited by the room's enchantments. Those who linger in the Passion Room in search of the trove will know lust and be tempted by it. In truth, lust is indeed a component to physical passion. Consequently, most who linger in the Passion Room will succumb to its powerful allure. Yet mere lust alone will not serve to reveal the trove of the Passion Room to those who seek it. Only passion borne of a true love—of two souls everlastingly entwined—only then will the true nature of the trove of the Passion Room be recognizable and its true nature and infinite value revealed.

"Thus, be forewarned of this: the Passion Room will claim any man and woman who enter into it and dare linger in the enchantment that pervades it. The power of the Passion Room cannot be escaped. Passion will enfold whatever man and woman tempt it. It will consume them.

"Therefore, if a hope is held within a man or woman—a deep desire to find the trove of the Passion Room—then the visitor must enter only with a companion to whom one is not averse to succumbing to—to surrendering all to—even virtue. For the visitors will succumb, either to lustful, physical passion or to the pure, abiding, soul-wrenching passion of true, true love.

"That is the way of the Passion Room and the decree of the trove. Hence, tempt the Passion Room if you dare desire to find the trove—tempt the Passion Room just as the Fates have so long been tempted. Yet know this: far better it would be to care little for the trove and instead discover your soul's faithful, beloved mate—to discover truth, loyalty, and sheer, perfect love amidst the enchanted walls of the Passion Room."

Sharlamagne sighed and returned the pages to the leaves of Mrs. Tanner's poetry book. "Wow," she sighed. "Heavy stuff." She smiled and added, "Ridiculous, maybe…and totally impossible. But heavy."

She was suddenly very tired then. Using the word *heavy* out loud seemed to influence her eyelids, and she felt overwhelmingly fatigued all at once.

"The trove of the Passion Room, huh?" she yawned as her head hit the pillow. Closing her eyes, she smiled as a vision of Maxim Tanner drifted into her mind. "Well, true or not…lust or love…I'd sure like to spend some time in the Passion Room with you, Mr. 'I Was Made for

Loving You' conductor, Maxim 'Hot-Stuff' Tanner." She sighed as sleep began to overtake her. "Indeed I would."

❦

"So? Which one did you choose?" Maxim asked as he popped a frozen cherry into his mouth.

Sharlamagne smiled as he handed her the bowl. They'd taken a break from sorting through the stuff in the old house and were now sitting on the back porch of the old Victorian eating a bowl of frozen cherries he'd retrieved from the freezer.

"I guess you'll just have to wait and find out," she teased. She chose a slightly thawed sweet cherry from the bowl and popped it into her mouth. "Mmm," she couldn't help sighing. "These really are so good!"

"I know," Maxim agreed. "Grandma has kept them on hand in the deep freeze as long as I can remember. She ordered them from somewhere in Oregon every fall, and we'd stretch them out all through the year until new ones came the next fall." He paused, momentarily melancholy.

Sensing his pain at remembering the loss of his grandmother, Sharlamagne smiled and said, "Well, I guess you'll just have to order them yourself from now on. In fact, if you find the number, let me know. My family would love these."

Maxim felt his eyes narrow as he studied Sharlamagne for a moment. She was trying to soothe his pain of loss—he knew she was. It was a sweet gesture, and the realization made him smile. He chuckled then, realizing that, one way or the other, she had soothed him. It seemed that Sharlamagne was always soothing him, whether it was intentional or not. He just felt good when he was with her—happy, confident, like the world was a great place.

In truth, he couldn't wait to take her to the World War II gala the following night. He couldn't wait to see her pretty face light up when she saw how awesome the decorations and the music would be. He couldn't wait to dance with her—slow dance with her. Part of him felt a little guilty looking so forward to taking Sharlamagne to the World War II gala—guilty because he knew he was going to enjoy

187

being with her. Part of him felt like he didn't have the right to enjoy something with someone else, something he'd always enjoyed with his grandmother. Yet another part of him wanted to be free of guilt—to just enjoy the fact that he'd be spending an entire evening lingering in nostalgia with a beautiful young woman he knew would appreciate it more than almost anyone else in the world—a beautiful young woman he wanted to hold in his arms and dance with. A beautiful woman he wouldn't mind carrying up to the Passion Room and…

"How much are they?" Sharlamagne asked, interrupting his thoughts.

"The frozen cherries? Like thirty bucks for a fourteen-pound box, I think," he answered, tossing a cherry up in the air and catching it in his mouth.

"Wow! That's cheaper than buying them fresh and freezing them yourself…not to mention a lot less time-consuming," she said.

Maxim watched as Sharlamagne chose a cherry from the bowl, tossed it into the air, and attempted to catch in her mouth. He laughed when it hit her forehead instead, bouncing off and into her lap.

"You should start with popcorn," he chuckled as he wiped the cherry juice off her forehead with his thumb. "It doesn't hurt when you miss like frozen fruit does."

Sharlamagne giggled and rubbed her forehead. "Thanks for the tip."

"You're welcome," he said, chuckling as he tossed another cherry into the air and easily caught it in his mouth.

"So," Sharlamagne began tentatively, "do *you* know what the trove in the Passion Room is? I mean, you must…being that you remodeled it and stuff. Right?"

Maxim shook his head. "Nope," he answered. "I really do not have any idea. I figure it's something Grandma just made up to intrigue guests and anybody else who visited the house. I've been in there a million times. I put in the new bathroom and all the fixtures and tile, including the footed porcelain bathtub. I painted, hung wallpaper, moved furniture, hung paintings, helped her drag all the heavy bedding and stuff up there, chopped wood for the fireplace. You name it, I did it…and I never saw anything treasure-ish looking."

"So you think it was just one of her yarns…one of her dreamy things she liked to think about?" she asked.

Maxim shrugged. "It has to be. I've really never seen anything too pricey in there. Unless the antiques are worth more than I know." He paused and looked at her inquisitively. "You'd probably know more about that than anything. Maybe the old bed is worth a million dollars and I just don't have the knowledge to recognize it."

Sharlamagne sighed and shook her head. "No. Mrs. Tanner had her limits on what she would spend…even on antiques. No, I think you're probably right. It's probably just some tale she spun to pique an interest in people." She laughed. "I mean, look at me. I'm all intrigued, right?"

Maxim smiled and nodded. "Yeah, that's true. It would be just like Grandma to plant something in people's minds just to agitate them." Yet he sighed and shook his head in the next moment. "But then again, I'm not so sure. She always told me everything. Any time she was about her little mischief things, she always told me. But the whole time I was redoing that room, she was adamant about the whole 'it's under a passion spell' thing. So I don't know."

All at once, a light leapt to his eyes—a light of his own mischief. "Hey, how about I show you the room right now? We could go up there together and see what happens—you know, test Grandma's claims that's its magic and we'll be swept away to me throwing you down on the bed and us having—"

"Do *not* say it!" Sharlamagne exclaimed, clamping her hand over his mouth for a moment. "Don't you dare say it! I'll spank you if you do!"

Maxim shoved her hand away from his mouth and teasingly asked, "Promise?"

"You are a bad, bad man, Maxim Tanner," Sharlamagne playfully scolded. Oh, her arms and legs were drowning in goose bumps, it was true! But she couldn't let him know that. She couldn't let him be too inappropriate—could she?

"But I thought you women liked us bad boys," he flirted. "And besides, now that I know the 's' word, as you put it, rattles your cage… you have to *know* I'm going to taunt you with it."

Sharlamagne blushed, and his smile broadened. "Look…it just makes me uncomfortable for some reason."

"The word or the actual act?" he teased again.

Sharlamagne smiled and rolled her eyes. "I told you that it's the word and that I wouldn't know about—"

"Yeah, yeah, yeah," he said. "You told me you don't like the word and that you're a virgin. I got that last time."

"Oh my gosh!" Sharlamagne exclaimed as her face turned overripe-radish red. "The 'v' word now? You're impossible!"

"Virgin?" Maxim laughed. "You've got to be kidding me! What, is there a whole list of words you can't handle?"

"Yes, actually…there is."

Maxim shook his head, obviously amused. "Well, I guess I'll have to be more careful tomorrow night at the World War II thing. I can't say sex, I can't say vir—"

"No 's' word and no 'v' word, Maxim!" Sharlamagne interrupted, clamping her hand over his mouth. "Besides, what reason do you have to even be using those kinds of words in the first place?"

Maxim wanted to roar with laughter, but he didn't. She was *too* adorable! So super sensitive about certain things. It was wildly endearing. Yet he also felt the time was perfect to offer something else to her—something reassuring that might actually cause her to maybe like him a little more—maybe.

"All right, all right," he began. "I'll watch my language around you, Miss Dickens."

"Thank you," she said, smiling at him, her cheeks as red as Rome Delicious apples.

"But you're not the only virgin sitting on the back porch right now, you know," he added.

He almost cracked up! The look of astonishment on her face was so thorough—she was so visibly shocked by his revelation—that she'd completely neglected to cover his mouth with her soft little hand.

"What?" he asked, feigning ignorance as she stared at him. "You're looking at me like I've got bugs crawling out of my nose."

"*You're* a virgin?" she breathed.

Instantly, Maxim put one hand at the back of her head, covering her mouth with his other. "Don't say the 'v' word out loud, Miss Dickens. People will think you're a hypocrite." He chuckled and released her. "And why are you acting so astonished?" He forced himself to frown at her. "You hadn't judged me as a womanizer or something before now, had you?" he asked, knowing perfectly well she had—at least to some extent.

"Of course not," she lied.

"Liar," he mumbled, smiling at her. "So you won't say the 's' word, but you're a liar?" he teased.

"Well, I might have thought you were…you know…" she stammered, shifting her weight because of her discomfort.

"You thought I was what?" he prodded, still having to struggle to keep from laughing. She was so uncomfortable. It was awesome!

"You know…" she stammered again. "I thought you were…you know…"

"What? 'S' word—ly active?" he offered.

"Well…yeah," she admitted, looking like a kid who'd just been caught stealing something from the toy store.

"Well, I'm not, Miss Dickens," he gently informed her. "I believe in saving the 's' word for marriage. And I can't believe you assumed differently. You know what they say about assuming, don't you?"

"What?" she asked, her cute little eyebrows puckered together with curiosity.

"To assume…well…all it does is make an ass out of 'u' and 'me.' Right?"

She continued to look at him with a puzzled expression for a moment. Then her face relaxed, and she grinned. "Oh, you're very funny, Maxim Olivier. Very funny. What a witty punster you are!"

"So I can say ass but not the 's' word?" he laughed. "You're the one who's funny, Sharlamagne Bronte. Not me."

"By definition, an ass is a long-eared, domesticated mammal related to the horse. Usually a beast of burden…which is exactly what you are going to be now, as payback for all this teasing you've been doing."

He watched her as she took the bowl of cherries, popped the last three in her mouth, set the bowl back down on the porch step, and stood up. "Come on, mule man. There's a trunk that needs to be carried to my car."

"I think a jackass is a male donkey, not a mule…if I'm not mistaken," he chuckled as she took his hand and started pulling him toward the old house.

"Well, you should know, I suppose," she giggled.

Maxim was wound up all of a sudden. His blood was pumping, and he was having to grit his teeth to keep from pulling Sharlamagne around to face him and kissing her. She was under his skin big time, and he wondered why his grandmother hadn't hooked him up with her a long time ago. But he humbled himself in the next moment. He hadn't been good enough for a girl like Sharlamagne before. That was probably it. For a moment, he wondered if it was because she had been so young when their paths had first crossed, but he quickly discarded the idea. Nope. Sharlamagne Dickens was a jewel—a lady—and she deserved a knight in shining armor—not an idiot like him.

Yet Maxim knew he wasn't as big an idiot as he had been several years before. Maybe he could shine up his tattered armor a little and attempt to sweep Sharlamagne off her feet—carry her away on his white steed slash old army jeep—sequester her in the Passion Room and…

"By the way, what time are we leaving tomorrow night again?" Sharlamagne asked.

"I'll…um…pick you up at six, if that's okay," Maxim answered.

She glanced back at him, realized she was still holding onto his hand, and quickly let go of it. She felt her cheeks heat up a little but managed to fight off a full blush. Oh, certainly she wished she could hold his hand forever—never let go of it. But she didn't want him to sense that about her and scare him off.

"Perfect!" she chimed, wondering if she appeared a little too exuberant. "I'll be ready."

"Oh, you think so, do you?" he asked, and she noticed the blue smolder of mischief in his eyes.

She couldn't figure out why it was there, however, and simply replied, "Of course! If you've learned nothing else about me by now, you should at least know that I'm fastidiously prompt."

"Six o'clock then," Maxim said, still grinning at her. "Now where's this trunk you need your 'beast of burden related to a horse' to move?"

Sharlamagne smiled. He was really fun to be with! Yep—really fun to be with and heavenly to gaze upon. She couldn't wait until he arrived the next night to take her to the World War II gala. She absolutely could not wait!

CHAPTER TEN

"I swear, Shar. It's like watching *U-571* Matthew McCona-hottie approach…only way, way, *way* better!" Gwen exclaimed in a whisper as she peeked out the window. "He's all decked out in a dress white Navy uniform. I'm practically panting over here!"

"Shut up, Gwen," Sharlamagne scolded. "I'm a nervous wreck as it is."

Inhaling a deep breath in an effort to calm her nerves, Sharlamagne studied herself in the mirror. She'd chosen to wear the coral-colored, sequin-bedazzled gown. It was the one Maxim had first removed from Mrs. Tanner's wardrobe—the first gown Sharlamagne had seen in its full glory. It was a gorgeous gown, and Sharlamagne felt relatively confident in her choice—relatively confident, that was, until Gwen said Maxim was arriving in a dress white Navy uniform!

Quickly she checked her hair—a perfect Betty Grable updo that boasted soft Victory Rolls on top. It hadn't been an easy style to accomplish, but even Sharlamagne's father thought she looked like she'd stepped out of a 1940s glamour magazine. She wore white elbow-length gloves and mid-high-heeled cabaret shoes (with a very feminine ruffle embellishment on the toe) that had also once belonged to Elisaveta Tanner. They were a little snug, but Sharlamagne hoped her feet wouldn't hurt too badly by the end of the evening. As a finishing touch, she'd decided to wear Mrs. Tanner's locket. It was amazing how perfectly it fit, so that the locket itself hung just below the hollow of her throat. She'd opened the locket to gaze on Mrs. Tanner's image many times since her friend had passed. She always found her attention lingering on the picture of Mrs. Tanner's husband as well, astonished at how much his grandson looked like him.

"You look ravishing, Shar," Gwen sighed. "So quit primping, and get downstairs before he rings the door—"

Sharlamagne gasped as she heard the doorbell ring. She'd wanted to be all ready so she could simply rush out the door without her family making a fuss. But she'd found she was too nervous and had taken too much time making sure the seams down the backs of her pantyhose were straight on her legs.

"Oh, no! He rang the doorbell already!" she whined to Gwen.

"It's fine, Shar. Settle down," her sister laughed. "Just because this is the date of your life—the *night* of your life, for that matter—doesn't mean you need to be all wound up like this."

"Gee, thanks," Sharlamagne said.

"Here. Blot your lipstick one more time," Gwen said, handing her a tissue.

"It's fine," Sharlamagne said. "Let's just go. I don't want him waiting on me."

Quickly she hurried out into the hallway and toward the stairs.

"Slow down!" Gwen whispered. "You'll go tumbling down the stairs and lay him out on the floor."

Sharlamagne's heart was pounding so hard she thought it might break free of her body and fly down the hall by itself. She tried to slow her step, but that only made her anxiety worse. As she neared the top of the stairs, she could hear Maxim's voice. She could hear her father's too and was thankful it was Van-Dyke Dickens who'd answered the door and not one of her brothers.

As she reached the top stairs, she looked down and saw Maxim. A quiet gasp caused her breath to catch in her throat. He was magnificent—tall, dark, handsome, and looking the perfect picture of a Naval officer in dress whites, clear down to the plethoric ribbons across his broad chest. She smiled as she noticed he'd gotten a haircut, delighted that he would spruce up so much for the event.

Her nerves leapt to a peak, and she felt her hands begin to tremble.

But then Maxim looked up at her. His eyes narrowed as he smiled—and his smile was that of sincere approval and admiration.

"Yikes!" he breathed as his eyes traveled over her several times as she descended the stairs, and Sharlamagne giggled at his endearing use of antiquated slang.

"Good night, Daddy," Sharlamagne said, kissing her father affectionately on the cheek. She retrieved her beaded evening clutch purse from the entry table and took Maxim's arm as he offered it.

"You kids have fun now," Mr. Dickens said as Maxim opened the front door.

Sharlamagne turned to see Gwen at the top of the stairs, fanning herself in a gesture of expressing how hot Maxim looked.

"Thank you, Mr. Dickens," Maxim said. "I'll have her home at a reasonable hour."

"I hope not," Van-Dyke chuckled as he ushered the couple out the door and closed it behind him.

"I've never had that response from a dad before," Maxim said, smiling as he escorted Sharlamagne to the dark car parked at the curb.

"Well, I'm sure he's kidding," Sharlamagne giggled.

"But what if he's not?" Maxim teased.

"I'm sure he is," she assured him.

As Sharlamagne approached the car, she smiled. "Wow! Look at it!" she couldn't help exclaiming. "It's perfect."

"Yep," Maxim agreed as he ran his free hand over the azure-blue paint on one fender. "It was Grandpa's pride and joy…next to me and Grandma, of course."

"Of course," Sharlamagne giggled.

Maxim opened the passenger door for her, and she slid into the smooth, cool seat of the car. "It really is incredible," she said once he was in the driver's seat.

"Yeah. It is. We worked a long time on it. I gave it a tune up this week…just for you," Maxim said, smiling as he turned the key in the ignition.

The car roared to life, and Sharlamagne couldn't help but laugh with nostalgic delight. "I can't believe this. I can't believe I'm going to a dance with a Navy officer in a blue 1943 Oldsmobile!"

"I can't believe I've got a gorgeous dish sitting next to me and permission from her father to keep her out late."

Sharlamagne giggled—sighed as she gazed at him for a moment. Could she really be sitting in a vintage Oldsmobile, wearing a vintage ball gown, with the most handsome man on the face of the earth taking her to a dance?

"Ready for the night of your life, sugar bee?" he asked.

Sharlamagne smiled. "Are you ready for the night of *your* life, sailor?" she flirted.

"Ooo, she's feeling frisky," Maxim chuckled. "I get the feeling you're not going to take my nonsense lying down tonight."

"Bring it on, handsome," she told him.

Maxim laughed and shook his head with being amused. "It's the uniform, isn't it? Why is it that dames always like a man better when he's in uniform?"

With that, he pulled away from the curb, and Sharlamagne Dickens knew she really was in for the cliché night of her life.

❦

She was dazzled! There was no other word for it. Sharlamagne was completely, entirely dazzled.

"It's awesome, right?" Maxim asked as they stood just outside the old airplane hangar looking in.

"It's astonishing!" Sharlamagne breathed.

And it was! The vintage airplanes parked outside the hangar were amazing enough, but the decor inside was nearly beyond belief. The ceiling of the hangar was strung with tiny, white, twinkling lights that cascaded down over the walls as well. There was a bandstand centered against the back wall, complete with a vintage-looking Benny Goodman–type band set up and already playing "Sing, Sing, Sing." The center of the hangar was obviously meant for dancing, and several couples were already showing off their swing dance skills. The perimeter of the dance floor was littered with tables and chairs, perfectly set with white tablecloths and flickering lamplight. American flags adorned the walls, and several elderly men dressed in uniforms of the various military branches were mingling with guests. It was overwhelming! Sharlamagne literally could not take it in all in at once.

"Well, how about first things first?" Maxim suggested, taking hold of her hand and tugging her toward one back corner of the hangar.

"What's that?" she asked, entirely too overwhelmed to think clearly.

"Our paper moon photo," he explained, smiling at her.

As Sharlamagne looked in the direction he was leading her, she smiled and bit her lip with marvelous delight. There, in one corner of the room, stood a photography setup—a vintage half-moon with a face paper moon nestled in a midnight black sky and twinkling stars background.

"I've always, always, always wanted a paper moon photo!" she exclaimed. "I can't believe it!"

Maxim turned and smiled at her. "So...are you saying I'm making your dreams come true, sugar bee?"

"Yeah...I guess so," she said. Wrinkling her nose, she asked, "Sugar bee?"

"That's my new nickname for you," he answered. "You once told me someone you know attracts people like bees to honey...and I told you I prefer sugar. Therefore, I'm hoping you're a sugar bee and not a honey bee. You know...that you prefer sugar too...specifically me."

Sharlamagne blushed and giggled—wished that she could feel as pretty and perfectly feminine every day as she did at that moment all dressed up in her vintage gown and gloves.

"How many poses would you like to take, sir?" the man standing behind the camera asked as Maxim gently ushered Sharlamagne toward the paper moon. The photographer was dressed in a perfect vintage army uniform, complete with triangle hat and army boots.

Maxim shrugged. "I don't know. Five or six?"

"You've got it, sailor," the man said.

The photographer walked over to Sharlamagne and Maxim. "Now, let's have you right here in the curve of the moon, honey," he instructed Sharlamagne. "And you, officer...let's have you right here on her left. That's it. Now, sailor...you hold on to that woman like you mean it, okay?"

A tremor of delight raced through Sharlamagne's body as Maxim's arms enveloped her, pulling her against him. She knew the smile the first photograph captured was one of the most sincere she'd ever smiled, for it really was a dream come true for her—and in more than one way.

Ever since she'd been a little girl, Sharlamagne had been fascinated by old paper moon photographs. The tradition stretched back as far as the Victorian times—the tradition of having one's photo taken on or with a novelty cutout half-moon. The height of the paper moon photo craze was between the early 1900s and roaring 1920s when photo postcards were popular. Still, even as late as the late 1940s, paper moon photographs were a popular novelty photo—especially at special occasions such as dances. Thus, Sharlamagne had always wanted her own paper moon photograph.

Add to that the fact that it was Maxim Tanner, the "I Was Made for Loving You" train conductor, Jeans Innovations washboard-abs model, and Victorian house restorer, who was her companion in her first paper moon photo, and Sharlamagne Dickens was—well—over the moon!

"You've got yourself a pretty lady there, sailor," the photographer said as he repositioned Sharlamagne and Maxim for another pose.

"Don't I know it, brother," Maxim agreed.

Sharlamagne smiled, amused by the way being dressed differently and lingering in a nostalgic atmosphere always brought out the vintage verbiage in people.

"It ain't such an ugly mutt you've got here yourself, Rita Hayworth," the photographer said, winking at Sharlamagne.

"He's handsome, isn't he?" she said, blushing. Over the years, several elderly men had compared Sharlamagne to the 1940s actress, dancer, and pinup girl Rita Hayworth. She'd always taken such comparisons as a great compliment. Still, she'd never had a young man make the comparison. It flattered her, and she blushed.

"There you go, honey," the photographer chuckled. "That's just the pearly white smile I was looking for."

"Rita Hayworth, huh?" Maxim said as the photographer nodded that he'd taken the five or six poses he'd been asked to. "With that hairdo…I was imagining you in a bathing suit—you know, more Betty Grable-ish, I guess."

"I can see that too," the photographer added.

Sharlamagne allowed her eyes to narrow with suspicion as glanced to the photographer and back to Maxim. "Okay. What do you want?"

Maxim shrugged. "Nothing. I was just saying—"

"What's with all the compliments, sailor?" she teased.

"Oh, so you can like my uniform, but I can't like your dress and stuff?" he countered.

She gave him one last suspicious glare and smiled. "I've always wanted a paper moon picture, you know. Thank you, Maxim."

"You're welcome, sugar bee," he said. He looked to the photographer then. "So, how do we order them, man?"

"They'll be ready to look at online on Monday, and you can order from there," the photographer said, handing Maxim a business card. "Just go to the website on the card and enter the code I've written on there, and you'll be able to access your digital proofs. Okay?"

"Yeah. Thanks," Maxim said. He retrieved his wallet from his back pocket and tucked the photographer's business card inside. "Are you ready to go check out the planes?" Maxim asked Sharlamagne.

"Very ready," she answered.

"Then come on, girl. The night has only just begun," he said, smiling as he took her hand and began to lead her away from the paper moon scene.

"Thanks," Sharlamagne called over her shoulder to the photographer.

"You bet, honey," the photographer said, winking at her.

"Looks like you won him over pretty quick," Maxim chuckled.

"I think that would be a fun job…taking pictures of people at things like this," Sharlamagne commented in return.

"Look!" Maxim said, pointing to the sky as they exited the hangar. "One of the B-52 bombers is landing."

Sharlamagne looked up into the sky, shading her eyes from the setting sun. She could hear the plane before she finally found it high among the clouds. As it descended toward the landing field, an uproar of cheering and applause erupted from the small crowd that had gathered outside while Sharlamagne and Maxim had been busy with the paper moon photographer.

"Here it comes," Maxim mumbled. "I love old airplanes."

Sharlamagne looked to him—studied him for a moment. He was so handsome! Even more handsome when relaxation and interest radiated from his expression. She wondered if she really was awake—if she really was there at a vintage World War II ball with Maxim Tanner as her Naval officer date! It all seemed surreal. But as the vintage B-52 landed on the airstrip close to the hangar—as the crowd roared with delight and Maxim cupped his hands around his mouth to shout his own kudos—Sharlamagne decided to quit wondering if she was dreaming and just jump into the evening with both feet. It really was a once-in-a-lifetime moment—the date of her life—and she wouldn't miss a moment of it over wondering how it had all come about.

"Do you wanna come see this P-51 Mustang over here with me?" Maxim said, nodding toward a vintage airplane nearby.

"Of course," Sharlamagne answered.

"Come on," he said, smiling. He was like a little boy in a toy shop. It was adorable!

Maxim and Sharlamagne wandered the airfield surrounding the old hangar for about an hour—admiring the old airplanes flown in for the event, touring the army tents sent up to look as they would have during World War II, and allowing other guests who admired their vintage attire to take their photo. It was all great, but Maxim was growing a little impatient to get to the dance floor and hold his pretty Betty Grable in his arms. It was like an itch he couldn't scratch—his desire to dance with her—to gaze down into her pretty face and hold her close.

Therefore, when the Andrews Sisters impersonators took the bandstand, he saw his chance.

"You'll like these ladies," he told Sharlamagne as he checked her gloves and purse at the hatcheck booth. "They're really good."

"I have no doubt of that," she giggled. "This is everything you said it would be…and way, way, way more!"

She smiled at him, and for a moment he thought he might not be able to resist the powerful urge he had to kiss her on her bright-red lipsticked, Rita Hayworth lips.

"Then come on. Let's cut a rug," he said, taking her hand and leading her to the dance floor.

"Cut a rug?" she giggled. "I might destroy a rug with my terrible swing dancing."

"Oh, don't worry. I stink at it too," he assured her.

As the band began to play "Boogie Woogie Bugle Boy," Maxim hoped he hadn't forgotten the basic swing and jitterbug steps he knew. He wanted Sharlamagne to have a good time, and he knew how much most girls liked to dance—and how much most boys didn't.

"Are you ready?" he asked, smiling at her when he realized her expression was that of a scared rabbit.

"As ready as I can be," she answered. She was a good sport. It was another thing he liked about her—one of the many, many things he liked about her.

As he took her in her arms and rather awkwardly began the windup steps to the jitterbug, he said, "I'm seriously warning you, shawty...I can do a mean krump, pop and lock, breakdance...even waltz...but watch your toes when I'm doing this."

She giggled and spun away from him as she began to jitterbug like a pro. He smiled as she said, "Don't worry about it, sailor. I'll do the work on this one, okay?"

"Okay," he laughed.

To his astonishment—very pleased astonishment—Sharlamagne then proceeded to go to town with the jitterbug, making it so all Maxim really had to do at first was match her, pull her, and spin her until he was more comfortable and was able to let loose a little more. He couldn't believe how lighthearted he felt. In fact, the more he thought about it, the more he wondered if he'd ever felt so lighthearted and free. She was like some weird magic potion or something—she made him feel happy, hopeful, excited, content, and worth something all at once. She was a good little swing dancer too.

By the time "Boogie Woogie Bugle Boy" had ended and everyone was applauding, Maxim's face hurt from smiling so hard. She'd taken it to town with him, and he was more than just a little impressed.

"I thought you said you stunk at this," he asked her.

"I thought you said you did," she giggled in response.

"Well, either way...I'm praying they slow it down for a minute so I can catch my breath."

"Me too," she agreed, putting her hand to her chest a moment. "I need to get more cardio...obviously."

As the music began again, Maxim sighed with relief. "We're saved," he said as "I Can Dream, Can't I?" began to play. "It's a slow one."

Sharlamagne smiled at him as her heart fluttered inside her chest. A slow dance with Maxim Tanner? Marvelous! As he took her in dance position, she felt her arms and legs break out in goose bumps.

"Again, I'm warning you...I'm clunky," Maxim told her.

But Sharlamagne shook her head. Not that he wasn't a little stiff and heavy-footed—but she wouldn't want it any other way. He as a manly, masculine dancer, and she wasn't a bit surprised. It fit him perfectly.

"You're perfect," she told him. Then, realizing her comment might have sounded a little too revealing of her overall opinion of him, she added, "You lead really, really well."

"Well, you're Ginger Rogers if you're anybody," he said, smiling down at her.

Sharlamagne continued to follow his lead, trying not to reveal how truly breathless with delight she was at being held so close to him. She tried to concentrate on how wonderful Mrs. Tanner's lovely gown felt as it swished with the rhythm of their dancing. She could feel the cool breeze wafting through the hangar from outside, caressing the back of her neck and blowing the few loose strands of hair that must've escaped her updo during their jitterbug. She thought it felt rather like a soft kiss on her skin, and as the sensation mingled with the sudden yet light fragrance of gardenia that suddenly scented the air, she thought there could never be a more perfect moment.

She looked up to see Maxim was grinning at her with approval.

"What?" she asked, blushing under his gaze.

"Nothing," he answered. "I was just wondering how I could get a pinup of you in that famous Betty Grable bathing suit. It would look great in my office."

She giggled. "What? Are you on a flattery binge tonight or something?" she asked playfully.

"Just telling you what I'm thinking," he answered.

His grin broadened, and as mischief leapt to his eyes, she asked, "What now?"

"I love watching all the old men here check you out," he whispered.

"What?" Sharlamagne gasped. She started to look around, but Maxim caught her chin in his hand that had been at her waist.

"Don't look!" he chuckled in a whisper. "You'll ruin the moment for them. They're probably all caught up in sentimental memories of their youth and how beautiful the women were back when they were younger men."

"And you're too busy noticing the elderly men to notice that every woman in the room is swooning over you, you handsome sailor, you," she whispered.

"It's different. With me, it's just the uniform," he argued. "But with you…it's you."

"Okay, okay," she giggled. "What do you want? You're too charming and complimentary tonight. You must want something. What is it?"

He chuckled. "I'm just telling you what I'm thinking," he said. "Well, *some* of what I'm thinking. You wouldn't want to know my other thoughts…though you couldn't help but be flattered by those too."

Sharlamagne softly slapped his shoulder. "Oh my gosh. You *are* a sailor!"

He laughed and very adeptly spun her around with him as they danced. He was magnificent—nothing short of truly magnificent! And Sharlamagne thought that the lyrics to the song the band was playing, "I Can Dream, Can't I?" were ironically apropos. She did dream of Maxim—always seemed to be dreaming of him—since the first day she met him at Mrs. Tanner's old house for him to show her the old house out back.

Maxim had scheduled his and Sharlamagne's meal at seven o'clock.

Once they were finished, he led her to the area on the wide side of the hangar dance floor, where a group of World War II veterans had gathered to share their own experiences of the war. He knew Sharlamagne would enjoy visiting with them. He always had. Every year, he and his grandmother had spent a significant amount of the evening in visiting with the men and women who had fought so hard and sacrificed so much for their country and fellow Americans. It was always one of his favorite parts of the evening—something he prized and always would. For the fact of the matter was World War II veterans were a vanishing treasure. Maxim had recently read that American World War II veterans were passing away at a rate of eight hundred fifty a day. When they were all gone, the world would never be the same, and true patriotism— understanding of sacrifice for freedom—would be lost forever. Something deep inside Maxim always felt somewhat fearful of the world being void of the valiant men and women who had seen the truths of the last World War, and he hung on every word and experience they shared. He knew Sharlamagne felt the same way he did. It was obvious in everything about her—her likes and dislikes, her priorities, her opinions. Thus, he led her over to the veterans group, pulled a chair out for her, and settled himself next to her.

Mere moments later, he smiled when she asked a question of a veteran who had been telling a story to those gathered around him. "The *Indianapolis*? You served aboard the *Indianapolis*, sir?"

"I did," the man proudly stated. "I went down with her, and I somehow managed to live through what followed…obviously."

Everyone chuckled—everyone except Sharlamagne. Maxim's smile broadened as he saw Sharlamagne reach across the space between her and the white-haired Navy hero and clasp his hand.

"Thank you, sir," she said. "Thank you for serving…for sacrificing… for making sure things were safe when the rest of us came along. I can't imagine what you endured. Thank you for doing that for us…for me."

Maxim felt an excess moisture fill his eyes as Sharlamagne leaned forward and kissed the old man on the cheek.

Maxim and everyone else sitting nearby chuckled as the old man blushed and said, "Well, that right there made it all worth it, honey."

Someone else asked the man a question, and Maxim took the opportunity to lean over and whisper to Sharlamagne, "You really know your stuff, shawty."

"The *Indianapolis*. Can you imagine?" she whispered in return.

"No. I can't," Maxim admitted. "Of course, I wouldn't know anything about the *Indianapolis* if it hadn't been for the movie *Jaws*," he added.

She smiled up at him. "I think most people are that way…especially now," she whispered. "But my dad told me about it. That's where most of my knowledge of war stuff starts…though then I get all voracious to know more. It's like he plants a seed in my mind and then I want it to grow, you know?"

"I do," Maxim answered.

They both returned their attention to the veterans at hand then— to the great men they were having the honor of spending time with. Yet even for the veterans surrounding them, Maxim couldn't keep his thoughts and mind from traveling back to Sharlamagne. He watched her—the way she was enraptured by what the true heroes had to say. He also noticed the way the old veterans stared at Sharlamagne—as if they'd just been transported back almost seventy years and were gazing at the perfect pinup girl of the era. His own grandfather had been a World War II veteran. He wondered what his grandpa would've thought of Sharlamagne Dickens. He smiled, knowing Alec Tanner would've probably been thinking the same things all the old veterans were thinking now.

He determined he'd share Sharlamagne's attention with the old heroes for an hour or so. It was the very least he could do for men who were unspoken heroes. But then he'd take her back. Maxim was a little surprised by the powerful possessiveness that had begun to overtake him during the evening where Sharlamagne was concerned. In truth, it was the first time he'd ever been with her that he really had to share her attention at all—and he found he didn't like sharing her attention.

Yep. He'd give it an hour or so, and then he'd whisk her off to the dance floor again—because he liked dancing with her. He liked holding her, laughing with her, spinning her around, seeing her brilliant smile light up the room—feeling it light up his soul.

❦

As the elderly man in a worn and ancient Navy uniform led her in dancing to the band's rendition of "Harbor Lights," Sharlamagne forced a smile to stay on her face. In truth, she wanted to sob. Here was a man—bent with age and the batterings of life, white-haired, and adorably wrinkled—who was a true and unsung hero. A man who slowly walked the aisle of whatever grocery store he shopped at, who deposited a pitifully small Social Security check into the bank every month—a man (a widower by his own account) who probably sat alone at the local coffee shop eating a muffin—a man who did all these things without being noticed, completely unappreciated by those around him. It broke her heart, the way true heroes were vanishing—and vanishing without gratitude. She only hoped she could finish dancing with the brave and heroic *Indianapolis* survivor before her tender emotions got the better of her and she burst into tears.

At last the music ended. "You're a beautiful young woman, Sharlamagne," the old war veteran said. His faded blue eyes were sparkling as he gazed at her. "Thank you for making an old man feel young again."

"Thank you, sir…for everything," she managed.

He leaned forward and placed a soft kiss at the corner of her mouth. "Thank you, darling," he mumbled as he stepped back from her. He glanced to Maxim a moment—Maxim, who had approached as the song began to end—and said, "You're a lucky man, sailor."

"Yes, sir," Maxim agreed.

The elderly man gazed longingly at Sharlamagne once more and then said, "You kids have fun now."

"Thank you for the dance," Sharlamagne said, still forcing her smile.

"You're welcome, honey."

The music started once more—another slow song, "Blue Hawaii"— and Sharlamagne felt herself melt against Maxim as he took her in his arms to start their dance.

Tears were welling in her eyes, and she couldn't keep them from spilling over onto her cheeks as Maxim asked, "What's the matter, shawty? Did that old vet get to you?"

Sharlamagne nodded, unable to speak for trying to hold back the sobs in her throat begging for release.

"They're precious, aren't they?" he asked, and she nodded as more tears escaped over her cheeks. "Well, don't you worry, sugar bee. I think I can prove that I know you pretty well."

"How's that?" she whispered, brushing the tears from her cheek with one hand. She didn't want to get makeup on his uniform.

"Here," he said, pulling a handkerchief from his pants pocket.

Sharlamagne giggled through her tears as she accepted the hanky. "A handkerchief? Not a tissue, but a handkerchief?" she asked.

"I wanted you to feel like you were with a real-life 1940s sailor," he explained. "And I don't think a sailor would've had a tissue on hand back then. He would've had a handkerchief."

Sharlamagne smiled as she wiped her tears on the soft white cloth. "Thank you," she said, smiling up at him.

He winked at her and then said, "How about we sit this one out? This uniform is getting hot. Would you care if I took off the jacket and left it with your gloves and stuff at the coat check place?"

"Not at all," she answered, wiping the rest of her tears.

"Good," Maxim said as he began to unfasten the fancy buttons on the front of his uniform.

Sharlamagne felt much better as she saw the white sleeveless T-shirt and black suspenders Maxim was wearing beneath his uniform jacket.

She giggled and said, "Now you look really ready to swing!"

"Well, I wanted it to, like, fit in with or without the jacket," he said. "I'll be right back."

By the time Maxim had returned from checking his uniform jacket, Sharlamagne had almost fully recovered from her sentimental meltdown with empathy and appreciation for the old veteran she'd danced with. And as the band began to play "All the Cats Join In," Maxim grabbed her hand and pulled her out onto the dance floor.

"This is one of my favorites," she told him as they started to dance.
"Mine too."

Dancing with Maxim lifted Sharlamagne's spirits once more. He was so wonderful! She loved dancing with him, touching him, smelling him, being with him, feeling him—just plain looking at him!

By the time "All the Cats Join In" was over, she and Maxim were both laughing, amused at their efforts to keep up with the semiprofessional swing dancers that had been dancing near them. As the band slowed the tempo, Maxim gathered Sharlamagne against him and began to slow dance with her.

"Grandma loved this song," he said, pulling Sharlamagne's body flush with his own.

"Yeah. I love it too," Sharlamagne sighed.

Maxim's eyebrows arched with mild disbelief. "You know this song?"

"Of course!" she giggled. "'I Remember You.' Though Helen Forrest's version is my favorite."

Sharlamagne began to sing along with the music, and Maxim shook his head, smiling with pleased approval. It seemed Sharlamagne Dickens would never cease to astound him.

She continued to hum for a few more measures and then smiled up at him.

"What?" he asked, for it was obvious he was amusing her somehow.

"Nothing," she answered. "It's just that...well...you know what they say about a man in uniform."

"No. What do they say?" he teased.

Sharlamagne shrugged. "I don't know exactly...something about...about..."

"Women love a man in uniform?" he offered.

"Yeah," she giggled.

"So you're admitting you like the uniform, huh?" he teased. "And why do you think that is? You know...that women like a man in uniform?"

She reached up and straightened his suspender at one shoulder a little. "I don't know. Maybe it's because they look so extra handsome and heroic in one. I mean, think about it. You can put the homeliest man in a military uniform or a firefighter uniform or a policeman's uniform…and all of a sudden, he's more attractive."

"Is that so?"

"Yeah. It's totally true."

"So I'm not as homely tonight as I usually am?" he baited her.

"Oh, you couldn't be homely if you tried!" she exclaimed. "But even you are…in a uniform you're even more…even more…"

"Even more what?" he prodded. She was blushing radish red—and Maxim loved it!

"You know…more…more…" she continued to stammer.

"Are you telling me you're having a hard time keeping your hands off me just because I'm wearing an old Navy uniform?" he suggested. "Even though I'm not even wearing most of it now?"

"Well…with or without the uniform…you're very handsome."

"Why, thank you, Miss Dickens," he said. He could tell by her blush that it had been a brave admission for her to make. Furthermore, it gave him the courage he'd been trying to find all night to do something he'd wanted to do for a long time.

"You know," he began, pulling her body flush with his, "I've been thinking about something all night."

"And what's that?" she asked. He liked the way she seemed to melt against him—as if she were somehow surrendering to him.

"I've been thinking about how I might kiss you tonight. You know, deciding where."

Her eyes widened with visible delight, and his courage mounted.

"Were you thinking here?" she asked. "Right here in the airplane hangar?"

Maxim grinned, letting his hand slide from her waist, slowly moving up over her back until he held her neck. He shrugged. "Well, kind of."

"What do you mean?" she asked in a breathless whisper.

"I was thinking the first place I'd kiss you…the very first place…

would be right on your pretty mouth," he mumbled as his head descended toward hers.

At the very first sense of Maxim Tanner's kiss, Sharlamagne thought she might never draw another breath! It wasn't a tentative, light kiss, but it wasn't a hard, demanding kiss either. His kiss was moist and warm, and although it wasn't a long kiss, it was instantly followed by another—and another. Maxim's hand went to her waist, pulling her body flush with his own, and there was nothing she could do but allow her arms to encircle his broad shoulders—allow her hands to travel the breadth of them to the back of his neck.

Sharlamagne was rendered breathless as his kiss deepened—not to anything too scandalous for public, but it *was* an open-mouthed, moist, and somewhat passionate sort of kiss. She felt her hands cling more tightly to the back of his neck—felt his hair beneath one palm and grasped it tightly, letting it feather between her fingers. She felt weak one moment—as if her knees might give way, causing her to crumple to the floor of the old plane hangar. Yet the next, her insides were filled with such a feeling of strength and vigor that she thought maybe she could take flight if she really tried. She was awhirl in literal ecstasy! Somewhere in the corners of her mind, she could hear the band playing "I Remember You." Somehow, she was still vaguely aware of the other people dancing around them, that Maxim wore his grandfather's Navy uniform (or at least part of it), and that she wore a vintage ball gown. But for the most part, all she could do was to surrender her every sense and emotion to the kiss she was sharing with Maxim Tanner.

Sharlamagne's beautiful body curved perfectly against the lines of his own, and the scent of the vanilla fragrance she wore filled his lungs. The skin around her mouth was soft; he was certain all her skin was soft—every inch of it. Maxim was sure that no matter where he kissed her—her neck, her lips, her shoulder—no matter where he kissed her, her skin would be soft. Furthermore, she tasted sweeter than anything he'd ever eaten. And he could sense something else—something that seemed to be simmering just beneath the surface of her kiss. He sensed that, were they not in a public forum the way they were, her response to him would be far more dramatic. Not that there was anything the slightest bit unsatisfactory about the way she was kissing him—it was just that Maxim somehow knew what would erupt between them were they isolated alone together. It would be…different.

It made him glad he'd chosen the World War II event as the venue of kissing her for the first time. Because with what was broiling inside him at that moment, he figured Sharlamagne Dickens was lucky they weren't alone. He wanted her—every inch of her—every aspect of her personality—every smile, every touch, every breath she breathed—he wanted all of her! He wondered if the kiss was ringing her bell the way it was ringing his. Oh, he'd kissed plenty of women (not that he was proud of it, however), and not one woman's kiss had ever done this to him! Not one had ever made him want to…

"Ladies and gentlemen," began the announcement from the bandstand. "Ladies and gentlemen," a man repeated as the music stopped. "It's over! The war is finally over!"

Everyone in the room cheered, applauded, and began hugging and kissing. But Maxim and Sharlamagne were already kissing. Even as the announcer began reading the details of the Japanese surrender aboard the USS *Missouri*, their kiss lingered.

Yet the celebratory chaos was too formidable, and Maxim ended their kiss slowly and at the same time with haste—for he was too affected in too many ways to continue in a public place anyway. He'd kissed her, and she'd kissed him back. It was enough for him to know she wanted him to kiss her. Therefore, he figured the next kiss they shared could wait for a more private circumstance.

He smiled when he saw the pink in her cheeks and the twinkle in her eyes as red, white, and blue confetti and balloons rained down upon them from above. She hadn't only wanted him to kiss her, she'd liked his kiss. He breathed a quiet sigh of relief. He'd been afraid he'd muck it up somehow and she'd never want to kiss him again. And, man oh man, did he hope she'd want to kiss him again!

Sharlamagne's eyes narrowed, and she studied Maxim's face for a moment. "Are you for real?" she asked. "Are you for real…or are you just putting on all this…this Mr. Marvelous stuff?"

Maxim frowned as he chuckled a little. "What? What do you mean?"

"Oh, the first place I'm going to kiss you is on the mouth," she said, attempting to mimic his deep, masculine voice. "I mean, what a line! How long did it take you to think that one up, sailor?"

He laughed then and answered, "All afternoon, baby. All afternoon."

Sharlamagne sighed as he pulled her close to him and continued their dance. It truly was the night to top all the other nights of her life. She moistened her lips and smiled, knowing that, only moments before, Maxim's lips had been pressed to hers. It was unbelievable! Divine, resplendent, and fantastically dreamy! Just like everything else about Maxim Olivier Tanner.

"You wear it well," Maxim said, nodding toward his grandmother's locket that hung at Sharlamagne's throat. He reached out and touched the familiar locket for a moment, unable to remember a time he hadn't seen it around his grandmother's neck. He'd changed the chain out, of course, before he'd given it to Sharlamagne. He'd figured the locket deserved a new chain since it was going to a new owner.

Setting down the large trophy he and Sharlamagne had won for best costume, Maxim leaned against a post on Sharlamagne's front porch and continued to consider the locket. "I mean it. It really looks like it belongs on you now."

"Really?" Sharlamagne asked, taking the locket between her thumb and forefinger as she glanced down at it. "Well, I thought it would be kind of neat…you know…to wear it tonight."

"Have you discovered the secret yet?" Maxim asked. Surely she had. Surely Sharlamagne had noticed the other part of the locket.

"Its secret?" she asked, however.

"Yeah." Maxim answered. "Here. Let me show you."

Taking Sharlamagne by the shoulders, he turned her around to face away from him, fumbling with the clasp of the gold chain at the back of her neck until he freed the chain and locket.

"Look," he said, holding the locket in his palm.

Sharlamagne watched as he pressed the tiny button on the right side of the locket. "See? Alek and Elisaveta Tanner, right?"

"Yeah…" Sharlamagne breathed.

Turning the locket over, Maxim began to twist the back gold panel the same way one would twist the back panel of some antique pocket watches. "A little twist left—you know, lefty loosey," he mumbled. "And there you have it," he announced as the back locket piece came free.

"What?" Sharlamagne exclaimed. "It has another compartment?"

"That it does," Maxim verified. "See?" he said, holding the locket out to her. "There's a piece of glass placed there, and under the glass you'll see…"

"It's like a mourning hair locket on this side!" she exclaimed.

Maxim chuckled. "Well, I'd say it *is* a mourning hair locket on this side, shawty. The darkest hair—the black hair there—that's my grandpa's hair. Grandma clipped it off him the day they were married. The blonde hair is Grandma's, also clipped the day they were married." Handing the locket to Sharlamagne so she could better see it in the low light of the Dickens's front porch, he added, "Grandpa had the locket made, like, a month later and gave it to Grandma for Christmas."

"I can't believe she would give this to me," Sharlamagne whispered. She looked up to him, and he could see the trepidation in her eyes. "You really should have this."

But Maxim shook his head. "No. She wanted you to have it, and I really do think you'll appreciate it more than anyone else would've… even me. I've got so many things of theirs." He leaned forward and whispered, "I even found a couple of my grandpa's teeth in the kitchen junk drawer when I was cleaning it out the other day."

She giggled and asked, "Really?"

Maxim nodded. "Yeah. I can remember how Grandpa hated dentists. He would always swear he would never go again. I remember him taking the pliers and yanking out a tooth that was hurting him when I was a kid. I guess he just tossed it in the junk drawer. There were three others in there, so I figured he kept his word and never did go to a dentist again."

Maxim watched as Sharlamagne replaced the removable back of the locket, clasped the locket with both hands, and held it to her chest for a moment.

"Thank you for this, Maxim," Sharlamagne said. She could feel the tender emotion rising in her. She didn't want to be reduced to tears in front of him twice in one night but took the chance she would be and added, "For the locket...for tonight...the dance...the airplanes... everything! It really was the most marvelous time I've ever had."

"Well, you're welcome, Sharlamagne," he said, reaching out and placing his hands on her shoulders. "It *was* really, really fun, wasn't it?"

"It was," she agreed. She was starting to feel let down. It was over—the beautiful evening, the beautiful dream was over.

"Are you going to be coming out to the house on Monday when you're finished at the antique store?" he asked.

Sharlamagne's heart suddenly soared with hope. Did he still intend to help her? Would she still get to see him now even though the house was half empty already?

"Of course," she said hopefully—and hoping she didn't appear too hopeful. "How about you?"

He grinned. "I'm off at five. So if you need me to come by, I can—"

"Oh, I do need you!" Sharlamagne interrupted. Aaarrgghh! She wanted to smack herself. Could she have been more obvious? Could she have appeared more desperate to see him again? She thought not. "I mean...if you're not too busy and stuff," she added—though it didn't dilute her feelings of stupidity very much.

"I'm not too busy," he assured her, smiling. He moved his hands from her shoulders to her waist—moved closer to her. "Can I...uh... can have a good-night kiss, Miss Dickens?"

Oh, you can have anything you want! is what her mind screamed—but thankfully her mouth said only, "Of course."

Slowly, he pulled her against him, and she liked the way the fabric of his white Navy uniform jacket felt beneath her palms as she slid her hands along his shoulders to the back of his neck.

"Thank you for a wonderful evening, Miss Dickens," he said. His voice was low and provocative; it caused her knees to weaken. "I hope we can do this again sometime."

"Yeah," she managed to breathe a moment before he kissed her.

He wouldn't press her for a long kiss—not tonight—not when the porch light might blaze forth at any moment. Maxim kissed Sharlamagne well enough for the moment—but not well enough. He didn't want to chance a father or a brother or anyone happening on them, even if it was two a.m. He didn't want Sharlamagne to have any uncomfortable memories of their evening together. So, with the self-control of a Tibetan monk, Maxim kissed her the same way he'd kissed earlier in the evening at the dance—well, but not great.

"See you Monday then?" he asked as he released her and stepped down one of the porch steps.

"Yep," she said, still blushing.

"Good night then, shawty," he said, as he turned and head toward his car. "And you take good care of our trophy."

"I will. Good night," Sharlamagne called as she watched Maxim saunter toward the Oldsmobile parked at the curb. When he was far enough away that she knew he couldn't hear a whisper, she breathed, "Good night, Maxim. And thank you for asking me to go…for actually taking me…for dancing with me. And thank you, thank you, thank you for kissing me like I really was some fabulous forties pinup girl."

CHAPTER ELEVEN

All day Sunday, and every moment at work on Monday, Sharlamagne was torn between simultaneous feelings of elation at the thought of seeing Maxim again after work and anxiety at wondering if there would be any discomfort between them because of what had happened—the kissing. Saturday night had been bliss, pure wonderment, for Sharlamagne. And the kisses she'd shared with Maxim at the World War II dance and her parents' front porch when he'd taken her home had been causing randomly timed tremors and goose bumps to race over her body ever since.

Oh, Sharlamagne had been kissed by a few guys over the years; she'd kissed them back too. But nothing—nothing—had ever affected her the way Maxim Tanner's kisses had! She'd been nervous when he'd first kissed, of course. After all, they'd been dancing in the middle of a hundred other couples. Yet in her soul she knew that the public place of their first kiss wasn't really the cause of her nerves—it was Maxim himself. When he'd kissed her, she'd literally thought for a moment that she might drop dead of the physical and emotional delight that instantly overwhelmed her.

Sharlamagne had always figured Maxim would kiss as well as he looked like he would, but she'd really never imagined how thoroughly devastating his kiss would be to her. He'd owned her—totally owned her in those moments! He owned her heart, her mind, her soul, her body; any part of her that existed to be owned, Maxim had owned it. The sensation was a little frightening, yes. But more so, it was fantastic!

She'd hardly been able to think of anything else since it had happened.

Kissing Maxim had also taught Sharlamagne something else about herself. It was a rather humbling notion, as well as somewhat unsettling. The way Maxim had completely owned her with one kiss—the way he'd made her feel—the emotional and physical desire he'd triggered in her—had given Sharlamagne the rather conscious reprimanding experience of knowing that her strength in resisting seduction was perhaps not foolproof.

Oh, she knew there was no way she'd ever succumb to anything too intimate—well, she'd never succumb to finding herself involved in the ultimate act of intimacy between a man and a woman before she was married. At least she'd always known it before. Yet there had been an instant—several instants, in truth—that Sharlamagne's feelings and desires toward the ethereally gorgeous, attractive, alluring Maxim Tanner had caused her to think—rather, to understand—how people could more easily find themselves in deeply intimate situations they hadn't planned to find themselves in. It had humbled her a great deal, knowing that the right man might tempt even her to stumbling into…

"What in the world are you thinking about, Sharlamagne?" Louisa Dickens asked, interrupting Sharlamagne's train of thought—thankfully.

"Oh. Sorry, Mom," Sharlamagne answered. "Just a little tired, I guess."

"Well, I'm not surprised," Louisa said. "Staying out 'til all hours of the morning." Smiling and offering a wink of understanding to her daughter, Louisa teased, "And with a sailor. How scandalous!"

"I know, right?" Sharlamagne giggled. "Even Gwen was impressed."

Louisa laughed. "Oh, you girls and your boys. It's so entertaining. It keeps me young." Louisa paused in polishing the silver platter she'd been shining up. "So…um…are you going over to your house tonight? You know…to gather up some more things for the store or your storage unit?"

"Yeah," Sharlamagne sighed. "Though I probably need to take a break. You and Dad have got so much stuff piled out in the back rooms of the shop that you'll never sell it all as it is."

"Oh, don't take a break now, darling!" Louisa exclaimed. "Not when you have...you know...so much help in going through things every evening. Why let a good thing go? Good help in antiquing is hard to find, you know."

Sharlamagne grinned at her mother, quickly surveyed her crimson and plum outfit, and giggled.

"You mean good-looking help, Mom? Right?"

"Exactly, darling," Louisa admitted. "Maxim might not always have the time to lift and move things with you the way he seems to now. So wait until he *doesn't* have the time...and *then* you can take a little break. Do you see what I mean?"

"Of *course* I see what you mean, Mom. I just don't want him to get tired of me or something."

Setting down the silver tray and polishing cloth, Louisa took Sharlamagne by the shoulders and said, "Sharlamagne...darling. If he was tired of you, don't you think he would've stopped showing up to help you long before now?"

"I suppose so," Sharlamagne admitted—though her mother had unwittingly planted a huge seed of doubt in her mind. What if Maxim didn't show? What if—when she was finished with her shift in ten more minutes—what if she drove out the old house and Maxim never came to meet her there?

"Exactly," Louisa said. "Now why don't you just end your shift now so you can run a brush through your hair and things?" She looked Sharlamagne up and down and frowned a little. "Are you really going to wear those worn-out jeans and this...this lumberjack shirt?"

Sharlamagne smiled as she looked down at the old brown and ivory plaid shirt that had once belonged to her brother Cristo. "It's a great shirt to go digging around in an old house with, Mom. What? Do you want me to wear one of Mrs. Tanner's old ball gowns or something? Don't you think Maxim might wonder if I'd lost my marbles?"

Louisa smiled. "You're right. You're off to work in dust and cobwebs. This outfit you're wearing is perfect."

"Thanks," Sharlamagne said. "And since you were dissing my outfit...I will take you up on that offer to clock out early."

"You do that, darling," Louisa said as she and Sharlamagne exchanged cheek kisses. "And don't lift anything too heavy. I don't want you hurting yourself."

"Okay. Love you," Sharlamagne said as she headed to the bathroom at the back of the store.

"Love you too, sweetie," Louisa called after her.

Sharlamagne studied herself in the bathroom mirror a moment. She certainly looked a lot different than she had Saturday night. Yet she figured if she redid her pony tail and freshened up her makeup a little, she'd look somewhat presentable for Maxim. Not kissable, perhaps— but presentable.

As she pulled the hair tie from her hair and began to brush her hair out with the brush she and Gwen kept in an antique cabinet in the store bathroom, she thought for a moment that she'd be more than willing to wear one of Mrs. Tanner's vintage ball gowns—ruin one even—if it meant Maxim might kiss her again. But she rolled her eyes at her own stupid thoughts and pulled her hair back into a ponytail.

"I am what I am," she said out loud. She smiled then, thinking she sounded like she was quoting the old MGM version of *The Ten Commandments.*

What the hell is she wearing? Maxim thought, and he headed for the old house. Didn't she know how mouth-watering she looked in her ratty old jeans and brown plaid boys' shirt? For a moment, Maxim was fully convinced that Sharlamagne was trying to seduce him. Didn't she understand that he was a man? Didn't she understand that men were very visual beings—that dressing in any provocative manner affected them? Geez!

"Hi," she called as he approached from across the lawn. "I wasn't sure you'd be able to make it."

"Of course I was able to make it," Maxim said, pasting on a smile in an effort to hide the fact that he was nearly drooling at the sight of her in her cute little outfit. "There's work to be done, ain't there?"

Sharlamagne smiled, and he felt somewhat settled down— somewhat. "Wait until you see what I've unearthed in that one larger bedroom," she said. He could see by the twinkle in her eyes that whatever it was must really be good. She was looking at him like she'd never been happier to see anyone in all her life. Yep—whatever his grandmother had left in the large bedroom, it must be something she knew would really catch Sharlamagne Dickens's eye.

"What?" he asked. "More doilies?"

She giggled. "No, you smart aleck. They're these really great prints of, like, romantic scenes and stuff. They're framed, and they're huge… so I didn't dare try to get them out myself."

"Oh, I knew it," Maxim said, shaking his head. "You just want me for my body."

She rolled her eyes, even though she blushed with delight. "I just want you for your muscles, you dork."

He chuckled. She seemed a little more bubbly than he would've expected after she'd already worked a full day at her parents' shop. On the other hand, he felt like crap. He'd gotten up at four a.m. and started working early so he could get enough done to justify leaving work by five to help Sharlamagne.

"Well, lead the way," he said. "Use me for whatever you want to."

She rolled her eyes again and shook her head—though her smile told him she was delighted by his flirting. He'd hoped she would be. He'd worried ever since he left her on her porch Saturday night (in truth, Sunday morning) that he'd pressed her too far with all the kissing. He'd worried she'd feel weird around him now. But she seemed fine. In fact, she seemed more than fine.

"I already pulled a few of the smaller ones out," she began as he followed her to the bedroom. "But the big ones are just too big."

They stepped into the largest of the bedrooms on the bottom floor of the old house, and Maxim smiled. "Ahh! I see you've found copies of the Passion Room pictures."

"What?" she asked, whirling around to face him. "What do you mean?"

"These paintings or prints…or prints of paintings or whatever," he said as he finished pulling the already torn heavy brown paper away from the framed artwork, "they're the same ones that Grandma had me hang in the Passion Room. She told me she had others tucked away somewhere…in case the ones in the room got damaged or something."

Sharlamagne smiled and studied the framed print as Maxim finished removing the brown paper from it. "Really?" she asked. "I love these! And I can totally see why she'd hang them in the infamous Passion Room."

She reached out and gently touched the glass protecting the print. It was a gorgeous print with a medieval theme, depicting a knight carrying a beautiful woman in his arms. The knight did not wear a helmet but was donning the rest of his armor. The woman had long brown braided hair that hung nearly to the knight's knees as he carried her. Her dress was a soft red, and she wore no slippers. The woman gazed up into the handsome knight's face as he gazed down to hers, and their mutual expression of desire caused butterflies to flutter around in Sharlamagne's stomach.

"They're *so* in love," Sharlamagne sighed.

"There's *so* much sexual tension," Maxim said.

"Maxim!" Sharlamagne scolded, turning to face him.

He chuckled. "Oh, right. Sorry. There's so much 's' word–ual tension."

"You are so bad," Sharlamagne pouted. "Can't you see they're in love? He probably just rescued her from some terrible, evil king, and he's whisking her away to—"

"To the Passion Room in his house, so they can—" Maxim chuckled as Sharlamagne's hand clamped over his mouth.

"You are being nasty," she playfully scolded. "Now stop!"

"I'm not being nasty," he laughed, shrugging broad shoulders. "I'm just telling you what's happening. He's carrying her home so he can—"

"He's rescued her, and he's carrying her to the parsonage, or the vicarage or wherever, so they can be married," she explained.

Maxim frowned, studied the print a moment, and then nodded. "Yeah. Yeah, I can see that now," he said. "The only thing is…if you look right here…behind them in the background…" He indicated a place in the distance of the print. "What's that look like to you? That building they're walking *away* from?"

Sharlamagne sighed. "A church. They're walking away from a church."

"Exactly. He's carrying to his house so he can—"

"He's carrying her to the threshold of his house…because they just got married and they're on their way—"

"To the Passion Room in his house," Maxim interrupted with finality. "See? I told you there was a lot of ssss—"

"Don't say it!" Sharlamagne giggled, clamping her hand over his mouth again.

"Okay, okay. I won't say it," Maxim chuckled. "Now where do you want me to haul these paintings to? They won't fit in your car, will they?"

"No. I'll have to have my dad bring the truck. But I just want to put them in a safer place so they don't get damaged while we're moving all this other stuff out."

"Okay," Maxim agreed. "How about I just put them in the front parlor…against that north wall? They should be fine there, right?"

"Yeah." Sharlamagne sighed as she gazed at the print again. She loved romantic art—not modern romantic art, but the old kind—the knights and ladies kind. "I'm going to keep all of these. I'm going to hang them up someday when I have my own house."

"That reminds me," Maxim began as he started to move the painting, "how about helping me move on Saturday?"

"Move?" Sharlamagne asked, suddenly panic-stricken. He was moving? Moving away? "Where are you moving?"

He smiled. "You won't believe me if I tell you."

"Try me," she said as her heart began to hammer with anxiety. Was he moving far away? Would she ever see him again?

"Right down the street from this place. Twenty-one sixteen Whippoorwill Lane. That's me as of Saturday," he answered.

"You're moving down the street?" she asked, overcome with relief. "Why? You already have a big old fancy house."

"I did," he said, his smile fading. "It's ridiculously big and worth a ridiculous amount. I sold it and bought a place I remodeled for a guy down the street a couple of years ago. It's an old Victorian…more like this one than Grandma's though. And smaller. I've always liked it."

"How wonderful for you!" Sharlamagne exclaimed now that her anxiety had been vanquished. Maxim wasn't moving away; he was just moving. "Of course I'll help. After all, it's the least I can do—"

"For using me for my body?" he teased.

"Yeah," she giggled.

He chuckled and took hold of the print's frame once more. "Here," he instructed. "If you help me just slide it out, I can take it the rest of the way."

"Are you sure?" she asked. "It's a lot heavier than it looks."

"What? Are you doubting me now?" he teased as Sharlamagne squeezed between two trunks stacked in front of the print.

"Ouch!" she squealed as she heard the sound of tearing fabric and felt something dig into her flesh.

"Are you all right?" Maxim asked.

"Yeah," she fibbed. "It's just a scratch, I think." Looking down, she saw that she'd neglected to notice that a large piece of metal bracket was sticking out from one of the trunks. Her shirt had caught on it and torn, and the metal had put a pretty mean scratch on the left side of her tummy. Still, she didn't want Maxim to think she was a sissy, so she tried to ignore it.

"Okay then…just push your side of the frame this way, slide it a little, and then I can get it out the rest of the way," he instructed, having bought her downplay of the injury.

Sharlamagne did as he instructed, and soon the print was free.

"Now just show me right where you want it," he said as he maneuvered the print so that his arm span could lift it.

"Just…just right out here," she said, brushing past him as she headed toward the front of the house. She pressed her hand against the aching flesh on her tummy and wiped the little bit of blood on her jeans. "Just right where you said…against that north wall. Thanks, Maxim."

She watched as Maxim carefully set the large frame and print down. "There," he said. "Next?"

He turned around then, his gaze falling to her torn shirt, and she knew she was busted.

"You did hurt yourself," he rather growled, striding determinedly toward her. "What happened?"

"Oh, it's not that bad," she said. "There was just a piece of old metal sticking out off one of those trunks and—"

"Come outside so I can see it better," he ordered, taking her arm and nearly hauling her out of the house.

Once they were outside, Maxim tried to move her shirt out of the way so he could see the wound. But Sharlamagne was shy—greatly unsettled at the thought of his seeing her side and tummy—and pushed his hand away.

He frowned at her and growled. "Here," he said, dropping to one knee. "Let me see it."

"No, no. I'm sure it's nothing," Sharlamagne assured him. However, the sensation of his fingers brushing aside the torn fabric of her shirt caused her entire body to erupt into continuous waves of goose bumps. His touch was too affecting, and she gritted her teeth to keep calm.

"It's not all right," Maxim mumbled, frowning. "It's a pretty bad scratch."

Sharlamagne watched as Maxim simply stripped the shredded fabric from her old plaid shirt and used it to dab at the wound on her stomach. "You don't need stitches or anything...but since that was a pretty rusty piece of metal, we should clean it good."

"I'm sure it will be fine," Sharlamagne said.

Maxim had managed to bury the fiery attraction he was feeling toward Sharlamagne—until the moment he'd dropped to his knee, that is. Instantly, the fragrance of her clothing and skin had washed over him, consuming him like a warm ocean wave. She smelled like vanilla, berries, and fabric softener. To make matters worse, when he put his hands at her waist to steady himself, one hand had inadvertently come to rest on the bareness of her flesh where her shirt had been torn away. The sensation was instantly conquering!

Sure, Maxim had seen plenty of girls in bathing suits, bikinis, and every other manner of revealing attire. But something about this girl—something about Sharlamagne Dickens in an old button-up plaid shirt and ratty jeans—was fascinatingly affective to every sense he owned, both physically and emotionally.

"Looks like that old trunk scratched you when it tore your shirt," he said, allowing his thumb to trace the slightly bleeding welt on Sharlamagne's tummy. She shivered, and he couldn't help but smile—because he sensed it was a pleasurable shiver and not one caused by any pain of his touching the scratch. He pressed the torn-off piece of fabric to the wound for a moment, applying pressure in an effort to slow what very little bleeding there was.

Maxim then reinspected the red, swelling area. "It's not bad at all," he mumbled. He blew on the wound—more out of habit than anything else, just the way his grandmother used to blow on the scrapes he had constantly accosted his knees with when he'd been little. Yet his attention was drawn to the flesh surrounding the wound when he saw goose bumps crop up on Sharlamagne's skin surrounding it.

"What're you doing?" Sharlamagne asked. Maxim sensed her voice held a slight tone of apprehension.

"People always blow on scrapes," he explained. He softly blew on the wound on Sharlamagne's stomach again, this time grinning as he saw more goose bumps appear on her skin. A sudden vision of his grandmother kissing his scraped-up kindergartner's elbow flashed before his eyes, and before he could think better of it, Maxim tucked the piece of torn, bloody fabric in the waistband of his jeans, took Sharlamagne's waist between his hands, and pressed his lips to the scrape at her tummy.

"There now," he said, allowing his thumbs to softly caress her near the scratch. "Supposedly that makes it all better, right?" He blew on the wound one more time, grinning as he saw the lingering goose bumps on Sharlamagne's smooth, warm skin.

"S-supposedly," Sharlamagne managed to answer. She couldn't believe he'd kissed her stomach! She couldn't believe he was touching her skin! Her entire body was still riddled with goose bumps, and she silently prayed he hadn't noticed.

She fought the sudden urge to bury her hands in his hair, drop to her own knees, and lay one heck of an impassioned kiss on him. Instead, she gritted her teeth, attempting to appear unaffected as he rose to his feet once more.

"We really should clean it though. You know, pour some peroxide on it and let it sizzle…smear some antibacterial ointment around," he suggested.

Sharlamagne sighed with disappointment. She had hoped to spend several more hours working at sifting through the stuff in the old Tanner house with Maxim. It miffed her that she'd let herself get injured, thereby ruining her own fun.

"Well," she began, glancing up at the sun, "I suppose it's almost suppertime anyway. I guess I can quit early and go home now instead of working awhile longer."

"Naw. We don't have to quit yet. Grandma has all that first-aid stuff in the main house," Maxim said, smiling at her and gesturing with one thumb over his shoulder toward the big house. "We should take care of it now. You don't want to wait and let it get all swollen and infected. And besides, I've got stuff in the fridge we can make for dinner. Ham, cheese, bread. We can make sandwiches."

"Are you sure?" Sharlamagne asked, delighted that he was willing to allow her to stay—to feed her dinner and let her tend to her scrape.

"Oh yeah," he assured her. "Come on," he said, taking her arm. "We both need a break anyway, right?"

"Yeah," Sharlamagne agreed, hoping she didn't look as wildly anxious as she felt. "After all, you did move that one painting."

He laughed. "Exactly. And I need to eat so I can keep my strength up and move the rest of them, right?"

"Right," Sharlamagne giggled. "You're sure you don't mind?"

Maxim grinned and tried to ignore the little red devil on his left shoulder that was whispering to him that he should whisk Sharlamagne up into his arms and carry her off to his house the way the knight in the damn framed print was doing.

"Of course not," he said. "And anyway, I always wanted to play doctor with you." He chuckled when she smiled at him. He thought it was funny—the way she thought he was kidding.

CHAPTER TWELVE

"I should show you the rest of the house before we go back out," Maxim suggested as he tossed his paper plate in the garbage can in the cupboard under the kitchen sink. "You've never seen the upstairs, have you?"

"Nope," Sharlamagne answered. She was nervous—insanely nervous, for some reason.

She figured it was the residual and delightful aftershocks of having been medically tended to by Maxim. Once he'd seen the scratch on her tummy, he'd insisted they go into the house and tend to it. Sharlamagne had found Maxim's intrigue with peroxide hilarious. As he'd used a cotton ball to saturate her cut with peroxide, his eyes began to glow with an intense interest and anticipation. He'd explained how, as a child, he'd beg his grandmother for a bottle of peroxide and then spend an hour or two pouring it on his scabs, his scrapes, the dirt, moss—anything he thought might give cause for the peroxide to do its magic and begin to fizz. Sharlamagne had giggled when he'd sighed with disappointment when her scratch only produced a mild fizzing. Maxim had sighed and said that the lack of foam and fizz was a good sign—just not as fun as he'd hoped.

He'd used his index finger to rub antibacterial ointment over the welted scratch and then carefully placed two large adhesive bandages over it. The entire experience had been fabulous, wonderful, and marvelous and had left Sharlamagne oddly glad she'd been injured. Maxim's attention was absolutely divine, but it had left her somewhat

231

unsettled. His touch had sent wave after wave of goose bumps rippling over her body, and she worried that she enjoyed it a little too much—that she should have minded a little more that he was touching her stomach.

After Maxim had seen to her miniscule wound, they'd made ham sandwiches and enjoyed light conversation about peroxide and the way slugs oozed out when someone poured salt on them. Yet all through their meal, Sharlamagne felt agitated, nervous, and unable to relax. She couldn't reason why she felt so nervous. She just did. And now that their meal was over and they'd be getting back to work, she was almost glad, hoping that whatever the feelings were that were stirring around inside her would eventually resolve.

"Well, you have to see the upstairs, shawty," Maxim said, taking her paper plate as she handed it to him and tossing it in the garbage with his own. "It's awesome. I mean, admittedly a couple of the bedrooms are a little too girlie for my taste…but Grandma was nothing if not girlie. Right?"

Sharlamagne smiled and nodded. "I was surprised to find this house wasn't fairly dripping in prisms and velvet."

Maxim chuckled. "Well, obviously you've never been upstairs." Sharlamagne smiled as he motioned to her and said, "Come on. You'll love it. It's *very* Elisaveta Tanner."

Sharlamagne smiled at Maxim and said, "Thank you," as he moved aside and gestured that she should precede him.

"I won't tell you what she's named each one," he said as he climbed the stairs behind her. "It'll be more fun to watch your expression when you see for yourself."

"Named what? The rooms?" she asked

"Yeah. Each one has a name…like a bed-and-breakfast would."

"Which reminds me," Sharlamagne began, "what have you decided to do with the house? I mean, you've bought your house down the street, so I'm guessing you've decided not to live in it."

"I'm still thinking along the museum–slash–historical-landmark line," he said. "I just need to find out a little more about it all. I haven't had time yet. I've been too busy being someone's muscle slave in the old house out back."

Sharlamagne stopped in her tracks, just a few steps below the second-floor landing. "If I'm keeping you from stuff, Maxim...you don't need to help me every night. I can do it on my own. Really."

He grinned. "I was teasing you, Sharlamagne," he said. "I like to help you. It gives me something fun to look forward to every day."

Sharlamagne smiled and couldn't help but breathe a little sigh of delight. "Well...if you're sure."

"I'm sure," he confirmed, still grinning up at her. "So...are you ready for your first Elisaveta Tanner room?"

Sharlamagne giggled. "I was born ready."

"You think so, huh?" he said, nodding forward to indicate she should go ahead and climb the last few stairs.

Once they were both on the landing, he said, "Well, do you want to start to the right or the left?"

"Ummm," Sharlamagne said, glancing to either side and seeing that the closest door was to their left. "The left. Like reading...left to right."

"Okay," Maxim said. He took a few steps ahead of her, bowed, and indicated a door that stood ajar to her left. "You might want to read the plaque thing above the door before entering, my lady."

Sharlamagne giggled and moved toward him. As Maxim reached out and lightly shoved the door, causing it to slowly swing inward, Sharlamagne looked up and read the ornately crafted wooden plaque hanging above it.

She giggled. "Ooo! The Lilac Bower?" she whispered. "Sounds very...fragrant."

"Yes, ma'am, it does," Maxim said as he followed her into the room.

Sharlamagne's eyes widened as she gazed around the stunning room. "So...the Lilac Bower. The perfect lady's boudoir!" she giggled.

"I know, huh?" Maxim said. "I still can't believe all the lilac stuff Grandma found for this room. The day I finished the remodel, I thought the lilac paint on the accent wall and the white-based wallpaper with the little lilac pattern would be the end of it. But, no! I came back a week later to find the queen canopy bed totally drenched in a white lace canopy, complete with lilac-themed quilt and pillow thingies." He nodded toward the wall to their left. "And the romantic couple kissing near the lilac tree painting there? Where do you find that? She's even had doily things made in the shapes of lilac bunches to place under the hurricane lamps that have lilacs painted on the shades." He pointed to two beautiful Queen Anne chairs positioned near the windows. "I mean...where did she find an upholsterer to reupholster those chairs in lilac stuff? And naturally, when they were in bloom like they are now, she had tons of fresh lilac bunches sitting around in here...you know, in crystal vases and stuff. At which point it *was* very fragrant."

Sharlamagne's smile broadened—for sure enough, both Queen Anne chairs were upholstered in a beautiful lilac tapestry-type cloth. The bed *was* totally drenched in lilac-themed bedding, and the hurricane lamps with little lilac embellishments on their shades *did* sit on doilies crocheted in a lilac pattern.

"So...she was holding out on me where the doilies were concerned, eh?" she teased.

"What is it with women and doilies?" Maxim asked, shaking his head with feigned exasperation. He smiled then and walked across the room. "Now, if you'll follow me, madame, to the window seat here— also upholstered in lilac crap—you'll see the wonderful view from the window."

Sharlamagne laughed when she looked down to see that even the throw rugs in the room had lilac patterns on them. She admired Elisaveta Tanner all the more in that moment, for to decorate an entire room in a lilac theme and not have it feel noisy to linger in was a true gift. And this room was not at all noisy; rather, it owned a loveliness that soothed the senses somehow.

"Here," Maxim said, nodding toward the window seat. "Sit down for a minute and enjoy the view."

Sharlamagne did as he instructed, bursting into giggles when she saw that the room overlooked the house Mrs. Tanner had left to her— the house that was now totally surrounded by gorgeous lilac trees in full bloom.

"I see she was very into detail, your grandma," she said to Maxim.

She sighed with melancholy. "And if there's one thing I know about Elisaveta Tanner…it's that she could find anything in any theme she ever wanted."

"No kidding," he said, striding toward the mantel. "Which leads me to believe that you're the only person, other than me, who will appreciate this little detail."

Sharlamagne followed him to the mantel, smiling with amused pleasure when she saw the brass-based, crystal, dangling-prism-drenched compote adorning the center of the mantel. The crystal bowl of the compote was filled with dried lilac blooms, but it was the base— the brass lilac sprigs pedestal poised on its marble base—that was so astonishing.

"A lilac pedestal compote?" Sharlamagne giggled.

"Complete with prisms," Maxim added. Sharlamagne looked to him then—saw that his blue eyes were sparkling with both the pain of losing his grandmother and the joy of what she had meant to him.

"I've never seen one like this before," Sharlamagne remarked as she studied the piece. "She must've paid an arm or a leg for it."

"More likely it cost her a kidney," Maxim chuckled under his breath. Striding to a door to their right, Maxim opened it to reveal a small bathroom, also entirely lilac-themed. "Grandma was in to private bathrooms. She thought every person or couple should have their own bathroom."

"I agree with her," Sharlamagne said. She looked to Maxim and smiled. "And I'm sure you do too…considering your aversion to public restrooms."

"Har har, sugar bee. You're a real scream," he mumbled as he turned to leave the room.

Sharlamagne sighed, not wanting to leave such a lovely setting. She thought she could probably linger in the lilac room—the Lilac Bower—for days and not grow weary of its serene beauty. Still, she followed him out of the room, wondering—if the Lilac Bower was so fabulous, what did the other upstairs rooms look like?

"So you wanna just zigzag back and forth?" Maxim asked her as they stepped into the upstairs hallway once more.

"Sure," she answered.

"Then enter at your own risk, baby," he said, striding to a door standing ajar just a little further up the hallway. "Because next on the tour is the infamous Passion Room."

A strange thrill traveled through Sharlamagne as she watched Maxim give the door a little shove so that it slowly swung inward.

Pausing at the entrance to the room, Sharlamagne looked up to the wildly ornate plaque above the door. "*The Passion Room*," she mumbled. Then, as Maxim pointed to a small brass sign fixed to the wall to the right of the doorframe, she read, "*To Those Who Seek the Trove: Seek what you desire and leave only as two who shared fleeting passion. Find the trove and leave as lovers—and consorts of the soul.*" As Sharlamagne's eyebrows arched, she looked to Maxim and said, "Ooo! That's serious stuff."

"Very serious," Maxim said. He grinned, his eyes narrowing with mischief as he looked at her and asked, "Are you sure you want to go in there with me? What if the room takes us over and we find ourselves embroiled in—"

"Don't say it!" she scolded, clamping a hand over his mouth.

He pushed her hand away and chuckled. "I was only going to say sssizzling passion. That's all I was going to say."

"Sure you were," she giggled.

"So…I dare you to go in with me," he teased. "Unless you're afraid you can't resist whatever supernatural power Grandma always claimed hangs out in there."

Inhaling deeply and forcing an expression of triumph to her face as she looked at Maxim, Sharlamagne reached out, took his hand, and stepped into the room.

"Wow!" she breathed as she looked around. "Wow!"

"I know, huh?" Maxim chuckled. "It's pretty awesome."

"I mean, wow!" Sharlamagne said, shaking her head with disbelief.

The room was incredible. She'd never imagined it would look so beautiful—so passionately beautiful! In her wildest dreams, she'd never seen such a gorgeous room. A huge four-poster bed, the head of which was against the wall to her left, drew her attention first. It was a magnificent piece. The wood boasted a dark stain, which was so perfectly complemented by the deep, crimson comforter, crimson and gold throw pillows, and sheer, golden head canopy hanging from the ceiling that it made Sharlamagne want to turn around, grab the front of Maxim's shirt, and pull him down to sharing passionate kisses on it!

Her attention next fell to the fireplace on the opposite wall from where she now stood. The stone used for it was lovely, and the stonework was even lovelier. A chaise lounge, again upholstered in crimson, was placed before the fireplace, accompanied by a large, crimson velvet chair. A small, low-legged table was situated between the chaise lounge and the larger chair, and an absolutely breathtaking, chandelier-type lamp (simply dripping with dangling prisms) was the only thing setting on it. The mantel above the fireplace boasted a crystal, prism-adorned compote to one side, filled nearly to overflowing with what looked like a combination of dried hydrangea blossoms, red and golden rose leaves, and several small pinecones. Along the rest of the mantel stood several vintage Edwardian wedding portraits in authentic time-period folders, pinecones and rose petals neatly strewn between them.

Sharlamagne's attention was drawn back to the bed—to the wonderful end tables on each side of the bed at its head. Each little table boasted drop-leaves on either side, a small drawer at its front, and elaborately carved legs. Small hurricane lamps with red globes sat on the surface of each table, and again the rose petals, hydrangea petals, and small pinecones added to the romantic, vintage feel of the lamps and tables.

"And there's your picture from the old house," Maxim said.

"What?" Sharlamagne asked, so overwhelmed by the beauty of the room that she couldn't quite comprehend what he was referring to at first.

"Right there," he said, striding to the wall opposite of the bed. "There's your knight and his...um...bride."

Sharlamagne smiled as she looked up to see another copy of the print she'd been helping Maxim move when she injured herself on the old trunk. Yes—it was the same handsome knight, carrying the same beautiful woman *away* from the church.

"Oh, it's so much more affecting in here," she said as she approached it. "Look at that frame! I think it's authentic Edwardian."

"Of course it's authentic...whoever Edwardian was," Maxim teased. "My grandmother bought it, didn't she?"

"And this print...well...it actually is a painting," Sharlamagne observed out loud. "She must've really loved it...to commission someone to do a repro of it. That's expensive stuff."

"Like I said," Maxim began with a smile, "my grandmother bought it, didn't she?"

"It's beautiful! The frame is...it's astonishing," Sharlamagne added as she touched the vintage, gold-painted frame.

"I actually like this one better though," Maxim said.

Sharlamagne turned to see him looking toward the wall that owned the entrance door. She gasped when she saw the print—rather reproduced painting—hanging against the crimson accent wall.

"Wow!" she breathed! "I love that one!"

"Here," Maxim said, going to a row of light switches near the door. "It's hard to see it at dusk like this. But here." He flipped a switch, and not only did the beautiful lamps in the room turn on to create a soft glow, but two prismed sconces on either side of the painting he'd drawn Sharlamagne's attention to lit up. Combined with the small recessed lighting in the ceiling above the painting, the light perfectly displayed the work.

"It's so beautiful," Sharlamagne said, shaking her head as she approached. "Again...a vintage frame and a repro painting. I really do love it."

"I figured you would," Maxim said as he stood next to her studying the painting.

The painting on the wall before her was the most romantic she'd ever seen. There was something about it—something different than others she'd seen of the same style and period. For one thing, the knight in the picture was very, very masculine—not soft and wistful-looking like most portrayals of knights, but strong, broad-shouldered, square-jawed, and handsome. The woman the knight held in his arms was lovely as well. She wore a crimson gown and seemed to be desperately clutching the knight's armored arms as his head was poised ready to kiss her. Their lips were so close—so close to meeting in a kiss—that it was nearly frustrating to Sharlamagne. She wanted to shout, *Kiss her!* but simply bit her tongue and gazed at the beauty of the art.

"And wait until you see the bathroom in here," Maxim said, taking her hand and pulling her away from the beautiful scene of a knight ready to kiss his lady.

"What is it with you and bathrooms?" she giggled as he opened the door and flipped on the light as they stepped in.

Maxim looked at her, an expression of being perplexed on his face. "They're the hardest part of the remodel, woman!" he informed her. "And this one was a bast—monster."

Sharlamagne giggled. He was so funny.

"So? What do you think?" he asked.

"It's incredible. Just like the entire room!" she told him.

And it was! First of all, the standing, lion-footed porcelain tub was enormous. Sharlamagne pointed to it and arched her eyebrows with awe.

"Yeah…special ordered, and it cost a mint," Maxim confirmed. He winked. "Big enough for two, if you know what I mean."

Sharlamagne blushed, rolled her eyes, and stepped further into the bathroom.

"What?" he chuckled. "Grandma's the one who wanted it that way. Not me."

"And there's a shower too?" she asked as she saw the shower, complete with beautifully stitched, crimson shower draperies.

"Yep," Maxim answered. Lowering his voice, he leaned over and whispered in her ear, "Complete with two showerheads…if you get the implication."

"Stop it!" she playfully scolded, shoving an elbow back into his stomach.

"Two standing porcelain sinks, with individual mirrors above," he pointed out. "A little toilet 'closet,' as my grandmother always called them…so that you don't have to actually look at the toilet when you're bathing or getting ready for the day. Grandma hated toilets. She couldn't stand looking at them and always insisted they were in their own little 'closets,'" he explained.

"So your toilet thing originally stems from her, huh?" Sharlamagne teased.

He laughed a little. "Yeah, I guess."

"Well, Maxim," she began, "I can honestly say that—with all the compotes in here filled with dried roses and hydrangeas and all the little cherub statues and romantic art on the walls—this is by far the prettiest bathroom I've ever been in."

"Joke if you want…but Grandma took it very seriously," he told her.

"I can see that," she giggled.

Maxim turned off the light, and they left the beautiful bathroom. As they stepped back into the main bedroom once more, Sharlamagne's attention was again drawn to a painting, this one hanging on the wall across from the bathroom, to the right of the bed.

"She had a way of finding wonderful things, didn't she?" Sharlamagne thought aloud as she studied the third painting of a knight and his lady, this time entwined in each other's arms and sharing a very passionate kiss.

"She did," Maxim agreed.

Sharlamagne sighed, turned to Maxim, and asked, "So what is so special about it…this Passion Room?" she asked. "I mean, the pages I found in the book profess it has magical powers or something. But where did that all come from? Did she just make it up? Or were, like, two lovers murdered in here or something? Was some great artist conceived in here or what?"

"See?" he said, smiling at her. "That's one of the things I really like about you—that imagination you have. Murdered lovers and the conception of artists? I would've said something like maybe it was once a honeymoon suite or something."

"That's because you're a guy," Sharlamagne teased. "And what does that mean…*the trove*? It kind of really piques your curiosity, huh?"

"Well, I've been in this room a thousand times, and I just don't get it either. Grandma never told me, so I just always assumed it was a gimmick she'd made up for when the house was a bed-and-breakfast or something one day. I still think it looks like a honeymoon suite," he explained. He looked at her then, grinning the same grin of mischief Sharlamagne had seen him grin so many times over the past weeks—the grin that always sent goose bumps prickling her arms and a delightful shiver racing up her back.

"Do you want to stay in here a little while and talk? You know, see if the ghost of some dead lover or Passion Room–conceived artist shows up to explain it all?" Maxim asked, taking hold of Sharlamagne's arm. She turned to look at him, rendered breathless by the smoldering mischief apparent in his eyes as he reached beyond her, closing the door and isolating them in the Passion Room. "Don't you think we should test it? You know…see if Grandma was right about this room or if she was just being theatrical as usual."

"Test it?" Sharlamagne squeaked as her heart's rhythm increased times ten.

"Sure," Maxim mumbled, taking her hands in his and leading her further back into the room. "Come on, Sharlamagne Dickens. Let's see what happens. Live on the edge for a minute or two. Let's linger in the Passion Room and see if some sort of magic overpowers us."

Sharlamagne smiled, wildly enraptured by his flirting. "But we've already been in here for, like, fifteen minutes," she reminded him.

"So? It's dark outside now. Maybe the room works better at night or something."

Sharlamagne smiled at him. How could she resist smiling at him? He was so very, very handsome—so very, very alluring—so very, very delicious from head to toe, and inside and out.

"So you're saying you want me stay in a room now that it's night… to stay in a room that's notorious for leading to…to…"

"To sss—" Maxim began to tease.

But Sharlamagne's hand over his mouth silenced him. "Don't say it!" she scolded, blushing.

Pushing her hand away from his mouth, he said, "I was only going to say ssscandalous passion."

"Sure you were," she whispered, still blushing. Her blush deepened as a sudden and nearly uncomfortable heat washed over when she felt his hand at her waist—as he pulled her against him.

"So what do you say, sugar bee? Wanna test the supernatural with me?" he mumbled. "Do you wanna tempt fate and see what really happens in here? Let's kiss and see what happens, Sharlamagne. Just one kiss. If all Grandma's hype about the room is true…we should know it with just one kiss, right?"

Sharlamagne felt his hand against the bare skin of her waist where her shirt was torn. His touch was warm and affecting. She could sense the calluses on his palms—the strength in his fingers. He lightly kissed her cheek—softly blew on her neck.

"Well, I…I'm not sure we should," she stammered, breathless and trembling. She felt she had to put up a resistance of some sort—though, in truth, she had no desire to resist him—none whatsoever.

"Wrong answer," he mumbled a moment before his mouth pressed to hers.

There was no timid spark of affection between them the way there had been the night of the World War II ball—only an instantaneous eruption of driven, fiery desire! In the space of one mere instant, Sharlamagne found herself wrapped in Maxim Tanner's powerful arms, her own arms resting at his shoulders as her hands caressed the back of his neck, her fingers weaving up through the hair at the back of his head.

She was immediately swept away in breathless ecstasy as they kissed, and she briefly wondered what had happened to propriety, coyness, or any fiber of social timidity between them. But as Maxim's hot, moist mouth demanded wild reciprocation from hers, Sharlamagne's rational thoughts disappeared as quickly as did her inhibitions.

His hair between her fingers felt like the softest sable. The scent of his skin in her nostrils was like some intoxicating zephyr, and the feel of his mouth—the feel of his mouth was some savory dessert—a warm, moist, tempting indulgence. The rough stubble of his whiskers chafed the tender flesh of her chin, but she wouldn't have cared if it abraded her skin to bleeding—for the euphoric delirium his mouth was working over her was far too blissful to give up.

A low moan escaped Maxim as he ground his open mouth more savagely against Sharlamagne's. Holy hell, he wanted to devour her! For a moment, he was astonished at her response—the way she met the endeavors of his mouth, demanding kiss for demanding kiss. His mouth was watering with an insatiable thirst for hers—the palms of his hands burning from the feel of her flesh beneath them where he held her. He was glad she'd torn her shirt—glad the entire lower half of one side of it was gone so that his hands could rove over the warm, smooth skin of her waist.

Maxim's every sense could feel Sharlamagne Dickens. She smelled of warm vanilla and taunting flavor. Her skin was like the smoothest, soft satin, and the curves of her body fit perfectly to the lines of his. Her mouth tasted like sugar and spice and everything that was ever possibly nice, and he could not quench his thirst for the essence of it.

He literally wanted to throw her on the bed and ravage her! Instead, he opted for breaking the seal of their lips long enough to push her back against one large bedpost at the foot of the bed. She gasped as he tasted her neck, placing long, moist kisses at the hollow of her throat as her hands fisted in his hair. He thought an imp must have surely possessed him then, as he grinned a moment and adhered his mouth to the soft flesh at the side of her neck, coaxing the blood beneath her skin to rise and gently bruise her there.

But even the brief moments necessary to leave his mark on her neck were too long for his mouth to be absent from hers, and wrapping his arms around Sharlamagne and the bedpost behind her, Maxim crushed his wonting kiss to her mouth again.

He paused only long enough to growl, "Kiss me," and chuckle with triumph as she clutched the collar of his shirt in her fists and pulled his mouth tight against hers in obeying him.

Sharlamagne couldn't breathe! And yet, she felt her lungs might burst with being so filled with unparalleled pleasure. Could it be that Elisaveta Tanner had been right? Was there something about the Passion Room that drizzled a hypnotic spell of unbridled excitement and physical fervor over its occupants? Surely Maxim wouldn't be kissing her like this if there wasn't some bewitching thing about it. And she certainly would never have had the courage to kiss him if there weren't.

She paused, taking his face in her hands and gazing at him a moment. Could it really be? Could she really be captured up against a bedpost kissing Maxim Tanner? His eyes were a sapphire smolder, their expression conveying that he was not finished with her yet.

Again with an unfamiliar courage burning in her chest, Sharlamagne slowly drew his head toward hers once more, kissing his lower lip in a lingering, teasing manner. He allowed her to toy with him for a moment, though she felt his hands leave the bedpost and slide to her waist once more. His touch was irresistible, and she slowly pressed a moist kiss to his mouth.

"Kiss me," she breathed against his lips, and she felt him smile as his mouth melded to hers with renewed enthusiasm.

Maxim's blood was literally boiling! He wanted her like he'd never wanted anything in all his life. The physical effect she was having on him was almost unbearably taunting. Her kisses provoked a hunger in him he wasn't so sure he could deny, and taking her by the waist, he quickly lifted her, sweeping her feet out from under her so that she toppled back onto the soft, red comforter on the bed.

He'd lost his mind, and he didn't care. As he hovered over her a moment, the way a lion might hover over its recently incapacitated prey, he quickly studied her face. Maxim saw nothing but welcome in her eyes—encouragement and desire. Therefore, he crushed his lips to hers once more, grinding such an impassioned kiss against her tender mouth as to render her entirely breathless.

Sharlamagne did not know how it came to be that she was lying on her back on the bed, comfortable and warm on the velvety surface of the crimson comforter. The way she'd arrived there did not register in her recklessly distracted mind. She had no conscious recollection of how Maxim had managed to maneuver them both to the bed. She only knew that he now hovered over her—kissing her—caressing her stomach with one hand as he supported his weight with the other.

Maxim's kisses were masterful! Sharlamagne had never before imagined she could know such searing passion—such overwhelming desire! In all her life, she had never experienced anything the likes of what Maxim was causing her to feel—euphoria, bliss, fervent, desperate longing!

Suddenly she felt the weight of his body relax onto hers. Taking her face between his powerful hands, he deepened their kiss—though she would have thought it impossible to deepen what was already so ablaze. His mouth lingered at her neck for several moments, and then, without warning, he suddenly rolled his body from hers to lie on his back next to her.

"Sorry," he mumbled, resting one arm across his eyes and forehead as his broad, muscular chest rose and fell with the labored breathing of restrained passion. "I'm not usually such a...such a panther."

Instantly Sharlamagne was humiliated by her own unguarded behavior. He must think she was a total skank—making out with him as if she were his girlfriend—or more even than a girlfriend.

"It wasn't your fault," she began. "I-I don't know what my deal is. I hope you don't think I'm—"

She gasped when he rolled to his side, took her chin firmly in one hand, and growled, "What I think is that *you* are delicious. I swear, I wanna eat you up."

His mouth was hot and demanding. It was as if he wanted to consume her somehow, and any resistance she had melted. She clutched at the fabric of his shirt, fisting it in her hands and pulling him closer to her.

Maxim knew he had to stop. Thoughts of tearing her clothes from her body, of keeping her there all through the night, were ricocheting around in his brain. He was out of control—he had to stop. Thus, abruptly he broke the seal of their mouths and fairly leapt up from the bed, taking her hand and pulling her to her feet as well.

"It's getting late," he explained. "And you know what Grandma always used to say. The devil does his best work in the dark."

"Yeah," Sharlamagne breathlessly whispered. "My mom always says the same thing."

He led her to the door—to their means of escaping the Passion Room. Yet he paused before opening it. Pressing her back against the wall next to the door, Maxim couldn't resist taking one last, powerful drink of her mouth. Goose bumps broke over his arms as Sharlamagne sighed and relaxed against him while returning his kiss.

He wondered for a moment if there were actually something to his grandmother's claims concerning the Passion Room. Would he be unable to control himself if he lingered longer in the room with Sharlamagne in his arms—with their mouths so perfect in the rhythm of their kiss? Would all their shared moral values—all their determination to save the most intimate happening between a man and a women for their individual marriages—be sacrificed as the legend of the Passion Room claimed?

"Have you had enough of me for today?" he asked, hoping Sharlamagne was feeling stronger than he was at that moment.

Maxim winced with shattered hope, yet knew simultaneous euphoria, when breathlessly she whispered, "No."

"Then we'll stay close to the door. That way we can leave whenever we're ready...right?" he breathed.

"Right," she mumbled as their mouths met in a renewed sharing of passion.

I love you! Don't you realize that I love you? Sharlamagne's mind silently shouted as Maxim kissed her, as his powerful body kept hers prisoner against the bedroom wall. *I love you! I want you to love me! I want you to marry me! I want to sleep with you, have a family with you! Maxim! Don't you know how perfectly I love you?* her mute heart cried.

She felt him tremble—or shiver suddenly. But then she wasn't certain whether it was Maxim who was trembling or her.

"Sharlamagne," he mumbled as he broke the seal of their lips and began to step back from her.

"No," she breathed, however, wrapping her arms under his and pulling him to her once more. "I don't want you to stop kissing me," she whispered against his mouth.

She felt his arms enfold her—felt his hands slide over her back until he finally buried them in her hair, fisting it almost uncomfortably. His mouth was voracious when he kissed her again, as if some insatiable thirst or hunger had gained control of him—a thirst or hunger he could neither quench nor satisfy in any regard.

Freshly cut wood—cedar, pine, and something her reeling senses couldn't identify—that's what he smelled like. Maxim smelled like wood and her favorite manly cologne—like trees and grass with a hint of motor oil. Sharlamagne felt her heart swell all of a sudden, and she was having trouble catching her breath.

I love you! her mind screamed in silence. *That's why I'm here with you...because I love you!*

His mouth left hers, traveling hungrily over her neck to her collarbone.

"I'm losing it, Sharlamagne," he mumbled against her neck. "You're doing something to me, and if I don't get away from you...I can't promise I'll be able to let you out of here without—"

"It's not me," she whispered. "It's the room. That's all it is."

Sharlamagne wanted to cry. It *was* the room—she knew it was! For all her reputation of being overdramatic, Mrs. Tanner was right—there was something about the Passion Room—something that had caused a man the perfect likes of Maxim Tanner to think he wanted to seduce Sharlamagne.

She felt tears welling in her eyes as he took her chin in his hand, kissed her softly on the mouth, and said, "It's not the room."

One last playful tug at her lower lip, and Maxim released her, reached beyond her, and opened the door. "It's getting late," he said.

"Y-yeah," she stammered, still breathless. "I-I guess so."

They stepped into the hallway, and the cool breeze wafting in from the room across the way served to calm Maxim's body somewhat.

"Th-thanks for your help today," Sharlamagne offered. She was blushing, uncertain as to what to say to the man she'd just spent she didn't know how long making out with. "I couldn't have done all that without you."

Maxim shrugged, raking a strong hand through his ebony hair. "I like helping you out there. It's like a treasure hunt or something… waiting to see what Grandma tucked away for you to find."

"It is fun, isn't it? Almost like she's still here in a way."

Maxim nodded, and Sharlamagne blushed again as he stared at her, grinning. "Well?" he asked. "What do you think?"

"About what?" she asked, feigning ignorance. She knew darn well what he meant. He was asking her what she thought about the legend of the Passion Room.

"About Grandma's infamous Passion Room," he explained unnecessarily. "Do you think it's bewitched or enchanted or anything? Or do you think our mouths just fit together that well naturally?"

Sharlamagne couldn't imagine Maxim Tanner would've kissed her the way he had if the room truly wasn't under some sort of supernatural hold. But of course she didn't believe in such things as a room holding paranormal powers of persuasion. Yet what he'd said about their mouths—fitting together so well. She was rattled. Entirely rattled—and still trembling from being in his arms.

"I-I don't know," she managed at last. "I can't imagine that you would really want to…I mean…I'm not normally so…so…"

"Uninhibited?" he offered, smiling at her. "Me neither," he added with a smile. It soothed her a little. He shrugged. "Anyway, if nothing else, I took care of one of your 'I've never done such-and-such' things, now didn't I?"

Sharlamagne frowned, entirely puzzled. What was he talking about?

"What?" she asked.

Maxim chuckled. Reaching out, he moved the collar of her shirt a little and frowned.

"Of course, it's not a very good one. Hardly visible," he said. "Will you let me fix it?"

"Fix what?" Sharlamagne asked. Her senses were still reeling, and with the way his thumb was caressing her neck, she couldn't think straight.

"Come here," he said, pulling her against him.

Sharlamagne gasped with delirium as she felt him kiss her neck— and they weren't even in the Passion Room! It only took a moment, however, for her to realize exactly what Maxim was doing. He was no longer kissing her neck—he was sucking on it!

"What are you doing?" she exclaimed, struggling until he released her.

"Fixing it," he answered. "You could hardly see it before, and I wanted to make sure you couldn't say you've never had a hickey anymore."

"What?" she squealed, rushing to the hanging mirror at the end of the hall. "You did *not* do that!"

"And now I can never say I've never given one," he laughed. "That's my first one, you know."

Sharlamagne pulled aside her collar—her mouth gaping open in mingled horror and delight as she studied the nickel-sized bruise on her neck.

"Maxim!" she breathed, uncertain as to which emotion broiling in her was strongest—desire, worry, delight, or guilt.

"Yeah?" he asked, smiling as she turned around to face him.

She felt the heat of humiliation rising to her cheeks. What must he think of her? How could she let herself be so carried away like that? She was a level-headed girl—wasn't she? What he did to her—the way he knocked down every one of her defenses every time she was around him—the way he made her mouth water, her heart smolder, and her arms ache to hold him—it was dangerous. *He* was dangerous!

"Did you lie to me?" she asked, suddenly angry and hurt inside.

"What?" he asked, frowning. "About what?"

"About...about the 'v' word," she mumbled. "You said I wasn't the only...last week when we were sitting on the back porch...when we were eating cherries…and you said I wasn't the only…the only…"

"That you weren't the only virgin sitting on the porch?" he finished for her. "It's not a bad word, Sharlamagne."

"I know," she said, glancing down to the floor.

"But what do you mean by asking me if I lied about it?" he asked. He looked irritated—nearly angry.

Sharlamagne paused in explaining. But what had happened between them in the Passion Room—the emotion and physical desire he'd evoked in her—she had to ask him.

"Did you lie about it? I mean…I can't imagine that you're that good at making a woman feel…you know…like, lose control and stuff…if you're not…you know…experienced in…you know…seducing them," she sputtered. "I mean…you must think I'm a tramp! The way I acted in there…you must think…"

Maxim was flattered and offended at the same time. She thought he was promiscuous—experienced in making women lose control? That's what she meant? He was hurt. And yet, obviously she'd experienced something herself that she never had before, and by that, he was flattered.

Thus, even for the frustration he was feeling, he interrupted her. "I think you're hot, Sharlamagne. I think you're smart, funny, sensitive… and secretly very passionate." She blushed, and he knew she needed reassurance. He'd pushed her too far in the Passion Room—that was his own fault. Why wouldn't she think he was intent on seducing her— that he was experienced at seduction?

"You drive me wild," he mumbled, reaching out and wrapping his arms around her waist. "Like, literally drive me wild. And I just want to return the favor…that's all." He pressed a soft kiss to her neck and felt her breathing increase. "And as far as being experienced in seducing women," he mumbled against her neck, "I was telling the truth when we were sitting on the porch that day. You're actually the only girl I've ever wanted to seduce." He felt her begin to relax in his arms—felt her hands travel over his biceps to his shoulders. "But I won't seduce you right now. I promise…okay?"

"Okay," she breathed as their mouths met.

Her hands caressing the back of his neck sent goose bumps racing over his arms and legs. He'd have to be careful—not press her too much—or she wouldn't believe him. But he sighed and ground his mouth to hers as she pulled him tightly against her as she rather stumbled back against the wall. He could feel it in her—that her desire was nearly as rich and ripe as his—and they weren't even in that damn Passion Room.

CHAPTER THIRTEEN

"So don't try moving anything too heavy by yourself, okay?" Maxim instructed.

"Okay," Sharlamagne promised, wiping a tear from her cheek as she held her cell phone to her ear.

He wasn't coming. For the first time in weeks, Maxim wasn't meeting her after work to help her sort through the things in the old house. Every heartbreaking reason her mind could possibly concoct was running through her brain tissue—she'd been too easy with him the day before—too perfectly easy to conquer during their time together in the Passion Room and afterward, when they'd spent two hours in the hallway kissing, hugging, talking, and then kissing.

When Sharlamagne had detailed what had happened between her and Maxim to Gwen early that morning, Gwen had assured her that all was well.

"Finally!" she'd exclaimed. "Finally you've found the one guy in the universe that you can totally be yourself with."

Naturally Sharlamagne was a little uncertain about the level of propriety of the entire event. After all, her lips were still nearly numb from so much kissing, not to mention the purple bruise on her neck— proof positive that Maxim Tanner was always full of mischief in any given situation.

Yet Gwen had reassured her. "Look, Shar. Without that kind of attraction, the human race would've been wiped out long ago. It's natural, after all. And when you keep it in check like you did last night…I mean, there you guys were in a house—an empty house, I might add—filled with nothing but empty bedrooms stuffed with empty beds. And what did you do? You made out in the hallway, with no inappropriate groping, no rolling around on the floor…nothing beyond kissing. You're fine. You just like him so much you're worried about everything, that's all."

Gwen had been right—Sharlamagne knew she was. It was everything she'd already told herself. But now—now that Maxim was on the phone telling her he couldn't make it that evening—the ugly dark dinginess of doubt began to overwhelm her.

"I want to be sure everything's ready so that I really can move in on Saturday," Maxim was explaining. "And I'm just now at Carl Rowlands's office. He had some stuff I needed to look at, and I've got to meet with the real-estate agent in forty-five minutes to get the keys to the new place. So…will you be okay there by yourself tonight?"

"Oh, sure!' Sharlamagne managed to answer.

She was trying to believe him—trying to believe he wasn't just ditching her and chalking her up as a conquest. Still, she knew him better than that—she did. He wasn't like a lot of other guys. He was sincere. Gritting her teeth, she turned her thoughts from doubt and suspicion to determination not to let fear and discouragement muddy everything up.

"And I won't do any heavy lifting," she added.

"Good," he said. "But if you tear your shirt or anything…call me, and I'll drop whatever I'm doing and come and kiss it better for you, okay?"

Sharlamagne giggled. With one sentence, he'd vanquished almost all her uncertainties.

"Okay," she said. "I will."

He chuckled, and the sound warmed her. "Okay then. I'll see you tomorrow at about five thirty. All right?"

"All right."

"Okay. Bye, Sharlamagne," he said.

"Bye," she sighed.

Sharlamagne smiled and tucked her cell phone in her back pocket.

It was okay; everything was all right between them. Maxim simply had things to do after work. She couldn't expect to him to help her every day for the rest of his life, could she?

With more confidence in the fact that what had happened between them the night before really *wasn't* because of mystical power of the Passion Room—that there was more to it than mere lust—Sharlamagne opened a box in the room she'd been working in. Instantly, she giggled when she saw that whatever was causing the box to feel heavy was protected by a layer of doilies.

"Everything okay?" Carl asked.

"Yeah," Maxim answered. "Everything's great."

"I'm glad to hear it," Carl said. "No problems with your parents or anything?"

Maxim shook his head. "I haven't heard one word from them since you cut them their checks and they hightailed out your door to start spending Grandma's money."

"Well, as warped as it may sound…I'm glad to hear that too," Carl mumbled. "Now, I've got just a few more things to go over with you." Maxim watched as Carl withdrew a large manila envelope from his desk drawer. Reaching inside, he withdrew three smaller manila envelopes and a small, ancient-looking key and laid them all on his desk, returning the larger envelope to its drawer.

Maxim instantly recognized his grandmother's handwriting on the front of each envelope and on the small tag on the key, and his heart began to race. "What is all this?" he asked, feeling rather desperate to handle the items.

"These are things your grandmother entrusted to me…to hold for you until today, actually," Carl explained.

"Okay," Maxim said. "But what are they?"

"Well, first let's go with the key here," Carl began. He handed the old brass key (looking to be approximately two inches in length) to Maxim. "Go ahead and read the note," Carl instructed.

Maxim felt a pang of pain pinch his heart as he looked at his grandmother's beautiful handwriting. It was so familiar. He loved it; he missed seeing it.

"*Maxim, darling. Put this key on your key ring this minute, and keep it with you always. You'll know when and where to use it one day,*" Maxim read. He grinned and shook his head. "She always liked to string me along with little mysteries," he explained to Carl. "I'm glad she still does."

Carl laughed. "Me too. Me too. I miss her," he said. "I've never known anyone like Elisaveta…and I know I never will again."

"Ain't it the truth?" Maxim said as he pulled his key ring from his pocket and proceeded to add the old brass key to it.

"So that's it?" Carl asked. "You'll just put it with the rest of your keys…and then what?"

Maxim chuckled. "Oh, you know Grandma. There's no trying to outguess her plans. If she says I'll know when to used it and where… she's got some way planned for me to just trip over it someday and figure it out."

"Wow! That would drive me crazy," Carl chuckled.

"It used to drive me crazy…when I was a kid," Maxim agreed. "But Grandma was big on teaching moments, and this kind of thing was how she always displayed 'lessons in patience, Maxim, darling.' So I've just learned to deal with it."

Carl laughed. "Oh, yeah. I guess I actually know what you're talking about. She always said to me, 'Good things come to those who *patiently* wait, Carl, dear.'"

"That's Grandma." Maxim smiled and returned his keys to his jeans pocket. "Now what other kind of mischief is she up to here?" he asked, studying the envelopes on Carl's desk.

"Well, first we have this one." Carl handed Maxim one of the envelopes.

"*To my Maxim,*" Maxim began reading aloud. "*To be opened whenever you like…especially if you're missing me.*" Maxim felt moisture rise to his eyes. "Well, that one's gonna have to wait until I'm alone and willing to get in touch with the child within, right?"

"That would be my suggestion, yes," Carl agreed. "And next…" He handed Maxim another envelope.

"Hmm…intriguing," Maxim said, grinning. "*To my Maxim. To be opened on the first morning following your wedding night.*"

"Wow!" Carl chuckled. "Following your wedding night, eh? So I guess she's not offering any advice on, or last minute explanations of, the ol' birds and the bees, huh?"

Maxim shook his head, entirely amused by his grandmother's familiar antics. Oh, how he missed her! He ached with missing her. He knew he always would.

"Nope. I guess I'm on my own with that one," Maxim said.

"And last but not least," Carl said, offering the third envelope to Maxim.

"*To my Maxim,*" he read. "*To be opened in Carl Rowlands's office, in Carl Rowlands's presence, on the last occasion you have to meet with him concerning my estate.*"

Carl shook his head. "Okay, I'll admit that *that* one about put me in the nuthouse with curiosity."

Maxim smiled. "I can imagine." Looking to Carl, he asked, "Want me to open it?"

"Hell yes I want you to open it!" Carl exclaimed. "It's been on my mind ever since she gave it to me before she passed!"

Maxim laughed. "What do you think it is?"

Carl shrugged. "Well, I *hope* it's one of those famous Elisaveta Tanner love letters. You know, one of those letters she sometimes wrote to people telling them things about…about…"

"About how much you meant to her and how the world was a better place with you in it?" Maxim finished for him.

"Exactly," Carl admitted. "I know it sounds corny. But I miss her. And even though she told me I'd been a great help in straightening out things so they wouldn't be so messy with your parents and stuff once she was gone…I'd like to hear that she really cared for me, you know. Just one more time."

"I know," Maxim mumbled. He would miss his grandmother's love letters too. She'd always believed in taking the time to sit down and really pour your heart out over someone special. He'd kept every letter and note she'd ever written to him, and he was saddened in knowing he'd never get another one.

"So?" Carl prodded impatiently. "Are you gonna sit there just messing with me, man? Or are you going to open it?"

"Good things come to those who *patiently* wait, Carl, dear," Maxim teased.

Carl laughed as he watched Maxim slit the envelope with a pocketknife he had in his pocket.

"Well?" Carl asked, leaning forward over his desk.

Maxim smiled. "Your dreams have come true, Carl," Maxim said, removing a sealed envelope he recognized as being from his grandmother's favorite stationery. "It says, '*To my dearest Carl*' on the front. I think you've got your love letter."

"Awesome!" Carl exclaimed, fairly snatching the envelope from Maxim's hand. "And it's nice and thick. My own piece of Elisaveta Tanner's affections."

Maxim smiled even though a frown of curiosity wrinkled his brow. "Dude! Were you in love with my grandmother?"

Carl smiled as he studied the envelope. Maxim was touched as he saw moisture in Carl's eyes.

"I think I was in a way," he said. "If I'd been born sixty years earlier…I might have given your grandpa a run for his money."

"Man! I had no idea you were so sappy," Maxim teased.

"Well, we all have our little secrets, don't we?" Carl asked.

"We certainly do," he said, thinking of the night before—of the way he'd barely managed to resist temptation where Sharlamagne was concerned. Oh, he'd managed it—but he had spent the whole day wondering how he had. "There's something else in here for you too, Carl," Maxim said then. He'd seen what else was in the envelope for Carl. He'd seen it the moment he'd opened the envelope. But he knew the letter would be what Carl would treasure the most, so he'd saved the other item for last.

Maxim removed the money order from the envelope and read the sticky note attached to it out loud. "*Carl, dear…quit dragging your feet!*

Love doesn't need to wait for money, but just so you'll quit worrying about it…buy that girl of yours a ring!"

Maxim smiled as he watched Carl's eyes widen when he saw the two digits followed by six zeroes on the amount line of the money order.

"What?" he exclaimed. "What? Why would she do this? Why would she leave me eleven million dollars? I don't need eleven million dollars to buy a ring for Kathy."

"But you might need eleven million dollars if you ever hope to break away and start your own law firm with your brother, right?" Maxim suggested.

Carl shook his head. "Elisaveta already paid me for taking care of her estate. I can't accept this," he said, offering the money order to Maxim.

"Dude…it's a money order with your name on it. You can't refuse. You can't even sign it over to a charity or anything," Maxim reminded him. "Not this kind of money order. So take it and break away from this big firm. Grandma knew you hated working for it. All she did was give you start. You'll have to work hard to keep it going."

"Maxim," Carl said, still shaking his head. "Why would she do this?"

"Because she loved you, man," Maxim explained. "She loved you. You were her tried-and-true friend for, like, six or seven years, right? She loved you, and she wanted to do something good with her money. My parents will blow through Grandma and Grandpa's money like crap through a goose. But you won't…and she knew that."

Carl nodded, was silent for a moment, and then said, "It's weird, isn't it?"

"What?"

"That someone can hand you eleven million dollars and all you can think about is that you miss her and you're glad she took the time to write a personal letter to you," he answered.

"It's not weird, man," Maxim said. "It's the way it should be."

As Maxim left the large office high-rise downtown and stepped into the orange light of the setting sun, with an old key added to his key ring and two manila envelopes under his arm, he sighed. Carl Rowlands was a good man. By giving him the money to break away and start his own law firm—excel or fail—his grandmother had freed Carl in a similar manner to which she'd freed Maxim. What a wonderful gift—freedom.

As he walked to the parking garage to get into his jeep and drive to the real estate agent's office, he decided he'd take the keys to his new house on Whippoorwill Lane, go on in, sit down, read his grandmother's "open when you miss me" envelope, and have himself a good, cleansing man-weep. He needed it. Even though life was good, the future was bright, and Sharlamagne Dickens was digging him enough to spend some time kissing him, he needed to purge some lingering emotions of hurt—hurt at his grandmother's passing, hurt that his parents hadn't called, e-mailed, or contacted him at all since Carl had handed them their checks, and hurt that some good things in life were as painful as they were joyous.

Still, as he drove out of the parking garage on his way to the real estate agent's office, a vision of the expression that had leapt to Sharlamagne's face when they'd won the best costume trophy at the World War II ball popped into his mind. Instantly, he smiled. She was adorable! Adorable, funny, compassionate, smart, deliciously sexy, and everything else he'd ever dreamed of in a wife.

He'd been so startled at his own thoughts he'd nearly ran a red light. As he slammed on the breaks, the jeep screeching to a stop, he shook his head.

"What the hell were you thinking, man?" the driver in the car next to him asked through the open window of his SUV. Maxim simply shrugged and wondered the same thing himself. He'd known Sharlamagne—what—a few weeks? Kissed her—what—on two occasions? How had the word *wife* managed to find its way into his thoughts? Yet in the next moment, he was reminded of something his grandmother had said to him on several occasions.

"Maxim, darling," she'd begun each time, "it is my very correct opinion that if you're with someone—you know, dating them or otherwise associated with them...and in your case, a woman—and you aren't wanting to marry her by three to four weeks into the relationship, then you're wasting your time by dragging it on. You'll know, darling, when you've found the right woman for you. You'll know quickly… within a month. Mark my word, dear. All these ridiculous couples who stay together for years and years without thoroughly committing to one another through marriage vows…they're not meant to be together. The woman you're meant to be with—the woman who'll make your happiness—you'll know her within a month of your association."

Maxim parallel parked in front of a parking meter near the real estate agent's office. But he didn't jump right out of his jeep. Rather he paused a moment, considering the astonishing, yet not surprising, thoughts he'd been having about Sharlamagne—considering his grandmother's advice. But it seemed crazy! It was too fast—wasn't it? Hell! All they'd ever done together was unload crap from his grandmother's old house. That, and they'd been on one date—and they'd made out in the Passion Room—and out of the Passion Room.

He shrugged, raised his eyebrows, and said aloud, "But we didn't cave into temptation and mess up," he reminded himself. "I didn't rip her clothes off and throw her down on the bed…even though I wanted to. And why *is* that, do you think?"

But he already knew the answer to his own question. He knew it because his grandmother had told him he'd know—and he knew it because he knew it. Sharlamagne Dickens was the one—the one he wanted—and not just physically. Dammit! He loved her! He was totally in love with her!

Rather stumbling out of the jeep and heading toward the office, he began to chuckle to himself. "And you were right, Grandma," he mumbled. "The woman for me does have real bosoms."

You didn't do any heavy lifting, did you, sugar bee? Sharlamagne smiled as she read Maxim's text message.

You told me not to, didn't you? she texted in return.

She giggled when her text message alert sounded.

Yes, I did. So does this mean that anything I tell you to do, you'll do? he flirted via cell phone.

Yes, she bravely texted back.

Another alert sounded, and Sharlamagne found her heart was pumping so hard she could hear it ringing in her ears.

Then go home. I don't want you there alone this late, he texted.

Sharlamagne's heart sunk. She'd hoped for another flirtatious text.

But then her text alert sounded again almost instantly, and she smiled when she read, *But on your way, stop by my new house. I'm having trouble getting my clothes off tonight...need some help.*

Sharlamagne laughed and texted, *You are being naughty!*

Sorry. But seriously...I don't want you there this late, came Maxim's responding text. And then another. *I'll be able to help tomorrow...so call it a night and get home safe and sound. Text me when you're all tucked snug in your bed...unless you'd rather come on over and be all tucked snug with me in mine ;)*

"*Actually,*" Sharlamagne brazenly texted, speaking out loud as she did so, walking toward the front door of the old house, intent on leaving. "*I WOULD rather be tucked in with you in yours.*" It was so much easier to text scandalous flirtations than it was to say them face to face. There were no consequences with texting.

"Then come on over and make it happen."

A startled squeal escaped Sharlamagne's throat at the sound of Maxim's voice. She looked up, blushing as she saw him standing in the doorway, shoving his cell phone in his pocket.

"Hi," she said, tucking a loose strand of hair behind her ear and wondering how truly sweaty and dusty she was.

"Hi," he said. His blue eyes were simmering with roguery mischief.

"You scared me," she admitted. "I didn't even hear you come up."

"That's why I don't want you here by yourself after dark, shawty," he explained. "Anybody can sneak up on you and...you know...startle you."

Sharlamagne reached back, slipping her cell phone into one back pocket as Maxim's hands went to her waist and pulled her against him.

"I mean, anybody could just sneak up on you, take hold of you like this," he said as his hands released her waist and quickly took hold of her shoulders. "Shove you against the wall, like this," he said, gently pushing her back into the old house and up against the nearest wall. "And kiss you like this."

She gasped with pleasure a moment before Maxim's mouth took hers in a long, moist, expertly applied kiss. Her hands went to his shoulders as he continued to kiss her a moment.

When he broke the seal of their mouths, drew back, and gazed at her, smiling with triumph, she stammered, "You say anybody could do that...but you're wrong. I'm more wary when you're not around. But when you're here..."

"You lower your guard...is that it?" he asked, kissing her cheek.

"You have no idea," she whispered as he kissed her neck.

He chuckled and drew her away from the wall and into his arms. "Good," he said. His voice was low and alluring—provocative in tone.

"You kind of bring out the worst in me or something," she said, letting her hands gently embrace his neck.

"I bring out the worst in you?" he teased, feigning offense.

"Well...no. I mean...you make me weak," she whispered. "I trust you too much or something. Last night...I should've been more...I should've been less...I shouldn't have let myself be so easily..."

"You trust me too much?" Maxim asked. "How can you trust someone too much, Sharlamagne?"

Oh, he knew what she meant—knew that she'd trusted him not to seduce her to sacrificing her virtue. But he wanted to hear her say it; he needed to hear her say it. He felt that if she said it out loud to him, if she professed to owning a trust of him that was strong—that if she told him she trusted him not to press her too far, to sleeping with him—then maybe he'd be strong enough not to.

"I trust you," she said, gazing up into his eyes. Her expression was warm and welcoming. She was as physically attracted to him as any woman could be to a man. Her eyes told him so. "I trust you to not... you know...to not..."

"I know what you mean, Sharlamagne," he said, deciding to let her off the hook. "But you know what?"

"What?" she breathed.

"I need to trust you to be my wingman on this," he answered. "You know…to let me know if I start to go too far. Last night, there was a moment when I thought…"

"When you thought what?" she asked, a frown of concern wrinkling her brow.

It was time for a confession—he knew it was. She needed to understand it.

"I like you, Sharlamagne," he said.

"I like you, too, Maxim. But—"

He covered her pretty mouth with his hand to keep from kissing her for a moment. "I like you. And I'll just flat out tell you…I want you. And to avoid any word that might make you uncomfortable…I want you—intimately." She blushed—her eyes flashed with the light of being pleased. "Like and want—it's a very dangerous combination."

"I do know," she said as he removed his hand from her mouth. She smiled at him, and he wondered if he should turn and walk away. But he didn't.

"Do you now?" he asked instead. He brushed a strand of hair from her face and then studied her for a moment. Reaching to the back of her head, he pulled the hair tie from her hair, flicked it across the room, and buried his hands in her hair as he ground a kiss to her mouth that he knew took her breath away—for he felt her gasp.

It was the same detonation of passion Sharlamagne had experienced with Maxim the night before in the Passion Room. It was instant, blazing, irresistible, nearly out of control! Wrapping her arms around his neck, she pulled her body against his, kissing him with such a loving and wanton intensity she thought she might burst apart. She loved him! Her heart loved him, her mind loved him, her body loved him.

Suddenly, she released him and pushed at his chest until he released her. It was too much! She loved him—not just liked him—*loved* him. And if like and want were dangerous, then love and want combined were perilous. She knew she would never succumb to a purely carnal desire—she knew she wouldn't. But what bothered her was that she had to keep reminding herself that she wouldn't.

"What?" he asked, breathless. "Did I...did I do something?"

Sharlamagne shook her head. "No...no. It's just...you know...dark and late, and we're both tired from a long day and—"

"You're right," he said. He puffed a sigh. "I'm sorry."

"No," she said, taking his face in her hands. "It's me."

Maxim smiled and began to laugh.

"What?" Sharlamagne asked. "It *is* me."

"Baby, if we get carried away, it's never gonna be *your* fault," he said, taking her face between his hands and kissing her forehead. He was still smiling when he added, "And that 'it's me' excuse?" He kissed her nose. "You don't have to try and take responsibility for my predatory behavior."

"I'm not," she told him. "I'm just...too comfortable with you... which is ridiculous, considering you're the Jeans Innovations hottie model...the conductor of the 'I Was Made for Loving You' train."

"What?" he asked, obviously unable to make sense of her emotional babble.

"I mean...I talk to you about anything and everything...and now I'm throwing myself at you like some...like some..."

"I wish you'd throw yourself at me," he teased, grinning at her.

"Maxim...I'm serious," she scolded.

"So am I," he countered, kissing her cheek. Sharlamagne watched as Maxim took his cell out of his pocket and checked the time. "Look," he began as he slipped the phone back into its place. "It's ten to nine. Let's make out for...mmm...ten more minutes, okay? Then I'll let you go home." He shrugged, adding, "What can get out of hand in ten minutes?"

Sharlamagne laughed, rolled her eyes, and shook her head.

"What?" Maxim asked, perplexed.

"You talk like...as if I'm really the girl who could tempt you," she explained. "I've seen the kind of woman you hang out with—"

"*Used* to hang out with," he interrupted, correcting her.

"Whatever. Used to hang out with then. But…I'm just the antique dealer's daughter."

Sharlamagne wanted to cry. She loved him; she wanted him to love her. But as well as they'd gotten to know each other—for as much physical chemistry that exploded whenever they kissed…

"Give me ten minutes, Sharlamagne," he mumbled, taking her in his arms. "Ten minutes and I'll show you just how much you tempt me." He placed a light kiss on her lips. "And I'll prove that you can trust me too…*again*."

"But why me?" she asked as Maxim gathered her in his arms.

"Hey, lady!" he exclaimed, pretending to be seriously scolding. "I've only got ten minutes here. We can talk later."

"But—" she began.

"Shut up and let me kiss you, Sharlamagne," Maxim mumbled a moment before his mouth captured her in a ravenous exchange of affection, passion, and mutual desire.

"Do you want to explain this text, Sharlamagne Dickens?" Gwen asked as Sharlamagne exited their bathroom wrapped in a towel.

"Who is it from?" Sharlamagne asked—though from the look of delight on Gwen's face, she knew exactly who it was.

Gwen cleared her throat, held up Sharlamagne's phone, and read, "*Thanks for the ten minutes in heaven, sugar bee. And see? Your virtue is still intact. Do you trust me now?*" Gwen held Sharlamagne's cell out toward her, arched her eyebrows, and asked, "Well?"

Snatching her phone, Sharlamagne answered, "Well…maybe it's time you quit reading my texts every time my phone beeps, Guinevere. They might be misinterpreted when you read them out of context."

"Ten minutes in heaven?" Gwen asked. "Do I need to check you for more hickies?" she teased.

"Of course not," Sharlamagne grumbled. "That was just a…he was just being funny last night when he did that."

"Oh, is that what Maxim 'Abs-God' Tanner was doing last night—being funny?" Gwen giggled. "I'm your sister, Shar. You can tell me anything. You can tell me everything. So tell me."

Sharlamagne took a deep breath. It would feel good to say it out loud—to vocalize what her heart had been screaming to her mind for so long.

"Okay, Gwen," she began. "I'll tell you." Sharlamagne smiled and said, "Someday." She giggled when Gwen growled with frustration.

Responding to Maxim's text, she simply said, *Yes ;) I trust you.* Then, sighing, she whispered to herself, "It's myself I don't trust sometimes."

CHAPTER FOURTEEN

"I kind of like having you as *my* moving slave," Maxim teased as Sharlamagne handed him two more jars full of marbles.

"Har har," she said, reaching into the box at her feet and retrieving two more jars. "And I wish you would've had me help you sooner. I can't believe you packed up everything all by yourself. And now I feel even worse about asking you to help me in the evenings. I didn't know you were going home and packing every night afterward. You should've told me…and you should've asked me to help long before now."

"Naw," Maxim said, placing the two jars on the shelves he'd built in his new workshop. "I hate messing with my own stuff. It was way more fun messing with yours. I mean, seeing the vast collection of Grandma's doilies alone was worth it."

"And what's the big difference between marbles and doilies?" Sharlamagne teased him.

"Marbles are cooler," he chuckled.

"But not cool enough to be in the new house?" she asked.

Maxim shrugged. It was true. He had decided not to put his marble collection in his new house. He wanted something different in his new house. He'd known he'd wanted something different in this house from the moment he bought it—something besides marbles and expensive furniture. He hadn't known exactly what at first, but he did now, and he smiled at her.

"Which reminds me," he began, "I think I have decided what I want to do with Grandma's house."

Sharlamagne found herself holding her breath, afraid he might have decided to sell the beautiful restored Victorian after all. "And what's that?" she ventured.

"I think I do like the museum idea," he said. "I mean, I'm sure I can get it put on a protected historical site thing, but then I wouldn't have control over it like I want. I think I just want to keep it the way it is…call it the Elisaveta Tanner House or something. I know Grandma wasn't a well-known poet anymore. But it's so perfect for tourism, and I feel like she'd probably want other people to see it—to have the chance to feel the past…how important it was. Do you know what I mean?"

Sharlamagne was fighting tears. Of course she knew what he meant! Was he even kidding? Elisaveta Tanner's home was beautiful— something that people nowadays rarely ever had the chance to experience. It was a glimpse not only into the past but into the heart of a woman who appreciated the past—who knew how important it was that the people and history that went before were remembered. It was a perfect idea—the Elisaveta Tanner House—and she told him.

"It's perfect, Maxim," she said. "I'm sure you're right and that it's just what she would've wanted. And that way, you keep the property and everything. You can decide what will be done to the house, how many days it's available to the public…it's perfect."

Maxim sighed—grinned with a sort of relief washing over him. "I'm glad you approve. Thanks," he said. "Which leads me to my next question. I was wondering if you'd be willing to do me a favor—you know, use your antique expertise to make some decisions for me."

"What decisions?" she asked. He had entirely piqued her curiosity. What decisions could he possibly need help making? Maxim Tanner was one of the most independent people she'd ever known.

"I need you to go through Grandma's house for me and, you know, decide if there's anything in there that would be a possible theft target," he explained. "As much as I want to share Grandma's essence with the world, I don't want anyone vandalizing or stealing her precious memories. Do you know what I mean?"

"I know exactly what you mean," Sharlamagne agreed. "But you do realize that everything in there is probably a target for theft, right?"

He nodded. "Yeah. But just help me decide what I should remove—you know, just to minimize the ease and temptation to rip Grandma off for money."

Sharlamagne smiled, reached up, and placed a hand on his cheek. "You are quite a tenderhearted man, aren't you?"

Maxim frowned, growled, straightened his posture, and said, "No, I'm not. I'm just smart."

But Sharlamagne giggled. He was adorable, like a little boy guarding a ramshackle tree house.

"Well, I can tell you what the first thing is you should take out of there…before *anybody* goes in," she said.

"What?"

"That family portrait hanging in the entryway area. It's the first thing you see when you come into the house, and although it's beautiful and emotionally stirring, it's also incredibly valuable…and you wouldn't want to lose an heirloom like that. That picture…you need to hang onto that with both fists for your entire life."

Maxim smiled. "Excellent point, Miss Antique Expert Lady."

"It doesn't take an expert in anything to know that photograph is priceless…and in a lot of ways."

Maxim nodded, took the two jars of marbles Sharlamagne had been holding, plopped them on the shelf, and said, "Okay then. Let's go get it now."

"What?" she giggled.

"Let's go get it and bring it back here," he repeated. "Now you've got me all freaked out that someone might actually break into the house and try to steal it. It is visible from one of the front windows, you know."

"Yes, it is," Sharlamagne agreed, feeling a sudden sense of urgency herself.

"Then let's go get it. We'll just walk over there. It's, what, ten houses down?"

"Okay," she said, dusting her hands on the seat of her pants. "Let's go."

"And then you can help me find a place to hang it," he suggested.

"You do like my new house, don't you, sugar bee?"

Sharlamagne smiled. "You know I love your new house," she admitted. "I love it so much I'm almost breaking one of the ten."

"One of the ten?" he chuckled. "You mean like in Moses? Like in, 'Thou shalt not covet thy neighbor's house' Ten Commandments–type stuff?"

"Yes," Sharlamagne giggled, delighted at the way he'd deepened and broadened the tone of his voice when he'd quoted the Tenth Commandment. "Only I said I'm *almost* breaking it. And what is it they say about almost?"

"That almost only counts in horseshoes and hand grenades," he answered. Then he added, "But I think the Ten Commandments have a similar almost-clause too."

"Okay, okay," Sharlamagne playfully relented. "I won't covet your house. I'll just admire it. Will that do?"

"Yeah," he said. Then, taking her chin firmly in one hand, he mumbled, "But I'd like it better if you admired its owner more."

Sharlamagne sighed and smiled up into the handsome face of the man she was in love with. "Well, I do admire its owner more."

"Good," he said, kissing her. "Keep that up, will you?"

Maxim couldn't resist Sharlamagne then. After all, it had been almost twelve hours since he'd kissed her last—eleven o'clock the night before when they'd finally pulled themselves away from each other and gone home. Twelve hours. He figured it had been a long enough break. So he gathered the tasty little morsel that was Sharlamagne Dickens into his arms and took a few long drinks of her more than willing kisses.

He wondered if she owned the same desperate feelings for him that he owned for her—if she thought of him every minute of every day, dreamt of him every night. He couldn't get Sharlamagne out of his head anymore—not for a moment. Not that he wanted to anyway, but he hoped she was as strung out over him as he was over her. Her behavior would suggest that she was. After all, she was a girl, and girls were a lot less likely to kiss a guy the way Sharlamagne kissed him if they weren't strung out too. But still, he doubted. It was probably his own insecurities. Actually, it was absolutely his own insecurities, and he wanted to get over them. He knew Sharlamagne was the girl to help him get over them too, but he had to get past them enough on his own to get close enough to her to let her help him. He was freaked out about the "l" word—love—and the fact had begun to crack him up at himself. He kept thinking he was akin to Sharlamagne in that regard too; she had her "s" word, and he had his "l" word. It was comical.

But he did "l" word her. He did. He loved her—he was in love with her—and he was fairly certain she was in love with him. Now all that was left to do was to find the courage to reach out and take her, no matter what his fears were, no matter what the world would think of such a seemingly quick romance. Yep. Maxim knew he just needed to drop the "l" word once, and he'd be free. Yet he didn't sense this was the moment. He needed a better moment.

Slowly lessening the demanding nature of his kiss, Maxim eventually broke the seal of their lips, brushed a strand of hair from Sharlamagne's cheek, and said, "Come on. Let's go get my priceless family photograph. Okay?"

"Okay," she whispered.

Taking her hand, Maxim led Sharlamagne out of the workshop and out to the sidewalk that lined Whippoorwill Lane. He liked walking with her—liked the way she had to take two steps to each one of his—the way her ponytail bobbed back and forth in rhythm.

"Let's use the backdoor," Maxim suggested as they reached Mrs. Tanner's old house. "That way I can grab a snack in the kitchen. Are you hungry?"

"Nope," Sharlamagne answered. And she wasn't—not for food anyway. She was hungry for Maxim's continued attention, his constant company, and his kiss, but not for food.

As they crossed the lawn and headed for the back of the house, however, Sharlamagne gasped. "Look! Look at that enormous lilac tree back there behind my house. I've never noticed it before, but from this angle...look how enormous it is! And it's all in bloom too."

"Yeah," Maxim said. "It's been there forever. It was there before

Grandma and Grandpa moved in. Grandma always said it was probably nearly as old as the house. I used to play inside it all the time when I was a kid."

"Play inside it?" Sharlamagne asked.

"Yeah. I'll show you."

Sharlamagne followed Maxim as he walked to the very back of the property. The lilac tree was indeed enormous, and as Maxim ducked down and forced his way through an opening in the branches, Sharlamagne understood why the tree was so enormous.

"See?" he said. "It's awesome in here! I used to get my army guys and the hose and make little forts out of mud and rivers and stuff and play in here for hours and hours and hours. Grandma and Grandpa always knew where to find me."

Sharlamagne smiled, gazed up into Maxim's beaming face, and said, "I used to play under our lilacs when I was little," she told him.

"It's the ultimate place to play," he said, smiling. "Cool and shady, private…and at certain times of the year, like now, it smells good." He frowned a little. "But I could never quite figure out why there was this empty space in here. I mean, either I've grown a lot since I last climbed in here or the trees have because the space does seem smaller than it used to. But why is it here at all? It seems like the tree would've grown from the center, right?"

Sharlamagne giggled. "Did you know, Maxim, darling," she began, impersonating Elisaveta, "that lilacs are sometimes called outhouse flowers?"

"Outhouse flowers?" he asked, puzzled.

"I'm guessing that if you dug down in the center here about eight feet, you'd find all kinds of marvelous little artifacts—broken toys, pieces of glass, old bottles," she explained. "People used to throw their broken things away…down the outhouse hole. And they used to plant lilacs around the outhouse, you know, to dress it up a bit and…well… hide any unpleasant odors that might emanate from it."

Maxim's eyes widened with understanding. "You mean I used to play army men over a sh—"

"An outhouse hole," she interrupted, clamping her hand over his mouth. "Yes."

Maxim laughed. He laughed and laughed until moisture filled his eyes. Sharlamagne laughed too—because his was contagious.

"No wonder Grandma never told my why there was a space inside the lilac tree," he said at last.

"She knew how much you hated public restrooms, and she didn't want to ruin the escape for you," Sharlamagne said as Maxim chuckled and nodded. "This isn't one tree. It's several that have grown together over the past hundred years or so."

"Holy cow," Maxim said, wiping the mirthful moisture from his eyes with the back of his hand. "That's hysterical."

Unexpectedly then he reached out, wrapping his powerful arms around her and pulling her against him in a warm, affectionate embrace.

"You're good for my soul, Sharlamagne Bronte Dickens," he mumbled into her hair. "You're good for *me*...all of me."

Clutching at the back of his shirt, she sighed. "I'm glad you think so," she said. "Because you're good for me too...all of me."

Maxim held her away from him for a moment—gazed down into her face with narrowed, smoldering blue eyes. Her heartbeat was speeding up. There was an expression on his face—a glint of mischief in his eyes she recognized. She'd seen it before—the night of the 1940s ball, the night in the Passion Room when they'd been swept away in the suggestion that the room owned paranormal influences, and every time he'd meant to kiss her since.

"I want to say something," he mumbled. "But...I need a little encouragement first."

"Encouragement?" Sharlamagne asked as goose bumps began to spring up over her arms. What was he going to say? Was he going to say he loved her? Did he love her? She could hardly breathe, for she could see in the sapphire simmer of his eyes that he did love her!

"Yeah," he affirmed. "You know...something to motivate me to tell you. Some kind of assurance that you won't think I'm an idiot... that you'll still like me once I've confessed the thing I need to confess."

"Oh," she breathed, hardly able to stay conscious. She was

overwhelmed with anticipation—blissful anticipation. "Oh…okay. Encouragement." She cleared her throat dramatically and said, "I swear to still like you after you tell me whatever it is you want to tell me."

Maxim smiled, chuckled a little, put his hands at Sharlamagne's waist, and gently eased her further back into the lilac bush. "That's really sweet…but it's not exactly the kind of encouragement I meant," he mumbled.

"Oh," Sharlamagne breathed. "Wh-what kind of encouragement did you mean then?"

Maxim's smile broadened. "That's one of the things that's so cute about you, you know."

"What?"

"The way you play dumb with me when you're nervous."

Pushing her even farther into the lilac bush, until they were both immersed in aromatic, lavender blossoms, Maxim pulled her into his arms and against his body.

Lightly kissing the corner of her mouth, he mumbled, "Encourage me, Sharlamagne. If you want to know my secrets, then show me a little—"

Instantly, Sharlamagne's arms slid around his neck, pulling his head to hers as she kissed him. And it was no timid kiss she offered. Surprised by her own daring, Sharlamagne clung to Maxim almost desperately as she endeavored to encourage him. And encourage him she did, for in the space it took for her to draw one deep breath, he was at her like a lion to its kill.

A low, soft growl escaped Maxim's throat as he ground his mouth to Sharlamagne's warm, inviting one. He could not believe the feelings, emotions, and desires she provoked in him! He thought of their night together in the Passion Room—thought he was no less attracted to her now—no less wanting. Even in the bright light of midday—even while shoved in the branches, leaves, and blossoms of an old tree—everything about this girl fueled a fire in him he nearly couldn't control.

Random reasons began to bang around in his mind as he kissed her. It was because she was so clever, witty, and smart. Or perhaps it was because she made him feel like life was wonderful—like the grass was greener and the sky was bluer. Maybe it was simply lust—the perfect way her body felt against his, the way goose bumps broke over his arms whenever he felt her warm flesh beneath his palm. Maybe it was her cute little jeans and T-shirt or the way her ponytail bobbed from side to side when she walked. Maybe it was because she simply made him feel good and happy—that when he was in her company, he loved being alive.

Sharlamagne broke the seal of their mouths a moment, sighing as she kissed his lower lip—slowly kissed his upper lip. She kissed him softly—toying with his pent-up passion and desire to ravage her—and he loved it! Maxim felt her fingers begin to caress the back of his neck—felt them slowly weave up through his hair. Again she kissed him—playfully—teasingly—as if she were daring him to maintain his self-control.

Over and over, his mind thought of the reasons for his attraction to her. As his body fought to best her at her teasing manner of kissing him, he thought of her smile and the way her eyes lit up when she found some battered old piece of something she thought was valuable. He pulled her more tightly against him, and she giggled, playfully kissing his lower lip.

Maxim Tanner was trembling with the effort of maintaining self-control. The lyrics to an old song about laying a lover down in a bed of roses leapt to his mind, and he thought how much more comfortable a bed of lilacs would be. He let his hands freely rove over her back and shoulders—considered slipping them under her shirt but then remembered that she was a sweet, innocent girl and that his grandma had raised him to be a gentleman.

All at once, he smiled as she kissed him, for a thought—a memory—had just occurred to him. He thought of all the girls who had kissed him over the years—of all the women who had tried to seduce him, tried to provoke him to the passionate point that Sharlamagne Dickens provoked him to—of all the girls who had failed. He nearly chuckled as he remembered the conversation he'd had with his grandmother the day he'd first met Sharlamagne all those years ago. Of all the women who had fought to own his true affection, Sharlamagne was the only one with real, God-given bosoms.

"What?" Sharlamagne said, drawing back from him slightly.

"Nothing," he lied, smiling at her. "But I dare you to do that again, shawty. Kiss me like that again…if you have the nerve."

Sharlamagne smiled at him. She was so comfortable in his arms—so confident. It was as if Maxim were the magic feather that made the elephant believe he could fly.

"You're daring me now?" she whispered. "Are you calling me a chicken?"

"Yeah," he mumbled. "Kiss me like that one more time. I dare you. Do you think you can handle the consequences? Or *are* you a chicken?"

"I can handle anything you can dish out, Mr. Tanner," she said.

"Oh, really?"

"Yes, really."

"Then I dare you. Do it again."

In truth, Sharlamagne was trembling from the topmost hair of her head to the soles of her feet. But she trusted him. Something in her trusted him. And so, she leaned forward, gently kissing his upper lip. She smiled, however, as she softly kissed him again, allowing her tongue to ever so lightly taste the space between his lips.

Her heart soared with delight as his fingers dug into her shoulder blades, his powerful hands and arms pulling her so tight and flush with his muscular body that she could hardly breathe. If this was the consequence of her playful kisses—such steamy, wet, demanding, devouring kisses from him—then she would tease him that same way every chance she could! She felt as if she'd broken into a sudden fever, for she was overheated, and found it hard to draw a breath that wasn't ragged and labored.

Sharlamagne began to silently scold herself—for giving into lust. After all, that's what it was between them at that moment, wasn't it? Just a physical desire that he somehow unleashed in her? Yet she kept thinking of Maxim the day he'd come to the shop to tell her of his grandmother's death—thought of the pain in his eyes that day. She thought of his championing her at the reading of Elisaveta's will—against his own family, his own flesh and blood. She thought of his sense of humor and teasing behavior—of his somewhat old-fashioned manners in everything (well, everything save when he was kissing her, that was). She thought of how safe she felt whenever she was with him, how often he made her laugh, how confident he made her feel. In his arms, she felt as if she were the most beautiful, desirable woman on the face of the earth—as if she were just as wonderful as all the supermodel types he'd kept social company with all his life. In fact, she felt more beautiful and desirable than they appeared.

Was it simple lust she was feeling? Or was it something far deeper—far more divine? She loved him—oh, how she loved him! She didn't doubt that for one moment. But what defined true love? What made it different from easy lust? Her body wanted to be always touching his, it was true. Yet even more powerful was her very soul's desire to meld with his. It was in that moment that Sharlamagne understood that Maxim truly did love her—he loved her! Love—it was why she could trust him, because she somehow knew that, no matter how powerful their mutual desire was to push the tethers of passion beyond delicious kisses, Maxim would never press her too far—because he loved her.

As Maxim continued to command her mouth to reciprocate the passion his was raining on her, Sharlamagne consciously began to allow herself to hope—to dream of a future with Maxim Tanner. Tears filled her closed and burning eyes as she silently told herself she'd found the one man ever born on the face of the earth who could evoke such physical and emotional passion in her. It was almost surreal to realize that she was in love with Mrs. Tanner's grandson!

Sharlamagne fought to keep the moisture in her eyes from escaping, but she couldn't. She was thankful, however, that when they did find their way out, they traveled down over her temples and the sides of her face—not over her cheeks to mingle with the melding kisses she was sharing with Maxim.

Maxim wanted her! More than that, he needed her. Every cell in his body was aware of her—of the physical thirst he had for her. Yet he knew his heart was hammering so savagely in his chest not merely because of his carnal desires for Sharlamagne but because he wanted to own her heart. Sure, she lit a fire in him he'd never imagined could be lit. But he'd begun to realize it was so much more than that. Yes, he loved her mouth and the feel of her body in his arms—loved the way she teased him with her playful kisses and touch. But what he most wanted—what he truly desired to have from her—was her heart—her soul. He wanted her soul to love his—to love who he was with as much passion as she physically shared with him whenever they kissed. But it couldn't be that easy, could it? It couldn't be that the one woman his grandmother had inadvertently put in his path would actually be the one woman she'd spoken of—the one woman to unlock the passion and capacity for loving he'd been bottling up his entire adult life. It just couldn't be that easy.

Maxim hugged Sharlamagne more tightly—felt her breath be forced from her lungs and into his mouth as his arms bound her to him. Yet she didn't struggle or make any move to free herself. She simply tightened her own embrace of him, sighing with pleasure as he kissed her again. She trusted him. She trusted him. He allowed the phrase to echo through his mind—to keep him from making a mistake he'd regret for the rest of his life if he made it.

Maxim broke the seal of their lips abruptly, and Sharlamagne opened her eyes to see him frowning at her. "Did you hear that?" he asked.

"Hear what?" she breathed. The only thing Sharlamagne could hear was the sound of her blood pumping through her body with the vigor induced of passion.

"I hear voices," he whispered. "Come on."

Taking her hand, Maxim led Sharlamagne out of the ancient lilac grove and to the back of the house Mrs. Tanner had bequeathed to her. "Listen," he whispered, and Sharlamagne heard them then. Someone was there. But why did she feel so suddenly anxious about the fact? And why did Maxim?

She looked up to him—saw the scowl that overtook his handsome brow as he inhaled an angry breath. "Stay here," he growled, releasing her hand.

But Sharlamagne had no intention of letting him leave her there wondering what was going on. Therefore, as Maxim angrily strode toward the back of Mrs. Tanner's Victorian, she followed, her heart sinking with a thud in her stomach when she saw none other than Maxim's father and mother and a large, muscular man standing on the back porch of the main house, and apparently messing with the doorknob.

"The key does not fit, Julia," Mr. Tanner grumbled to his wife.

"It has to fit!" Mrs. Tanner whined. "We have got to get in there! What did he do? Change the locks?"

"You're damn right I changed the locks!" Maxim growled as he approached the trio. It was obvious his mother and father and whoever the big, burly guy was were trying to get into Mrs. Tanner's house.

All three intruders whirled around, glaring at Maxim.

"What are you doing here?" Mr. Tanner demanded.

Maxim chuckled with disbelief. "I own it," he reminded him. "What the hell are you doing here?"

Sharlamagne bit her lip. It was disturbing to hear someone talk to one's parents the way Maxim was talking to his. Yet she understood as well. They were arrogant, entitled, demanding people, and dealing with them gently would've been a waste of time.

"Darrell," Mr. Tanner said, pointing from the big, buff, bar-bouncer-looking man to Maxim.

The large man who was accompanying Mr. and Mrs. Tanner stepped down off the porch and started toward Maxim.

"Really, Dad?" Maxim asked. "You're really going to sic Darrell on me?" Maxim turned his attention to the man named Darrell then. "And you really want to go there, Darrell?" Darrell paused in his advance, and Maxim asked his father, "What're you doing? There's nothing in there that belongs to you. You have no reason to be here."

"There's a discrepancy somewhere, Maxim," Mrs. Tanner began to explain. "The checks your father and I were given? Well, they were supposedly the conglomeration of all Grandma's money—the liquidation of her estate…other than these two houses, of course. But our people assure us that it is only half the amount it should be. There's a thirty million dollar discrepancy somewhere, Maxim. Somewhere Grandma has thirty million more dollars, and we aim to find out where."

"Knowing my mother as I do," Mr. Tanner interjected, "she most likely kept it in cash and hid it somewhere…probably in the house."

"So what?" Maxim said. "She could have it buried in the damn ground, and I don't care. If it's here—whether it's in the house or buried in the backyard—it doesn't concern you. If you'd listened to her will, Grandma left the big house, all its contents, and the property it sits on to me. The other house and all its contents are Sharlamagne's. So you have no right to be here. You took your checks and ran. So run now. Get off my property, and take your pit bull with you," he demanded, pointing to Darrell.

"We are not leaving until we see what's in this house, Maxim," Mr. Tanner shouted.

Maxim inhaled deeply. Glancing back over his shoulder to Sharlamagne, he asked, "Baby…will you please call 911 and tell them we have not only three trespassers but people attempting to break and enter with the intention of theft?"

"Of course," Sharlamagne said without pause. His parents were vile! She couldn't believe how warped they were. Quickly, she pulled her cell phone from her pocket and dialed 911.

"Nine one one. What is your emergency?" the woman's voice on the other end of the call inquired.

"Put that phone down, girl!" Mr. Tanner shouted, starting toward Sharlamagne. But nothing would have induced her to hang up. Furthermore, she knew Maxim wouldn't allow his father to get to her.

"Hi. I'm at 2022 Whippoorwill Lane. It's my boyfriend's house, and we have three people here trying to break in and steal things. Could you send someone right away please? They have a man with them, and I think they mean to hurt us."

"Boyfriend?" Mrs. Tanner and Maxim exclaimed in unison. Maxim smiled at Sharlamagne, obviously pleased by what she'd said. Mrs. Tanner, however, looked enraged.

"Give me that phone, young lady!" Mr. Tanner ordered, marching toward Sharlamagne.

"Please hurry," Sharlamagne said to the 911 operator.

"I have a unit en route, miss. Please stay on the line until it arrives," the operator said.

"Dad," Maxim said, reaching out and taking hold of his father's arm to stop him. "Don't make me do it."

Mr. Tanner yanked his arm out of Maxim's grasp, however, looked to Darrell, and said, "Darrell…take care of my son, will you? I will get into my mother's house…one way or the other."

"Yes, sir, Mr. Tanner," Darrell said.

"Really, Darrell? Really?" Maxim chuckled.

"You haven't been at the fights for a couple of years now, Maxim," Darrell said. "You've gone soft."

"Give me that phone!" Mr. Tanner shouted as he ran toward Sharlamagne, intent on getting the phone from her.

"Please hurry!" Sharlamagne yelled to the 911 operator as she sprinted away.

"Dad! Don't you touch her!" Maxim shouted.

Sharlamagne heard someone cough and turned to see that Maxim had somehow laid his father out on the grass.

"Let this go, Dad. I mean it," Maxim said.

Darrell, however, was not incapacitated yet, and Sharlamagne screamed, "Maxim!" as she saw Darrell throw a cheap-shot punch at Maxim's head. It was a cheap shot, but it was brutal, and Maxim staggered.

"Really?" Maxim asked Darrell as he quickly stripped off his shirt and tossed it to the ground. "Did you really just sucker punch me, man?"

"It weren't no sucker punch, boy!" Darrell said, throwing another fist.

Sharlamagne winced as Maxim easily blocked the punch and threw an elbow up into Darrell's face. Darrell reeled back enough for Maxim to hit him repeatedly in the rib cage. In the next moment, she watched in awe as Maxim simply spun around, delivering a brutal tornado kick to Darrell's head and laying the bully out on the ground.

"Maxim?" she asked in a whisper as she watched him pick his shirt up from the lawn, twist it into a length, roll Darrell over, and secure his hands behind his back by knotting the shirt around his wrists.

Maxim turned to his father then. "Okay, Dad. Do you wanna fight your own fight now?" he asked.

"Do not threaten your father that way, Maxim!" Mrs. Tanner ordered.

But Maxim laughed, obviously overcome with disbelief.

"Are you kidding me, Mom?" he asked. "You have got to be kidding me."

Sharlamagne heard the sirens then and sprinted to the front yard. "They're here," she told the 911 operator. "The police are here."

"Thank you, miss," the operator said. "When the situation is contained, would you please hand the phone to one of the officers?"

"Yes," she said as she gestured to the backyard and watched the two police officers hurry to aid Maxim.

Following them, she heard one officer inquire, "Do you want to explain the situation to me, sir?"

"Yes! My son is keeping me from what is rightfully mine!" Mr. Tanner bellowed. "He is—"

"Are you the owner of this property, sir?" the officer interrupted to inquire of Mr. Tanner.

"Yes! Well…now. It was my mother's house." Mr. Tanner stammered.

"Then who is the owner of this property?" the officer asked.

"That would be me, sir," Maxim offered.

The officer who wasn't asking the questions studied Darrell for a moment, grinning and nodding with admiration.

"Did you call about an attempted robbery, sir?" the officer asked Maxim.

"Yeah. My girlfriend called for me," Maxim said. "I was too busy fending off an assault."

Even with all that was going on—all that would go on—Maxim glanced to Sharlamagne, smiled, and winked. She was his girlfriend—officially his girlfriend.

She didn't care what happened next in regard to Maxim's parents. All she cared about was that she was Maxim Tanner's girlfriend—the girlfriend he was in love with.

CHAPTER FIFTEEN

An hour later, Maxim and Sharlamagne were still sitting in the local police station. Maxim shook his head with disgust. "Can you believe them?" he growled. "I mean, seriously...can you believe them?" He looked up at her, and Sharlamagne could see the pain mingled with his anger. She could not begin to imagine what it must feel like to have parents who valued money and things more than their child. Again she was thankful Elisaveta Tanner had been Maxim's grandmother. She had loved him—obviously more than anything.

"She left them everything," Maxim continued to vent. "Everything...all her money and properties. The only two things she didn't leave them were our houses, their contents, and the property. From a purely mercenary standpoint, they're probably the least valuable properties she owned." He ran his fingers through his hair and sighed with discouragement. "When I have kids of my own, they're going to know they're loved...that they're more important than anything in the world. They'll be hugged and kissed, nurtured and taught." He groaned a little—buried his handsome face in one hand for a moment. "I sound like an idiot, don't I?"

"Not at all," Sharlamagne assured him.

"My darlings!"

Maxim was surprised when he looked up to see Sharlamagne's father and mother enter the police station. He was even further surprised by their reactions to him.

Sharlamagne's mother, whom he'd met only twice, breezed into the police station in graceful waves of red and purple clothing, scarves, and jewelry, immediately throwing her arms around his neck.

"Sharlamagne explained everything to us on the phone, Maxim," she said as she hugged Maxim so tightly he could hardly breathe. "Are you all right, dear?" she asked, taking his face between her soft hands and gazing up at him with the sincerest sympathy he'd ever seen.

"Yeah," he managed to answer.

"Oh. I'm so sorry," she sighed. "Well, you'll be fine, sweetie. You'll be fine. Van-Dyke and I are here now. Everything will be fine."

She'd turned her attention to Sharlamagne then. "I'm glad you called us, darling," Mrs. Dickens told her daughter as she hugged her. "This is a ridiculous situation! I hate that these kinds of things go on," she whispered. "Poor little Maxim."

Maxim almost laughed out loud at Mrs. Dickens's maternal reference to him—poor little Maxim.

"You holding up all right, son?" Mr. Dickens asked him, placing a reassuring arm around Maxim's shoulders.

"Yeah. It's just so...stupid," he said. He couldn't believe how instantly comfortable he felt with the man. He hardly knew him.

"So Sharlamagne explained to us that your folks think there's some big money hoard hidden in your grandmother's house...is that it?" Mr. Dickens asked.

"Yep," he answered. "And I'm not quite sure what to do about it. I don't want Grandma's house being at constant risk of intrusion. I know my grandmother...and she wouldn't have just left thirty million dollars in cash lying around in the house somewhere." He thought for a moment and then added, "Though...I *can* see her burying it in the backyard or something like that."

Mr. Dickens chuckled. It was a warm, comforting sort of sound, and Maxim grinned when the man said, "Oh, so can I." He paused for a few moments, dropped his arm from Maxim's shoulders, and asked, "What have you decided to do? Are you going to go ahead and press charges?"

"No," Maxim said, shaking his head and running a weary hand

through his hair. "No. I can't do that. But I did call my attorney and have him start working on a light restraining order—you know, so they can't come on the property and stuff." He looked to Mr. Dickens and asked, "Do you think that's okay?" He couldn't believe he was asking advice from a man he didn't even really know. But he was—and he felt good about doing it.

Van-Dyke Dickens smiled, patted Maxim on the back, and answered, "Absolutely. They're your parents, Maxim. Whether or not you approve of them or they approve of you, they are still your parents. It's a show of respect to that fact on your part not to press charges and yet a strong, necessary stance you've taken with the restraining order." He smiled with sympathy and added, "It'll all work out one day. Things will eventually settle down, and you can try to find some sort of comfortable relationship with them again."

Mrs. Dickens reached out, clasping his hands then. "All parents make mistakes, dear. Even the best parents," she offered. "The trick is not to make the same mistakes your own parents did...and to be humble enough to admit that you will make your own. You'll never do this kind of thing, of course. But every parent goofs up. Still, if merely for the fact that they are the reason you began as a zygote and were able to enter this world...try to soften your feelings toward them if you can. Don't let this eat at you. That's in your power to control. Okay?"

"A zygote, Mom?" Sharlamagne whined. "Did you even just really say that?"

"Of course, sweetheart," Louisa Dickens confirmed. "A zygote is the preliminary cell that is formed when two gamete cells are united when a man and woman—"

"I know what it is, Mom!" Sharlamagne interrupted, covering her ears and blushing a brilliant red.

Maxim couldn't help himself—Sharlamagne was too cute—and he laughed. He couldn't help himself even further and reached out, pulling her into his arms and kissing her.

"Now we have a 'z' word to contend with?" he asked as she smiled up at him.

She giggled and shrugged, and he couldn't help but kiss her again.

Maxim suddenly released Sharlamagne when he heard Mr. Dickens chuckle. "I respect a man who isn't afraid to kiss his woman in public, Maxim," Van-Dyke said.

"His woman?" Mrs. Dickens asked. "You make it sound like he's a caveman…grabbing Shar by the hair and dragging her back to his cave to—"

Mrs. Dickens's scolding was interrupted by her husband pressing a quick kiss to her mouth. "Van-Dyke Dickens!" she scolded when their kiss ended. Louisa playfully slapped her husband on the chest and whispered, "We are in a police station! Or hadn't you noticed?"

"Oh, I noticed," Van-Dyke said, winking at her.

Maxim's eyes narrowed as he watched Sharlamagne's parents tease one another. This was a healthy family, at least from all outward appearances. Yet he knew it wasn't a fluke; he knew what the Dickens family appeared to be was exactly what they were. Because if there was one thing his own experience had taught him, it was to spot pretense as easily as a knife cut through pudding.

"We're finished, Mr. Tanner," a police officer said as he approached. "If we need anything else, we'll call you."

"Do you think they've taken me seriously?" Maxim asked. Sharlamagne felt his arm tighten around her waist. He was afraid his parents would still try to attempt to invade his grandmother's home in search of cash. Careless of her parents or the police officer, she hugged him, placed a reassuring hand on his whiskery cheek, and smiled at him.

"Well, if they haven't, the temporary restraining order will put them right back in here…and with far more severe consequences," the officer explained.

"Thank you," Maxim said, shaking the policeman's hand. "I'm sorry we had to bother you."

"No problem," the officer said. "Call us if you need anything else."

Maxim nodded, and Sharlamagne shook the policeman's offered hand as well.

"Yes. Thank you so much, dear," Louisa said, suddenly throwing her arms around the policeman's neck.

"Mom!" Sharlamagne scolded in a whisper.

But the officer only smiled and said, "You're welcome, ma'am."

"Sharlamagne," her mother whispered as they all left the police station, "everyone needs an extra hug now and then. Even policemen."

"You're lucky he didn't cuff you and lock you up for assaulting an officer, dear," Van-Dyke teased.

As her parents continued their playful banter, Sharlamagne exchanged amused glances with Maxim. "I'm sorry," she whispered. "They can be kind of embarrassing sometimes."

But Maxim shook his head and quietly said, "They're awesome. You're a lucky girl."

"I know," she admitted.

Sharlamagne thought then how wonderful it would be to share not only her life with Maxim but her family. He could use some good, old-fashioned, quality family time with a quality family. Especially now that both his grandparents were gone, now that he would be estranged from his parents—obviously—at least for a time. Yep. It was time to invite him to dinner at the Dickens's house. She knew he'd feel warm, safe, and happy in the company of her family. And besides, if nothing else, they'd keep him amused.

"We'll see you at home later, sweetie," Mrs. Dickens said as she hugged and kissed her daughter.

Maxim accepted Mr. Dickens's offered handshake. "If you need anything, Maxim…do not hesitate to call Louisa or I. Okay?"

"Yes, sir," Maxim said, smiling. It was amazing how parental they were toward him—how comfortable he felt around them.

He watched Mr. Dickens kiss Sharlamagne goodbye, accepted the hug and kiss on the cheek Mrs. Dickens offered to him, and then stood with Sharlamagne, watching as they drove away.

"Now where were we?" Sharlamagne asked.

Maxim gazed down into the bright, loving light of her pretty eyes. "Ironically, we were on our way to get Tandie Thomas's family photo out of Grandma's house before someone tried to break in and steal it," he said, brushing a hair from her face.

Sharlamagne giggled. "Oh yeah. We were on our way to prevent the temptation of theft. So I say, before we do anything else, we finish what we started."

"Roger that, shawty," Maxim agreed. He let his hands go to her waist as he kissed her forehead. "But when we're finished with that little errand…promise me we'll just sit down somewhere for the rest of the day and do nothing."

"Nothing?" she teased him. "Nothing at all?"

Maxim chuckled. She was growing more and more comfortable with him—more and more confident in her flirting. He thought of the night she'd attended his stupid birthday party—how nervous she appeared—how he (for whatever reason) rattled her. He never would've guessed then how quickly they were meant to fall in love. But now—now he couldn't see how it could have happened any other way.

"Well, maybe not nothing," he answered with a wink. "Maybe just things that don't require moving dusty boxes and jars of marbles…or ending up at the police station."

"Okay then…let's get that photograph to your new house and get busy doing nothing," Sharlamagne said, taking hold of his hand and pulling him toward his jeep.

"Be careful, you little temptress," he teased as he helped her into the passenger's seat of his jeep. "If you're gonna go swimming, you're gonna get wet."

❦

"Do you see anything else I should be worried about?" Maxim asked, glancing around as he stood in the entryway of the old Victorian.

"Well, this would be the thing I'd steal first if I were going to burglarize you," Sharlamagne said, still studying the ancient family photograph hanging before her. She looked to Maxim. "Are there any other family heirlooms within reach we could take with us while we're getting this one?"

"I don't know right offhand…but there is a photograph of Tandie hanging in one of the other bedrooms upstairs. I should probably take that now too," he answered.

"Oh yeah! I forgot there were more bedrooms upstairs," Sharlamagne said. "I never saw the others. Only the Lilac Bower and the Passion Room."

"Oh, yes," Maxim said, grinning and pulling her into his arms. "The good old Passion Room. That's a night I'll never forget."

Sharlamagne blushed at the wonderful, perfect memory of the evening that she and Maxim were lost for a time in the passionate bliss of kissing in the Passion Room itself. Her mouth began to water at the memory, and she found her gaze lingering on Maxim's lips.

"What are the other rooms upstairs called?" she asked in an effort to distract them both.

"Well, come on, sugar bee," he said, releasing her, taking her hand, and leading her toward the stairs. "We'll go up and get Tandie's photograph, and I'll let you see them for yourself."

Sharlamagne giggled as she hurried up the stairs with Maxim. She wondered how she could feel so perfectly happy after what had transpired between Maxim and his parents, but she did. It was still hard for her to believe—that she was actually Maxim Tanner's girlfriend—that he loved her—that if she asked him to kiss her that very second, he would.

"The two other bedrooms have themes as well, of course," Maxim said as they reached the upstairs landing. "And they're both just as perfectly Grandma as the first two."

Sharlamagne glanced to her left—into the Lilac Bower room as they walked past it. It was so beautiful! She had the urge to step in and linger there.

Then, as they approached the Passion Room, Maxim paused. "Hmm," he mumbled. Pausing in front of the Passion Room, he leaned in a little.

"What is it?" Sharlamagne asked, curious.

"I don't know," Maxim said. "I thought I heard something. Wait! There it is again. Do you hear that?"

Sharlamagne leaned into the room as well. A slight anxiety was beginning to rise in her. Was there someone in the house? Had Maxim's parents found a way in after all?

"I don't hear anything," she whispered.

"You don't hear that?" he asked, frowning as he glanced down at her.

"No. What do you hear?"

"It's a voice," he whispered. "It's saying, 'Take her now, Maxim.'"

Sharlamagne gasped as Maxim suddenly pulled her into the Passion Room, closed the door, and backed her up against one bedpost at the foot of the bed. He administered a hot, smoldering kiss to her willing mouth, and every inch of Sharlamagne's body tingled.

"One of these days," he breathed as their lips parted a moment. "One of these days, I am gonna rock your world, shawty."

"You already have," she whispered a moment before he kissed her again.

Sharlamagne surrendered to Maxim. Her arms endeavored to embrace him with more strength than she owned. She loved the scent of his skin—loved the feel of his holding her against the bedpost. Her mind began to whirl as they kissed. Images of Maxim flashed through her mind: images of their moments together, of his laughter when he opened a box in the old house to find more doilies, of the way he'd laid out his parents' bouncer so quickly. She could see the family photograph downstairs—see Maxim's resemblance to his ancestor Tandie. She could see the bed in the Passion Room in her mind's eye— the beautiful chaise lounge and red upholstered chair. She thought of the romantic paintings on the wall—of knights and their ladies—of how truly beautiful they were and how they evoked emotion—passion.

"Maxim!" she gasped, breaking from him suddenly.

"What?" he asked, frowning at her. "What's wrong? Did I do something?"

"No...but...but I think I just realized...I think I might know what the trove of the Passion Room is, Maxim. I'm not even kidding," she explained.

"What?" he asked, his frown fading and his narrowed eyes widening. "You have to be kidding me, right?"

"No," she told him, shaking her head. "Turn on the lights...the sconces next to this painting," she said, releasing him and pointing to the painting sharing a wall with the door.

As Maxim quickly flipped the light switch near the door, Sharlamagne shook her head with disbelief. "It can't be that simple," she breathed.

"What can't be that simple?" Maxim asked, joining her to stare at the painting.

"At the police station...when your parents were going on and on about their financial people or something...about how they said your grandma withdrew thirty million dollars two years ago...thirty million dollars that hasn't been accounted for..."

"Yeah," Maxim prodded, though Sharlamagne could see understanding beginning to wash over him.

Slowly, Sharlamagne looked to the lower-right corner of the painting. "It can't be," she whispered. "It seriously cannot be this obvious."

"Manolito?" Maxim read. "The artist's name was Manolito?"

"Holy cow!" Sharlamagne exclaimed. "Darrow Manolito was one of the most famous artists of the Edwardian period!" She turned to Maxim and took hold of his shoulders. "Of course, his paintings were not valuable at all until after his death." She looked back to the painting of the knight and lady poised ready to kiss. "So many artists' works are only appreciated posthumously."

"Posthumously," Maxim mumbled. "I always thought that word sounded like it had something to do with compost piles."

"If this painting is a real, original Manolito...I'm sure it's worth..." Sharlamagne mumbled. Quickly she turned and hurried across the room to check the artist's signature on the other two paintings in the room. Her heart was hammering so hard it hurt!

"Maxim," she said, returning to the first painting, "they're all signed Manolito! And...and though I'm not expert on paintings, I can tell you that these frames are from the Edwardian era...maybe 1910 to 1915."

"Are you telling me these three paintings are collectively worth thirty million dollars?" Maxim asked.

"I don't know," Sharlamagne admitted. "I'm not an art expert. But if they really are Manolito originals…then yes."

Maxim shook his head with disbelief. "But I remember when Grandma bought them. I was working on this room, and she said she'd found the perfect art for it. She hired a photographer and had prints made—the ones you have out in the older house. And when I was finished with the room, she just had me hang them. She told me she loved them more than any other art she'd ever seen, that they spoke to her soul, and that they belonged here. I just assumed they were something she picked up at an antique auction somewhere." He frowned a moment, an inquisitive expression puckering his brow as he looked at her. "But if you're no art expert…how do you know so much about this Manolito guy?"

Sharlamagne smiled. "Because I've always loved his work. When I was in middle school, we had some antique prints come into the store. They were beautiful! I was completely fascinated with them. Only the subjects were different—a masked highwayman stealing a kiss from a servant girl, a pirate kissing a bar wench…that kind of thing. There were no knights and ladies. I just always thought his stuff was so romantic…that it just caught that very moment before a kiss… the one the takes the woman's breath away." She looked at him. "Do you know what I mean?"

Maxim grinned. "Well, I'm not a woman…so not really. But I know just how that knight up there feels right now…like he'll die if he doesn't have her kiss this very second."

Sharlamagne blushed, delighted by his implication that he felt as desperate to kiss her as she did him each time.

"So we've found the trove of the Passion Room *and* the missing thirty million Mom and Dad were all messed up about," he said, taking her waist in his hands. "So can we get back to doing nothing now?"

"You don't care that we've just discovered the legendary trove of the Passion Room?" Sharlamagne giggled as he playfully kissed her neck.

"Nope," he said.

"You don't care that we've solved the mystery of where the thirty million dollars went?" she breathed as he kissed her mouth.

"Nope," Maxim said. "Grandma liked to buy things with cash sometimes…so that no one could nag her about how much she was spending on stuff. I figure that's what she did here—took thirty million in cash out of the bank and bought the paintings she wanted for this room." He kissed her cheek. "Now will you quit talking and kiss your boyfriend?"

Sharlamagne giggled. "If I do…will you let me call my dad to come over and look at these so I can see if I'm right?"

"Kiss me like you want me as badly as I want you right now, and I will," he dared.

"Okay, Mr. Jeans Innovations man," Sharlamagne whispered. "Pucker up and hold on."

Maxim sighed as Sharlamagne kissed him—kissed him like there was nothing on the earth more important to her than him. Her soft hands were at the back of his neck, caressing his skin, then gently moving up into his hair. Her kiss was warm, feminine, alluring, and entirely overwhelming to his self-control.

"Okay," he breathed, stepping back from her. "Call your dad. It might be a good idea for him to come over here and look at the paintings. I won't be tempted to have my way with you if your dad's standing in here with us."

She giggled, thinking he was kidding—but he wasn't.

Maxim watched as she took her cell phone out of her pocket and pushed the number two. "Who's number one on your speed dial, baby?" he asked.

"This hot, to-die-for, sexy jeans model I know," she said.

Maxim gasped dramatically. "Sharlamagne Dickens! You just uttered a derivative of the 's' word! Out loud!"

She smiled at him, and he couldn't resist gathering her into his arms again, kissing her neck, and relishing the sound of the sigh he'd caused to escape her lungs.

"Hi, Dad," she said, sounding a little too breathless. Maxim kissed her again. "Um…it's me…Sharlamagne. Yeah…I guess you did know that. Um…I'm wondering…" she stammered as he kissed the soft flesh at the hollow of her throat. "Can you come over to Mrs. Tanner's old house and look at something for us?"

Maxim was feeling powerfully driven to own her—to own all of her. He kissed her mouth, and it made a smacking sound.

"No…no, I'm not eating. I just need you to look at something," Sharlamagne said. "Could you drop by? Okay…thanks, Dad. See you in a few minutes."

Maxim smiled as he felt Sharlamagne's cell phone slide down his back and onto the bed as her arms went around his neck to join him in the kiss. He'd been moving her backward the entire time she'd been on the phone, and she hadn't noticed.

"I like doing *nothing* with you," she whispered as their lips parted a moment.

He chuckled. "Just imagine how much you'll like doing *something* with me," he teased.

"You are being naughty," she scolded, breathless in his arms.

Their mouths met again, blending together, melding. He had to have her! He couldn't wait it out much longer. He hoped her dad arrived quickly. He hoped her dad didn't have a heart attack when Maxim asked him if he could marry his daughter after such a short acquaintance. Maxim wanted to do *nothing* with Sharlamagne for the rest of his life—forever, actually.

"I love you, Sharlamagne," he whispered in her ear. "You know that I love you, don't you?"

Sharlamagne felt tears spring to her eyes. "I love you, Maxim," she breathed as he kissed her neck. "Oh, you don't even know how much."

He'd said it! He'd said he loved her! They were standing in the Passion Room, surrounded by thirty million dollars, and all he cared about was her. Tears spilled over her cheeks as Maxim kissed her again—ravaged her mouth with such an impassioned, loving kiss she thought she might faint. Maxim Tanner loved her, and no matter what happened next, in that moment, Sharlamagne Dickens felt free—free to be herself—free to love without fear.

Silently she thanked Elisaveta Tanner—thanked her for Maxim—for love.

CHAPTER SIXTEEN

"I think it's a little tipped, baby," Sharlamagne said as she stood back from the framed print Maxim had just hung on the wall in place of one of the Passion Room paintings.

"Which way?" Maxim asked.

"Push the lower-right corner up a little," she instructed. Maxim did as she instructed, and she said, "There! That's it. Come see what you think."

Maxim strode to stand next to her. He studied the print of the knight and lady poised to kiss and nodded. "I think it's straight now," he agreed. "It looks good. Not as good as the original maybe, but good."

As Maxim put one muscular arm across Sharlamagne's shoulders, she put her arm around his waist and laid her head against him. She was so content in that moment—so blissfully happy.

Three days before, when her father had arrived at the house and confirmed that, to the best of his knowledge, Mrs. Tanner's Manolito paintings were authentic originals, she'd been nearly overwhelmed with a giddy sort of delight in knowing she'd solved the mystery of the Passion Room. Yet almost immediately, she'd also realized that Mrs. Tanner's notes concerning the mystery and magic of the Passion Room—the pages she'd found in the poetry book Mrs. Tanner had bequeathed to her—were most definitely at least fifty years old. Thus, both Maxim and Sharlamagne were left wondering how it could be that she would have written about the paintings decades and decades before she owned them.

Still, in the end, it didn't matter. In the end, Sharlamagne had Maxim's arms around her, owned his heart, and really didn't care about anything else.

As Maxim stood looking at the professional, framed print that now hung where one of the Manolito originals had hung, he decided that he liked the Passion Room all the better now that the paintings were safe with the museum curator.

When Mr. Dickens's art appraiser had informed Maxim that the Passion Room paintings were now worth monetarily more than they had been when his grandmother had laid out thirty million dollars to buy and insure them (the insurance documents insuring the paintings and stating Maxim O. Tanner as their owner were attached to the back of each painting and discovered when the museum curator was having them taken off the Passion Room walls), he knew he didn't want them in the house. He didn't want something risking the house's safety. Furthermore, they were beautiful paintings and should be shared. He and Sharlamagne both realized that Mrs. Tanner must've felt the same way. Why else would she have had such elaborate prints made and framed in vintage frames similar to those that embellished the paintings? She'd obviously intended for Maxim to discover the value of the paintings one day—yet she also just as obviously wanted the Passion Rom to boast the same passionate emotion the paintings had added to its magic.

In truth, he was glad the paintings were gone—glad he could linger in the Passion Room with the woman he loved and not have to worry about thirty million dollars staring down at them all the time. Again he owned a sense of having been untethered, unleashed, and freed. He also owned a sense of urgency, impatience, and desire.

"Well, that's done," he said. "I really do like this room."

"Me too," Sharlamagne agreed. "It is so perfectly romantic."

"Yeah," Maxim agreed. "Even though I am a guy, I can see that about it. It's why I've been reconsidering my plans. Maybe this should be a bed-and-breakfast after all."

Sharlamagne gasped. "Are you serious? But it's our room," she accidentally let slip. Her thoughts were becoming more and more unguarded in Maxim's presence. She blushed a little, but he smiled.

"I'm glad you think of it that way," he said, turning her to face him. "But don't you think this would make the best bridal suite in the city?" he asked.

Sharlamagne tried to hide her disappointment. She didn't want anyone else in their room—in hers and Maxim's Passion Room. She wanted it to be theirs and only theirs. And yet what could she say? It wasn't her decision to make.

"Well, yes...but..." she began.

"I mean, I'd want to have my honeymoon here," he said. "Wouldn't you?"

"Well...yeah...but..."

"In fact," he began, "why don't we?"

"Why don't we what?" Sharlamagne asked. A strange heat was overtaking—the heat of desire and anticipation. Was he saying what she thought he was?

"Why don't we have our honeymoon in the Passion Room?"

Tears instantly filled Sharlamagne's eyes as Maxim held up one hand. A beautiful marquise-cut diamond solitaire engagement ring rested above the first knuckle of his index finger. Her hands flew to her mouth in an attempt to keep her from sobbing as tears trickled down her cheeks.

"Will you marry me, Sharlamagne Dickens?" Maxim asked. "I love you. I want you. I want you for my wife and the mother of my well-parented children," he said, smiling.

Sharlamagne couldn't speak—she couldn't breathe! Her throat had constricted with emotion.

As she endeavored to gain control of her senses and speech, Maxim added, "I want your answer now—yes or no. I don't want you telling me you need time to think. I need to know now...and don't hold back. I can take it."

Don't hold back. As Maxim's words echoed through Sharlamagne's mind, she leapt up, wrapping her arms around his neck and her legs around his waist.

"Yes! Yes, yes, yes, yes, *yes!*" she cried as he chuckled, holding her tightly to him.

Maxim laughed and put one hand at the back of her head as Sharlamagne dropped to her feet once more. "Now kiss me 'yes,'" he said.

"Yes," Sharlamagne breathed as Maxim's head descended toward hers. "Yes," she said, pulling away from him a moment. "Yes," she breathed as she pressed her mouth to his and drank deeply of his perfect kiss.

He chuckled, and she pulled back from him a moment. "What?" she asked.

Taking her left hand, Maxim pushed the engagement ring onto her finger. "I am so gonna rock your world, baby," he said.

"You already have," Sharlamagne whispered.

"Well, you ain't seen nothing yet," he told her, brushing the tears from her cheeks with the back of one hand. "And while we're at it, how about another hickey…just for good measure?"

"No!" Sharlamagne giggled, trying to pull away from him. But he held her arms tightly as he endeavored to press his mouth to her neck.

Gathering her into his arms and against his powerful form, Maxim breathed, "I love you, Sharlamagne. And Grandma knew I would."

"I think your grandmother knew everything…including the fact that I was yours the minute I saw you," Sharlamagne sighed.

Maxim grinned. "Don't you mean the minute you saw my stupid poster in the mall the day we met?"

"Nope," Sharlamagne giggled. "I mean the very minute I saw you. Though the poster didn't hurt any."

Maxim laughed. "I promise I'll take you somewhere else for the rest of our honeymoon, sugar bee…but I want our first night together to be here…right here."

Sharlamagne smiled and watched as Maxim took something out of the back pocket of his jeans. He held it up to her. It was a small manila envelope, and he tossed it on the bed.

"And I'll be interested to see what Grandma has to say about it the morning after," he said. "But for now, I'm gonna tell you something I discovered about this room."

"And what's that?" she asked.

"The trove of the Passion Room? It wasn't the paintings...at least not for me," he explained. "For me, the trove of the Passion Room is you."

"It's us," Sharlamagne whispered through her tears of joy. "For the visitors will succumb," she began to quote from Mrs. Tanner's notes, "either to lustful, physical passion—or to the pure, abiding, soul-wrenching passion of true, true love."

"Mmm...I like that lustful, physical passion stuff," Maxim teased.

"You are being naughty!" Sharlamagne giggled, playfully slapping Maxim's broad chest.

"Succumb to me then, shawty," Maxim said, kissing softly. "Marry me and share a life of true love and passion with me."

"Yes," Sharlamagne said. "I love you, Maxim."

"I love you, Sharlamagne," Maxim whispered as they shared such an impassioned, loving kiss that even the Passion Room itself seemed to blush crimson with confirming the presence of true, true love.

EPILOGUE

Sharlamagne slowly opened her eyes. It was light and bright in the Passion Room—obviously morning. She smiled and sighed as she saw Maxim's handsome face as he leaned over her, smiling. Then, realizing that she must look a mess, she grabbed the top of the gold bedsheet, pulling it up over her head.

"Oh, no! I have pillow hair and leftover makeup face!" she exclaimed.

Maxim's amused chuckle caused her heart to leap with delight, however, and she drew the sheet down to her nose and peeked out at him.

"You look beautiful," he said, brushing a strand of hair from her forehead. "I've been watching you sleep."

"Oh, no!" she whined. "How embarrassing."

Again, Maxim chuckled. "No...beautiful," he said. He kissed her forehead and tugged at the sheet to reveal her mouth. He pressed a soft kiss to her lips and then said, "I've been waiting for you to wake up. I didn't want to open it without you."

"Your grandmother's last envelope?" she asked.

Maxim had explained the envelope to her the night he'd proposed—explained that his grandmother had left it to him to be opened the morning after the day he was married. They'd both laughed at her continued mystique, even after having passed from this life to the next. But now, a tremor of curiosity traveled over her arms and legs. What did Elisaveta Tanner have to say to Maxim following his marriage?

"Yeah," he affirmed. "Should we open it now?"

"Yes!" Sharlamagne said, straightening the straps of her satin ivory negligee as she sat up in the bed.

She watched as Maxim retrieved the small manila envelope from the end table to his right. "*To my Maxim,*" Maxim read aloud from the front of the envelope. "*To be opened on the first morning following your wedding night.*" He looked to Sharlamagne and grinned, his blue eyes smoldering with mischief. "I wonder if she knew you'd be the one in my bed this morning."

Sharlamagne blushed, fantastically delighted by her husband's flirting.

Maxim none too gently tore open the top of the envelope and removed two other envelopes. Sharlamagne recognized their style—Elisaveta's favorite stationery.

Maxim smiled. "Well, well, well…not so sure of yourself after all, now are you?"

"What?" Sharlamagne asked.

Maxim chuckled and handed one of the envelopes to Sharlamagne. "*To be opened once you've married my Sharlamagne,*" she read. She gasped with delight. "Are you kidding me?"

"And yet," he said, handing the other envelope to her.

Sharlamagne smiled and read, "*To be opened if you're a blithering idiot and marry anyone other than Sharlamagne Dickens.*" She laughed and handed the envelope back to Maxim. He tossed it onto the end table as she returned the first envelope to him.

"Okay, baby," he began. "What insightful wisdom do you think Grandma has to impart to us this morning?"

Sharlamagne shrugged. She couldn't answer. She was too overwhelmed with her love for Maxim and the impassioned night of bliss they'd spent together in each other's arms—in the Passion Room.

Maxim sighed and began to read. "*Maxim, darling. You are my most beloved. I love you as you can never imagine being loved until you have children of your own. It is (and always has been) my greatest wish to see you loved the way you deserve to be loved, cared for the way you deserve to be cared for, and love and care for someone who is your equal in return. I knew the day you met Sharlamagne that she was meant for you and you for her. I knew it—as assuredly as I breathed, I knew it. I knew that she would be the one to free you—that only she could return upon you the physical and emotional love you could offer to her. That only she could be your counterpart in the level of passion that would consume you both."*

He paused, winked, and smiled at Sharlamagne, saying, "I like all this passion talk."

Sharlamagne blushed, slapped his arm, and shook her head. "Just read the letter, Mr. Passion."

Maxim smiled and continued, *"Maxim, you and Sharlamagne are meant for each other and only each other. I know that by now you know this…that by now you know what the true trove of the Passion Room is— yours and Sharlamagne's love. Oh, I'm certain my little Sharlamagne has already discovered the commercial value of my lovely Manolito paintings. But you know now that the paintings are not the trove…that the trove is your love—yours and Sharlamagne's true, soulful love.*

Years ago I was impressed to write my thoughts on a room—an inspiration that came to me almost fifty years ago, before the Passion Room even existed in mine and Alek's home. I was driven to write something that I did not understand—that I would not understand until fifty years later, the day you and Sharlamagne first set eyes on one another. The Passion Room text had always haunted me—made me wonder why it had come to me as it did—strong, firm, needing to be recorded.

Yet the evening of the day you and Sharlamagne were introduced—the evening following our day together at the antique fair four years ago— that evening I was sleeping and was awakened by a powerful dream and understanding of it all—of the Passion Room text I had been moved to write so long ago. This dream, and the understanding it offered me, became my solace. It became all my hopes for you, Maxim, my darling—and for Sharlamagne. Because of the Passion Room and this dream, I was able to leave this earth—to travel to the next life and be with Alek—for I knew assuredly, at last, that the greatest love God can gift any of us would be yours."

"A dream?" Sharlamagne asked when Maxim paused.

"Grandma dreamt a lot of things before they happened," he explained. "You knew that, right?"

"Kind of," she answered. "I knew she had visions or promptings or something. But I don't know if I ever knew they came to her in dreams."

"They did," he confirmed. "She even kept a dream journal on her nightstand. It was just a notebook, but she kept it there with a pen so she could write down her dreams…in case they were of consequence."

"Hmm. How wonderful," Sharlamagne said. "What a wonderful gift."

"Okay…she goes on," Maxim said. He smiled as he began to read. "*I wrote the dream for you, Maxim.*" He nodded to Sharlamagne, and she smiled. "*In the dream journal I had near me that night, I wrote my dream of you and Sharlamagne. I want you to have it—both of you. Let it be my wedding gift. Since I cannot be there to choose the perfect prisms and compote for your dining table, let my dream be my gift to you. Know that my heart is always with you and my Sharlamagne—that I love you, my Maxim—that I left this earth easy, knowing Sharlamagne would care for you and you for her.*

Carl Rowlands has given you an old key. You should have it with you now—in the pocket of your pants that are lying on the floor next to your bed."

Sharlamagne felt her eyebrows raise in astonishment.

"Holy cow," Maxim said as he leaned out of the bed and retrieved the trousers to the tuxedo he'd worn for his and Sharlamagne's wedding the day before. "How much of our being together did she dream anyway?" he chuckled.

"She left a key for you?" Sharlamagne asked.

"Yeah. Carl gave it to me the same day he gave me this envelope and the other one with Grandma's other letter I let you read."

Maxim cleared his throat and began reading the letter again. "*The key fits the lock of the drawer in the nightstand next to you, Maxim, darling. Unlock the drawer, and there you'll find my dream journal in which is recorded the dream I had of you and Sharlamagne the night after*" *the day you first met her. Read it with her, my darling—know that I knew you would be happy. It is my gift to you—peace of mind in knowing I am with your grandfather just as you are with Sharlamagne now. I love you, darling, and I do have more to say, but open the drawer, retrieve the journal, and save both the journal and this letter to reflect upon later. For this is your time to be only in each other's arms—to be lost in the passion borne of true love legally bound before man and God. Open the drawer, Maxim. Then take your beautiful young wife in your arms and…"*

Sharlamagne frowned as Maxim paused and smiled. "And what?" she asked. "And do what?"

Maxim shook his head. "It can wait. I want to be the one to make you blush." He winked at her, and she understood.

"Give me that key," she said, taking his key ring from him.

Leaning over him, she stretched her arm and unlocked the drawer in the nightstand. Maxim leaned over and retrieved the tattered spiral notebook that lay within. She watched as he opened it to the last entry. Shaking his head, he smiled and showed it to her.

Sharlamagne gasped. The date was exactly the date of the antique exhibition she'd helped her family with four years before. She remembered it perfectly, because she'd met Maxim that day and would never forget it.

"Let's see," he mumbled, flipping toward the back of the entry. "*I saw Maxim*," he read. "*I saw him with my pretty Sharlamagne in his arms—saw him kiss her throat and pull him to her—brush the strap of her lovely ivory nightgown from her shoulder and kiss her there. I saw take her in his arms, lay her on their bed, and—*"

"Okay, that's enough!" Sharlamagne said, snatching the notebook from him as he laughed. "I get it. She knew. I believe her."

"Give me that," he said, taking the notebook from her, returning it to the drawer in the nightstand, and dropping his keys to the floor with a thud. "You know," he mumbled against her mouth as his arms enveloped her and laid her back down on their bed, "I think I was *made* for loving you, Sharlamagne Tanner."

Sharlamagne smiled and ran a hand through his hair. It was all real. *He* was real! And the conductor of the "I Was Made for Loving

You" train really was going to whisk her away on a lifetime adventure of passion—passion borne not of just physical desire but of true love respected, cherished, and protected.

AUTHOR'S NOTE

First, let's talk about passion. The dictionary defines *passion* like this:

1. Any powerful, undeniable emotion or feeling, as in love or hate.
2. Love; strong amorous desire.
3. Strong "s" word–ual desire; lust. (Okay, yes, I paraphrased that one.)
4. An occurrence of powerful love.
5. A person toward whom one feels powerful love or "s" word–ual desire.

Now, if you will, please note that, of the five definitions given, emotional love is the binding thread throughout. See, I like the word *passion*. To me, it's a very expressive word—a more powerful word than affection, attachment, or feeling. Furthermore, it applies to many things in my own life. I own a passion for my family because they are the most important things to me. I love them with such a depth of emotion that it can be painful sometimes. Furthermore, I have a passion for history, photographs, autumn, pumpkins, Christmas, beautiful music, and the colors orange and brown—not the same passion I own for my family, of course, but a powerful love all the same. Do you see what I mean? We all have passions, and most of the time they have nothing to do with the "s" word–ual thing. (Naturally, I have a passion for my dead-sexy husband, Kevin, in many, many regards—but we'll talk about that later. Right?)

However, as much as I love and understand the word *passion*, the world has managed to cause it to be somewhat of an eyebrow-raiser. Thus, when I started to write *The Trove of the Passion Room*, I was a little nervous. I've been verbally slapped for allowing my heroes to cuss a little before, so I wondered what in the world would happen to me if I allowed the reader a little more insight into their intimate thoughts. But the story of Maxim and Sharlamagne—of their soul-saturating love and their strength in resisting temptation—was screaming to get out of my head! So I took the plunge: I wrote it. And as I wrote it, I knew I had to be true to myself and to the characters (because they're real to me, you understand). To me, the love story of Maxim Tanner and Sharlamagne Dickens is a *beautiful* one—and a passionate one, in every definition of the word. Maxim and Sharlamagne's story is also one of strength—strength in conviction, strength in selflessness, strength in loving someone else so much, in respecting them so much, that physical passions are kept in check.

And besides, as Gwen says, without the lustful definition of passion, the human race would cease to perpetuate. That physical passion between a man and a woman is a necessary and very wonderful aspect of true love. Thus, Maxim and Sharlamagne are tempted by it, and they're tempted by it from the first moment they kiss. Still, restraint and self-control—that's what sets their love apart from so many others, especially in a world where the "s" word has become a game—a trifle—something to do just because. Maxim and Sharlamagne's romance is a wonderful one and, in my opinion, admirable.

And yes, Maxim cusses some because that's who he is, especially at the beginning of the book—a rather angry, frustrated, neglected boy/man. Thank heaven for his grandparents, or who knows where he'd be right now. In fact, my friend Debra (after having read the book) tossed a little e-mail to me—a little supportive forewarning. I'd like to quote it here. Debra writes:

> One last thing—I want you to be prepared—this is the first book where you didn't have the hero catching himself each time he swore or have the heroine react in a "horrified" way each time it happened. I think it makes the book a bit more real and less fairylandish, but you might have those couple of readers who are offended. DO NOT change anything, but I want you to realize that you might just get that reaction from some of your readers. The swearing fits the Maxim character considering the horrible upbringing he had, and I would hope that readers would realize that.

Good ol' Debra (though she's not really old—that's just a term of endearment). She's been with me from the very beginning of my writing career (actually, before that), and she's always honest without being unkind. She also tries to protect me as much as she can, and this is a perfect example because I do *not* like to disappoint anyone! I will sometimes endure the worst thing possible for myself in order to keep from disappointing someone else, and Debra knows that about me (oh, the stories she could tell). She knows I love my readers—that I'm so grateful to them for even taking the time to read my books. She also knows I don't want to disappoint them/*you*. Yet she understands how desperately I love my characters (the passion I own for them, as it were), how real they are to me, and how it is better for me and my readers if I'm true to the characters and their story. Good ol' Debra! (Again—just a term of endearment there.) And therefore, it is what it is (as Kevin likes to say). Some people lie, some people are critical of others, some people gossip, and Maxim Tanner uses a few good old "farm-friendly" terms.

Okay, enough of that deep thinking, why this, and why that blah-blah-blahing. Let's have some fun!

One of the dedicatees of this book is my daughter Sandy (Sandy Ann, not to be confused with my bosom friend Sandy). Why? Well, because this book is *so* her! First of all, a year or so ago, while we were talking on the phone, Sandy said to me, "Mom! I just feel that somehow the entire responsibility of preserving history is on *my* shoulders!"

You see, Sandy has been working on an ongoing project—trying to collect as many stories and life details from as many family members as she can. It's an awe-inspiring project but also an overwhelming one. But that feeling of being responsible for preserving history all by yourself—I've always had that too. And that's when I realized that Sharlamagne and her family are antique dealers. It's also one reason why I see myself as Elisaveta Tanner. Elisaveta and I are true kindred spirits in more ways than I can tell you right now!

Thus, as I began to write this book with Sandy in mind, I began to nest on the idea of a World War II ball—the same kind of event that Sandy attended with her hottie husband, Soren, last Christmas in Boulder, Colorado. Yes, the World War II ball is an actual event! And to me it's a fabulous idea. There are actually two events every year—the World War II ball held in the summertime and the White Christmas event held in December. What a lovely thing, huh? I hope Kevin and I can attend someday.

Sandy and I both share the same reoccurring dream. Not the one where Keanu Reeves shows up looking for me at the Olympic figure skating pavilion that I have every year or so, but the fabulous dream wherein I find an old house with a secret passage that leads to a trove—rooms and rooms full of antiques that no one knows is there and that I can therefore pillage. I love that dream—though I do always wake up kind of sad and disappointed. Anyway, can you imagine a little elderly lady leaving you a house stuffed with beautiful antiques? Well, Sandy and I can—and so can Mallory (Sandy's bosom friend). Therefore, the old house Sharlamagne inherits from Elisaveta is a dream come true to us!

Now, I know you're asking the name question; a lot of people do. So, yes, I admit it—there are some stories behind the names in *The Trove of the Passion Room*. One of them you already know the story behind because it was in the story itself. Maxim Olivier—Maxim after Laurence Olivier's character in the movie version of *Rebecca* and Olivier after Sir Laurence Olivier himself. (I'm so transparent I scare myself sometimes.) Van-Dyke Dickens—well, I would think that would be obvious since you already know how my brain works. But in case you need further affirmation, then, yes, Dickens after Mr. Charles Dickens and Van-Dyke after Mr. *Chitty Chitty Bang Bang/Mary Poppins/The Dick Van Dyke Show* himself—Mr. Dick Van Dyke! (I *so love* Dick Van Dyke.) Another obvious one would be Louisa Dickens, after Louisa May Alcott, of course. Then there's the last name of Sharlamagne's biological father—Grinkov. Again, I'm so transparent it's pitiful! Gregory Grinkov—my secret little tribute to the beloved and "gone-too-soon" pairs figure skater Sergei Grinkov, who I adored and who died tragically at the age of twenty-eight on November 20, 1995. (Sniffle!) As for Sharlamagne—well, I've always liked the sound of the name Charlemagne, but never the spelling. And even though I know Charlemagne was a guy, I think it sounds like a girl's name, so voilà!

There you have some name histories for *The Trove of the Passion Room*. I hope you liked them as much as I did.

"Why does Elisaveta Tanner collect Uncle Remus books?" The answer is again obvious (I need to work on my mystique!). I *love* Uncle Remus books! My feelings are the same as Elisaveta's—that although they were written by a white man, the Uncle Remus stories are one of the few surviving attempts we have at capturing the valuable life lessons orally passed on by southern slaves in the morbid, horrid years before emancipation. The stories Joel Chandler Harris endeavored to preserve are beautiful, entertaining fables, filled with important moral lessons and frocked with humor. I love them, and I'm sad that more people don't value what they represent—the wisdom and personality of those early African-Americans who found escape and comfort in telling stories.

My friend Patsy (not to be confused with my mother, who is also named Patsy)—I once sat at her knee (literally) and listened while she told the story of how she came to possess several items that had once belonged to Baby Doe Tabor. She related Baby Doe's story to me as well in that wonderful moment, and I loved the way her eyes lit up with excitement and emotion. However, the actual Baby Doe artifacts Patsy owned—well, it had been so many years since I'd seen them that I just wasn't quite sure if I was remembering them correctly. So, naturally, I asked Patsy! Here's an excerpt of what she wrote to me concerning them:

> The Baby Doe items consist of three things: a perfume cask, a letter box, and a letter portfolio of sorts...I am not sure what it is really called, but the guy we got it from said it was where letters were stored as they were being written. All three items are the same burgundy velvet material. The letter portfolio has a silver plate on the front inscribed from Horace to Baby Doe. The perfume cask at one time held two bottles...there is only one bottle there. The story was that possibly one was buried with her. The perfume was thought to be

the first gift that her husband Horace Tabor gave to
her. Still gives me chills to think about that whole story!

How fun, right? Patsy is another one of my friends who values the past, antiques, and those who have already passed on. You remember Patsy from *The Touch of Sage*, don't you?

Now this little ditty might be the one that amuses you the most. Let me preface this by saying once more that you really never know what's going to inspire me where a book is concerned. The summer before I turned fifteen, my friend Amy and I took a driver's education course at a place here in Albuquerque. For the sake of anonymity for them, we'll call it John Smith's School of Driving. Now, the owner, John Smith, had two adult sons who worked at the driving school as instructors. "John Jr." was pushing thirty—a "husky," kind of brusque guy that Amy and I hated driving with. However, John Smith's younger son (we'll call him Max) was in his early twenties and way, way, way, way, *way* good-looking! Needless to say, Amy and I were always delighted when "Max" was our driving instructor. He was ridiculously flirtatious and probably could've been charged with something because of the age difference between us and him. However, we were fourteen, naïve, and googlie-eyed, so we loved it when he'd flirt with us. I remember driving with him once; he was in the passenger's seat, and one of us (I really can't remember which one) was driving while the other sat in the backseat. Max was wearing shorts (because it was summer, remember), and this was back in the '80s when shorts were pretty short, even for guys. So anyway, Max is sitting there, and he looks over at whichever one of us was driving and says, "It's okay. You can feel my thigh if you want to." I know! Scandalous, right? Well, we were too young to comprehend anything other than he was being flirty—which he always was with us—and so we just went merrily along. And then one day, we're at the mall, and we look up into the front windows of this store called Jeans West, and what do we see? That's right—Max Smith modeling Jeans West jeans! He was seriously the Jeans West model for quite a while. Hysterical, right?

So before we just move right on to trivia snippets, let me share one more insightful thing with you. When my little boy Mitchel was really little (potty-trained to four years old) he would *not* use any public bathroom that was in a gas station or rest area when we went on family trips. Would *not* use one—never—nope. He would only go in the wide open spaces off the highway. That was it. The end. He wouldn't go. Now, I have a theory as to where this little (though very understandable) OCD may have come from. You know my husband, Kevin? He has never—not since he was old enough to go by himself or to his memory—sat on a public toilet seat. Nope—never. Not with those tissue toilet seat covers, not with mounds of toilet paper placed up on it—nothing. Never. It's the truth. Thus, Maxim is the same way.

Oh, I could bore you for hours and hours with things in this book that were inspired by real life. But don't worry, I won't. As is always my mission when writing for you, I hope you enjoyed the story—that it swept you away on wings of delicious romance, that your heart felt lightened, your mind reassured of all that is good in the world, and that you closed this book with a contented sigh and a smile. Thank you for sharing Maxim and Sharlamagne's beautiful love story with me.

~Marcia Lynn McClure

The Trove of the Passion Room Trivia Snippets

Snippet #1—Last year, my friend Jean and her husband bought two new toilets for their house. Jean said (and I quote), "The only ring I got for Christmas came in a new toilet!" (Fear not, however. Jean and her husband also exchanged matching Mickey Mouse watches. Love it!)

Snippet #2—When my son Trent was little, we used to play the card game Old Maid using a deck of Disney princess cards. One of the jokers in the deck was Ursula from the Disney animated film *The Little Mermaid*. We used Ursula as the Old Maid card. And instead of saying, "Wanna play Old Maid?" we'd say, "Hey! Wanna play Ursula?" (Pronounced very enunciatively as ERR—syoo—laaah.) Thus, Sharlamagne and Gwen entertain themselves at the antique fair by playing "Ugly Old Witch"—i.e., "Ursula"!

Snippet #3—In 1984, my maternal grandfather, Wayne States, passed away. (You know him from the author's note in *The Heavenly Surrender*, remember?) In 1989, his wife, my sweet grandmother Opal Edith Switzler States, joined him. My Uncle Wayne purchased the home my grandma and grandpa had lived in during the last twelve to fifteen years of their lives, but when he got married in 1993, he decided to use the home as a rental property. Thus, my mom, my aunt, and my uncles met at my grandpa and grandma's house to sort through things. A couple of things are interesting about this event. First of all, my Uncle Wayne told me I could have anything I wanted from the house—anything. I chose the three white-and-blue enamel plates my grandma used to serve breakfast on (specifically the pound of bacon she would cook each morning when I was staying with my grandparents in the summer). I also asked for the large bowl my grandpa had always eaten his oatmeal out of each morning. I loved those breakfasts with Grandpa and Grandma, and to me those items were worth far more than gold. The other things I have tucked away are a few little items that we found in Grandma and Grandpa's kitchen junk drawer. One of the more interesting items is a piece of an artificial artery. It was a sample doctors had given to my grandpa and grandma back in the late sixties or early seventies when it was discovered that my grandpa needed to have an arterial repair in his leg. So I still have that little piece of artificial artery tucked away in my cedar chest, along with three other interesting items I found in the junk drawer that day—three teeth! Yep! I have either Grandpa's or Grandma's molars. I'm thinking they are my grandpa's and that when a tooth went bad, he just yanked it out and tossed it in the junk drawer in the kitchen. I *love* those teeth! I *love* that they were just sitting there in the junk drawer—treasure for me to find years after my grandparents were gone. Thus, there you have it—the inspiration for Maxim finding his grandpa's teeth discarded in his grandma's kitchen junk drawer.

Snippet #4—Both Sandy and my mother name lilacs as their favorite flower. I love them too, and you already know I used to play under a big lilac tree when I was a little girl.

Snippet #5—The paintings hanging in the Passion Room are inspired by prints I have hanging in the front room of my house: *Meeting on the Turret Stairs* by Sir Frederic William Burton, *La Belle Dame sans Merci* by John William Waterhouse, and *The Kiss* by Francesco Hayez, to name a few. Love them!

Snippet #6—My cherished friend Sandy (who you know as…well…) always said that a woman only feels as good as the lingerie she's wearing. I happen to believe this to be absolutely true! Wear ratty nightgowns or pajamas (which I often do), and you feel ratty. Wear an old, worn-out bra with no support left and underwire poking out through the fabric and digging a hole into your armpit, and you feel droopy and irritable. Wear raggedy old panties with the elastic ripping away from the fabric, and you feel raggedy, old, and stretched out. Thus, Gwen's advice to Sharlamagne considering her underwear—well, it's something I hold to still, to this very day. (Which reminds me—I have a few pairs of old pajamas that need to go straight into the trash can.) So pay attention to your lingerie, ladies—because a woman only feels as good as the lingerie she's wearing!

Snippet #7—When I was little (and I do mean little) I was in love with Manolito Montoya from the old TV series *High Chaparral*. (Hmm. This certainly dates me, considering that the series *High Chaparral* ran from 1967 to 1971—meaning, by the time it ended, I was only six years old!) Manolito and *High Chaparral* are one of my favorite memories of my mother too—the way she would sigh, smile, and say, "I think Manolito is *so* handsome!" Yep, Manolito Montoya and the *High Chaparral* theme music are two of my most vivid childhood reminiscences. Manolito was very handsome (at least to me and Mom), and I used to sigh and smile whenever he came on the screen, just like my mother did. I really can't explain how it was that Manolito's name popped into my head in the middle of the night as the name of the artist of the paintings that hang in the Passion Room; it just did. Therefore, the Edwardian artist Darrow Manolito is a figment of my imagination. However, in the movie-in-my-mind-version of *The*

Trove of the Passion Room, he is real, and he looks just like Manolito Montoya. (A little more information that you don't need is that the artist's first name is, in truth, is the last name of the actor who played Manolito in *High Chaparral*—Henry Darrow!)

My everlasting admiration, gratitude and love…
To my husband, Kevin…
My inspiration…
My heart's desire…
The man of my every dream!

ABOUT THE AUTHOR

Marcia Lynn McClure's intoxicating succession of novels, novellas, and e-books—including *The Visions of Ransom Lake*, *A Crimson Frost*, *The Rogue Knight*, and most recently *The Pirate Ruse*—has established her as one of the most favored and engaging authors of true romance. Her unprecedented forte in weaving captivating stories of western, medieval, regency, and contemporary amour void of brusque intimacy has earned her the title "The Queen of Kissing."

Marcia, who was born in Albuquerque, New Mexico, has spent her life intrigued with people, history, love, and romance. A wife, mother, grandmother, family historian, poet, and author, Marcia Lynn McClure spins her tales of splendor for the sake of offering respite through the beauty, mirth, and delight of a worthwhile and wonderful story.

BIBLIOGRAPHY

A Better Reason to Fall in Love
A Crimson Frost
An Old-Fashioned Romance
Beneath the Honeysuckle Vine
Born for Thorton's Sake
Daydreams
Desert Fire
Divine Deception
Dusty Britches
Kiss in the Dark
Kissing Cousins
Love Me
Saphyre Snow
Shackles of Honor
Sudden Storms
Sweet Cherry Ray
Take a Walk With Me
The Anthology of Premiere Novellas Romantic Vignettes
The Fragrance of her Name
The Heavenly Surrender
The Heavenly Surrender 10th Anniversary Special Edition
The Heavenly Surrender Hardcover Edition
The Highwayman of Tanglewood
The Highwayman of Tanglewood Hardcover Edition
The Light of the Lovers' Moon
The Pirate Ruse
The Prairie Prince
The Rogue Knight
The Tide of the Mermaid Tears
The Time of Aspen Falls
The Touch of Sage
The Trove of the Passion Room
The Visions of Ransom Lake

only stare up into his mesmerizing green eyes. His hand was strong and warm, powerful and reassuring.

"If it freaks you out so much…just kiss in the dark," he said.

Boston watched as Vance put the heel of his free hand to the light switch. In an instant the room went black.

Kissing Cousins
Contemporary Romance

Poppy Amore loved her job waitressing at Good Ol' Days Family Restaurant. No one could ask for a better working environment. After all, her best friend Whitney worked there, and her boss, restaurant owner Mr. Dexter, was a kind, understanding, grandfatherly sort of man. Furthermore, the job allowed Poppy to linger in the company of Mr. Dexter's grandson Swaggart Moretti—the handsome and charismatic head cook at Good Ol' Days.

Secretly, Swaggart was far more to Poppy than just a man who was easy to look at. In truth, she had harbored a secret crush on him for years—since her freshman year in high school, in fact. And although the memory of her feelings—even the lingering truth of them—haunted Poppy the way a veiled, unrequited love always haunts a heart, she had learned to simply find joy in possessing a hidden, anonymous delight in merely being associated with Swaggart. Still, Poppy had begun to wonder if her heart would ever let go of Swaggart Moretti—if any other man in the world could ever turn her head.

When the dazzling, uber-fashionable Mark Lawson appeared one night at Good Ol' Days, however, Poppy began to believe that perhaps her attention and her heart would be distracted from Swaggart at last. Mark Lawson was every girl's fantasy—tall, uniquely handsome, financially well-off, and as charming as any prince ever to appear in fairy tales. He was kind, considerate, and, Poppy would find, a true, old-fashioned champion. Thus, Poppy Amore willingly allowed her heart and mind to follow Mark Lawson—to attempt to abandon the past and an unrequited love and begin to move on.

But all the world knows that real love is not so easily put off, and Poppy began to wonder if even a man so wonderful as Mark Lawson could

Dusty Britches

Historical Romance

Angelina Hunter was seriously minded, and it was a good thing. Her father's ranch needed a woman who could endure the strenuous work of ranch life. Since her mother's death, Angelina had been that woman. She had no time for frivolity—no time for a less severe side of life. Not when there was so much to be done—hired hands to feed, a widower father to care for, and an often ridiculously light-hearted younger sister to worry about. No. Angelina Hunter had no time for the things most young women her age enjoyed.

And yet, Angelina had not always been so hardened. There had been a time when she boasted a fun, flirtatious nature even more delightful than her sister Becca's—a time when her imagination soared with adventurous, romantic dreams. But that all ended years before at the hand of one man. Her heart turned to stone…safely becoming void of any emotion save impatience and indifference.

Until the day her dreams returned, the day the very maker of her broken heart rode back into her life. As the dust settled from the cattle drive which brought him back, would Angelina's heart be softened? Would she learn to hope again? Would her long-lost dreams become a blessed reality?

Kiss in the Dark

Contemporary Romance

"Boston," he mumbled.

"I mean…Logan…he's like the man of my dreams! Why would I blow it? What if…" Boston continued to babble.

"Boston," he said. The commanding sound of his voice caused Boston to cease in her prattling and look to him.

"What?" she asked, somewhat grateful he'd interrupted her panic attack.

He frowned and shook his head.

"Shut up," he said. "You're all worked up about nothing." He reached out, slipping one hand beneath her hair to the back of her neck.

Boston was so startled by his touch, she couldn't speak—she could

Desert Fire

Historical Romance

She opened her eyes and beheld, for the first time, the face of Jackson McCall. Ruggedly handsome and her noble rescuer, he would, she knew in that moment, forever hold captive her heart as he then held her life in his protective arms.

Yet she was a nameless beauty, haunted by wisps of visions of the past. How could she ever hope he would return the passionate, devotional love she secreted for him when her very existence was a riddle?

Would Jackson McCall (handsome, fascinating, brooding) ever see her as anything more than a foundling—a burden to himself and his family? And with no memory of her own identity, how then could she release him from his apparent affliction of being her protector?

Divine Deception

Historical Romance

Life experience had harshly turned its cruel countenance on the young Fallon Ashby. Her father deceased and her mother suffering with a fatal disease, Fallon was given over to her uncle, Charles Ashby, until she would reach the age of independence.

Abused, neglected, and disheartened, Fallon found herself suddenly blessed with unexpected liberation at the hand of the mysterious Trader Donavon. A wealthy landowner and respected denizen of the town, Trader Donavon concealed his feature of face within the shadows of a black cowl.

When Fallon's secretive deliverer offered two choices of true escape from her uncle, her captive heart chose its own path. Thus, Fallon married the enormous structure of mortal man—without having seen the horrid secret he hid beneath an ominous hood.

But the malicious Charles Ashby, intent on avenging his own losses at Trader Donavon's hand, set out to destroy the husband that Fallon herself held secrets concerning. Would her wicked uncle succeed and perhaps annihilate the man that his niece secretly loved above all else?

house—Vivianna began to know—to know that miracles do exist—that love is never truly lost.

Born for Thorton's Sake

Historical Romance

Maria Castillo Holt...the only daughter of a valiant Lord and his Spanish beauty. Following the tragic deaths of her parents, Maria would find herself spirited away by conniving kindred in an endurance of neglect and misery.

However, rescued at the age of thirteen by Brockton Thorton, the son of her father's devoted friend Lord Richard Thorton, Maria would at last find blessed reprieve. Further Brockton Thorton became, from that day forth, ever the absolute center of Maria's very existence. And as the blessed day of her sixteenth birthday dawned, Maria's dreams of owning her heart's desire seemed to become a blissful reality.

Yet a fiendish plotting intruded, and Maria's hopes of realized dreams were locked away within dark, impenetrable walls. Would Maria's dreams of life with the handsome and coveted Brockton Thorton die at the hands of a demon strength?

Daydreams

Contemporary Romance

Sayler Christy knew chances were slim to none that any of her silly little daydreams would ever actually come true—especially any daydreams involving Mr. Booker, the new patient—the handsome, older patient convalescing in her grandfather's rehabilitation center.

Yet, working as a candy striper at Rawlings Rehab, Sayler couldn't help but dream of belonging to Mr. Booker—and Mr. Booker stole her heart—perhaps unintentionally—but with very little effort. Gorgeous, older, and entirely unobtainable—Sayler knew Mr. Booker would unknowingly enslave her heart for many years to come—for daydreams were nothing more than a cruel joke inflicted by life. All dreams—daydreams or otherwise—never came true. Did they?

battled with armor and blade—so the Scarlet Princess would battle in sacrifice and with secrets held. Thus, when the charge was given to preserve the heart of Karvana—Monet endeavored to serve her kingdom and forget her secreted love. Yet love is not so easily forgotten…

An Old-Fashioned Romance

Contemporary Romance

Life went along simply, if not rather monotonously, for Breck McCall. Her job was satisfying, she had true friends. But she felt empty—as if party of her soul was detached and lost to her. She longed for something—something which seemed to be missing.

Yet, there were moments when Breck felt she might almost touch something wonderful. And most of those moments came while in the presence of her handsome, yet seemingly haunted boss—Reese Thatcher.

Beneath the Honeysuckle Vine

Historical Romance

Civil War—no one could flee from the nightmare of battle and the countless lives it devoured. Everyone had sacrificed—suffered profound misery and unimaginable loss. Vivianna Bartholomew was no exception. The war had torn her from her home—orphaned her. The merciless war seemed to take everything—even the man she loved. Still, Vivianna yet knew gratitude—for a kind friend had taken her in upon the death of her parents. Thus, she was cared for—even loved.

Yet as General Lee surrendered, signaling the war's imminent end—as Vivianna remained with the remnants of the Turner family—her soul clung to the letters written by her lost soldier—to his memory written in her heart. Could a woman ever heal from the loss of such a love? Could a woman's heart forget that it may find another? Vivianna Bartholomew thought not.

Still, it is often in the world that miracles occur—that love endures even after hope has been abandoned. Thus, one balmy Alabama morning—as two ragged soldiers wound the road toward the Turner

A Better Reason to Fall in Love
Contemporary Romance

"Boom chicka wow wow!" Emmy whispered.

"Absolutely!" Tabby breathed as she watched Jagger Brodie saunter past.

She envied Jocelyn for a moment, knowing he was most likely on his way to drop something off on Jocelyn's desk—or to speak with her. Jocelyn got to talk with Jagger almost every day, whereas Tabby was lucky if he dropped graphics changes off to her once a week.

"Ba boom chicka wow wow!" Emmy whispered again. "He's sporting a red tie today! Ooo! The power tie! He must be feeling confident."

Tabby smiled, amused and yet simultaneously amazed at Emmy's observation. She'd noticed the red tie, too. "There's a big marketing meeting this afternoon," she told Emmy. "I heard he's presenting some hard-nose material."

"Then that explains it," Emmy said, smiling. "Mr. Brodie's about to rock the company's world!"

"He already rocks mine…every time he walks by," Tabby whispered.

A Crimson Frost
Historical Romance

Beloved of her father, King Dacian, and adored by her people, the Scarlet Princess Monet endeavored to serve her kingdom well—for the people of the Kingdom of Karvana were good and worthy of service. Long Monet had known that even her marriage would serve her people. Her husband would be chosen for her—for this was the way of royal existence.

Still, as any woman does—peasant or princess—Monet dreamt of owning true love—of owning choice in love. Thus, each time the raven-haired, sapphire-eyed, Crimson Knight of Karvana rode near, Monet knew regret—for in secret, she loved him—and she could not choose him.

As an arrogant king from another kingdom began to wage war against Karvana, Karvana's king, knights, and soldiers answered the challenge. The Princess Monet would also know battle. As the Crimson Knight

The Whispered Kiss
The Windswept Flame
To Echo the Past
Weathered Too Young

Still, fate often provides rescue by extraordinary venues, and Saphyre was not delivered into the hands of Death—but into the hands of those hiding dark secrets in the depths of bruised and bloodied souls. Saphyre knew a measure of hope and asylum in the company of these battered vagabonds. Even she knew love—a secreted love—a forbidden love. Yet it was love itself—even held secret—that would again summon Lord Death to hunt the princess, Saphyre Snow.

Shackles of Honor
Historical Romance
Cassidy Shea's life was nothing if not serene. Loving parents and a doting brother provided happiness and innocent hope in dreaming as life's experience. Yes, life was blissful at her beloved home of Terrill.

Still, for all its beauty and tranquility…ever there was something intangible and evasive lurking in the shadows. And though Cassidy wasted little worry on it…still she sensed its existence, looming as a menacing fate bent on ruin.

And when one day a dark stranger appeared, Cassidy could no longer ignore the ominous whispers of the secrets surrounding her. Mason Carlisle, an angry, unpredictable man materialized…and seemingly with Cassidy's black fate at his heels.

Instantly Cassidy found herself thrust into a world completely unknown to her, wandering in a labyrinth of mystery and concealments. Serenity was vanquished…and with it, her dreams.

Or were all the secrets so guardedly kept from Cassidy…were they indeed the cloth, the very flax from which her dreams were spun? From which eternal bliss would be woven?

Sudden Storms
Historical Romance
Rivers Brighton was a wanderer—having nothing and belonging to no one. Still, by chance, Rivers found herself harboring for a time beneath the roof of the kind-hearted Jolee Gray and her remarkably attractive yet ever-grumbling brother, Paxton. Jolee had taken Rivers in, and Rivers had stayed.

truly drive Swaggart Moretti from her heart. Would Poppy Amore miss her one chance at happiness, all for the sake of an unfulfilled adolescent's dream?

Love Me
Contemporary Romance
Jacey Whittaker couldn't remember a time when she hadn't loved Scott Pendleton—the boy next door. She couldn't remember a time when Scott hadn't been in her life—in her heart. Yet Scott was every other girl's dream too. How could Jacey possibly hope to win such a prize—the attention, the affections, the very heart of such a sought-after young man? Yet win him she did! He became the bliss of her youthful heart—at least for a time.

Still, some dreams live fulfilled—and some are lost. Loss changes the very soul of a being. Jacey wondered if her soul would ever rebound. Certainly, she went on—lived a happy life—if not so full and perfectly happy a life as she once lived. Yet she feared she would never recover—never get over Scott Pendleton—her first love.

Until the day a man walked into her apartment—into her apartment and into her heart. Would this man be the one to heal her broken heart? Would this man be her one true love?

Saphyre Snow
Historical Romance
Descended of a legendary line of strength and beauty, Saphyre Snow had once known happiness as princess of the Kingdom of Graces. Once a valiant king had ruled in wisdom—once a loving mother had spoken soft words of truth to her daughter. Yet a strange madness had poisoned great minds—a strange fever inviting Lord Death to linger. Soon it was even Lord Death sought to claim Saphyre Snow for his own—and all Saphyre loved seemed lost.

Thus, Saphyre fled—forced to leave all familiars for necessity of preserving her life. Alone, and without provision, Saphyre knew Lord Death might yet claim her—for how could a princess hope to best the Reaper himself?

Helplessly drawn to Paxton's alluring presence and unable to escape his astonishing hold over her, however, Rivers knew she was in danger of enduring great heartbreak and pain. Paxton appeared to find Rivers no more interesting than a brief cloudburst. Yet the man's spirit seemed to tether some great and devastating storm—a powerful tempest bridled within, waiting for the moment when it could rage full and free, perhaps destroying everything and everyone in its wake—particularly Rivers.

Could Rivers capture Paxton's attention long enough to make his heart her own? Or would the storm brewing within him destroy her hopes and dreams of belonging to the only man she had ever loved?

Sweet Cherry Ray

Historical Romance

Cherry glanced at her pa, who frowned and slightly shook his head. Still, she couldn't help herself, and she leaned over and looked down the road.

She could see the rider and his horse—a large buckskin stallion. As he rode nearer, she studied his white shirt, black flat-brimmed hat, and double-breasted vest. Ever nearer he rode, and she fancied his pants were almost the same color as his horse, with silver buttons running down the outer leg. Cherry had seen a similar manner of dress before—on the Mexican vaqueros that often worked for her pa in the fall.

"Cherry," her pa scolded in a whisper as the stranger neared them.

She straightened and blushed, embarrassed by being as impolite in her staring as the other town folk were in theirs. It seemed everyone had stopped whatever they had been doing to walk out to the street and watch the stranger ride in.

No one spoke—the only sound was that of the breeze, a falcon's cry overhead and the rhythm of the rider's horse as it slowed to a trot.

Take a Walk with Me

Contemporary Romance

"Grandma?" Cozy called as she closed the front door behind her. She inhaled a deep breath—bathing in the warm, inviting scent of banana nut bread baking in the oven. "Grandma? Are you in here?"

"Cozy!" her grandma called in a loud whisper. "I'm in the kitchen. Hurry!"

Cozy frowned—her heart leapt as worry consumed her for a moment. Yet, as she hurried to the kitchen to find her grandma kneeling at the window that faced the new neighbors yard, and peering out with a pair of binoculars, she exhaled a sigh of relief.

"Grandma! You're still spying on him?" she giggled.

"Get down! They'll see us! Get down!" Dottie ordered in a whisper, waving one hand in a gesture that Cozy should duck.

Giggling with amusement at her grandma's latest antics, Cozy dropped to her hands and knees and crawled toward the window.

"Who'll see us?" she asked.

"Here," Dottie whispered, pausing only long enough to reach for a second set of binoculars sitting on the nearby counter. "These are for you." She smiled at Cozy—winked as a grin of mischief spread over her face. "And now…may I present the entertainment for this evening… Mr. Buckly hunk of burning love Bryant…and company."

The Anthology of Premiere Novellas—Romantic Vignettes

Historical Romance

Includes Three Novellas:

The Unobtainable One

Annette Jordan had accepted the unavoidable reality that she must toil as a governess to provide for herself. Thankfully, her charge was a joy—a vision of youthful beauty, owning a spirit of delight.

But it was Annette's employer, Lord Gareth Barrett, who proved to be the trial—for she soon found herself living in the all-too-cliché governess's dream of having fallen desperately in love with the man who provided her wages.

The child loved her—but could she endure watching hopelessly as the beautiful woman from a neighboring property won Lord Barrett's affections?

The General's Ambition

Seemingly overnight, Renee Millings found herself orphaned and married to the indescribably handsome, but ever frowning, Roque Montan. His father, The General, was obsessively determined that his lineage would continue posthaste—with or without consent of his son's new bride.

But when Roque reveals the existence of a sworn oath that will obstruct his father's ambition, will the villainous General conspire to ensure the future of his coveted progeny to be born by Renee himself? Will Renee find the only means of escape from the odious General to be that of his late wife—death? Or will the son find no tolerance for his father's diabolic plotting concerning the woman Roque legally terms his wife?

Indebted Deliverance

Chalyce LaSalle had been grateful to the handsome recluse, Race Trevelian, when he had delivered her from certain tragedy one frigid winter day. He was addictively attractive, powerful, and intriguing—and there was something else about him—an air of secreted internal torture. Yet, as the brutal character of her emancipator began to manifest, Chalyce commenced in wondering whether the fate she now faced would be any less insufferable than the one from which he had delivered her.

Still, his very essence beckoned hers. She was drawn to him and her soul whispered that his mind needed deliverance as desperately as she had needed rescue that cold winter's noon.

The Fragrance of Her Name

Historical Romance

Love—the miraculous, eternal bond that binds two souls together. Lauryn Kennsington knew the depth of it. Since the day of her eighth birthday, she had lived the power of true love—witnessed it with her own heart. She had talked with it—learned not even time or death can vanquish it. The Captain taught her these truths—and she loved him all the more for it.

Yet now—as a grown woman—Lauryn's dear Captain's torment became her own. After ten years, Lauryn had not been able to help him find peace—the peace his lonely spirit so desperately needed—the peace he'd sought every moment since his death over fifty years before.

Still, what of her own peace? The time had come. Lauryn's heart longed to do the unthinkable—selfishly abandon her Captain for another—a mortal man who had stolen her heart—become her only desire.

Would Lauryn be able to put tormented spirits to rest and still be true to her own soul? Or, would she have to make a choice—a choice forcing her to sacrifice one true love for another?

The Heavenly Surrender
Historical Romance

Genieva Bankmans had willfully agreed to the arrangement. She had given her word, and she would not dishonor it. But when she saw, for the first time, the man whose advertisement she had answered…she was desperately intimidated. The handsome and commanding Brevan McLean was not what she had expected. He was not the sort of man she had reconciled herself to marrying.

This man, this stranger whose name Genieva now bore, was strong-willed, quick-tempered, and expectant of much from his new wife. Brevan McLean did not deny he had married her for very practical reasons only. He merely wanted any woman whose hard work would provide him assistance with the brutal demands of farm life.

But Genieva would learn there were far darker things, grave secrets held unspoken by Brevan McLean concerning his family and his land. Genieva Bankmans McLean was to find herself in the midst of treachery, violence, and villainy with her estranged husband deeply entangled in it.

The Highwayman of Tanglewood
Historical Romance

A chambermaid in the house of Tremeshton, Faris Shayhan well knew torment, despair, and trepidation. To Faris it seemed the future stretched long and desolate before her—bleak and as dark as a lonesome midnight path. Still, the moon oft casts hopeful luminosity to light one's way. So it was that Lady Maranda Rockrimmon cast hope upon Faris—set Faris upon a different path—a path of happiness, serenity, and love.

Thus, Faris abandoned the tainted air of Tremeshton in favor of the amethyst sunsets of Loch Loland Castle and her new mistress, Lady Rockrimmon. Further, it was on the very night of her emancipation that Faris first met the man of her dreams—the man of every woman's dreams—the rogue Highwayman of Tanglewood.

Dressed in black and astride his mighty steed, the brave, heroic, and dashing rogue Highwayman of Tanglewood stole Faris's heart as easily as he stole her kiss. Yet the Highwayman of Tanglewood was encircled in mystery—mystery as thick and as secretive as time itself. Could Faris truly own the heart of a man so entirely enveloped in twilight shadows and dangerous secrets?

The Light of the Lovers' Moon

Historical Romance

Violet Fynne was haunted—haunted by memory. It had been nearly ten years since her father had moved the family from the tiny town of Rattler Rock to the city of Albany, New York. Yet the pain and guilt in Violet's heart were as fresh and as haunting as ever they had been.

It was true Violet had been only a child when her family moved. Still—though she had been unwillingly pulled away from Rattler Rock—pulled away from him she held most dear—her heart had never left—and her mind had never forgotten the promise she had made—a promise to a boy—to a boy she had loved—a boy she had vowed to return to.

Yet the world changes—and people move beyond pain and regret. Thus, when Violet Fynne returned to Rattler Rock, it was to find that death had touched those she had known before—that the world had indeed changed—that unfamiliar faces now intruded on beloved memories.

Had she returned too late? Had Violet Fynne lost her chance for peace—and happiness? Would she be forever haunted by the memory of the boy she had loved nearly ten years before?

The Pirate Ruse
Historical Romance

Abducted! Forcibly taken from her home in New Orleans, Cristabel Albay found herself a prisoner aboard an enemy ship—and soon thereafter, transferred into the vile hands of blood-thirsty pirates! War waged between the newly liberated United States and King George. Still, Cristabel would soon discover that British sailors were the very least of her worries—for the pirate captain, Bully Booth, owned no loyalty—no sympathy for those he captured.

Yet hope was not entirely lost—for where there was found one crew of pirates—there was ever found another. Though Cristabel Albay would never have dreamed that she may find fortune in being captured by one pirate captain only to be taken by another—she did! Bully Booth took no man alive—let no woman live long. But the pirate Navarrone was known for his clemency. Thus, Cristabel's hope in knowing her life's continuance was restored.

Nonetheless, as Cristabel's heart began to yearn for the affections of her handsome, beguiling captor—she wondered if Captain Navarrone had only saved her life to execute her poor heart!

The Prairie Prince
Historical Romance

For Katie Matthews, life held no promise of true happiness. Life on the prairie was filled with hard labor, a brutal father, and the knowledge she would need to marry a man incapable of truly loving a woman. Men didn't have time to dote on women—so Katie's father told her. To Katie, it seemed life would forever remain mundane and disappointing—until the day Stover Steele bought her father's south acreage.

Handsome, rugged, and fiercely protective of four orphaned sisters, Stover Steele seemed to have stepped from the pages of some romantic novel. Yet his heroic character and alluring charm only served to remind Katie of what she would never have—true love and happiness the likes found only in fairytales. Furthermore, evil seemed to lurk in the shadows, threatening Katie's brightness, hope, and even her life!

Would Katie Matthews fall prey to disappointment, heartache, and harm? Or could she win the attentions of the handsome Stover Steele long enough to be rescued?

The Rogue Knight
Historical Romance

An aristocratic birthright and the luxurious comforts of profound wealth did nothing to comfort Fontaine Pratina following the death of her beloved parents. After two years in the guardianship of her mother's arrogant and selfish sister, Carileena Wetherton, Fontaine's only moments of joy and peace were found in the company of the loyal servants of Pratina Manor. Only in the kitchens and servants' quarters of her grand domicile did Fontaine find friendship, laughter, and affection.

Always, the life of a wealthy orphan destined to inherit loomed before her—a dark cloud of hopeless, shallow, snobbish people…a life of aristocracy, void of simple joys—and of love. Still, it was her lot—her birthright, and she saw no way of escaping it.

One brutal, cold winter's night a battered stranger appeared at the kitchen servants' entrance, however, seeking shelter and help. He gave only his first name, Knight…and suddenly, Fontaine found herself experiencing fleeting moments of joy in life. For Knight was handsome, powerful…the very stuff of the legends of days of old. Though a servant's class was his, he was proud and strong, and even his name seemed to portray his persona absolutely. He distracted Fontaine from her dull, hopeless existence.

Yet there were devilish secrets—strategies cached by her greedy aunt, and not even the handsome and powerful Knight could save her from them. Or could he? And if he did—would the truth force Fontaine to forfeit her Knight, her heart's desire…the man she loved—in order to survive?

The Tide of the Mermaid Tears
Historical Romance

Ember Taffee had always lived with her mother and sister in the little cottage by the sea. Her father had once lived there too, but the deep had claimed his life long ago. Still, her existence was a happy one, and Ember found joy, imagination, and respite in the sea and the trinkets it would leave for her on the sand.

Each morning Ember would wander the shore searching for treasures left by the tides. Though she cherished each pretty shell she found, her favorite gifts from Neptune were the rare mermaid tears—bits of tinted glass worn smooth and lovely by the ocean. To Ember, in all the world there were no jewels lovelier than mermaid tears.

Yet one morning, Ember was to discover that Neptune would present her with a gift more rare than any other—something she would value far more than the shells and sea glass she collected. One morning Ember Taffee would find a living, breathing man washed up on the sand—a man who would own claim to her heart as full as Neptune himself owned claim to the seas.

The Time of Aspen Falls

Contemporary Romance

Aspen Falls was happy. Her life was good. Blessed with a wonderful family and a loyal best friend—Aspen did know a measure of contentment.

Still, to Aspen it seemed something was missing—something hovering just beyond her reach—something entirely satisfying that would ensure her happiness. Yet, she couldn't consciously determine what the "something" was. And so, Aspen sailed through life—not quite perfectly content perhaps—but grateful for her measure of contentment.

Grateful, that is, until he appeared—the man in the park—the stranger who jogged passed the bench where Aspen sat during her lunch break each day. As handsome as a dream, and twice as alluring, the man epitomized the absolute stereotypical "real man"—and Aspen's measure of contentment vanished!

Would Aspen Falls reclaim the comfortable contentment she once knew? Or would the handsome real-man-stranger linger in her mind like a sweet, tricky venom—poisoning all hope of Aspen's ever finding true happiness with any other man?

The Touch of Sage
Historical Romance
After the death of her parents, Sage Willows had lovingly nurtured her younger sisters through childhood, seeing each one married and never resenting not finding herself a good man to settle down with. Yet, regret is different than resentment.

Still, Sage found as much joy as a lonely young woman could find, as proprietress of Willows's Boarding House—finding some fulfillment in the companionship of the four beloved widow women boarding with her. But when the devilishly handsome Rebel Lee Mitchell appeared on the boarding house step, Sage's contentment was lost forever.

Dark, mysterious and secretly wounded, Reb Mitchell instantly captured Sage's lonely heart. But the attractive cowboy, admired and coveted by every young unmarried female in his path, seemed unobtainable to Sage Willows. How could a weathered, boarding house proprietress resigned to spinsterhood ever hope to capture the attention of such a man? And without him, would Sage Willows simply sink deeper into bleak loneliness—tormented by the knowledge that the man of every woman's dreams could never be hers?

The Visions of Ransom Lake
Historical Romance
Youthful beauty, naïve innocence, a romantic imagination thirsting for adventure…an apt description of Vaden Valmont, who would soon find the adventure and mystery she had always longed to experience… in the form of a man.

A somber recluse, Ransom Lake descended from his solitary concealment in the mountains, wholly uninterested in people and their trivial affairs. And somehow, young Vaden managed to be ever in his way…either by accident or because of her own unique ability to stumble into a quandary.

Yet the enigmatic Ransom Lake would involuntarily become Vaden's unwitting tutor. Through him, she would experience joy and passion the like even Vaden had never imagined. Yes, Vaden Valmont stepped innocently, yet irrevocably, into love with the secretive, seemingly callous man.

But there were other life's lessons Ransom Lake would inadvertently bring to her as well. The darker side of life—despair, guilt, heartache. Would Ransom Lake be the means of Vaden's dreams come true? Or the cause of her complete desolation?

The Whispered Kiss
Historical Romance

With the sea at its side, the beautiful township of Bostchelan was home to many—including the lovely Coquette de Bellamont, her three sisters, and beloved father. In Bostchelan, Coquette knew happiness and as much contentment as a young woman whose heart had been broken years before could know. Thus, Coquette dwelt in gladness until the day her father returned from his travels with an astonishing tale to tell. Antoine de Bellamont returned from his travels by way of Roanan bearing a tale of such great adventure to hardly be believed. Further, at the center of Antoine's story loomed a man—the dark Lord of Roanan. Known for his cruel nature, heartlessness, and tendency to violence, the Lord of Roanan had accused Antoine de Bellamont of wrongdoing and demanded recompense. Antoine had promised recompense would be paid—with the hand of his youngest daughter in marriage.

Thus, Coquette found herself lost—thrust onto a dark journey of her own. This journey would find her carried away to Roanan Manor—delivered into the hands of the dark and mysterious Lord of Roanan who dominated it.

The Windswept Flame
Historical Romance

Broken—irreparably broken. The violent deaths of her father and the young man she'd been engaged to marry had irrevocably broken Cedar Dale's heart. Her mother's heart had been broken as well—shattered by the loss of her own true love. Thus, pain and anguish—fear and despair—found Cedar Dale and her mother, Flora, returned to the small western town where life had once been happy and filled with hope. Perhaps there Cedar and her mother would find some resemblance of truly living life—instead of merely existing. And then, a chance meeting with a dream from her past caused a flicker of wonder to ignite in her bosom.

As a child, Cedar Dale had adored the handsome rancher's son, Tom Evans. And when chance brought her face-to-face with the object of her childhood fascination once more, Cedar Dale began to believe that perhaps her fragmented heart could be healed.

Yet could Cedar truly hope to win the regard of such a man above men as was Tom Evans? A man kept occupied with hard work and ambition—a man so desperately sought after by seemingly every woman?

To Echo the Past
Historical Romance

As her family abandoned the excitement of the city for the uneventful lifestyle of a small, western town, Brynn Clarkston's worst fears were realized. Stripped of her heart's hopes and dreams, Brynn knew true loneliness.

Until an ordinary day revealed a heavenly oasis in the desert…Michael McCall. Handsome and irresistibly charming, Michael McCall (the son of legendary horse breeder Jackson McCall) seemed to offer wild distraction and sincere friendship to Brynn. But could Brynn be content with mere friendship when her dreams of Michael involved so much more?

Weathered Too Young
Historical Romance

Lark Lawrence was alone. In all the world there was no one who cared for her. Still, there were worse things than independence—and Lark had grown quite capable of providing for herself. Nevertheless, as winter loomed, she suddenly found herself with no means by which to afford food and shelter—destitute.

Yet Tom Evans was a kind and compassionate man. When Lark Lawrence appeared on his porch, without pause he hired her to keep house and cook for himself and his cantankerous elder brother, Slater. And although Tom had befriend Lark first, it would be Slater Evans—handsome, brooding, and twelve years Lark's senior—who would unknowingly abduct her heart.

Still, Lark's true age (which she concealed at first meeting the Evans brothers) was not the only truth she had kept from Slater and Tom Evans. Darker secrets lay imprisoned deep within her heart—and her past. However, it is that secrets are made to be found out—and Lark's secrets revealed would soon couple with the arrival of a woman from Slater's past to forever shatter her dreams of winning his love—or so it seemed. Would truth and passion mingle to capture Lark the love she'd never dared to hope for?

www.ingramcontent.com/pod-product-compliance
Lightning Source LLC
Chambersburg PA
CBHW060353260626
47160CB00006B/2296